Lincoln Peirce

HERE GOES NOTHING

BALZER + BRAY
An Imprint of HarperCollins*Publishers*

ABDOBOOKS.COM

Reinforced library bound edition published in 2021 by Spotlight, a division of ABDO, PO Box 398166, Minneapolis, Minnesota 55439. Spotlight produces high-quality reinforced library bound editions for schools and libraries.
Reprinted by permission of HarperCollins Publishers.

Printed in the United States of America, North Mankato, Minnesota.
042020
092020

THIS BOOK CONTAINS RECYCLED MATERIALS

Balzer + Bray is an imprint of HarperCollins Publishers.

BIG NATE is a registered trademark of United Feature Syndicate, Inc.

Typography by Andrea Vandergrift

Publisher's Cataloging-in-Publication Data

Names: Peirce, Lincoln, author. | Peirce, Lincoln, illustrator.
Title: Big Nate: here goes nothing / by Lincoln Peirce ; illustrated by Lincoln Peirce
Description: Minneapolis, Minnesota : Spotlight, 2021. | Series: Big Nate
Summary: Nate's not only the star of his own comic strip—he's the star goalie of his soccer team and he has to defend his goal from his school's rival team.
Identifiers: ISBN 9781532145278 (lib. bdg.)
Subjects: LCSH: Middle school students--Juvenile fiction. | Behavior--Juvenile fiction. | School--Juvenile fiction. | Friendship--Juvenile fiction. | Humorous stories--Juvenile fiction.
Classification: DDC [Fic]--dc23

Spotlight
A Division of ABDO
abdobooks.com

THE SHOW MUST GO ON

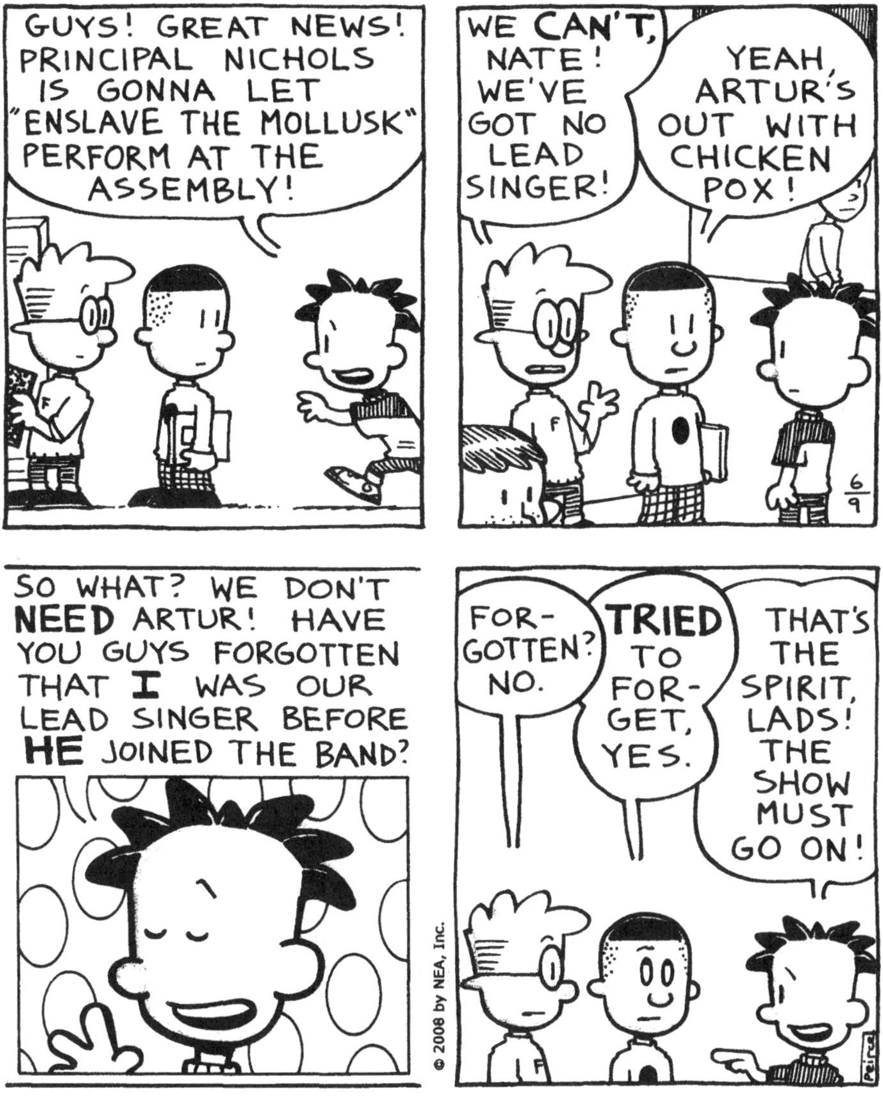

GUYS! GREAT NEWS! PRINCIPAL NICHOLS IS GONNA LET "ENSLAVE THE MOLLUSK" PERFORM AT THE ASSEMBLY!
WE **CAN'T**, NATE! WE'VE GOT NO LEAD SINGER!
YEAH, ARTUR'S OUT WITH CHICKEN POX!
6/9
SO WHAT? WE DON'T **NEED** ARTUR! HAVE YOU GUYS FORGOTTEN THAT **I** WAS OUR LEAD SINGER BEFORE **HE** JOINED THE BAND?
© 2008 by NEA, Inc.
FOR-GOTTEN? NO.
TRIED TO FOR-GET, YES.
THAT'S THE SPIRIT, LADS! THE SHOW MUST GO ON!
PEIRCE

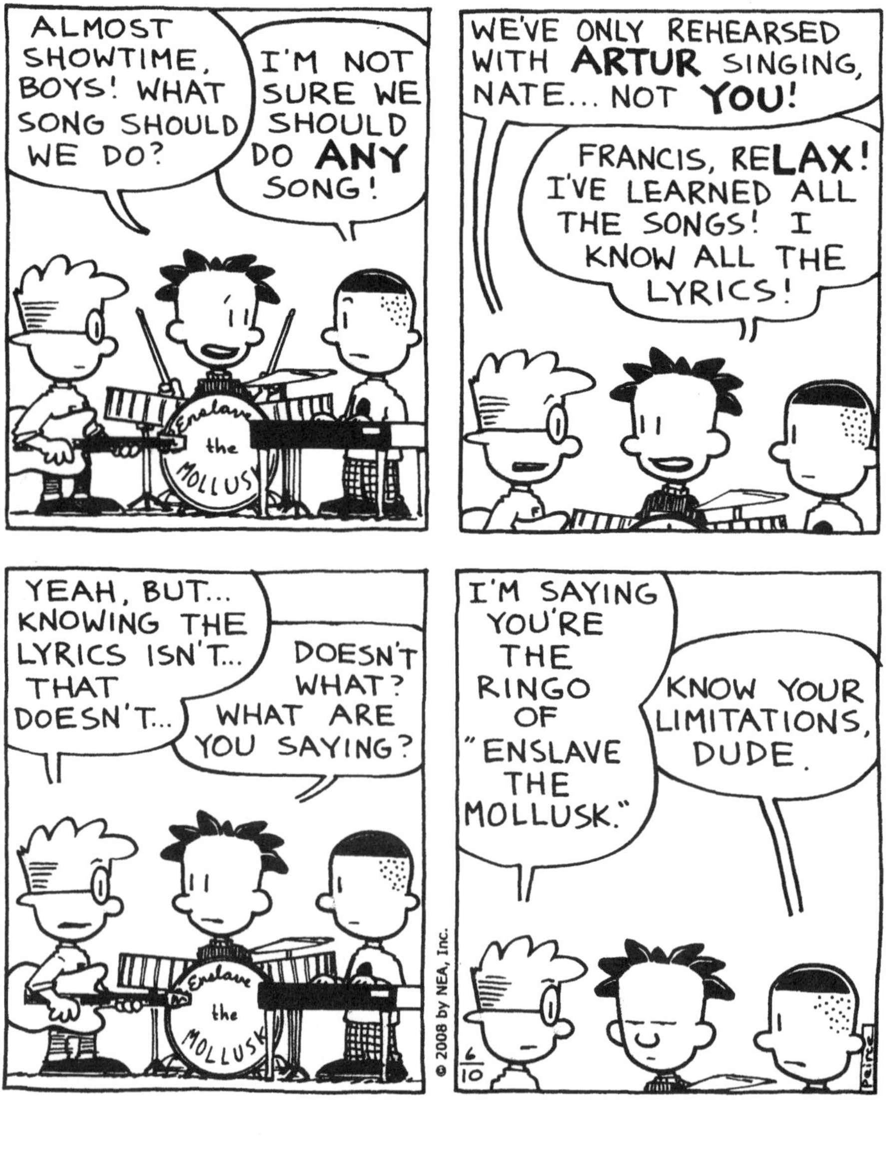
ALMOST SHOWTIME, BOYS! WHAT SONG SHOULD WE DO?
I'M NOT SURE WE SHOULD DO ANY SONG!
Enslave the MOLLUSK
WE'VE ONLY REHEARSED WITH ARTUR SINGING, NATE... NOT YOU!
FRANCIS, RELAX! I'VE LEARNED ALL THE SONGS! I KNOW ALL THE LYRICS!
YEAH, BUT... KNOWING THE LYRICS ISN'T... THAT DOESN'T...
DOESN'T WHAT? WHAT ARE YOU SAYING?
Enslave the MOLLUSK
I'M SAYING YOU'RE THE RINGO OF "ENSLAVE THE MOLLUSK."
KNOW YOUR LIMITATIONS, DUDE.
© 2008 by NEA, Inc.
6/10
Peirce

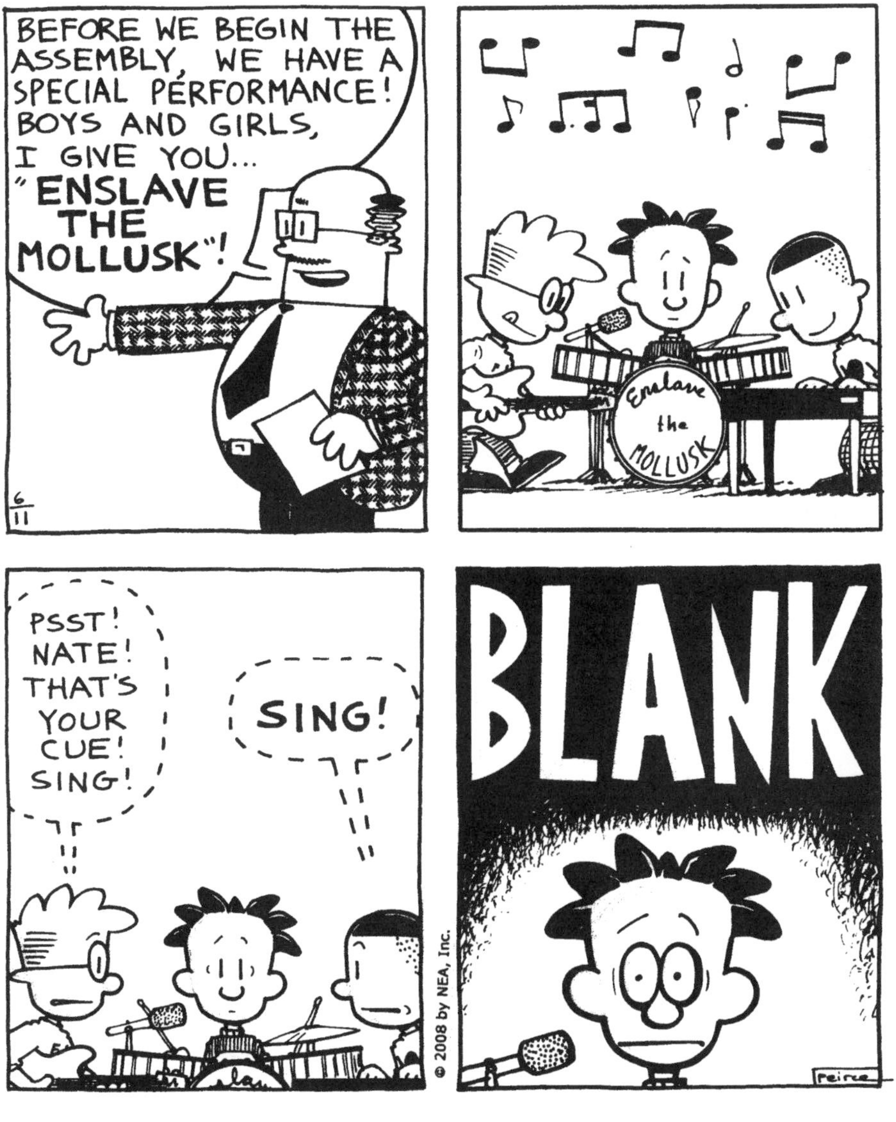
BEFORE WE BEGIN THE ASSEMBLY, WE HAVE A SPECIAL PERFORMANCE! BOYS AND GIRLS, I GIVE YOU... "ENSLAVE THE MOLLUSK"!
6/11
Enslave the MOLLUSK
PSST! NATE! THAT'S YOUR CUE! SING!
SING!
BLANK
© 2008 by NEA, Inc.
peirce

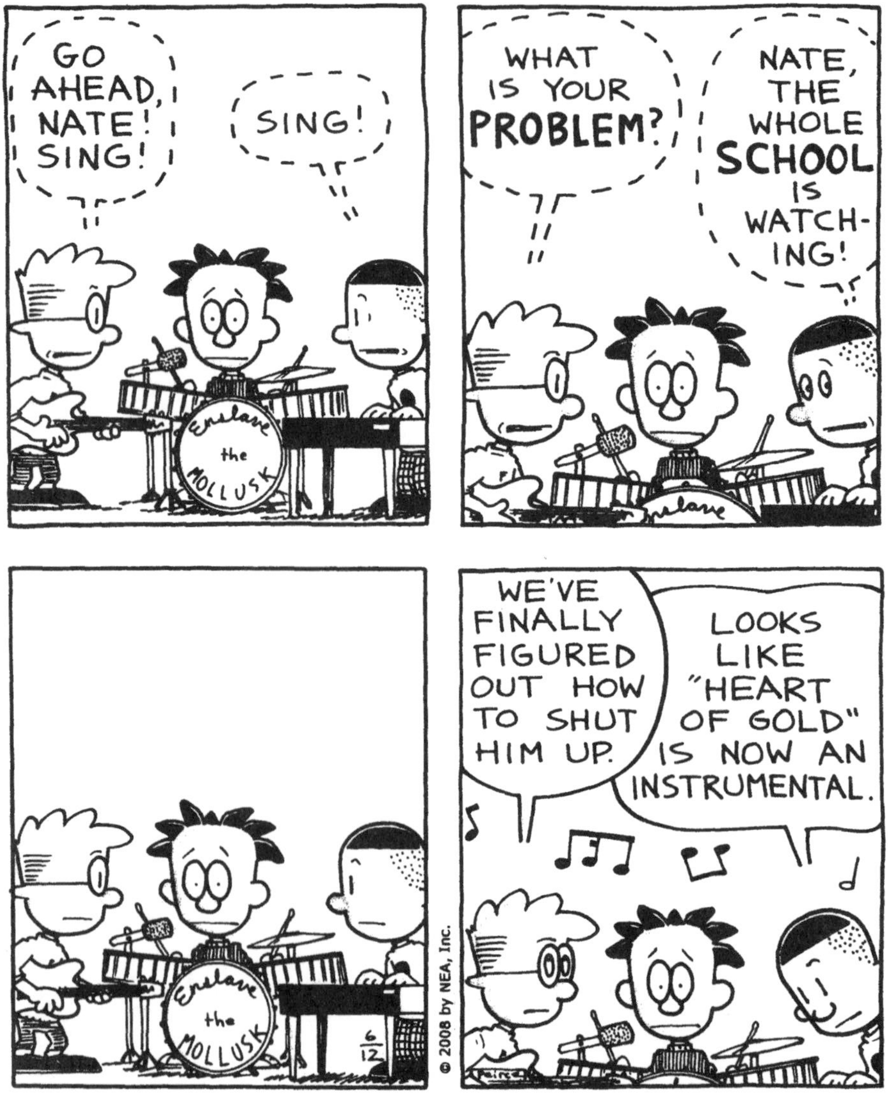
GO AHEAD, NATE! SING!
SING!
WHAT IS YOUR PROBLEM?
NATE, THE WHOLE SCHOOL IS WATCHING!
WE'VE FINALLY FIGURED OUT HOW TO SHUT HIM UP.
LOOKS LIKE "HEART OF GOLD" IS NOW AN INSTRUMENTAL.
Enslave the MOLLUSK
6/12
© 2008 by NEA, Inc.

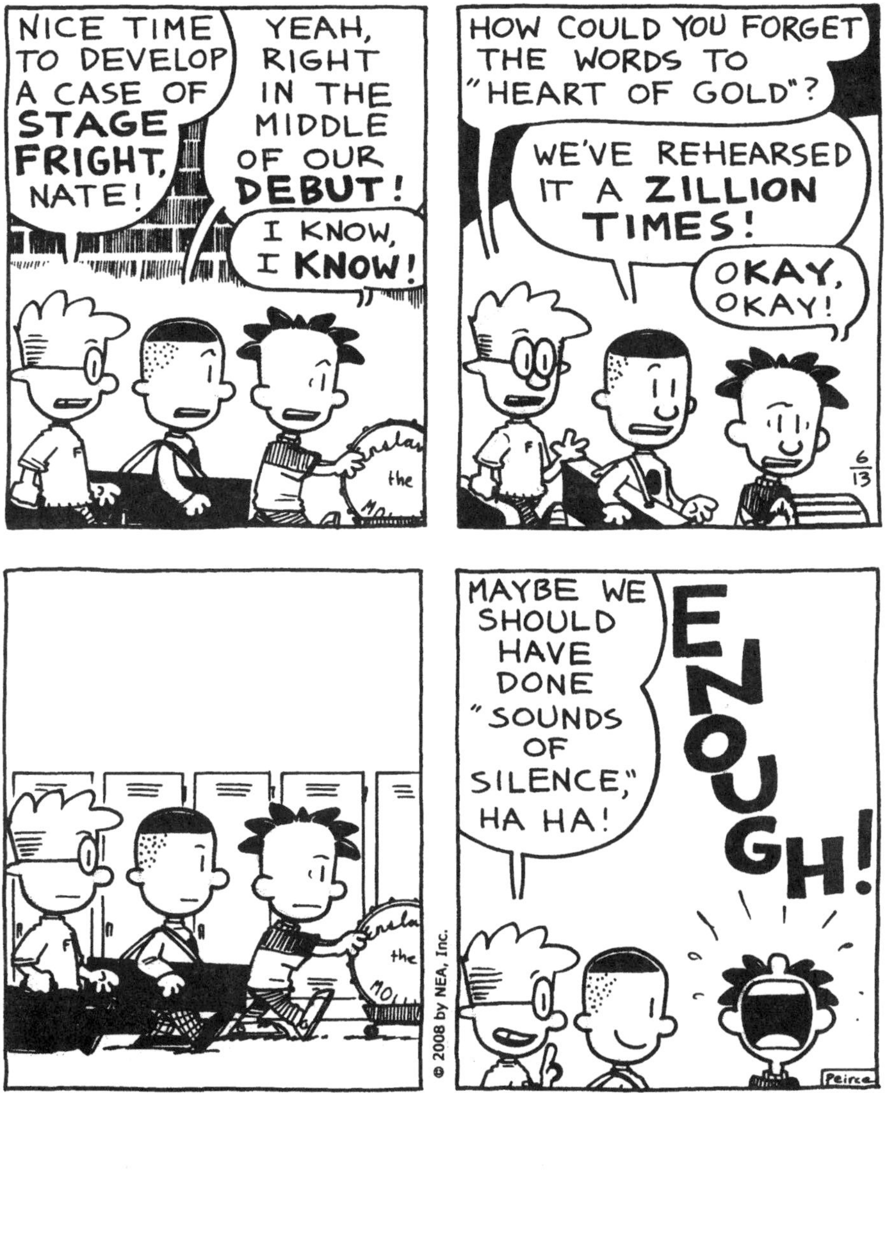
NICE TIME TO DEVELOP A CASE OF **STAGE FRIGHT**, NATE!
YEAH, RIGHT IN THE MIDDLE OF OUR **DEBUT**!
I KNOW, I **KNOW**!
HOW COULD YOU FORGET THE WORDS TO "HEART OF GOLD"?
WE'VE REHEARSED IT A **ZILLION TIMES**!
OKAY, OKAY!
6/13
MAYBE WE SHOULD HAVE DONE "SOUNDS OF SILENCE," HA HA!
ENOUGH!
Peirce

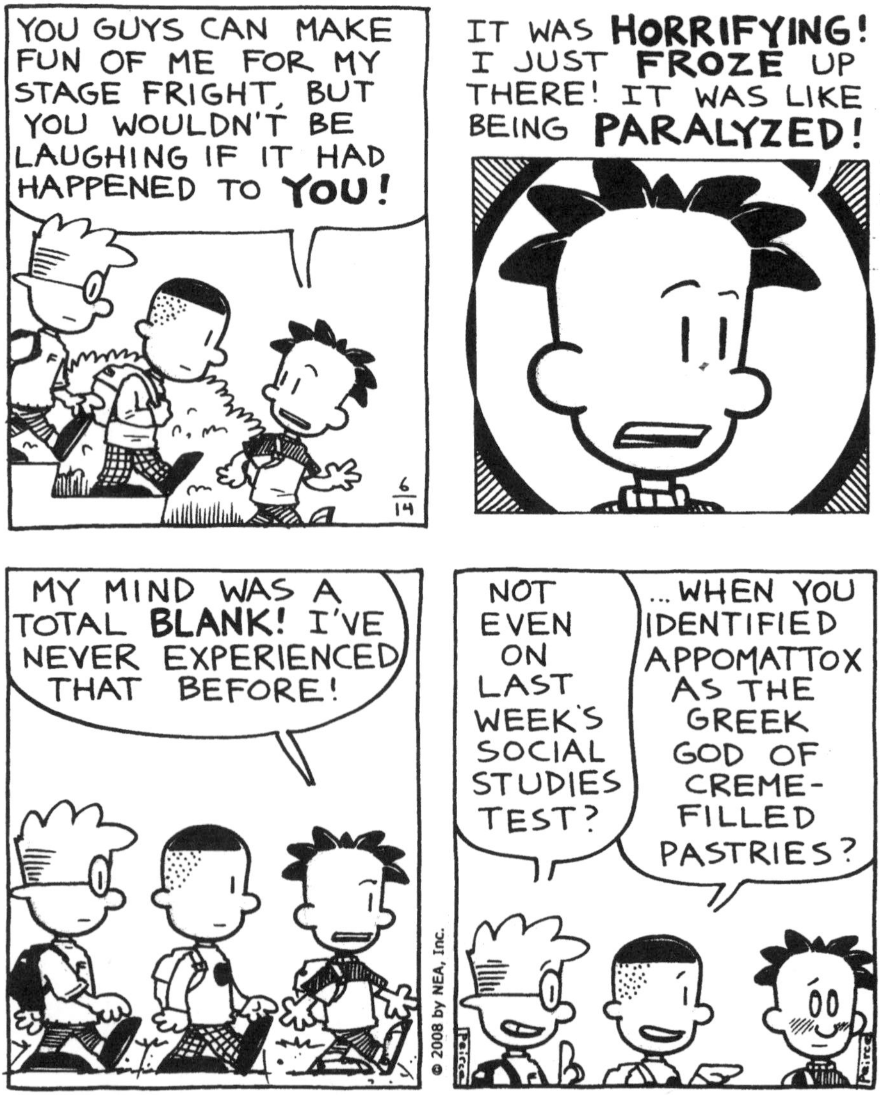
YOU GUYS CAN MAKE FUN OF ME FOR MY STAGE FRIGHT, BUT YOU WOULDN'T BE LAUGHING IF IT HAD HAPPENED TO YOU!
6/14
IT WAS HORRIFYING! I JUST FROZE UP THERE! IT WAS LIKE BEING PARALYZED!
MY MIND WAS A TOTAL BLANK! I'VE NEVER EXPERIENCED THAT BEFORE!
© 2008 by NEA, Inc.
NOT EVEN ON LAST WEEK'S SOCIAL STUDIES TEST?
...WHEN YOU IDENTIFIED APPOMATTOX AS THE GREEK GOD OF CREME-FILLED PASTRIES?

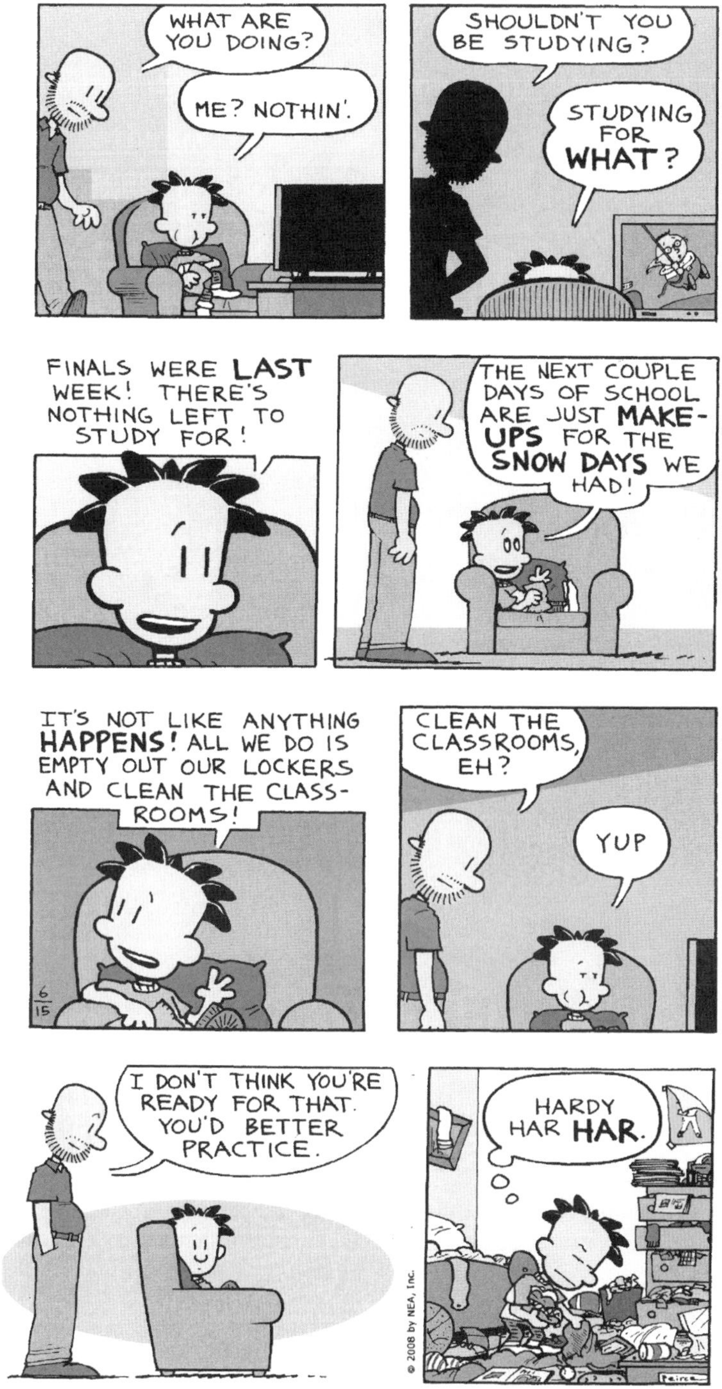
WHAT ARE YOU DOING?
ME? NOTHIN'.
SHOULDN'T YOU BE STUDYING?
STUDYING FOR **WHAT**?
FINALS WERE **LAST** WEEK! THERE'S NOTHING LEFT TO STUDY FOR!
THE NEXT COUPLE DAYS OF SCHOOL ARE JUST **MAKE-UPS** FOR THE **SNOW DAYS** WE HAD!
IT'S NOT LIKE ANYTHING **HAPPENS!** ALL WE DO IS EMPTY OUT OUR LOCKERS AND CLEAN THE CLASS-ROOMS!
6/15
CLEAN THE CLASSROOMS, EH?
YUP
I DON'T THINK YOU'RE READY FOR THAT. YOU'D BETTER PRACTICE.
© 2008 by NEA, Inc.
HARDY HAR **HAR**.

PRANKED!

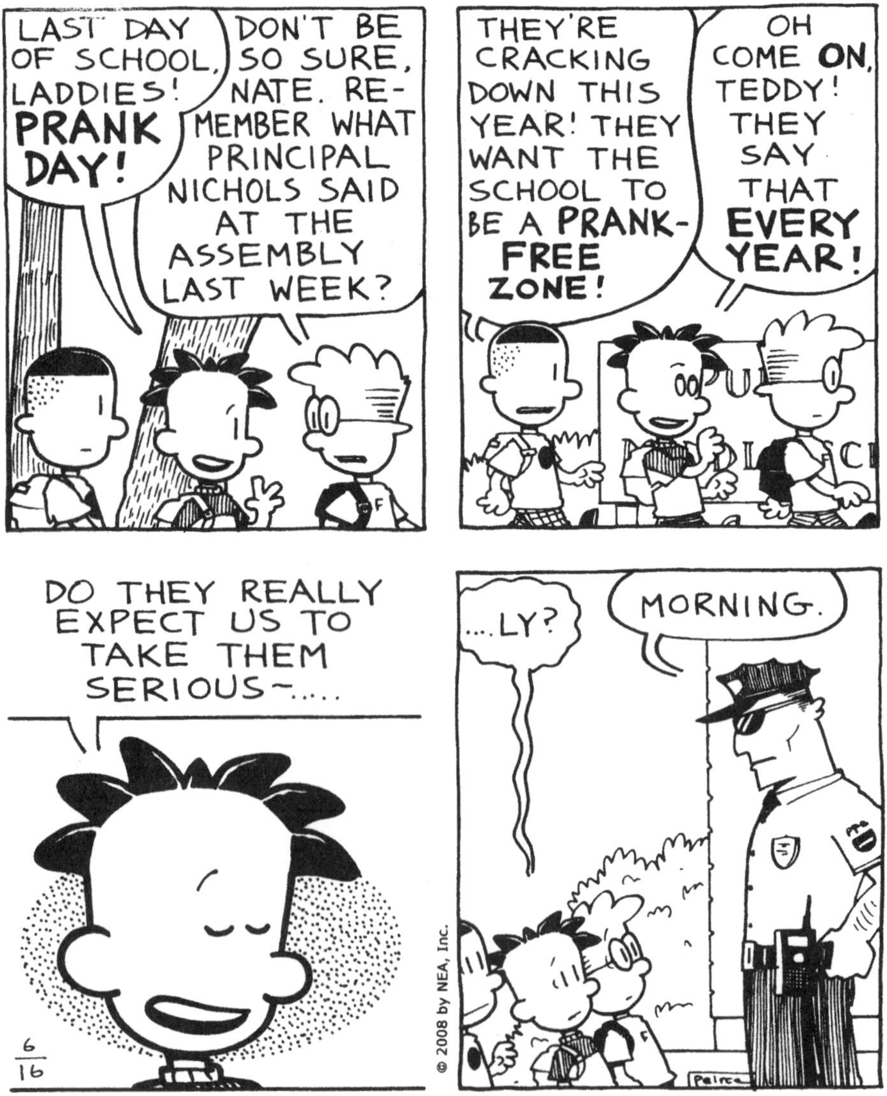
LAST DAY OF SCHOOL, LADDIES! PRANK DAY!
DON'T BE SO SURE, NATE. REMEMBER WHAT PRINCIPAL NICHOLS SAID AT THE ASSEMBLY LAST WEEK?
THEY'RE CRACKING DOWN THIS YEAR! THEY WANT THE SCHOOL TO BE A PRANK-FREE ZONE!
OH COME ON, TEDDY! THEY SAY THAT EVERY YEAR!
DO THEY REALLY EXPECT US TO TAKE THEM SERIOUS~....
6/16
...LY?
MORNING.
© 2008 by NEA, Inc.
Peirce

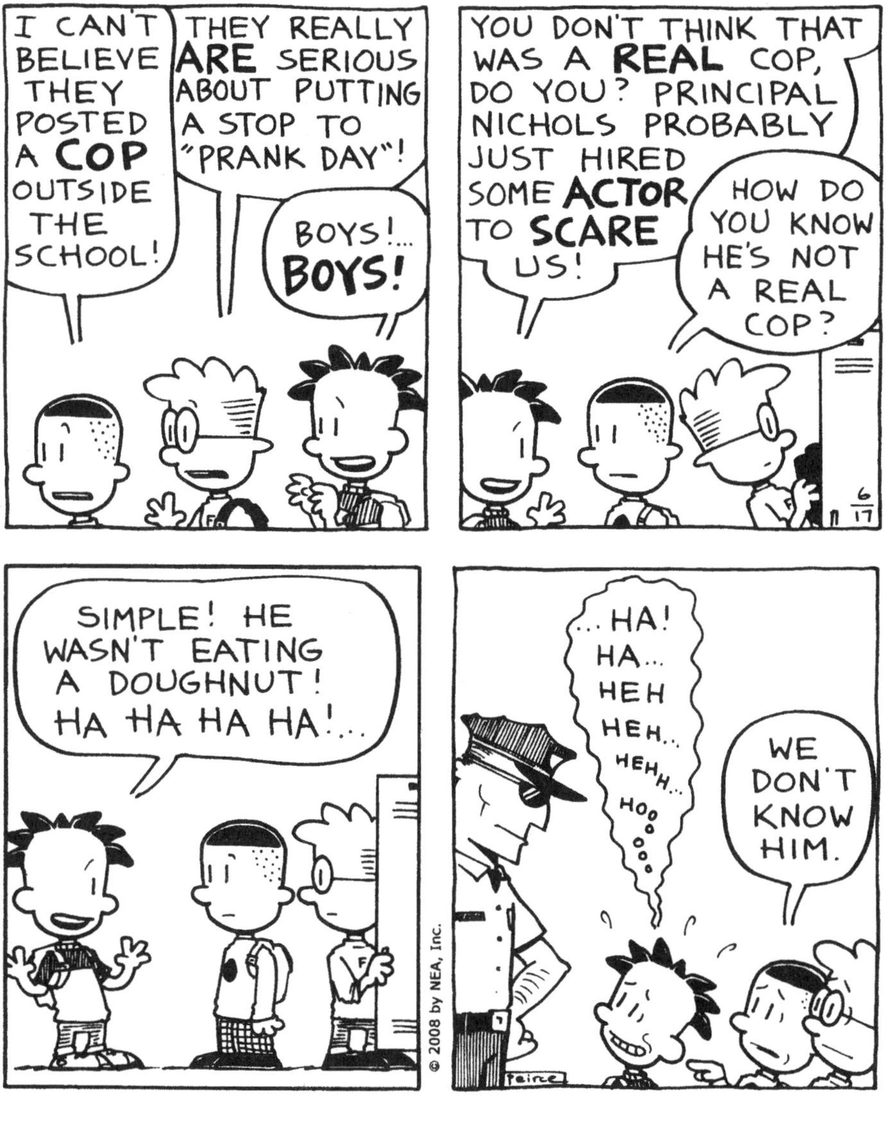
I CAN'T BELIEVE THEY POSTED A COP OUTSIDE THE SCHOOL!
THEY REALLY ARE SERIOUS ABOUT PUTTING A STOP TO "PRANK DAY"!
BOYS!... BOYS!
YOU DON'T THINK THAT WAS A REAL COP, DO YOU? PRINCIPAL NICHOLS PROBABLY JUST HIRED SOME ACTOR TO SCARE US!
HOW DO YOU KNOW HE'S NOT A REAL COP?
6 17
SIMPLE! HE WASN'T EATING A DOUGHNUT! HA HA HA HA!...
...HA! HA... HEH HEH... HEHH... HOOoooo
WE DON'T KNOW HIM.
© 2008 by NEA, Inc.

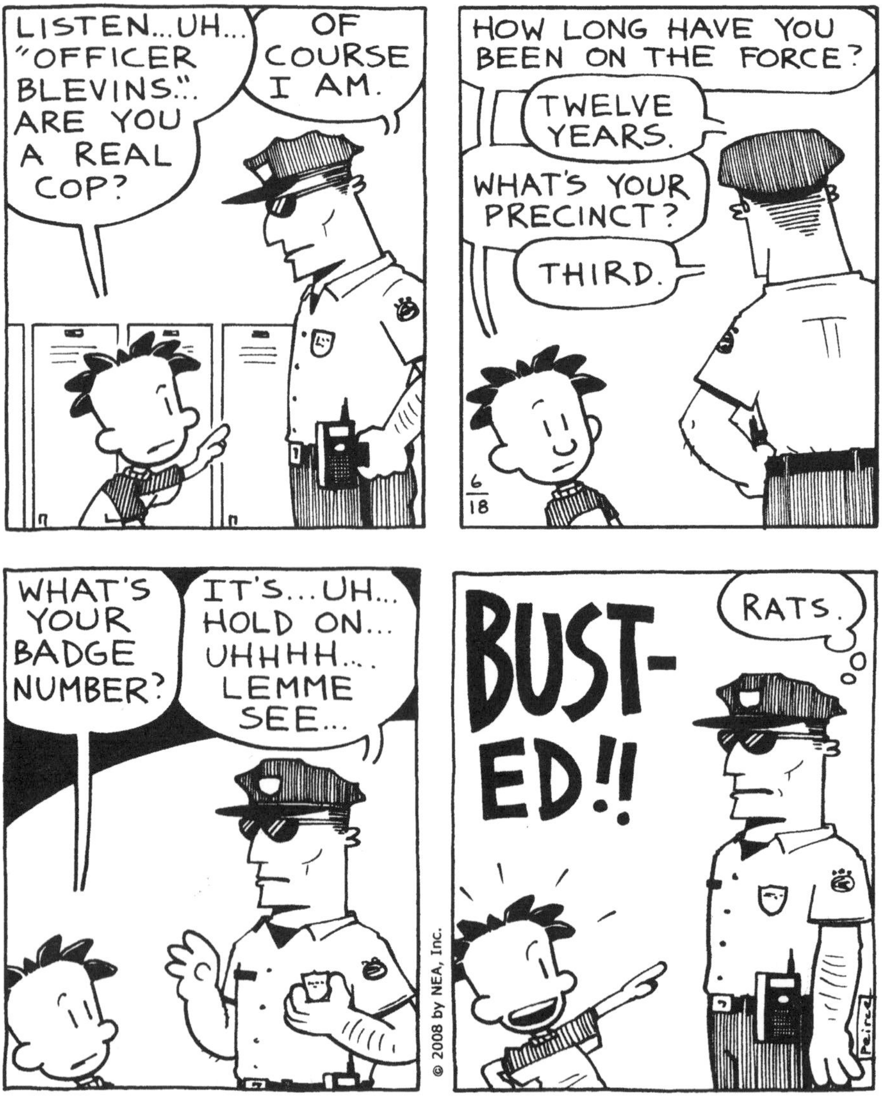
LISTEN...UH... "OFFICER BLEVINS"... ARE YOU A REAL COP?
OF COURSE I AM.
HOW LONG HAVE YOU BEEN ON THE FORCE?
TWELVE YEARS.
WHAT'S YOUR PRECINCT?
THIRD.
6/18
WHAT'S YOUR BADGE NUMBER?
IT'S...UH... HOLD ON... UHHHH... LEMME SEE...
© 2008 by NEA, Inc.
BUST-ED!!
RATS.
Peirce

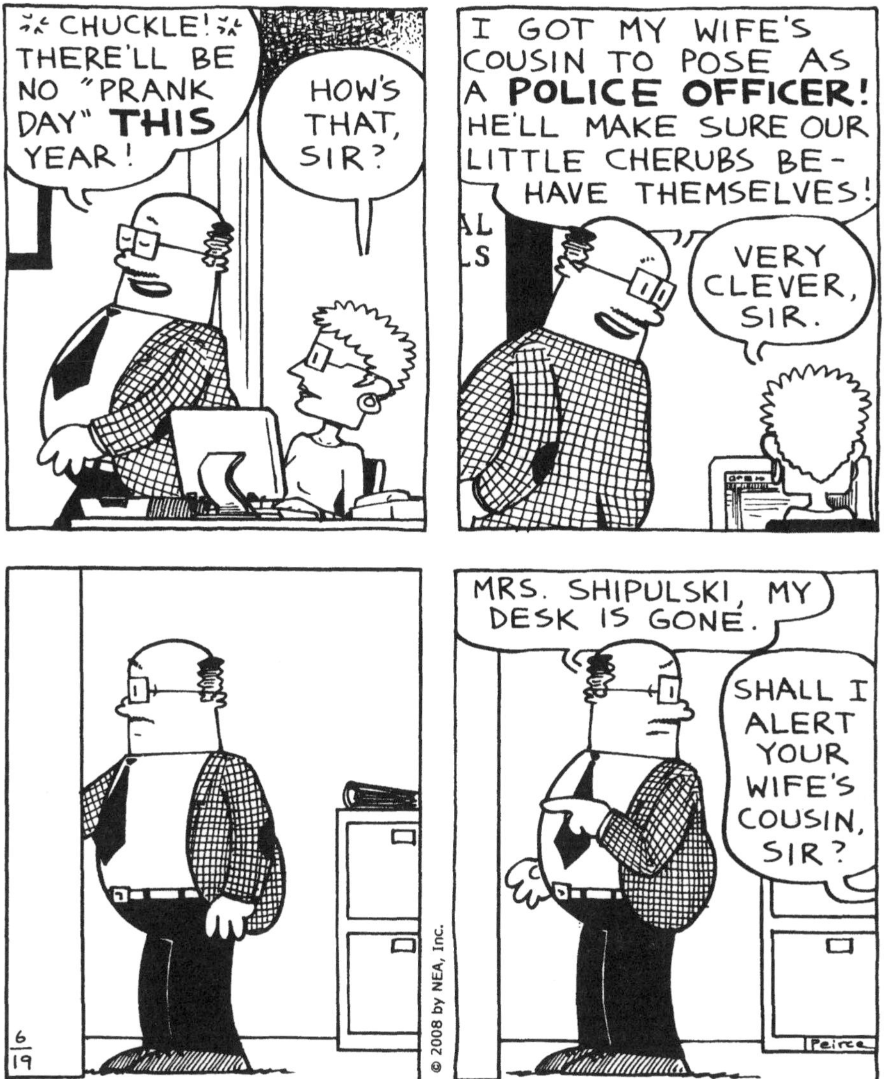
CHUCKLE! THERE'LL BE NO "PRANK DAY" **THIS** YEAR!
HOW'S THAT, SIR?
I GOT MY WIFE'S COUSIN TO POSE AS A **POLICE OFFICER!** HE'LL MAKE SURE OUR LITTLE CHERUBS BE-HAVE THEMSELVES!
VERY CLEVER, SIR.
6/19
MRS. SHIPULSKI, MY DESK IS GONE.
SHALL I ALERT YOUR WIFE'S COUSIN, SIR?
Peirce

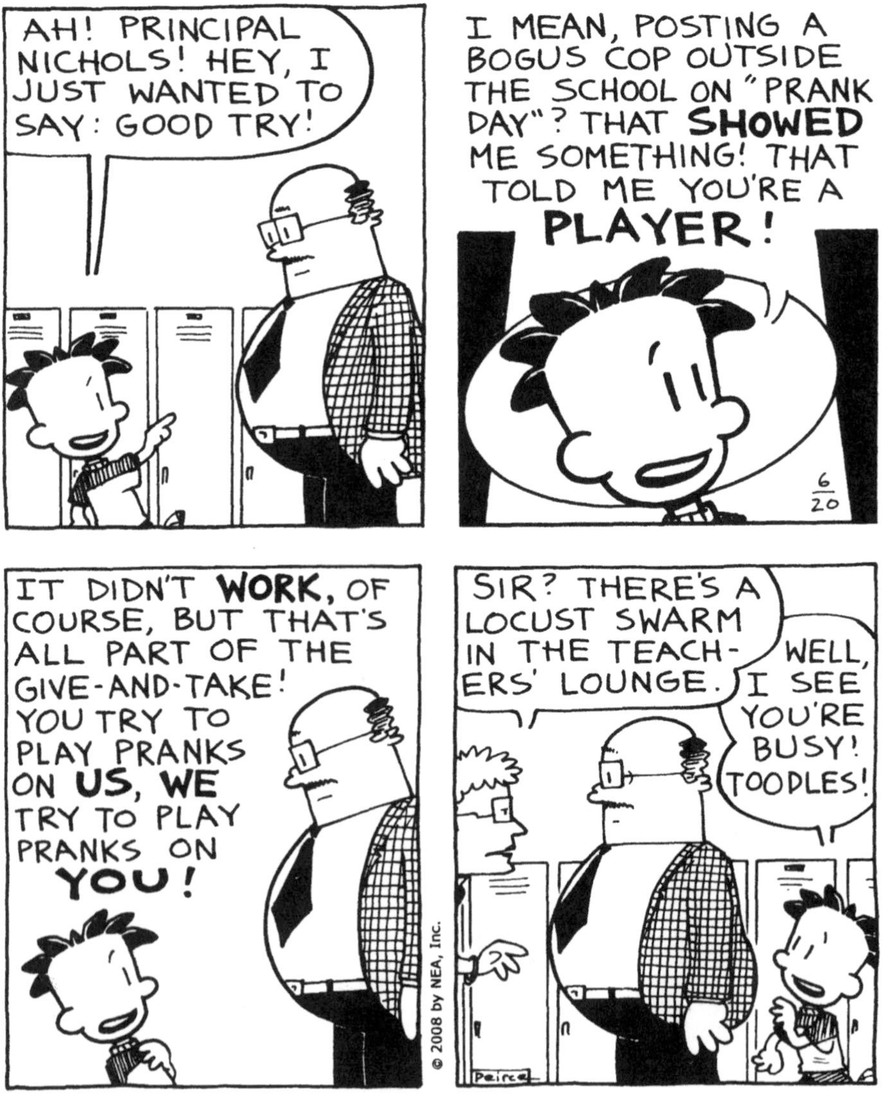
AH! PRINCIPAL NICHOLS! HEY, I JUST WANTED TO SAY: GOOD TRY!
I MEAN, POSTING A BOGUS COP OUTSIDE THE SCHOOL ON "PRANK DAY"? THAT SHOWED ME SOMETHING! THAT TOLD ME YOU'RE A PLAYER!
6/20
IT DIDN'T WORK, OF COURSE, BUT THAT'S ALL PART OF THE GIVE-AND-TAKE! YOU TRY TO PLAY PRANKS ON US, WE TRY TO PLAY PRANKS ON YOU!
© 2008 by NEA, Inc.
SIR? THERE'S A LOCUST SWARM IN THE TEACHERS' LOUNGE.
WELL, I SEE YOU'RE BUSY! TOODLES!
Peirce

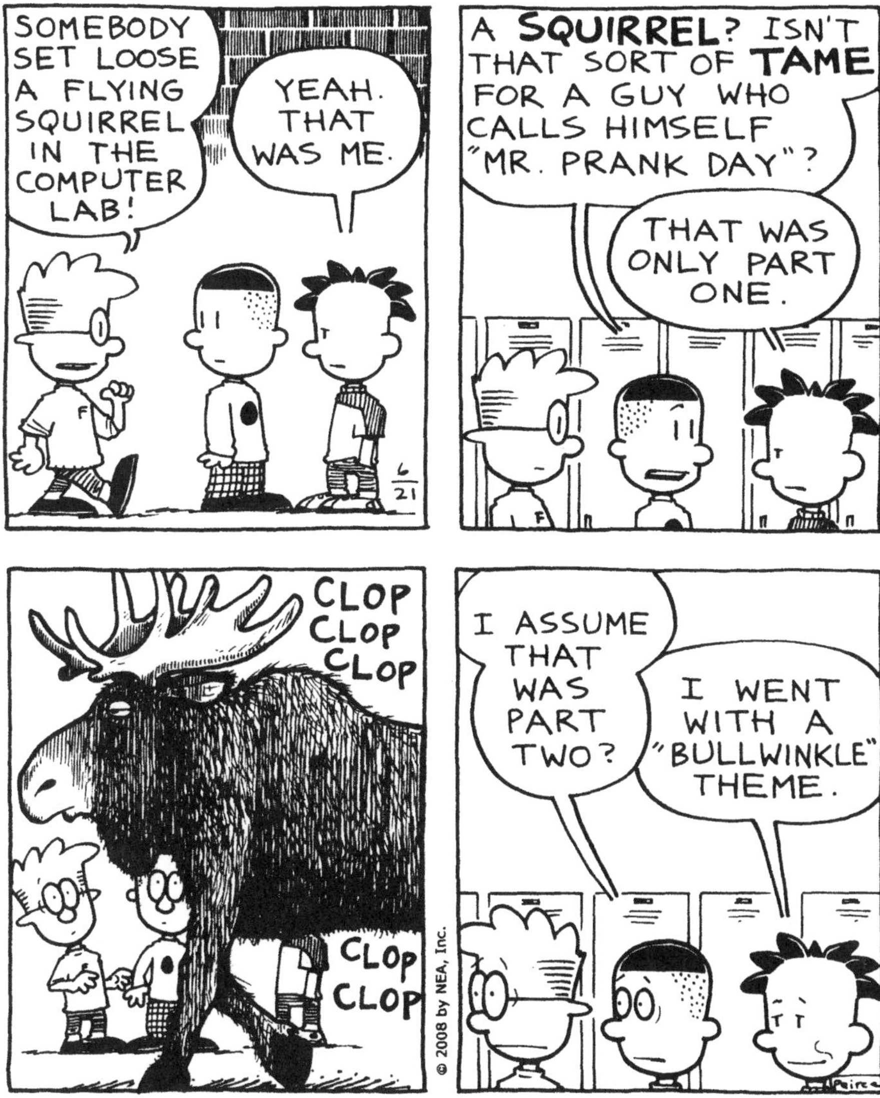
SOMEBODY SET LOOSE A FLYING SQUIRREL IN THE COMPUTER LAB!
YEAH. THAT WAS ME.
6/21
A **SQUIRREL**? ISN'T THAT SORT OF **TAME** FOR A GUY WHO CALLS HIMSELF "MR. PRANK DAY"?
THAT WAS ONLY PART ONE.
CLOP CLOP CLOP
CLOP CLOP
© 2008 by NEA, Inc.
I ASSUME THAT WAS PART TWO?
I WENT WITH A "BULLWINKLE" THEME.
Peirce

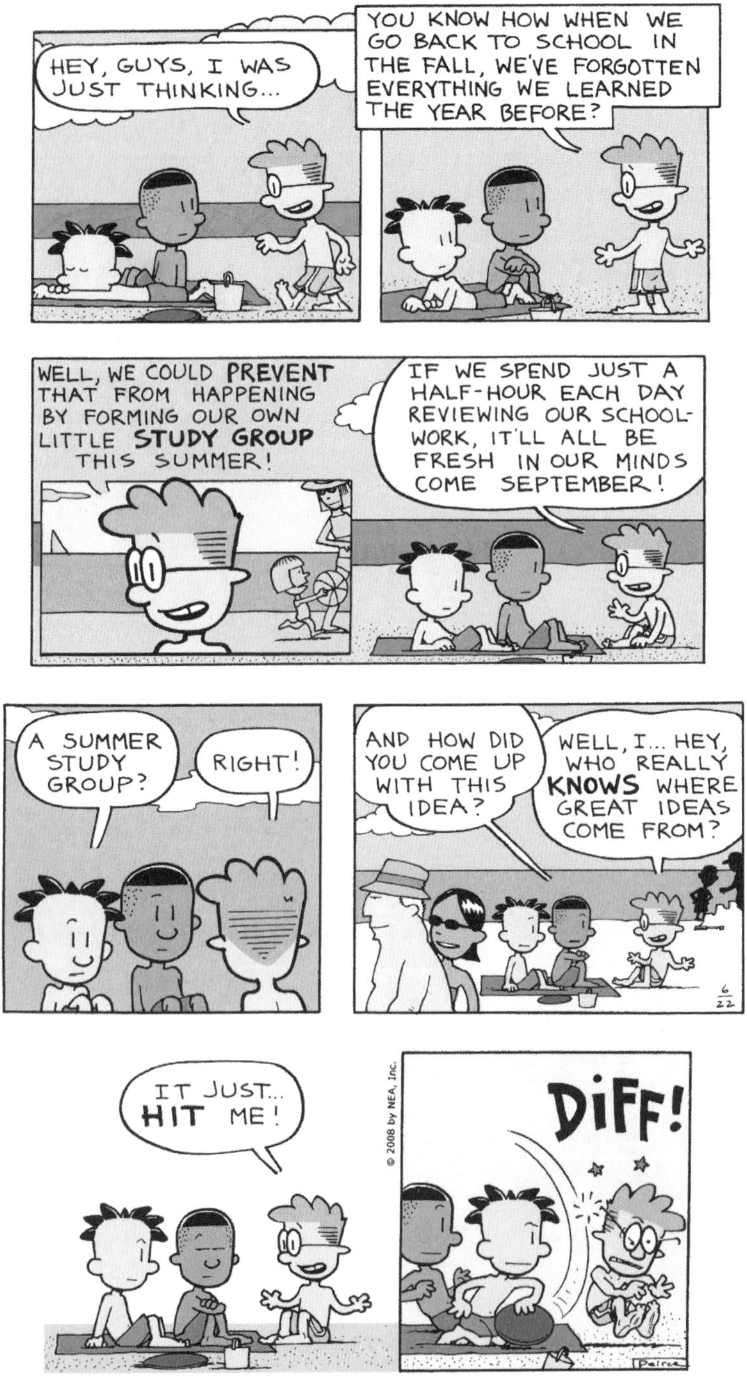
HEY, GUYS, I WAS JUST THINKING...
YOU KNOW HOW WHEN WE GO BACK TO SCHOOL IN THE FALL, WE'VE FORGOTTEN EVERYTHING WE LEARNED THE YEAR BEFORE?
WELL, WE COULD PREVENT THAT FROM HAPPENING BY FORMING OUR OWN LITTLE STUDY GROUP THIS SUMMER!
IF WE SPEND JUST A HALF-HOUR EACH DAY REVIEWING OUR SCHOOL-WORK, IT'LL ALL BE FRESH IN OUR MINDS COME SEPTEMBER!
A SUMMER STUDY GROUP?
RIGHT!
AND HOW DID YOU COME UP WITH THIS IDEA?
WELL, I... HEY, WHO REALLY KNOWS WHERE GREAT IDEAS COME FROM?
6
22
IT JUST... HIT ME!
© 2008 by NEA, Inc.
DiFF!
Peirce

THE SUMMER OF NATE

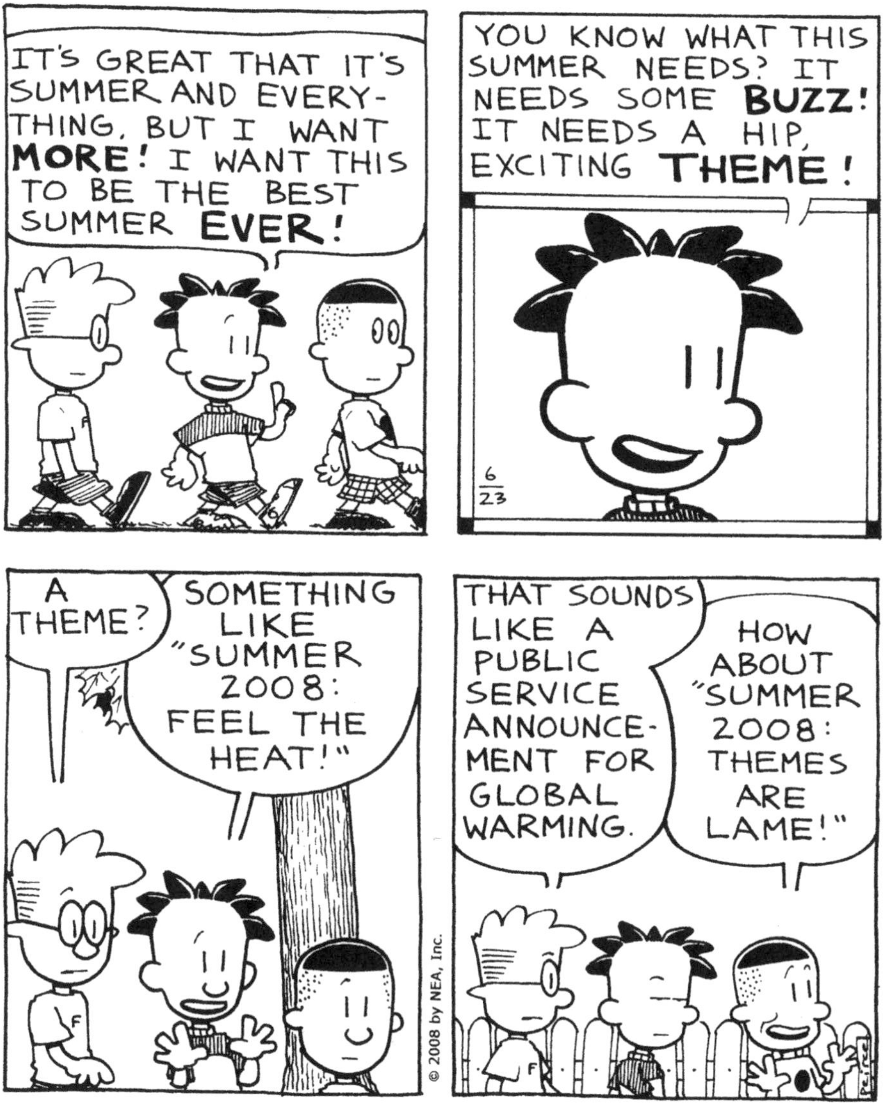
IT'S GREAT THAT IT'S SUMMER AND EVERYTHING, BUT I WANT **MORE**! I WANT THIS TO BE THE BEST SUMMER **EVER**!
YOU KNOW WHAT THIS SUMMER NEEDS? IT NEEDS SOME **BUZZ**! IT NEEDS A HIP, EXCITING **THEME**!
6/23
A THEME?
SOMETHING LIKE "SUMMER 2008: FEEL THE HEAT!"
THAT SOUNDS LIKE A PUBLIC SERVICE ANNOUNCEMENT FOR GLOBAL WARMING.
HOW ABOUT "SUMMER 2008: THEMES ARE LAME!"
© 2008 by NEA, Inc.
PEIRCE

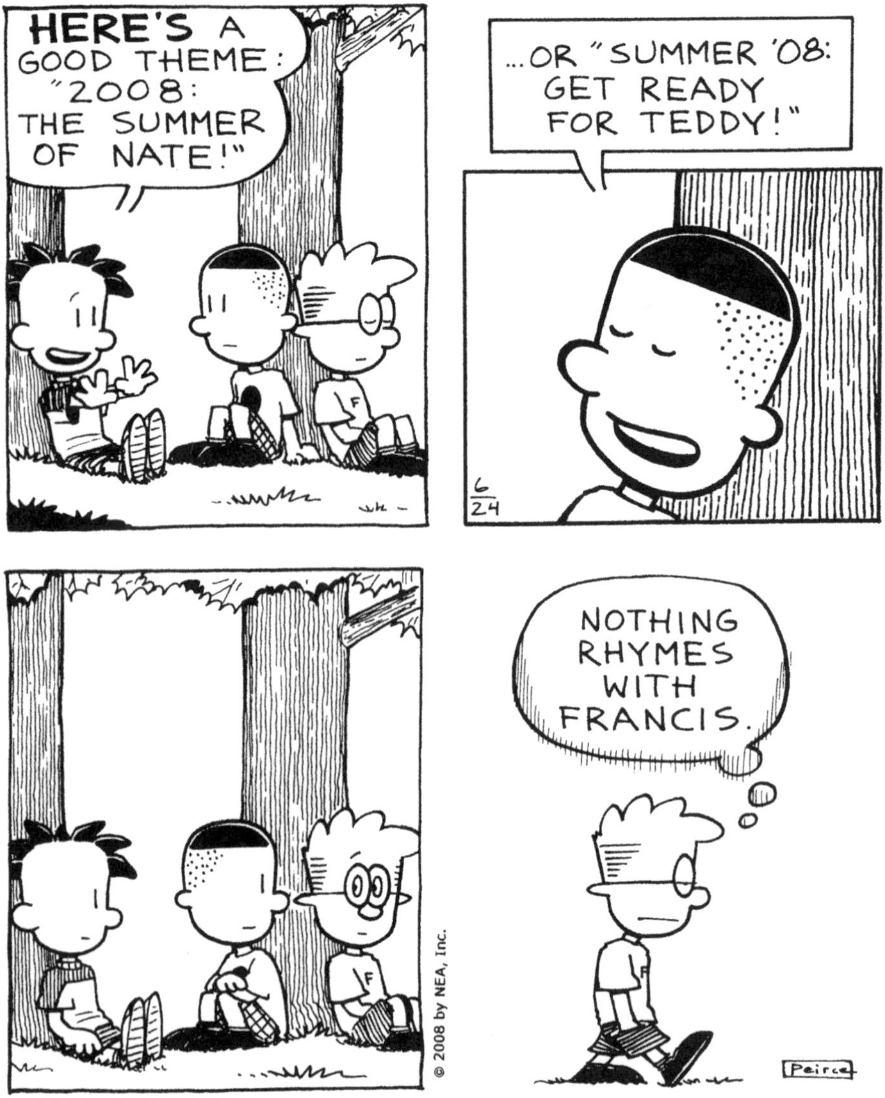
HERE'S A GOOD THEME: "2008: THE SUMMER OF NATE!"
...OR "SUMMER '08: GET READY FOR TEDDY!"
6/24
NOTHING RHYMES WITH FRANCIS.
© 2008 by NEA, Inc.
Peirce

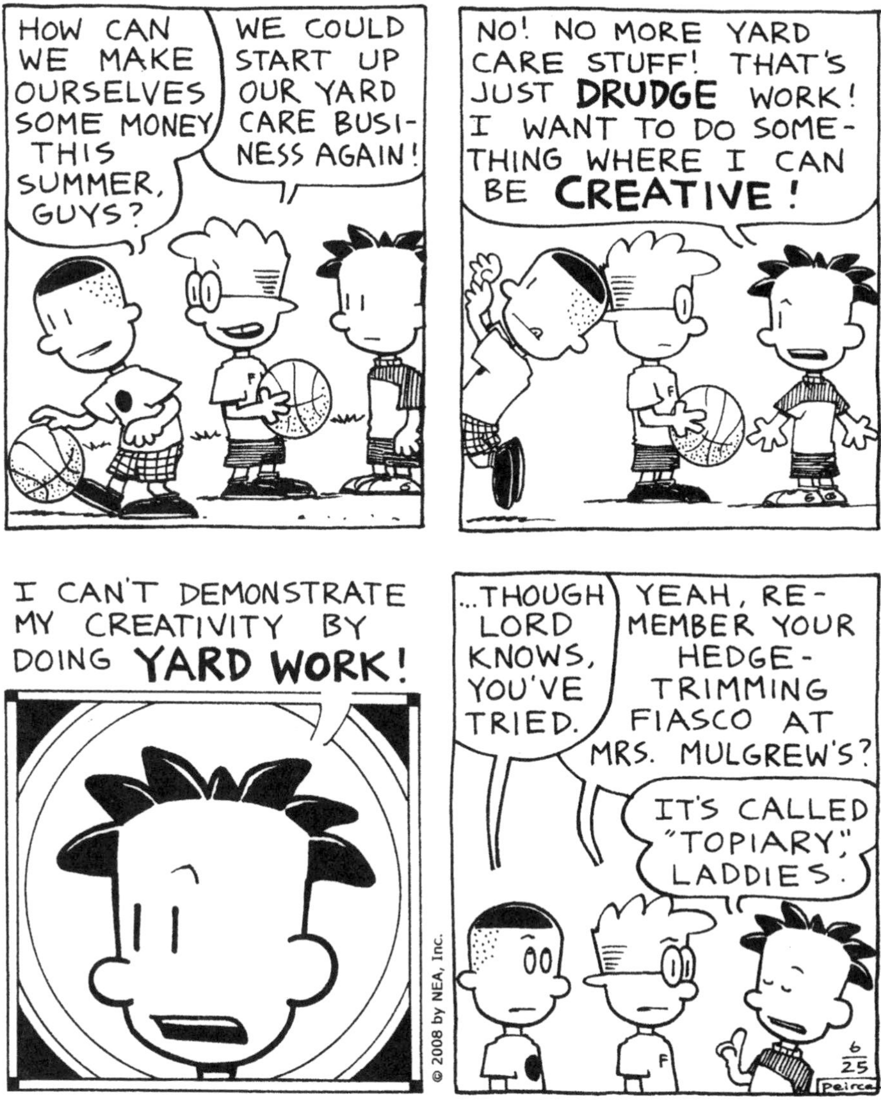
HOW CAN WE MAKE OURSELVES SOME MONEY THIS SUMMER, GUYS?
WE COULD START UP OUR YARD CARE BUSINESS AGAIN!
NO! NO MORE YARD CARE STUFF! THAT'S JUST DRUDGE WORK! I WANT TO DO SOMETHING WHERE I CAN BE CREATIVE!
I CAN'T DEMONSTRATE MY CREATIVITY BY DOING YARD WORK!
...THOUGH LORD KNOWS, YOU'VE TRIED.
YEAH, REMEMBER YOUR HEDGE-TRIMMING FIASCO AT MRS. MULGREW'S?
IT'S CALLED "TOPIARY," LADDIES.
6/25
Peirce
© 2008 by NEA, Inc.

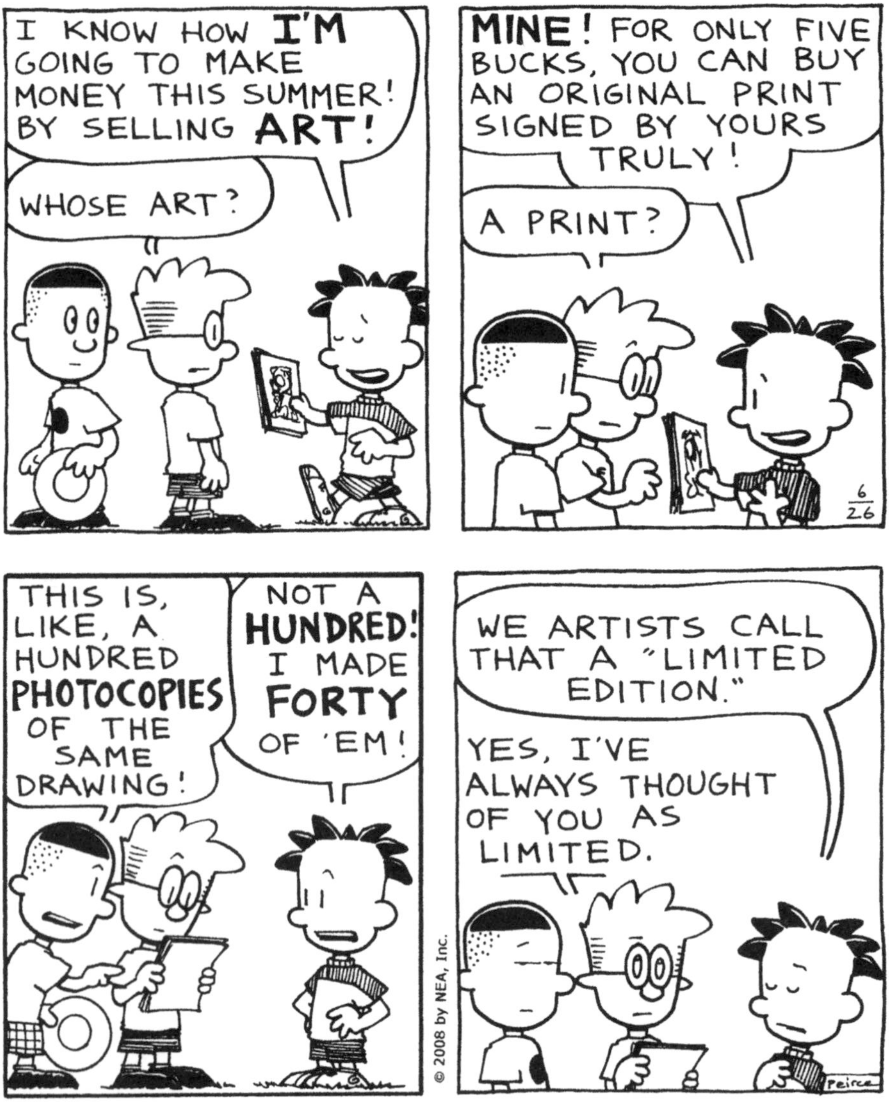
I KNOW HOW I'M GOING TO MAKE MONEY THIS SUMMER! BY SELLING ART!
WHOSE ART?
MINE! FOR ONLY FIVE BUCKS, YOU CAN BUY AN ORIGINAL PRINT SIGNED BY YOURS TRULY!
A PRINT?
6
26
THIS IS, LIKE, A HUNDRED PHOTOCOPIES OF THE SAME DRAWING!
NOT A HUNDRED! I MADE FORTY OF 'EM!
© 2008 by NEA, Inc.
WE ARTISTS CALL THAT A "LIMITED EDITION."
YES, I'VE ALWAYS THOUGHT OF YOU AS LIMITED.
Peirce

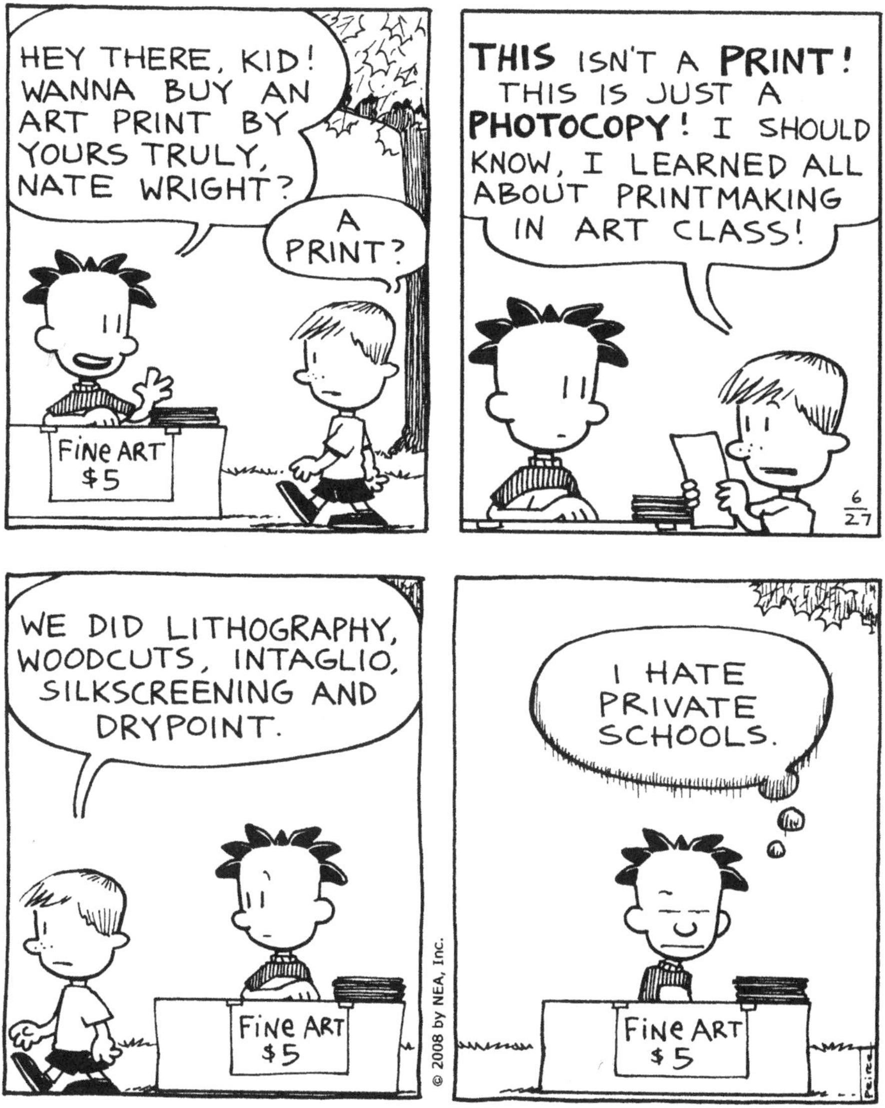
HEY THERE, KID! WANNA BUY AN ART PRINT BY YOURS TRULY, NATE WRIGHT?
A PRINT?
FINE ART $5
THIS ISN'T A PRINT! THIS IS JUST A PHOTOCOPY! I SHOULD KNOW, I LEARNED ALL ABOUT PRINTMAKING IN ART CLASS!
6/27
WE DID LITHOGRAPHY, WOODCUTS, INTAGLIO, SILKSCREENING AND DRYPOINT.
FINE ART $5
© 2008 by NEA, Inc.
I HATE PRIVATE SCHOOLS.
FINE ART $5

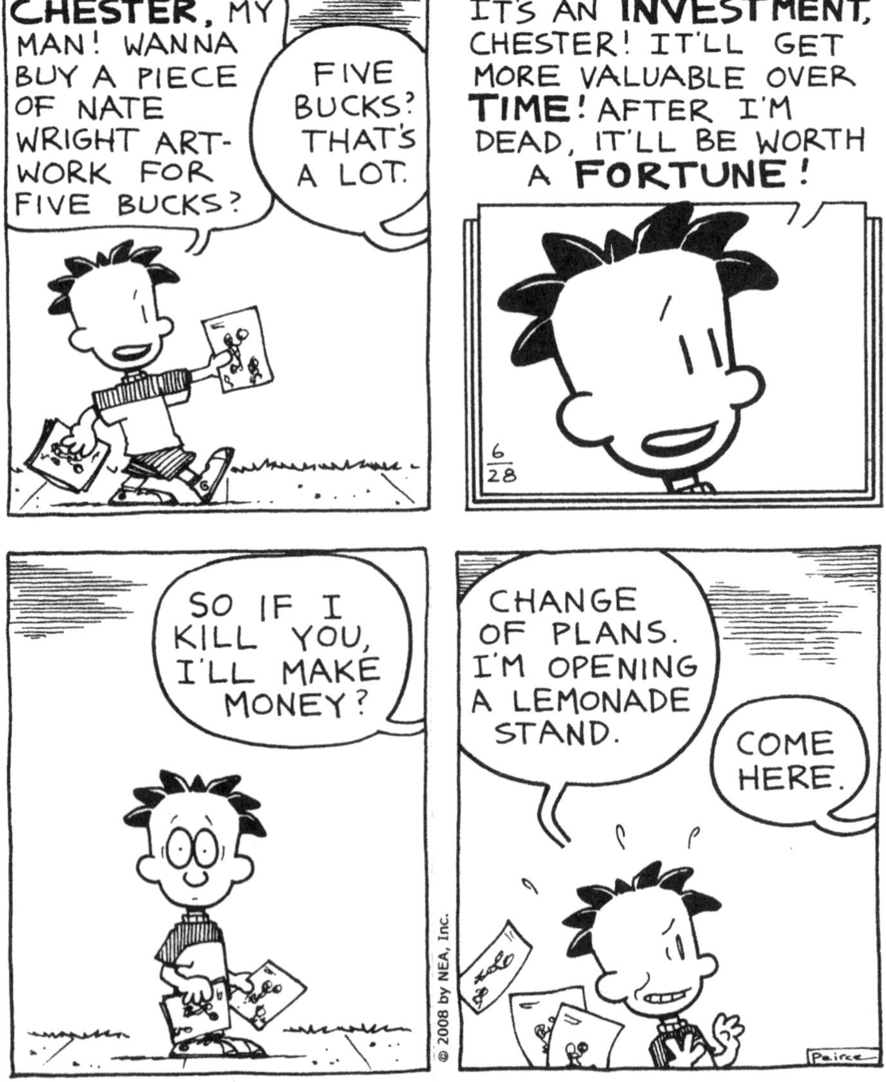
CHESTER, MY MAN! WANNA BUY A PIECE OF NATE WRIGHT ART-WORK FOR FIVE BUCKS?
FIVE BUCKS? THAT'S A LOT.
IT'S AN INVESTMENT, CHESTER! IT'LL GET MORE VALUABLE OVER TIME! AFTER I'M DEAD, IT'LL BE WORTH A FORTUNE!
6/28
SO IF I KILL YOU, I'LL MAKE MONEY?
CHANGE OF PLANS. I'M OPENING A LEMONADE STAND.
COME HERE.
© 2008 by NEA, Inc.
Peirce

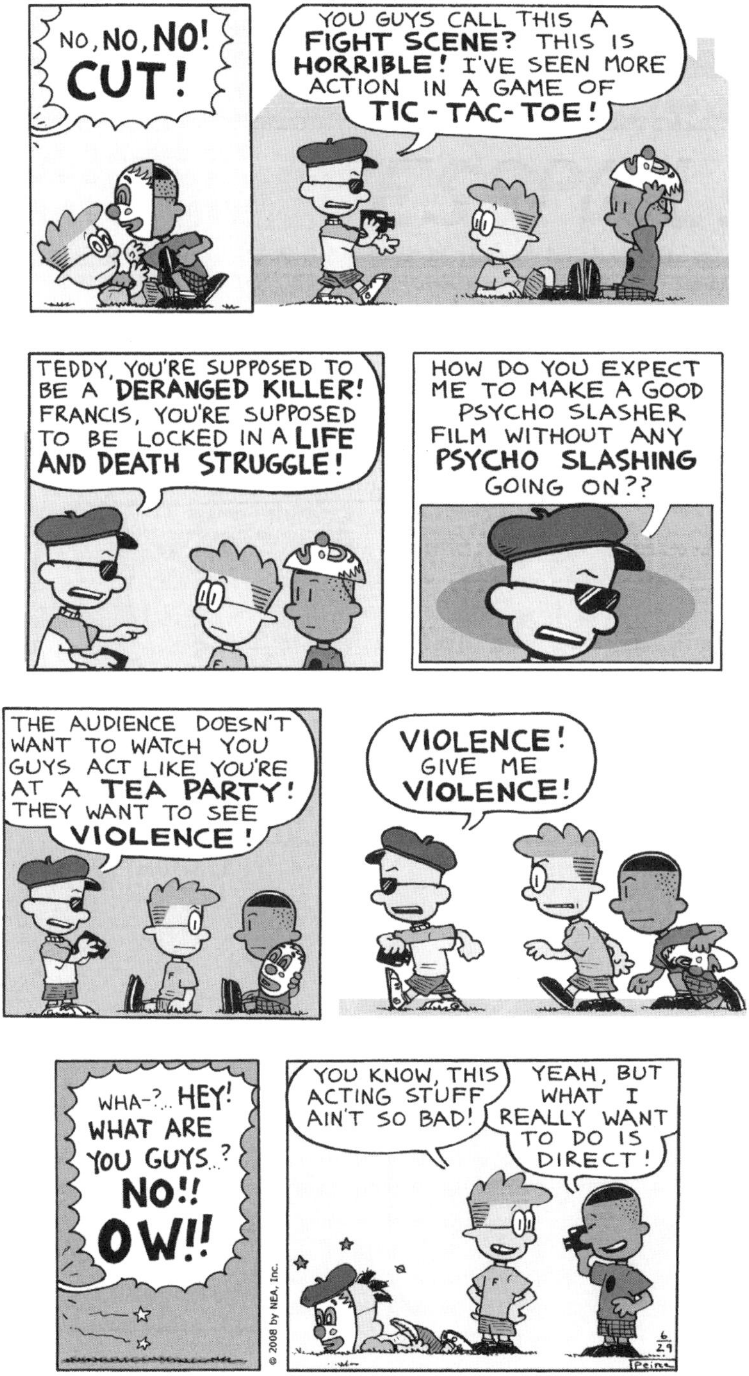
NO, NO, NO! CUT!
YOU GUYS CALL THIS A FIGHT SCENE? THIS IS HORRIBLE! I'VE SEEN MORE ACTION IN A GAME OF TIC-TAC-TOE!
TEDDY, YOU'RE SUPPOSED TO BE A DERANGED KILLER! FRANCIS, YOU'RE SUPPOSED TO BE LOCKED IN A LIFE AND DEATH STRUGGLE!
HOW DO YOU EXPECT ME TO MAKE A GOOD PSYCHO SLASHER FILM WITHOUT ANY PSYCHO SLASHING GOING ON??
THE AUDIENCE DOESN'T WANT TO WATCH YOU GUYS ACT LIKE YOU'RE AT A TEA PARTY! THEY WANT TO SEE VIOLENCE!
VIOLENCE! GIVE ME VIOLENCE!
WHA-?.. HEY! WHAT ARE YOU GUYS..? NO!! OW!!
YOU KNOW, THIS ACTING STUFF AIN'T SO BAD!
YEAH, BUT WHAT I REALLY WANT TO DO IS DIRECT!
6 29
Peirce

WILD RIDE

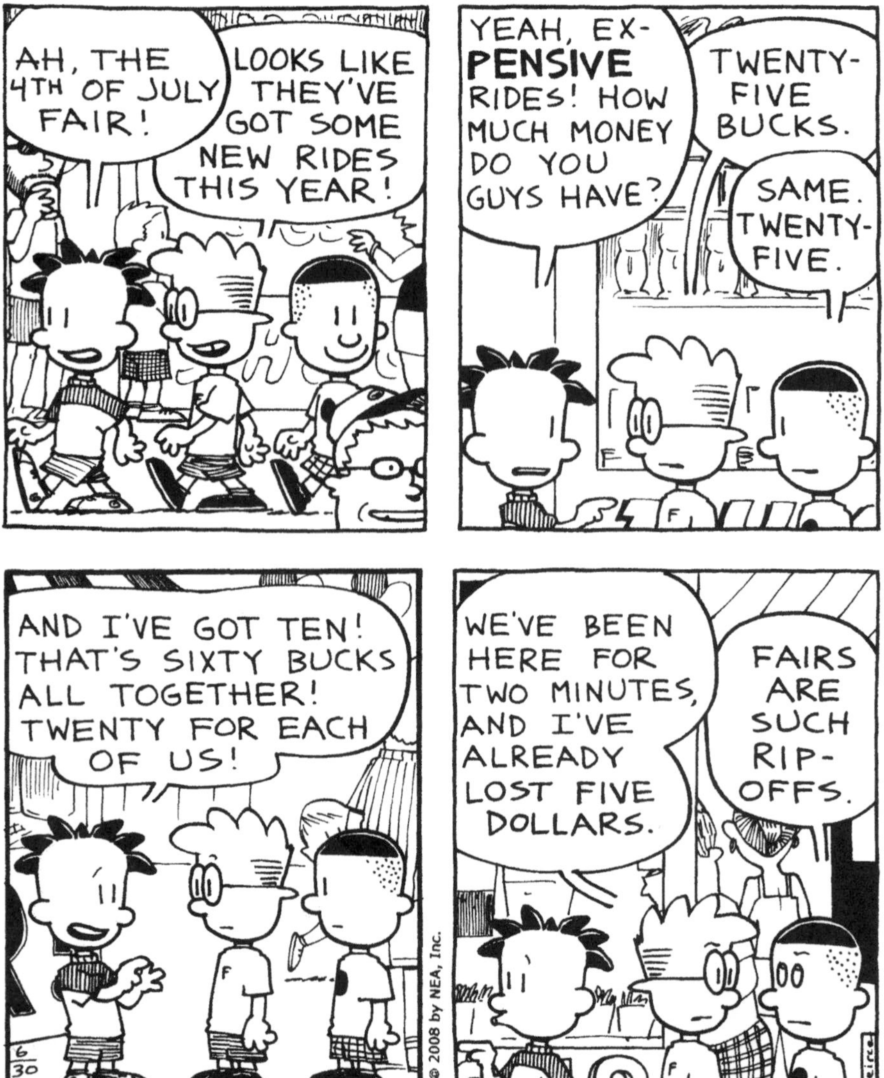
AH, THE 4TH OF JULY FAIR!
LOOKS LIKE THEY'VE GOT SOME NEW RIDES THIS YEAR!
YEAH, EX-PENSIVE RIDES! HOW MUCH MONEY DO YOU GUYS HAVE?
TWENTY-FIVE BUCKS.
SAME. TWENTY-FIVE.
AND I'VE GOT TEN! THAT'S SIXTY BUCKS ALL TOGETHER! TWENTY FOR EACH OF US!
6/30
© 2008 by NEA, Inc.
WE'VE BEEN HERE FOR TWO MINUTES, AND I'VE ALREADY LOST FIVE DOLLARS.
FAIRS ARE SUCH RIP-OFFS.
Peirce

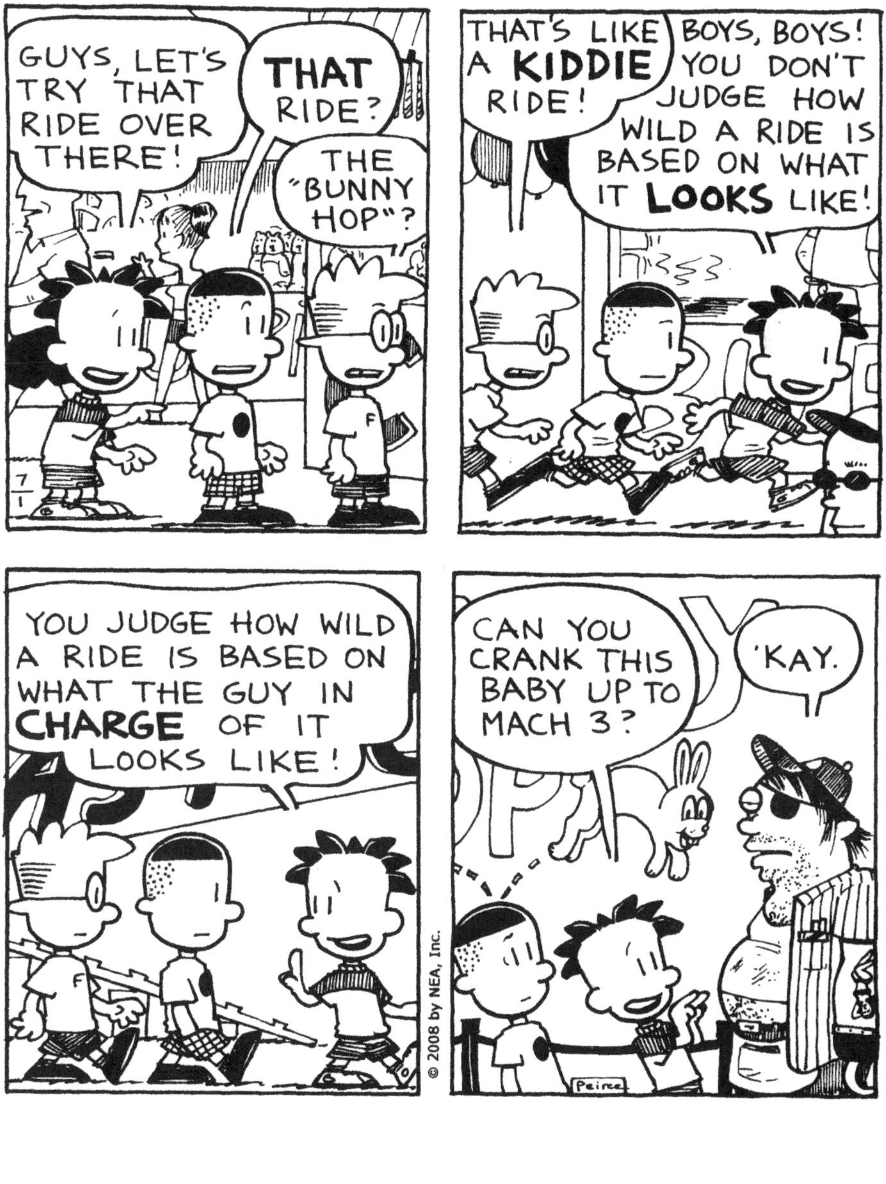
GUYS, LET'S TRY THAT RIDE OVER THERE!
THAT RIDE?
THE "BUNNY HOP"?
7/1
THAT'S LIKE A KIDDIE RIDE!
BOYS, BOYS! YOU DON'T JUDGE HOW WILD A RIDE IS BASED ON WHAT IT LOOKS LIKE!
YOU JUDGE HOW WILD A RIDE IS BASED ON WHAT THE GUY IN CHARGE OF IT LOOKS LIKE!
© 2008 by NEA, Inc.
CAN YOU CRANK THIS BABY UP TO MACH 3?
'KAY.
Peirce

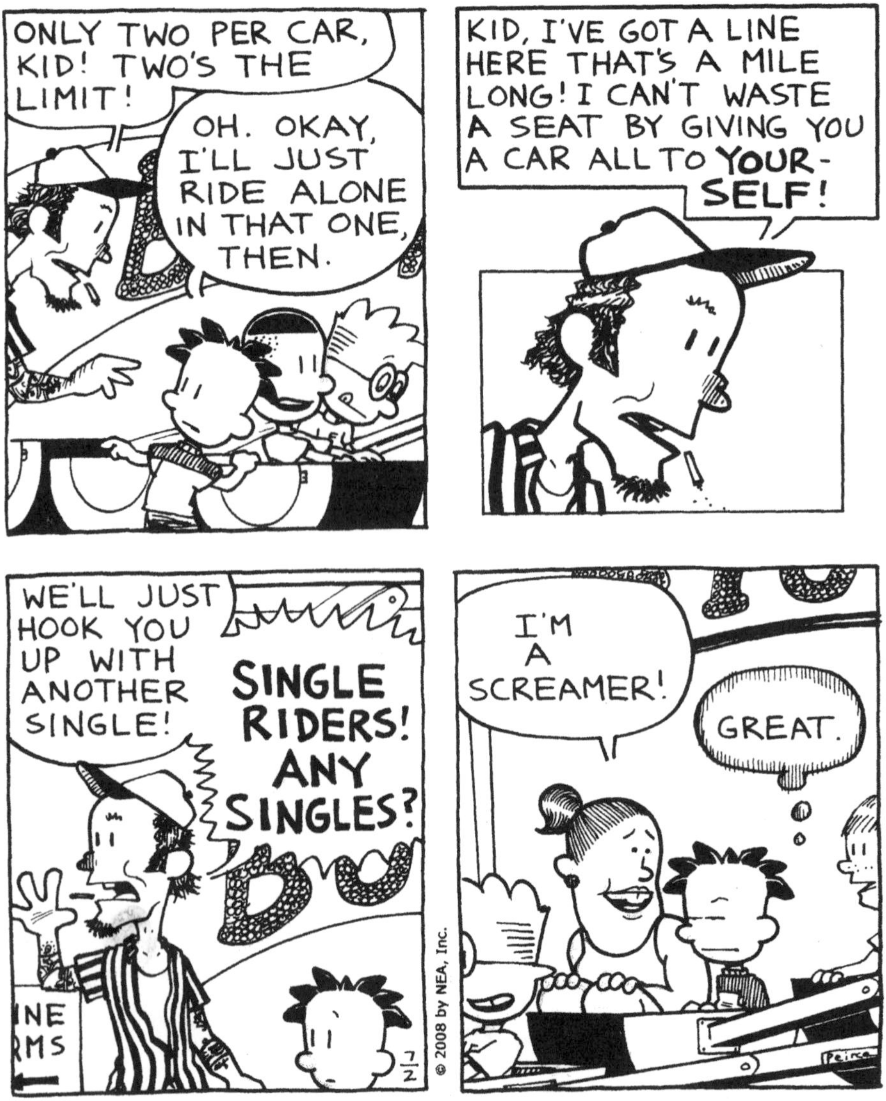
ONLY TWO PER CAR, KID! TWO'S THE LIMIT!
OH. OKAY, I'LL JUST RIDE ALONE IN THAT ONE, THEN.
KID, I'VE GOT A LINE HERE THAT'S A MILE LONG! I CAN'T WASTE A SEAT BY GIVING YOU A CAR ALL TO YOURSELF!
WE'LL JUST HOOK YOU UP WITH ANOTHER SINGLE!
SINGLE RIDERS! ANY SINGLES?
© 2008 by NEA, Inc.
I'M A SCREAMER!
GREAT.

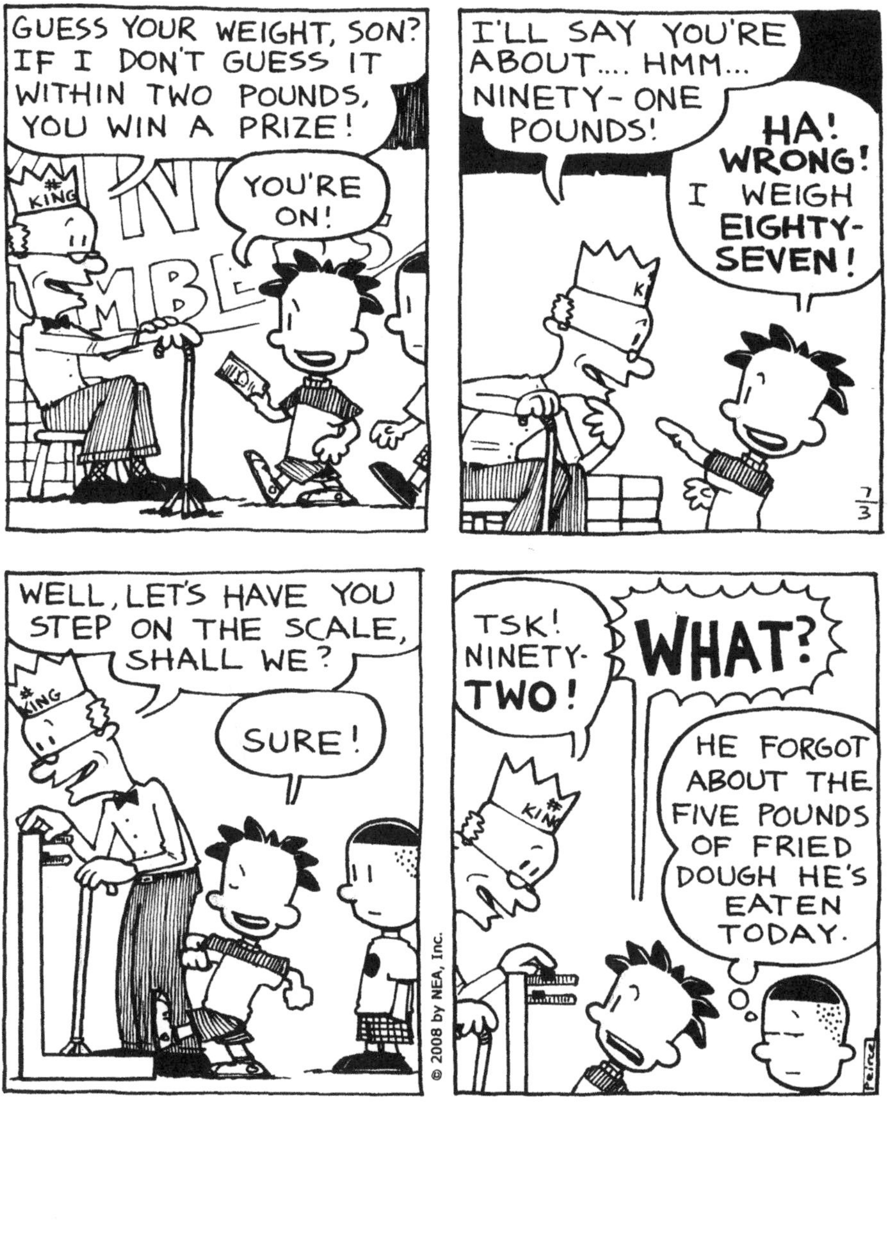
GUESS YOUR WEIGHT, SON? IF I DON'T GUESS IT WITHIN TWO POUNDS, YOU WIN A PRIZE!
KING
YOU'RE ON!
I'LL SAY YOU'RE ABOUT.... HMM... NINETY-ONE POUNDS!
HA! WRONG! I WEIGH EIGHTY-SEVEN!
7/3
WELL, LET'S HAVE YOU STEP ON THE SCALE, SHALL WE?
KING
SURE!
© 2008 by NEA, Inc.
TSK! NINETY-TWO!
WHAT?
HE FORGOT ABOUT THE FIVE POUNDS OF FRIED DOUGH HE'S EATEN TODAY.
Peirce

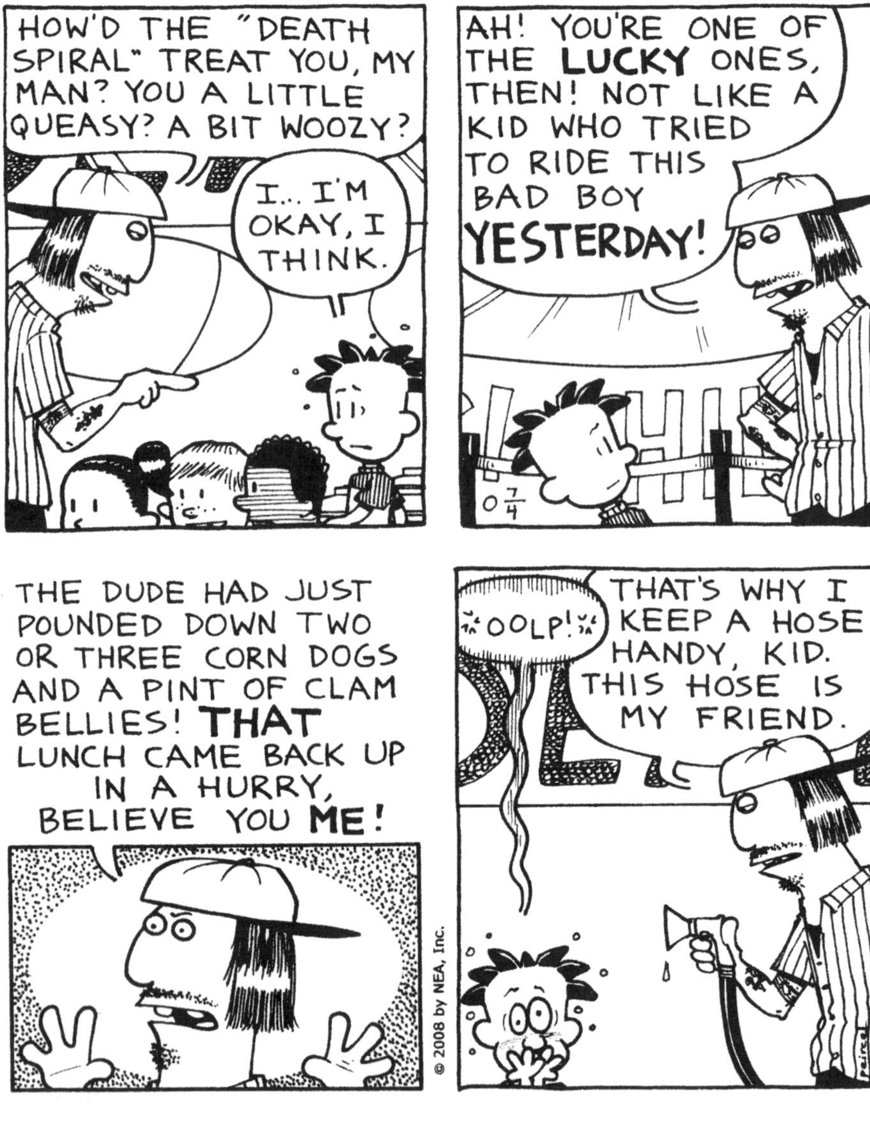
HOW'D THE "DEATH SPIRAL" TREAT YOU, MY MAN? YOU A LITTLE QUEASY? A BIT WOOZY?
I... I'M OKAY, I THINK.
AH! YOU'RE ONE OF THE LUCKY ONES, THEN! NOT LIKE A KID WHO TRIED TO RIDE THIS BAD BOY YESTERDAY!
THE DUDE HAD JUST POUNDED DOWN TWO OR THREE CORN DOGS AND A PINT OF CLAM BELLIES! THAT LUNCH CAME BACK UP IN A HURRY, BELIEVE YOU ME!
OOLP!
THAT'S WHY I KEEP A HOSE HANDY, KID. THIS HOSE IS MY FRIEND.
© 2008 by NEA, Inc.

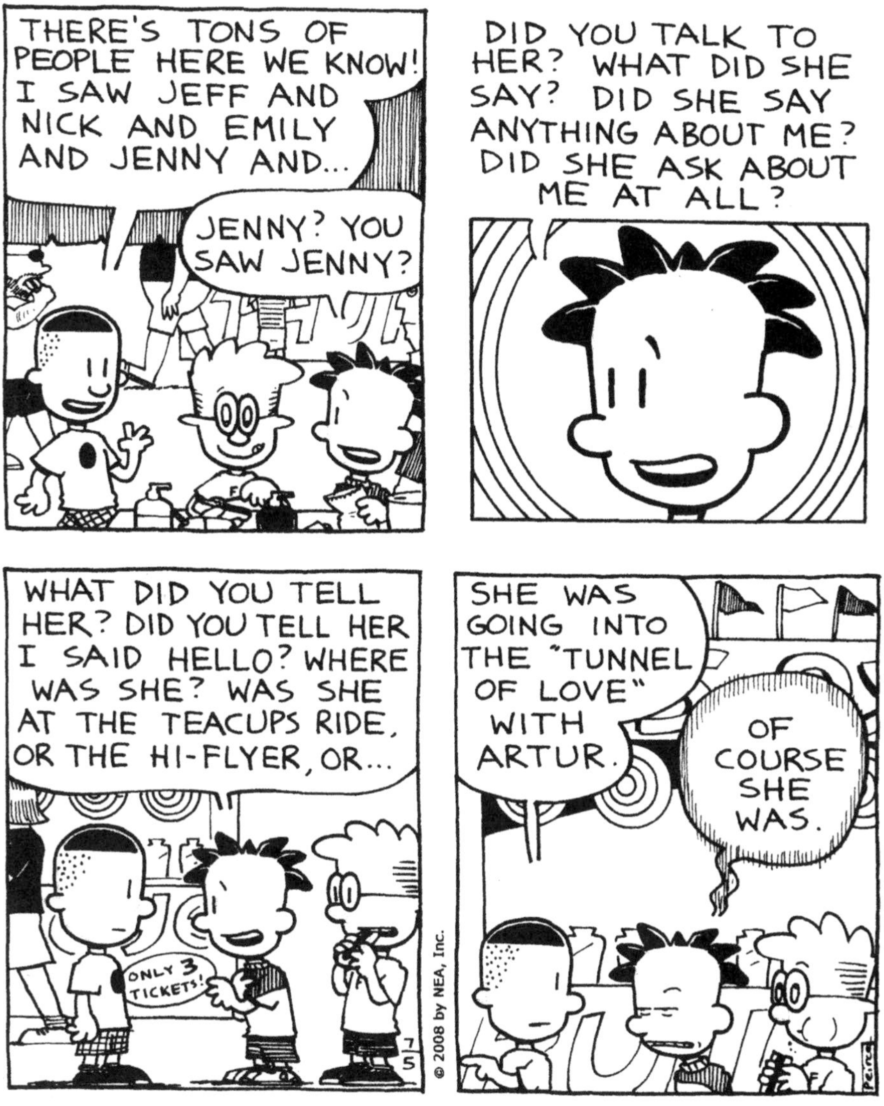
THERE'S TONS OF PEOPLE HERE WE KNOW! I SAW JEFF AND NICK AND EMILY AND JENNY AND...
JENNY? YOU SAW JENNY?
DID YOU TALK TO HER? WHAT DID SHE SAY? DID SHE SAY ANYTHING ABOUT ME? DID SHE ASK ABOUT ME AT ALL?
WHAT DID YOU TELL HER? DID YOU TELL HER I SAID HELLO? WHERE WAS SHE? WAS SHE AT THE TEACUPS RIDE, OR THE HI-FLYER, OR...
ONLY 3 TICKETS!
7/5
© 2008 by NEA, Inc.
SHE WAS GOING INTO THE "TUNNEL OF LOVE" WITH ARTUR.
OF COURSE SHE WAS.
PEIRCE

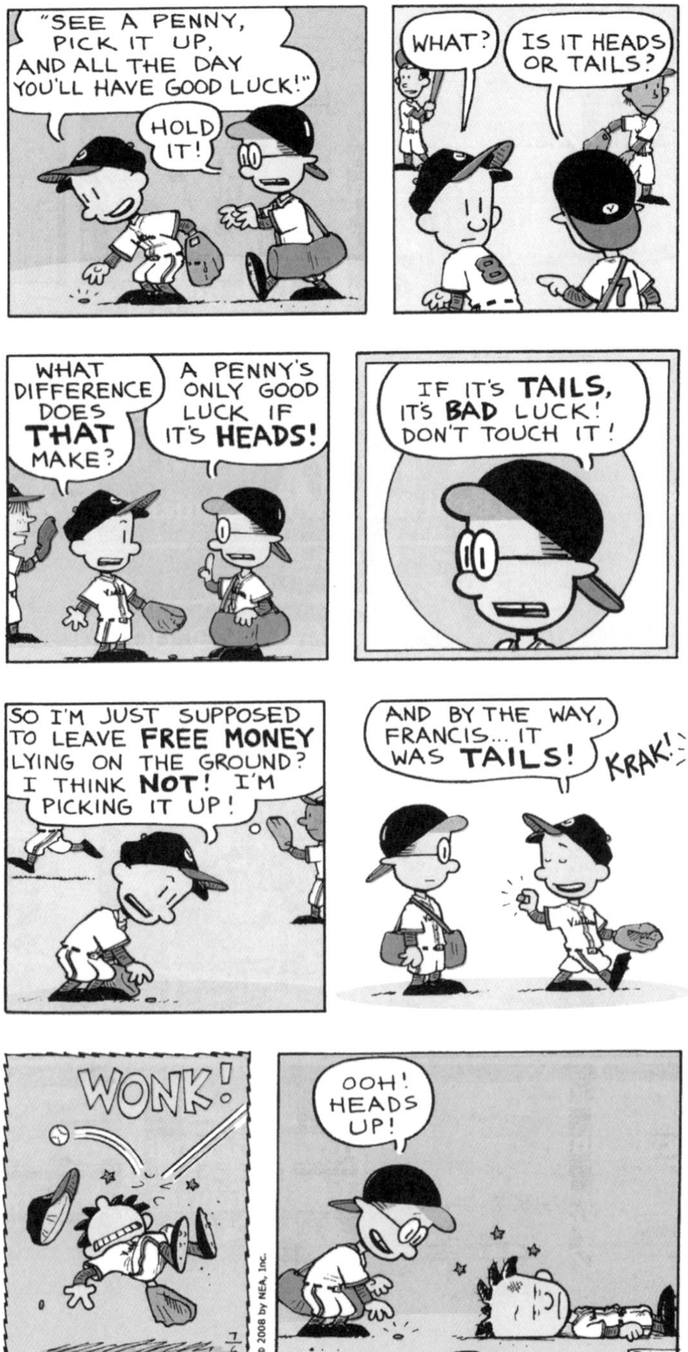
"SEE A PENNY, PICK IT UP, AND ALL THE DAY YOU'LL HAVE GOOD LUCK!"
HOLD IT!
WHAT?
IS IT HEADS OR TAILS?
WHAT DIFFERENCE DOES THAT MAKE?
A PENNY'S ONLY GOOD LUCK IF IT'S HEADS!
IF IT'S TAILS, IT'S BAD LUCK! DON'T TOUCH IT!
SO I'M JUST SUPPOSED TO LEAVE FREE MONEY LYING ON THE GROUND? I THINK NOT! I'M PICKING IT UP!
AND BY THE WAY, FRANCIS... IT WAS TAILS!
KRAK!
WONK!
© 2008 by NEA, Inc.
7/6
OOH! HEADS UP!
Peirce

WHAT BAD LUCK?

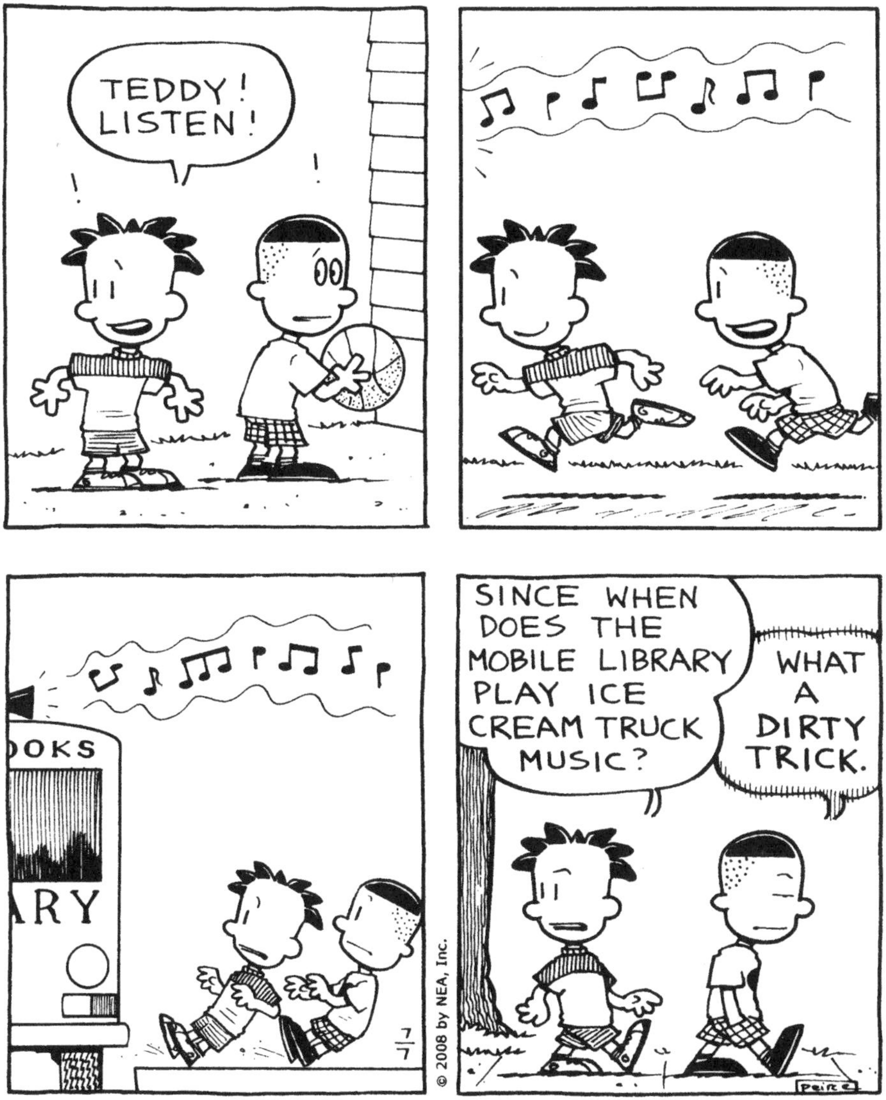
TEDDY! LISTEN!
!
!
SINCE WHEN DOES THE MOBILE LIBRARY PLAY ICE CREAM TRUCK MUSIC?
WHAT A DIRTY TRICK.

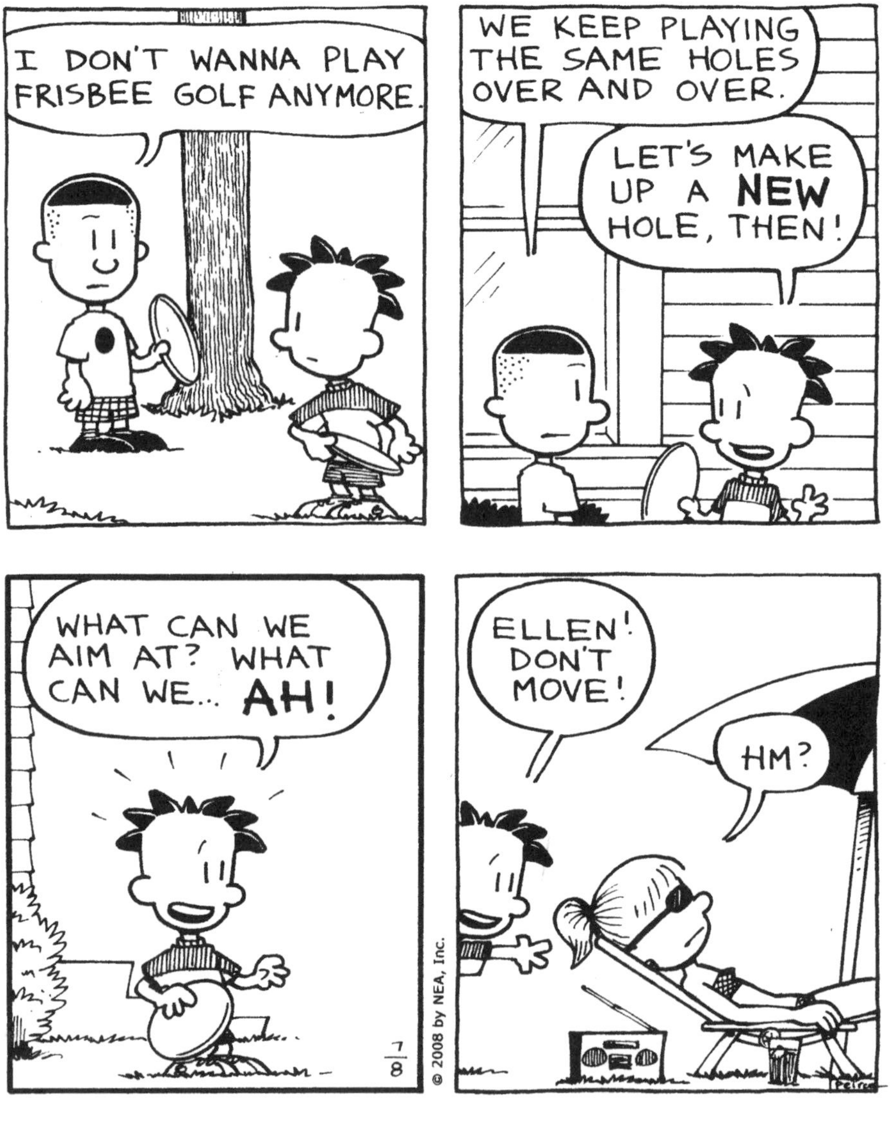
I DON'T WANNA PLAY FRISBEE GOLF ANYMORE.
WE KEEP PLAYING THE SAME HOLES OVER AND OVER.
LET'S MAKE UP A **NEW** HOLE, THEN!
WHAT CAN WE AIM AT? WHAT CAN WE... **AH!**
ELLEN! DON'T MOVE!
HM?
© 2008 by NEA, Inc.

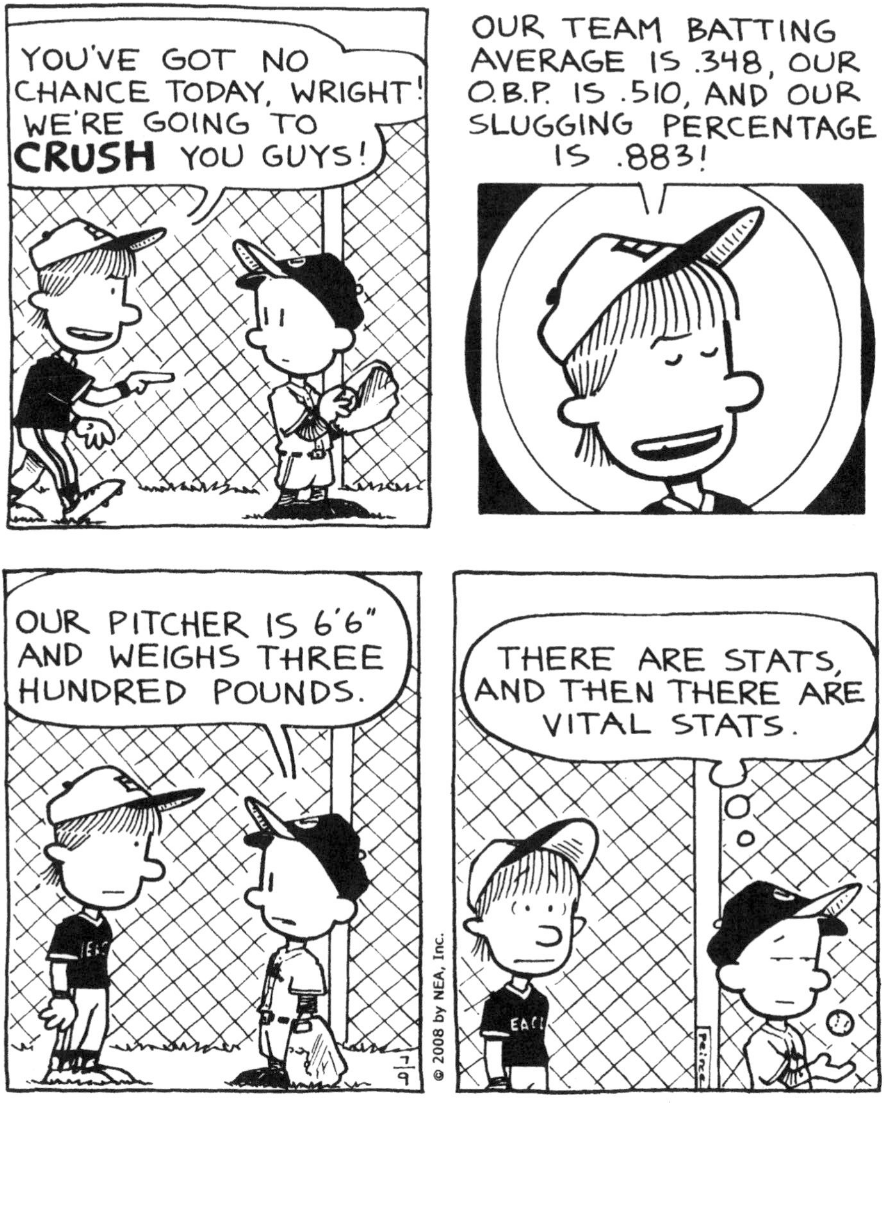
YOU'VE GOT NO CHANCE TODAY, WRIGHT! WE'RE GOING TO **CRUSH** YOU GUYS!
OUR TEAM BATTING AVERAGE IS .348, OUR O.B.P. IS .510, AND OUR SLUGGING PERCENTAGE IS .883!
OUR PITCHER IS 6'6" AND WEIGHS THREE HUNDRED POUNDS.
THERE ARE STATS, AND THEN THERE ARE VITAL STATS.
© 2008 by NEA, Inc.
7/9
Peirce

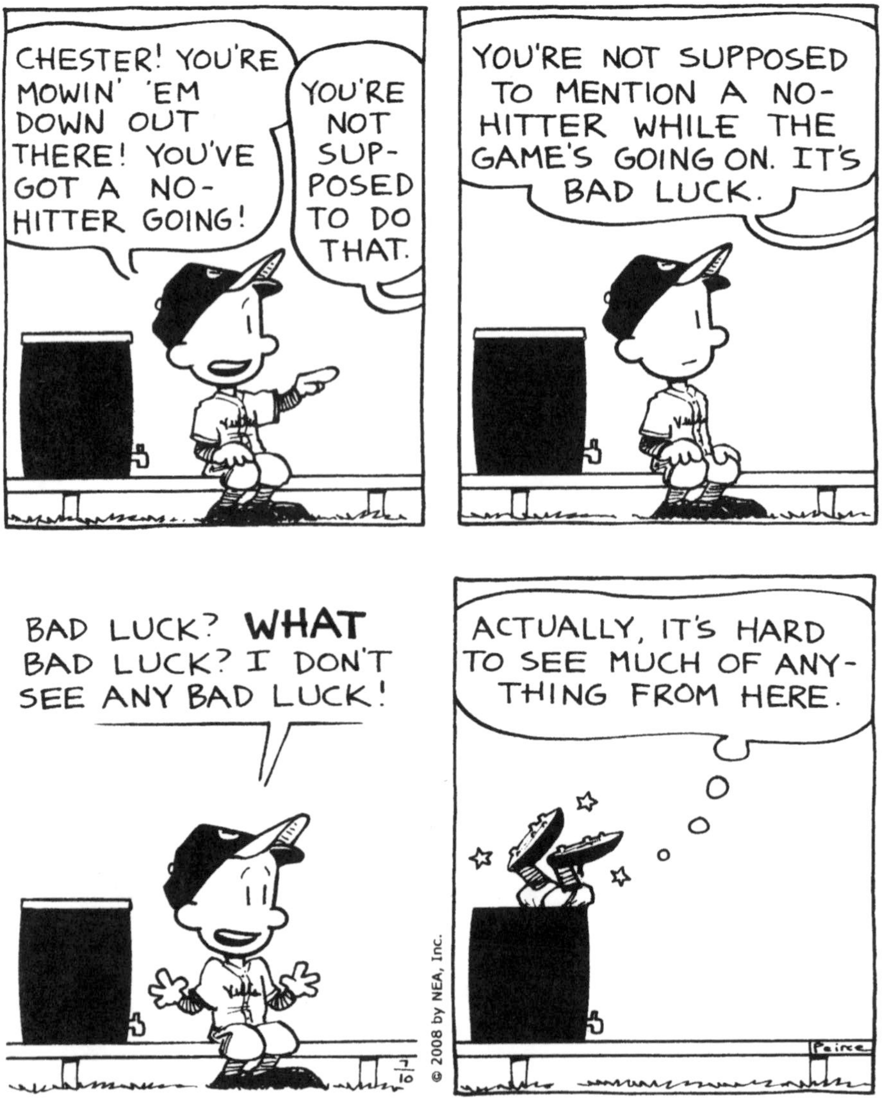
CHESTER! YOU'RE MOWIN' 'EM DOWN OUT THERE! YOU'VE GOT A NO-HITTER GOING!
YOU'RE NOT SUPPOSED TO DO THAT.
YOU'RE NOT SUPPOSED TO MENTION A NO-HITTER WHILE THE GAME'S GOING ON. IT'S BAD LUCK.
BAD LUCK? **WHAT** BAD LUCK? I DON'T SEE ANY BAD LUCK!
7/10
© 2008 by NEA, Inc.
ACTUALLY, IT'S HARD TO SEE MUCH OF ANYTHING FROM HERE.
Peirce

DOGS=AWESOME

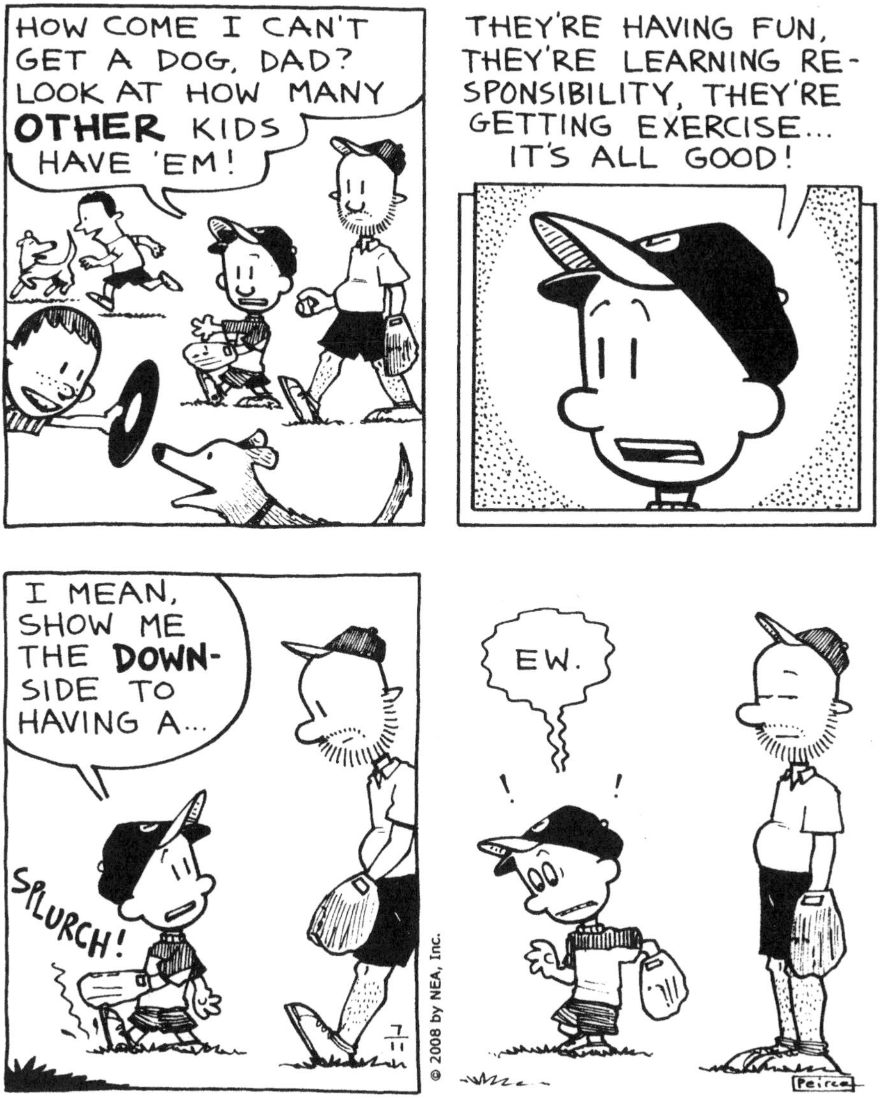
HOW COME I CAN'T GET A DOG, DAD? LOOK AT HOW MANY **OTHER** KIDS HAVE 'EM!
THEY'RE HAVING FUN, THEY'RE LEARNING RE-SPONSIBILITY, THEY'RE GETTING EXERCISE... IT'S ALL GOOD!
I MEAN, SHOW ME THE **DOWN**-SIDE TO HAVING A...
SPLURCH!
7/11
© 2008 by NEA, Inc.
EW.
! !
Peirce

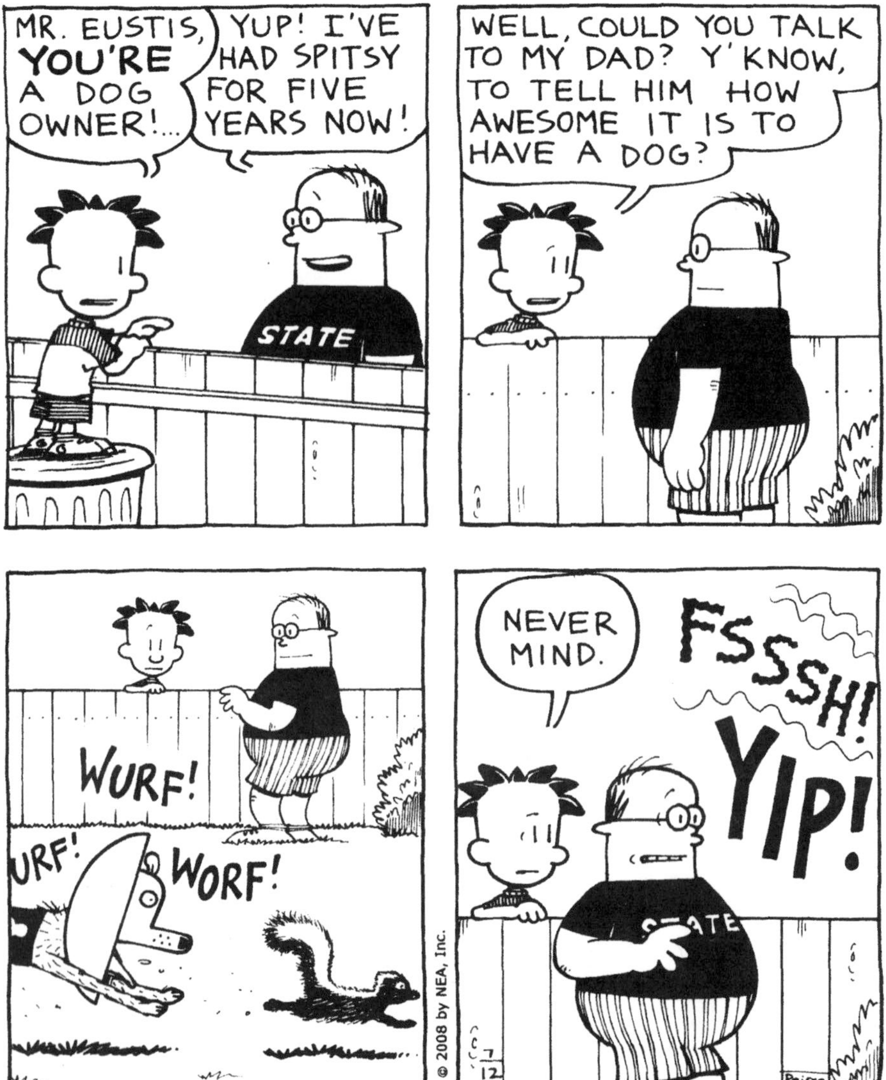
MR. EUSTIS, YOU'RE A DOG OWNER!...
YUP! I'VE HAD SPITSY FOR FIVE YEARS NOW!
STATE
WELL, COULD YOU TALK TO MY DAD? Y'KNOW, TO TELL HIM HOW AWESOME IT IS TO HAVE A DOG?
WURF!
URF!
WORF!
© 2008 by NEA, Inc.
NEVER MIND.
FSSSH!
YIP!
Peirce

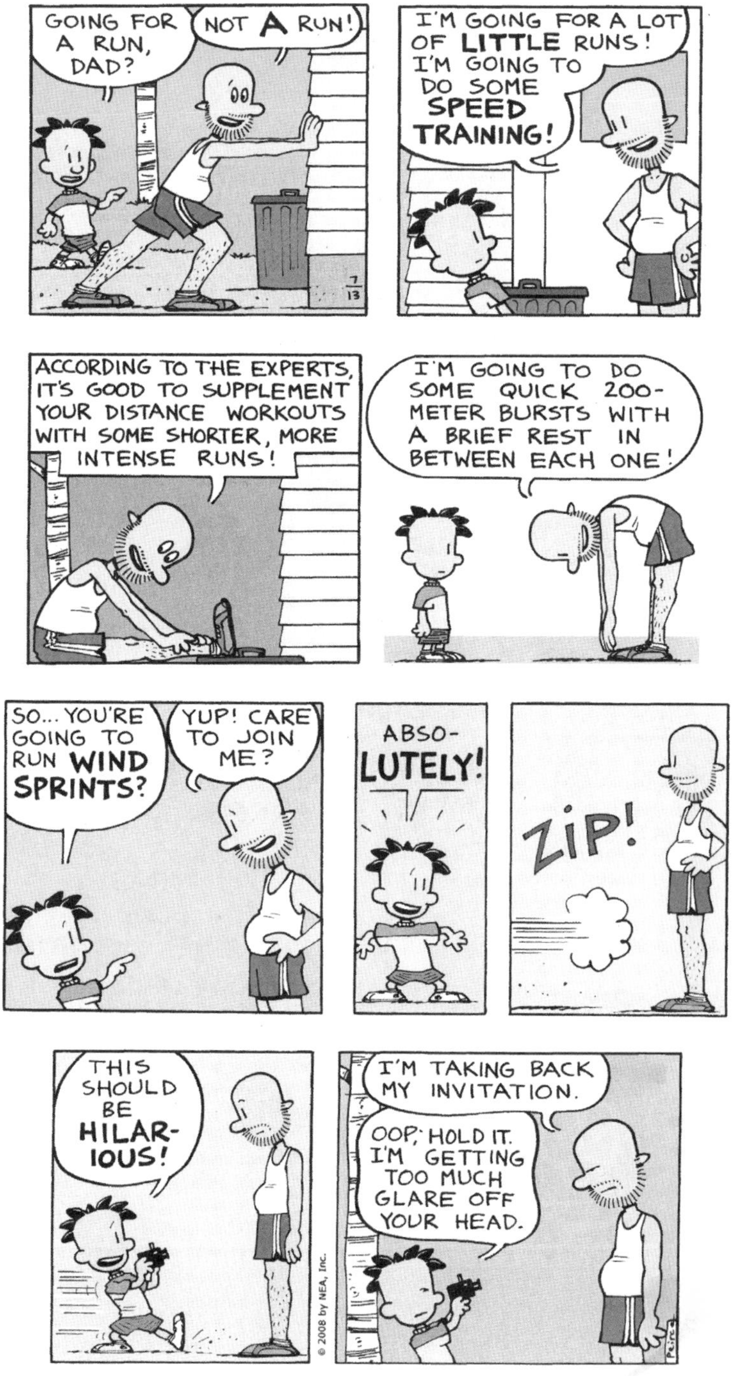
GOING FOR A RUN, DAD?
NOT A RUN!
7/13
I'M GOING FOR A LOT OF LITTLE RUNS! I'M GOING TO DO SOME SPEED TRAINING!
ACCORDING TO THE EXPERTS, IT'S GOOD TO SUPPLEMENT YOUR DISTANCE WORKOUTS WITH SOME SHORTER, MORE INTENSE RUNS!
I'M GOING TO DO SOME QUICK 200-METER BURSTS WITH A BRIEF REST IN BETWEEN EACH ONE!
SO... YOU'RE GOING TO RUN WIND SPRINTS?
YUP! CARE TO JOIN ME?
ABSO-LUTELY!
ZIP!
THIS SHOULD BE HILAR-IOUS!
© 2008 by NEA, Inc.
I'M TAKING BACK MY INVITATION.
OOP; HOLD IT. I'M GETTING TOO MUCH GLARE OFF YOUR HEAD.
Peirce

HUNGRY FOR VICTORY

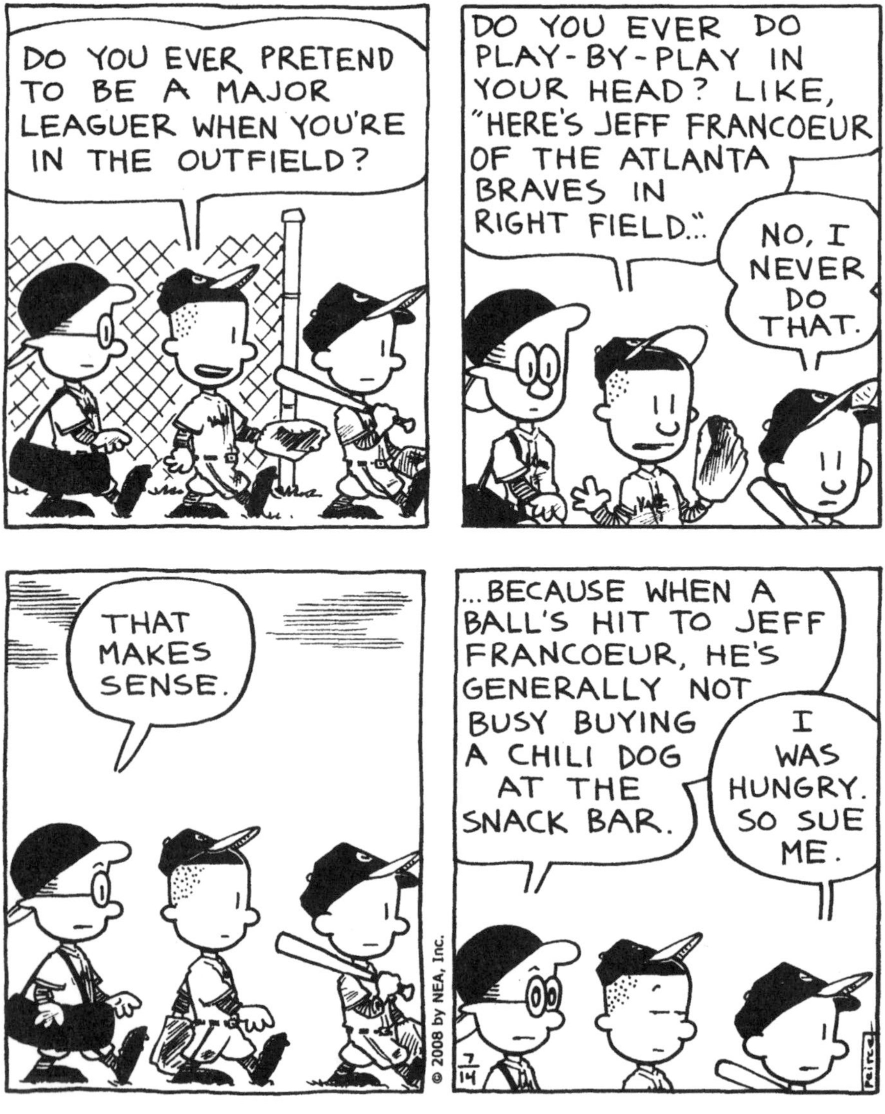
DO YOU EVER PRETEND TO BE A MAJOR LEAGUER WHEN YOU'RE IN THE OUTFIELD?
DO YOU EVER DO PLAY-BY-PLAY IN YOUR HEAD? LIKE, "HERE'S JEFF FRANCOEUR OF THE ATLANTA BRAVES IN RIGHT FIELD."...
NO, I NEVER DO THAT.
THAT MAKES SENSE.
...BECAUSE WHEN A BALL'S HIT TO JEFF FRANCOEUR, HE'S GENERALLY NOT BUSY BUYING A CHILI DOG AT THE SNACK BAR.
I WAS HUNGRY. SO SUE ME.
© 2008 by NEA, Inc.
7/14
Peirce

DOUBLE DATE

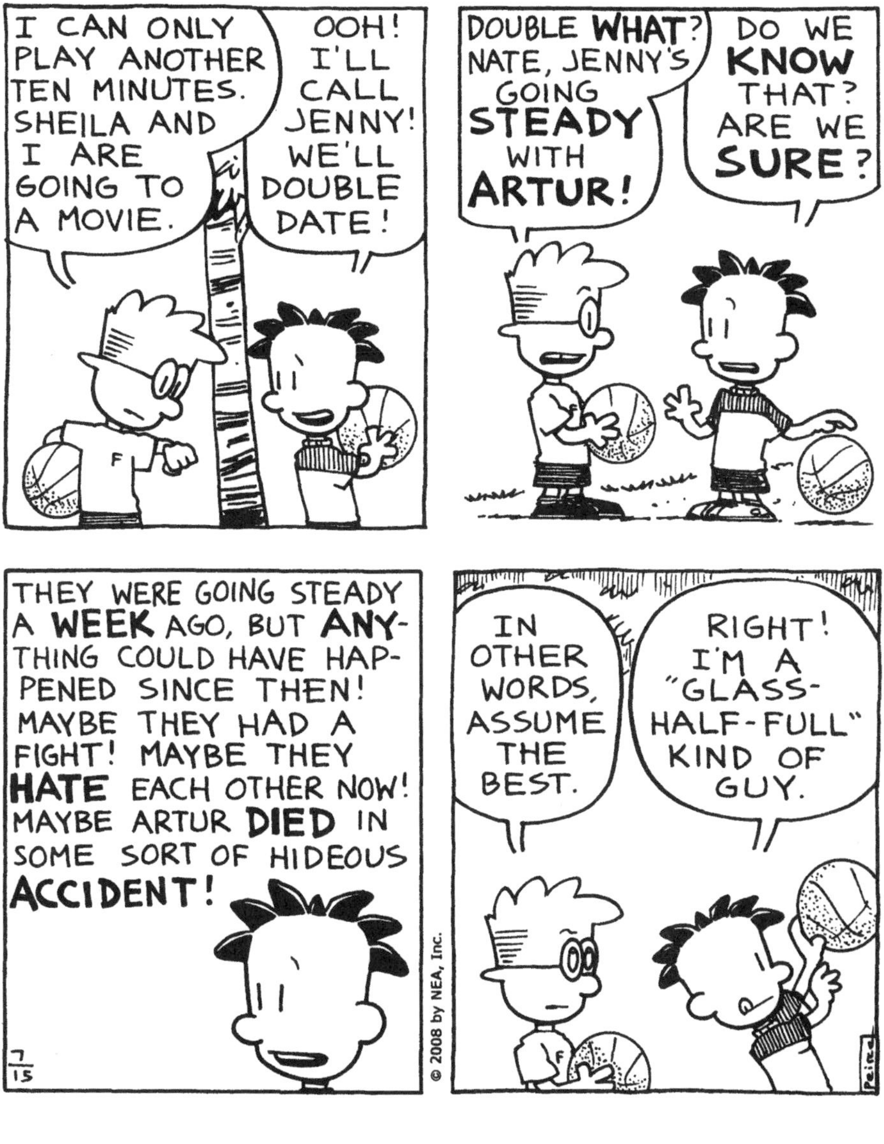
I CAN ONLY PLAY ANOTHER TEN MINUTES. SHEILA AND I ARE GOING TO A MOVIE.
OOH! I'LL CALL JENNY! WE'LL DOUBLE DATE!
DOUBLE WHAT? NATE, JENNY'S GOING STEADY WITH ARTUR!
DO WE KNOW THAT? ARE WE SURE?
THEY WERE GOING STEADY A WEEK AGO, BUT ANY-THING COULD HAVE HAP-PENED SINCE THEN! MAYBE THEY HAD A FIGHT! MAYBE THEY HATE EACH OTHER NOW! MAYBE ARTUR DIED IN SOME SORT OF HIDEOUS ACCIDENT!
7/15
© 2008 by NEA, Inc.
IN OTHER WORDS, ASSUME THE BEST.
RIGHT! I'M A "GLASS-HALF-FULL" KIND OF GUY.
Peirce

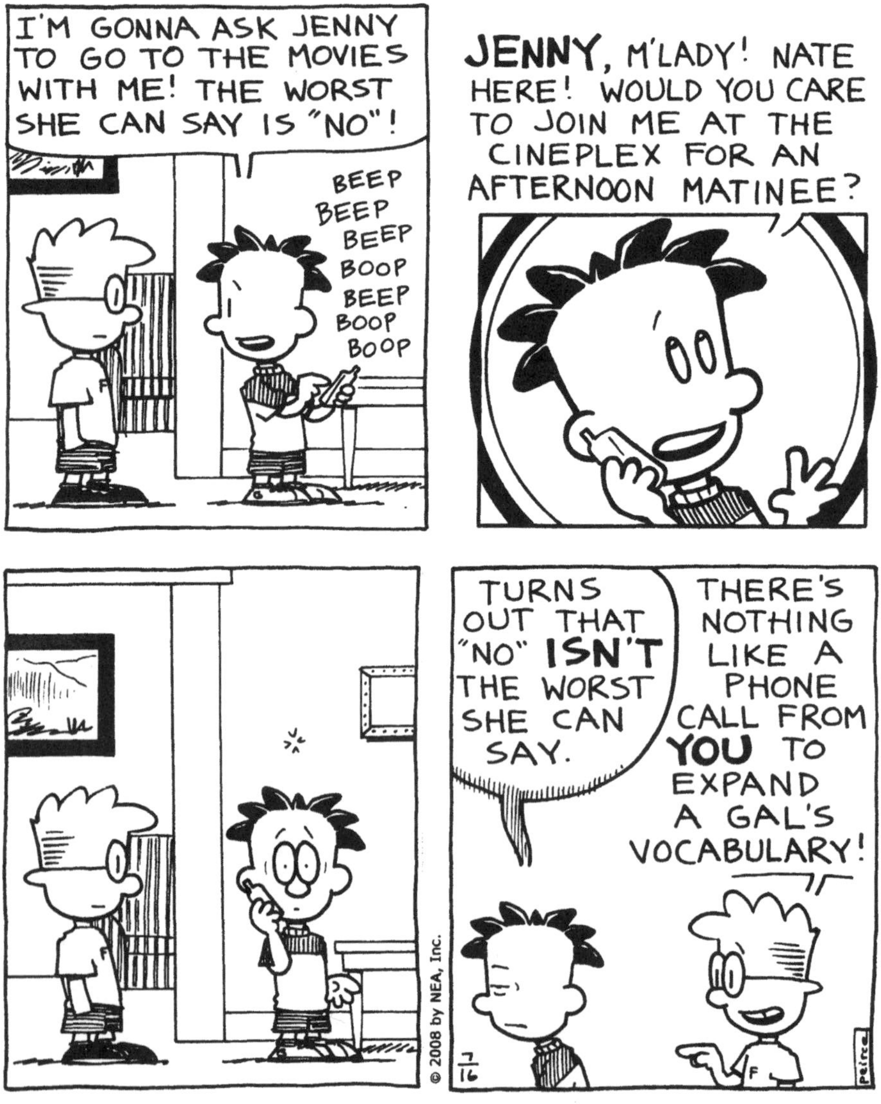
I'M GONNA ASK JENNY TO GO TO THE MOVIES WITH ME! THE WORST SHE CAN SAY IS "NO"!
BEEP BEEP BEEP BOOP BEEP BOOP BOOP
JENNY, M'LADY! NATE HERE! WOULD YOU CARE TO JOIN ME AT THE CINEPLEX FOR AN AFTERNOON MATINEE?
TURNS OUT THAT "NO" ISN'T THE WORST SHE CAN SAY.
THERE'S NOTHING LIKE A PHONE CALL FROM YOU TO EXPAND A GAL'S VOCABULARY!
7/16
peirce

SPECIAL DELIVERY

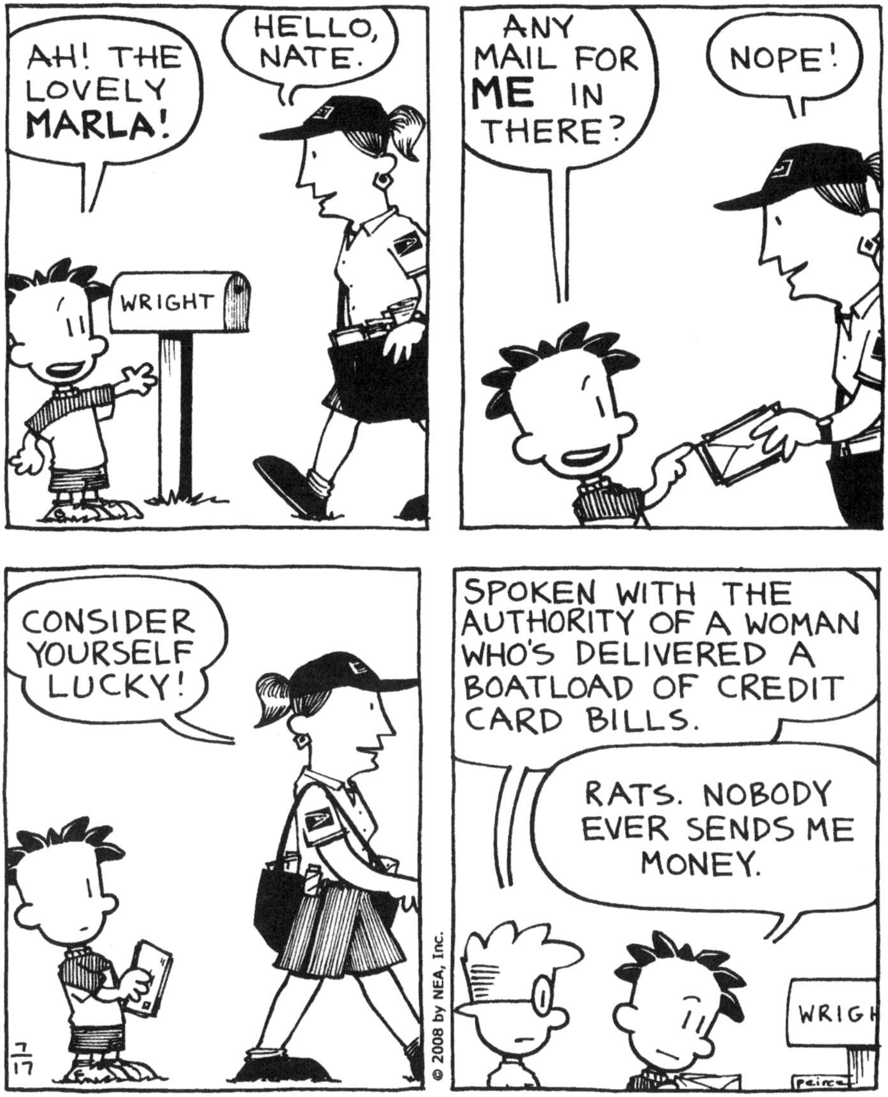
AH! THE LOVELY **MARLA**!
HELLO, NATE.
WRIGHT
ANY MAIL FOR **ME** IN THERE?
NOPE!
CONSIDER YOURSELF LUCKY!
7/17
© 2008 by NEA, Inc.
SPOKEN WITH THE AUTHORITY OF A WOMAN WHO'S DELIVERED A BOATLOAD OF CREDIT CARD BILLS.
RATS. NOBODY EVER SENDS ME MONEY.
WRIGH
peirce

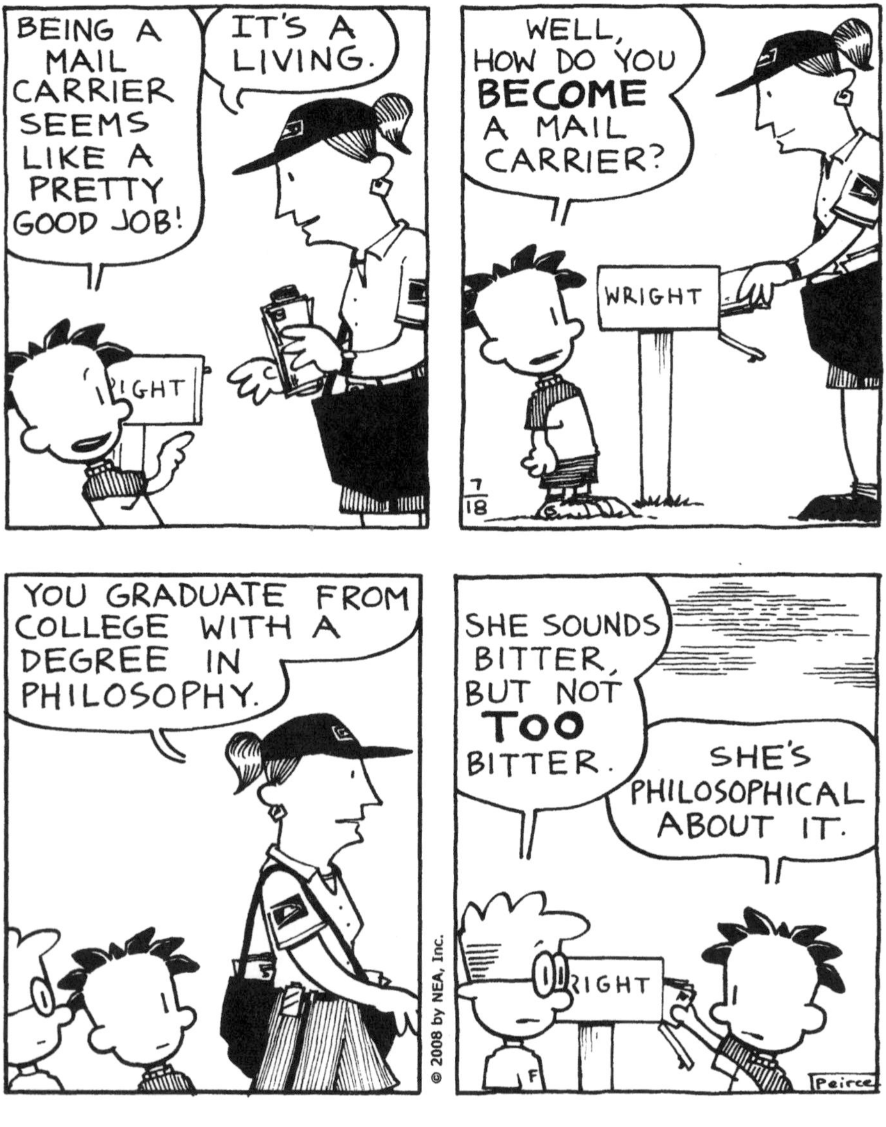

BEING A MAIL CARRIER SEEMS LIKE A PRETTY GOOD JOB!
IT'S A LIVING.
WELL, HOW DO YOU **BECOME** A MAIL CARRIER?
WRIGHT
7/18
YOU GRADUATE FROM COLLEGE WITH A DEGREE IN PHILOSOPHY.
© 2008 by NEA, Inc.
SHE SOUNDS BITTER, BUT NOT **TOO** BITTER.
SHE'S PHILOSOPHICAL ABOUT IT.
Peirce

DESTINATION VACATION

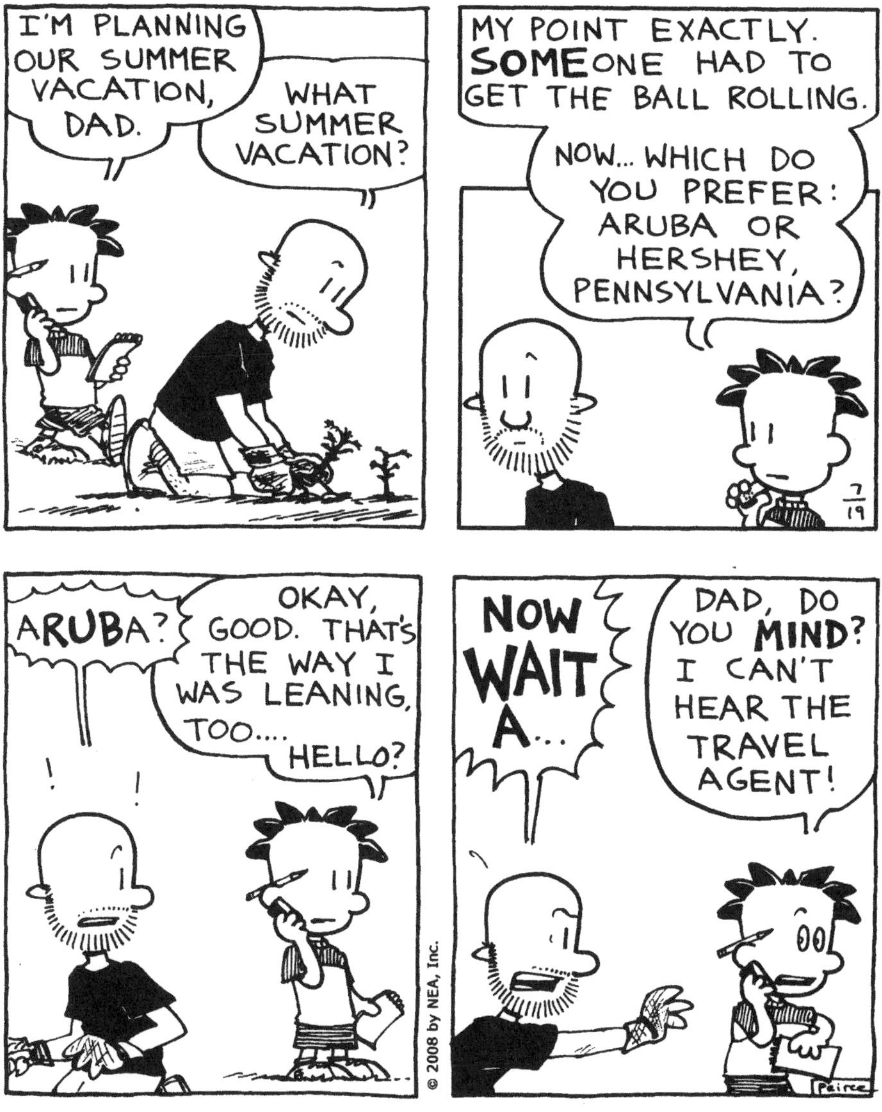

I'M PLANNING OUR SUMMER VACATION, DAD.
WHAT SUMMER VACATION?
MY POINT EXACTLY. SOMEONE HAD TO GET THE BALL ROLLING.
NOW... WHICH DO YOU PREFER: ARUBA OR HERSHEY, PENNSYLVANIA?
7/19
ARUBA?
OKAY, GOOD. THAT'S THE WAY I WAS LEANING, TOO.... HELLO?
! !
© 2008 by NEA, Inc.
NOW WAIT A...
DAD, DO YOU MIND? I CAN'T HEAR THE TRAVEL AGENT!
Peirce

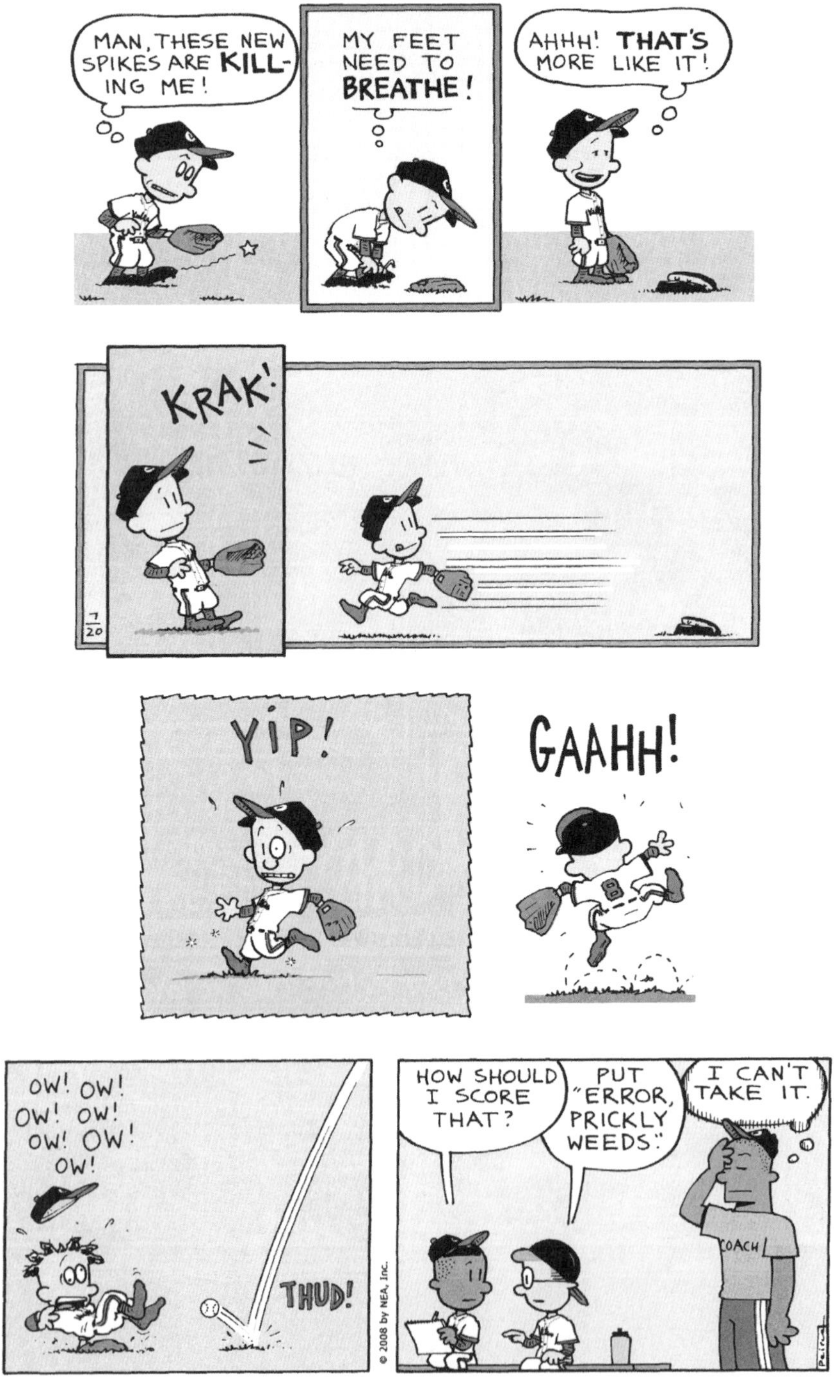
MAN, THESE NEW SPIKES ARE KILL-ING ME!
MY FEET NEED TO BREATHE!
AHHH! THAT'S MORE LIKE IT!
KRAK!
7/20
YIP!
GAAHH!
OW! OW! OW! OW! OW! OW! OW!
THUD!
© 2008 by NEA, Inc.
HOW SHOULD I SCORE THAT?
PUT "ERROR, PRICKLY WEEDS."
I CAN'T TAKE IT.
COACH

FAMILY (DYS)FUNCTION

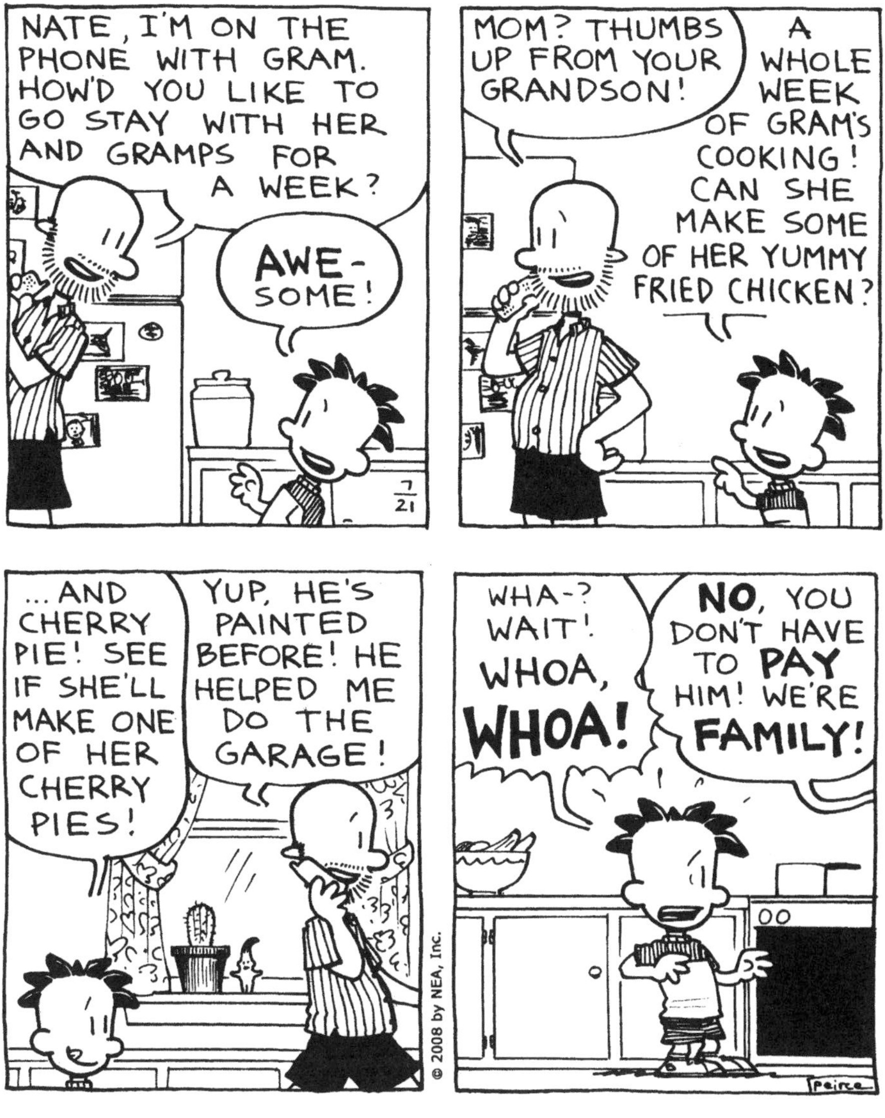
NATE, I'M ON THE PHONE WITH GRAM. HOW'D YOU LIKE TO GO STAY WITH HER AND GRAMPS FOR A WEEK?
AWE-SOME!
7/21
MOM? THUMBS UP FROM YOUR GRANDSON!
A WHOLE WEEK OF GRAM'S COOKING! CAN SHE MAKE SOME OF HER YUMMY FRIED CHICKEN?
...AND CHERRY PIE! SEE IF SHE'LL MAKE ONE OF HER CHERRY PIES!
YUP, HE'S PAINTED BEFORE! HE HELPED ME DO THE GARAGE!
© 2008 by NEA, Inc.
WHA-? WAIT! WHOA, WHOA!
NO, YOU DON'T HAVE TO PAY HIM! WE'RE FAMILY!
peirce

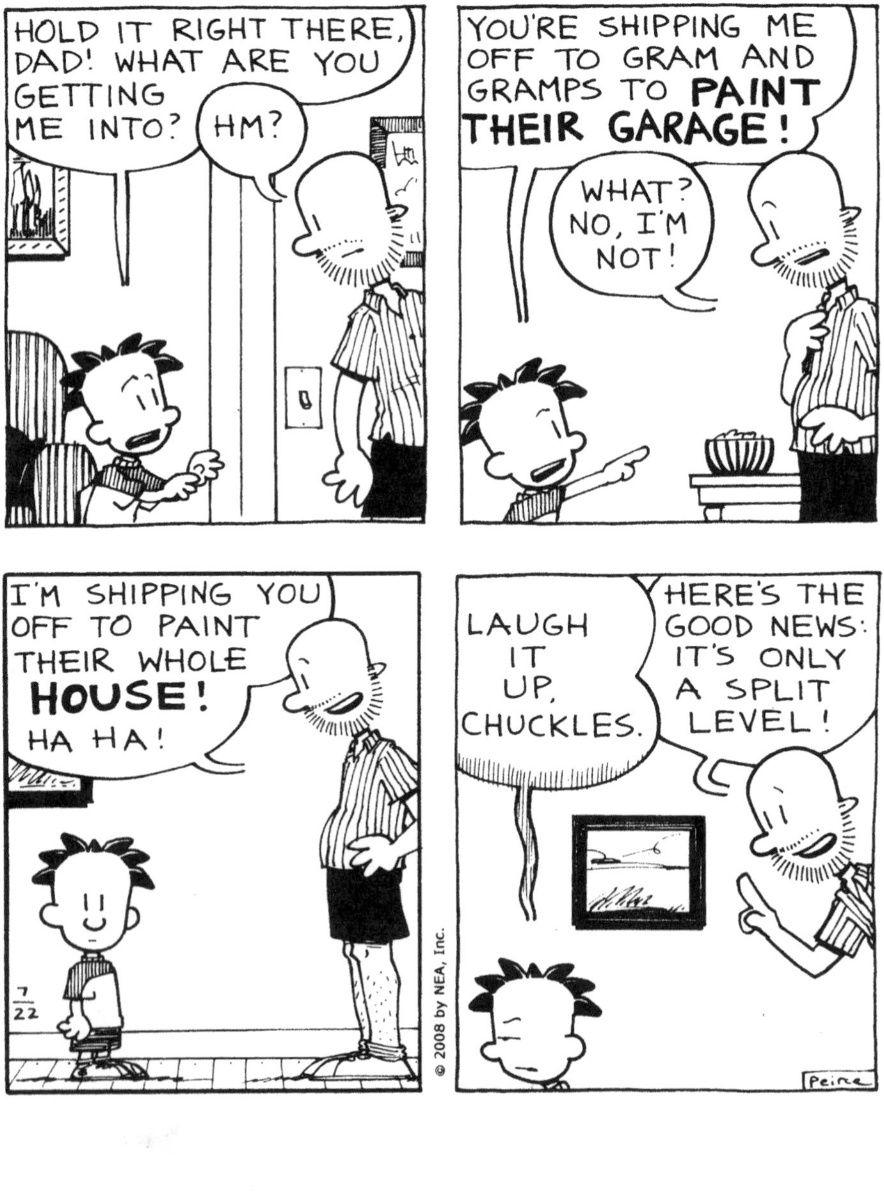
HOLD IT RIGHT THERE, DAD! WHAT ARE YOU GETTING ME INTO?
HM?
YOU'RE SHIPPING ME OFF TO GRAM AND GRAMPS TO PAINT THEIR GARAGE!
WHAT? NO, I'M NOT!
I'M SHIPPING YOU OFF TO PAINT THEIR WHOLE HOUSE! HA HA!
7/22
© 2008 by NEA, Inc.
HERE'S THE GOOD NEWS: IT'S ONLY A SPLIT LEVEL!
LAUGH IT UP, CHUCKLES.
Peirce

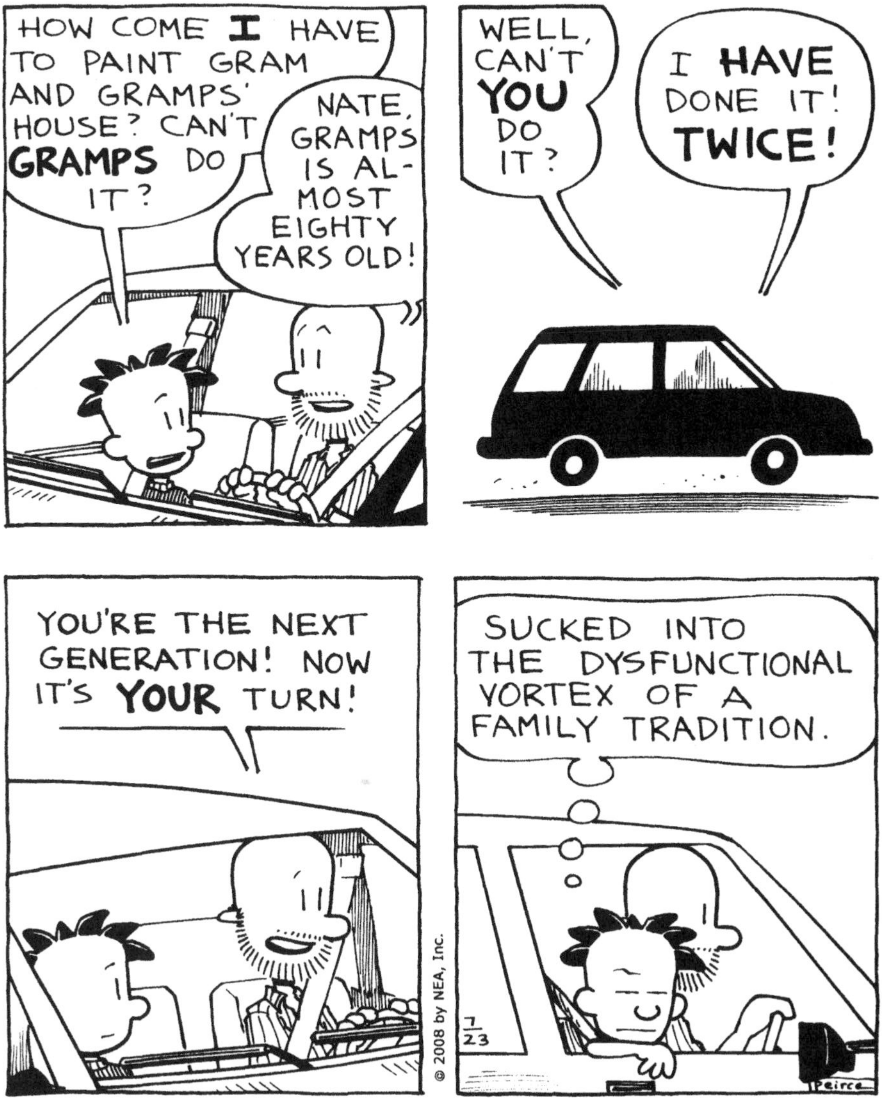
HOW COME I HAVE TO PAINT GRAM AND GRAMPS' HOUSE? CAN'T GRAMPS DO IT?
NATE, GRAMPS IS ALMOST EIGHTY YEARS OLD!
WELL, CAN'T YOU DO IT?
I HAVE DONE IT! TWICE!
YOU'RE THE NEXT GENERATION! NOW IT'S YOUR TURN!
© 2008 by NEA, Inc.
7/23
SUCKED INTO THE DYSFUNCTIONAL VORTEX OF A FAMILY TRADITION.
Peirce

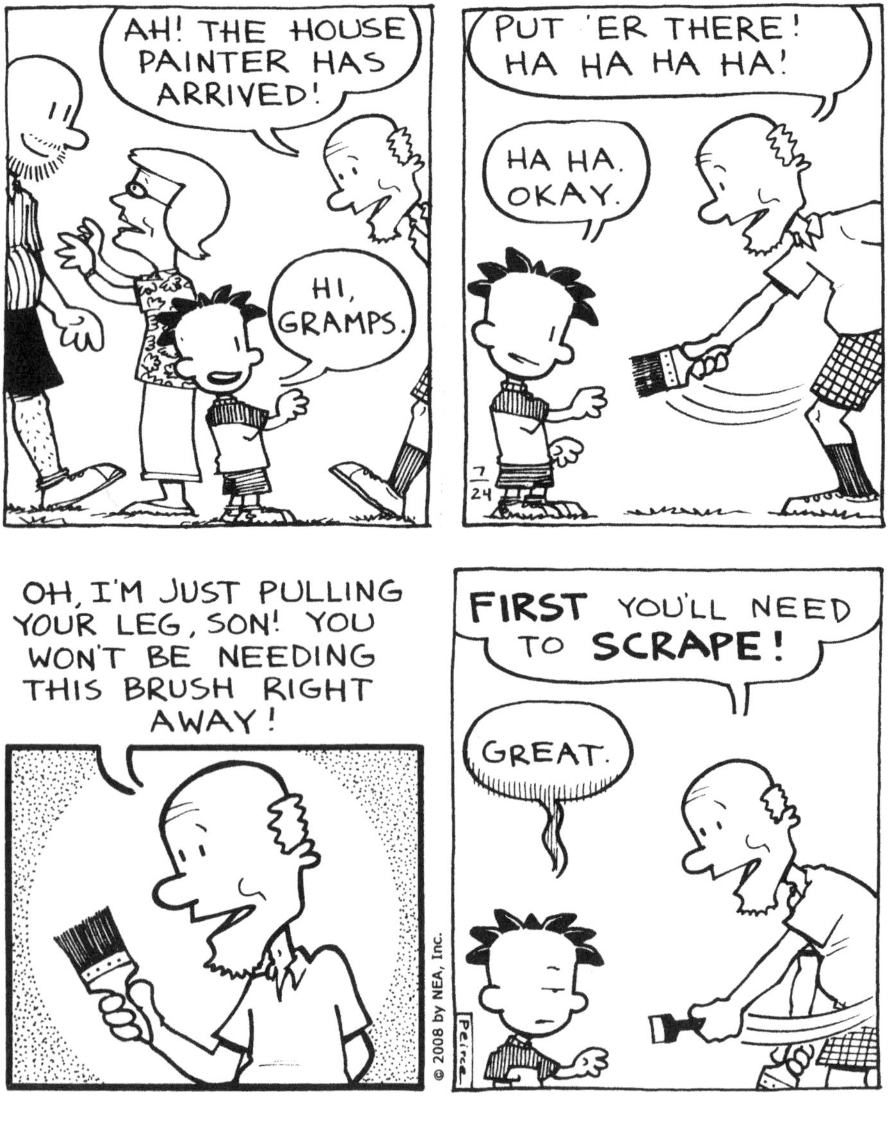
AH! THE HOUSE PAINTER HAS ARRIVED!
HI, GRAMPS.
PUT 'ER THERE! HA HA HA HA!
HA HA. OKAY.
7/24
OH, I'M JUST PULLING YOUR LEG, SON! YOU WON'T BE NEEDING THIS BRUSH RIGHT AWAY!
© 2008 by NEA, Inc.
Peirce
FIRST YOU'LL NEED TO SCRAPE!
GREAT.

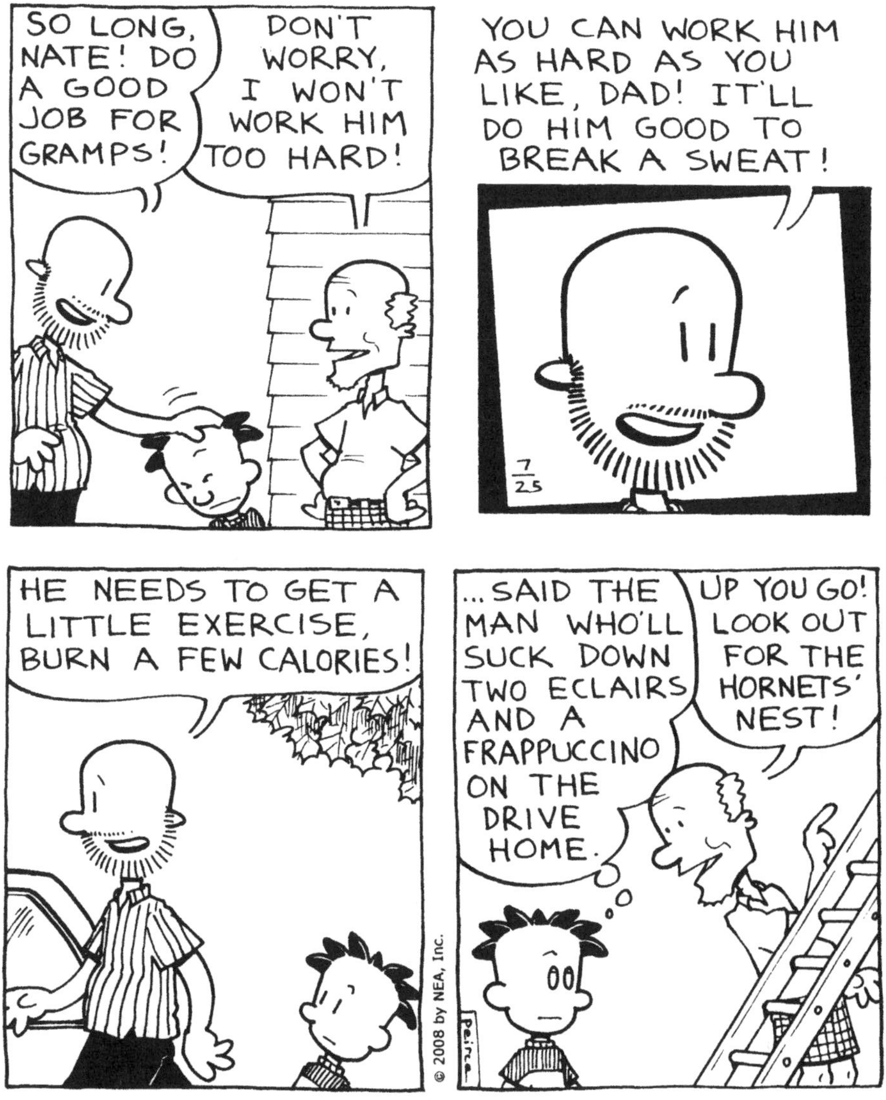
SO LONG, NATE! DO A GOOD JOB FOR GRAMPS!
DON'T WORRY, I WON'T WORK HIM TOO HARD!
YOU CAN WORK HIM AS HARD AS YOU LIKE, DAD! IT'LL DO HIM GOOD TO BREAK A SWEAT!
7
25
HE NEEDS TO GET A LITTLE EXERCISE, BURN A FEW CALORIES!
© 2008 by NEA, Inc.
...SAID THE MAN WHO'LL SUCK DOWN TWO ECLAIRS AND A FRAPPUCCINO ON THE DRIVE HOME.
UP YOU GO! LOOK OUT FOR THE HORNETS' NEST!
Peirce

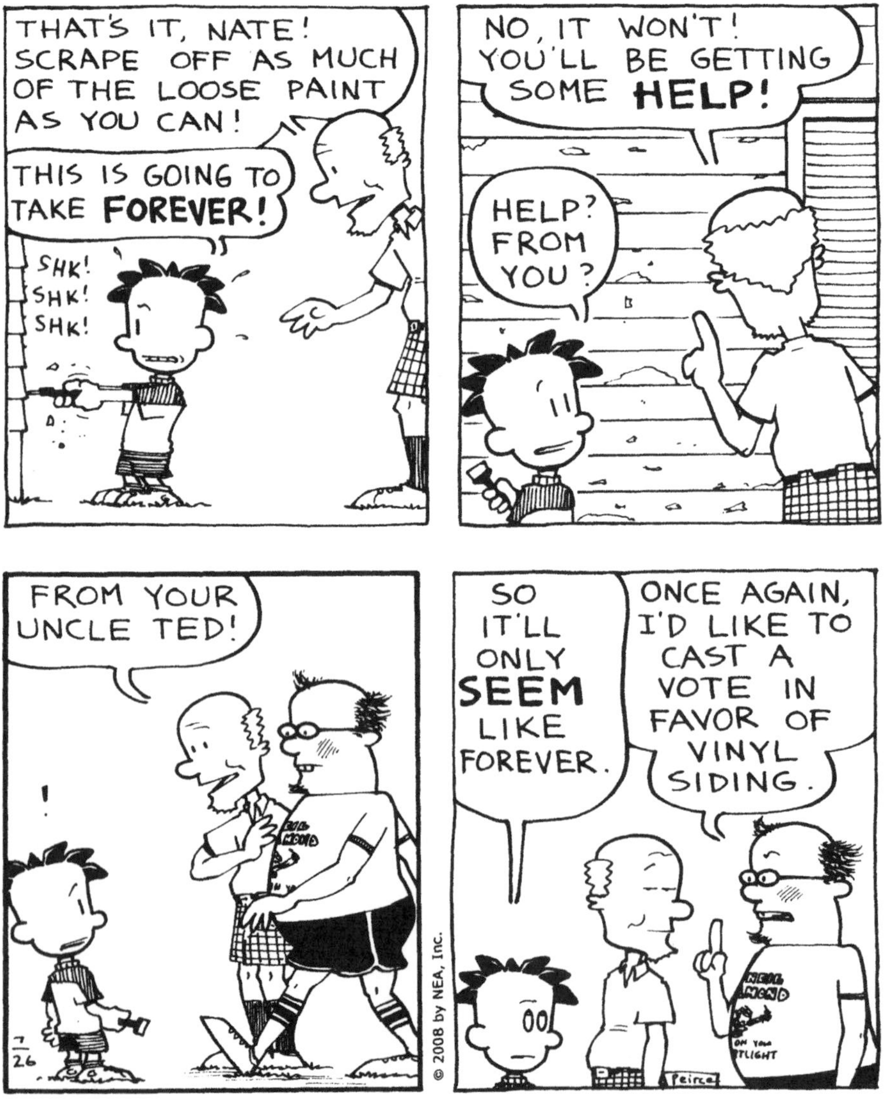
THAT'S IT, NATE! SCRAPE OFF AS MUCH OF THE LOOSE PAINT AS YOU CAN!
THIS IS GOING TO TAKE **FOREVER!**
SHK! SHK! SHK!
NO, IT WON'T! YOU'LL BE GETTING SOME **HELP!**
HELP? FROM YOU?
FROM YOUR UNCLE TED!
!
7/26
© 2008 by NEA, Inc.
SO IT'LL ONLY **SEEM** LIKE FOREVER.
ONCE AGAIN, I'D LIKE TO CAST A VOTE IN FAVOR OF VINYL SIDING.
Peirce

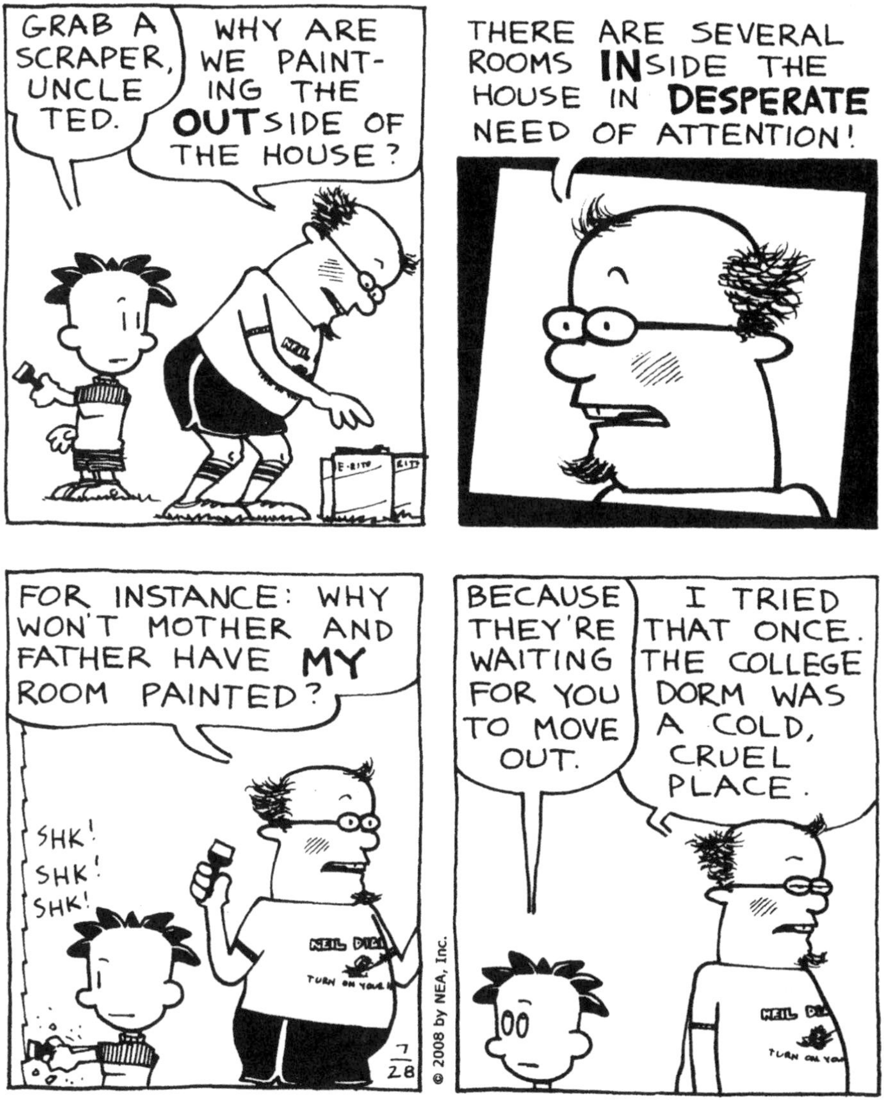
GRAB A SCRAPER, UNCLE TED.
WHY ARE WE PAINTING THE OUTSIDE OF THE HOUSE?
THERE ARE SEVERAL ROOMS INSIDE THE HOUSE IN DESPERATE NEED OF ATTENTION!
FOR INSTANCE: WHY WON'T MOTHER AND FATHER HAVE MY ROOM PAINTED?
SHK! SHK! SHK!
7/28
BECAUSE THEY'RE WAITING FOR YOU TO MOVE OUT.
I TRIED THAT ONCE. THE COLLEGE DORM WAS A COLD, CRUEL PLACE.

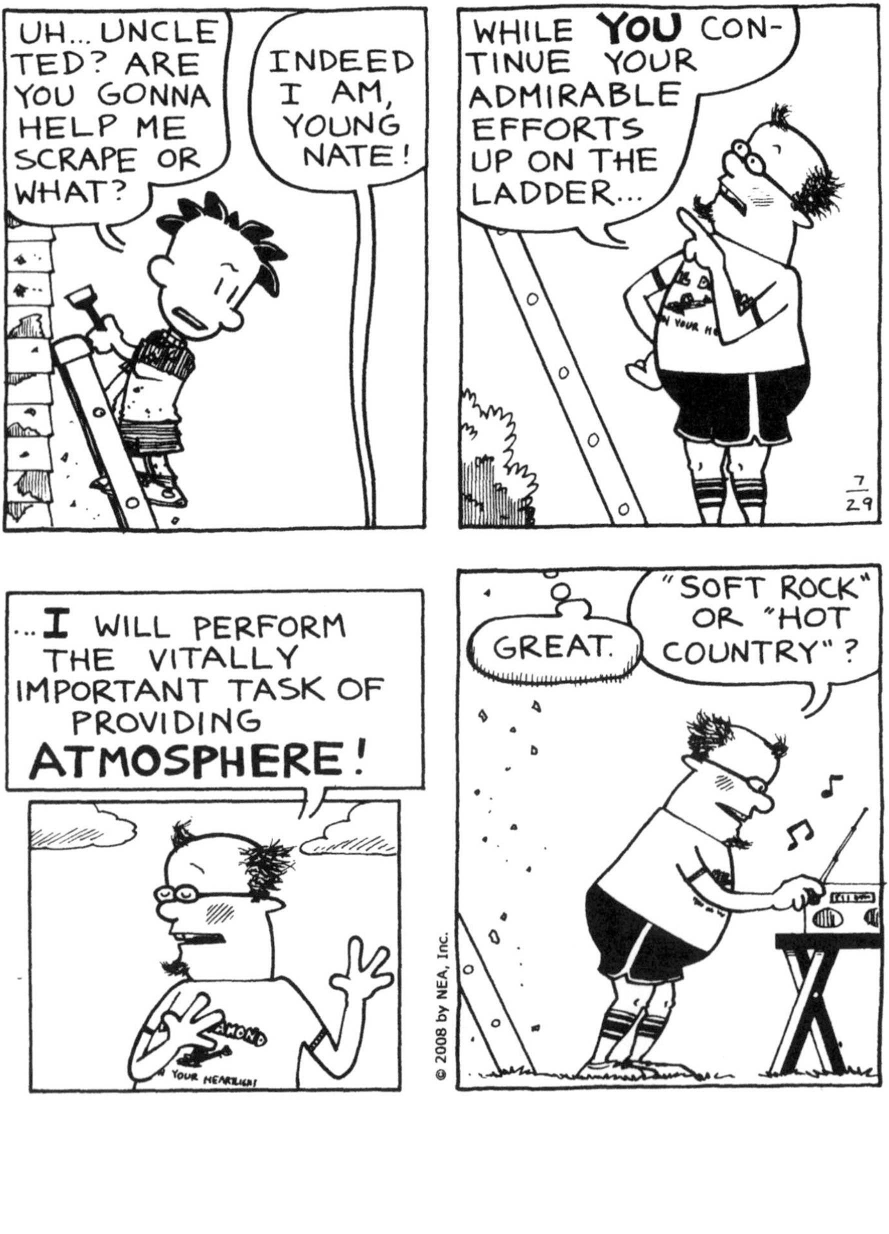
UH... UNCLE TED? ARE YOU GONNA HELP ME SCRAPE OR WHAT?
INDEED I AM, YOUNG NATE!
WHILE YOU CONTINUE YOUR ADMIRABLE EFFORTS UP ON THE LADDER...
7/29
...I WILL PERFORM THE VITALLY IMPORTANT TASK OF PROVIDING ATMOSPHERE!
GREAT.
"SOFT ROCK" OR "HOT COUNTRY"?

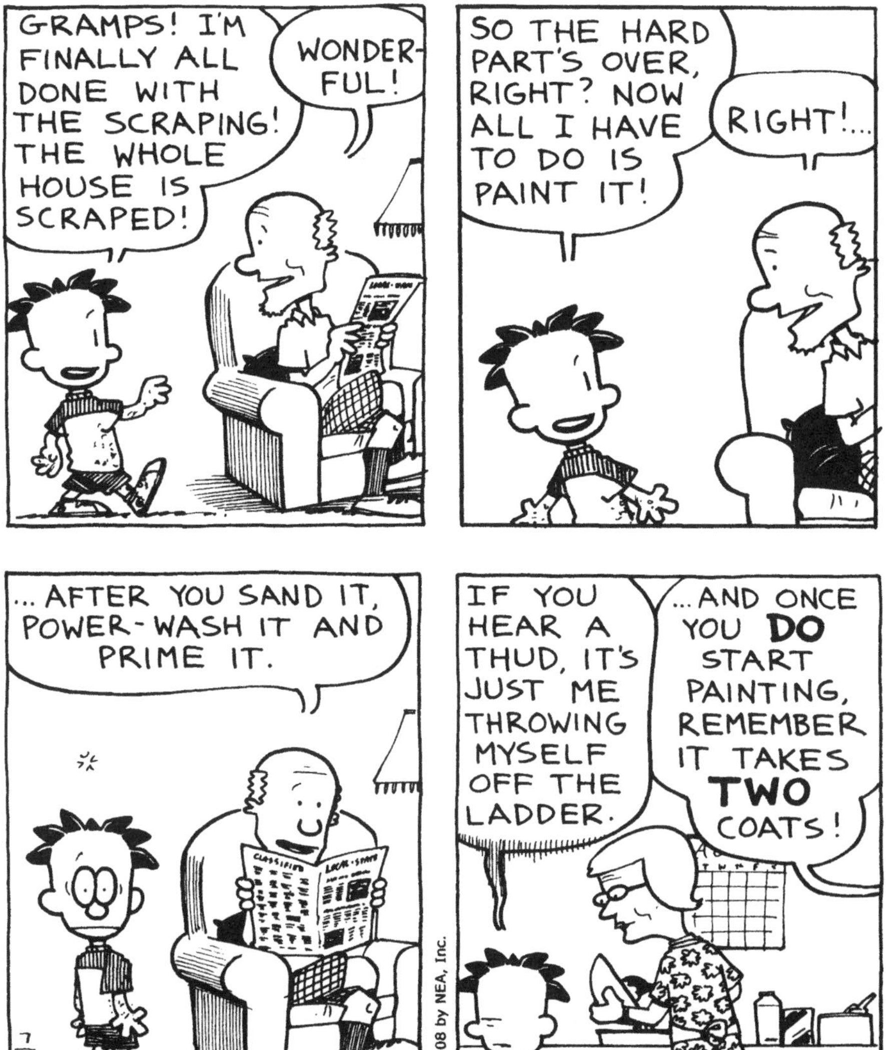
GRAMPS! I'M FINALLY ALL DONE WITH THE SCRAPING! THE WHOLE HOUSE IS SCRAPED!
WONDERFUL!
SO THE HARD PART'S OVER, RIGHT? NOW ALL I HAVE TO DO IS PAINT IT!
RIGHT!...
...AFTER YOU SAND IT, POWER-WASH IT AND PRIME IT.
IF YOU HEAR A THUD, IT'S JUST ME THROWING MYSELF OFF THE LADDER.
...AND ONCE YOU **DO** START PAINTING, REMEMBER IT TAKES **TWO** COATS!
7/31

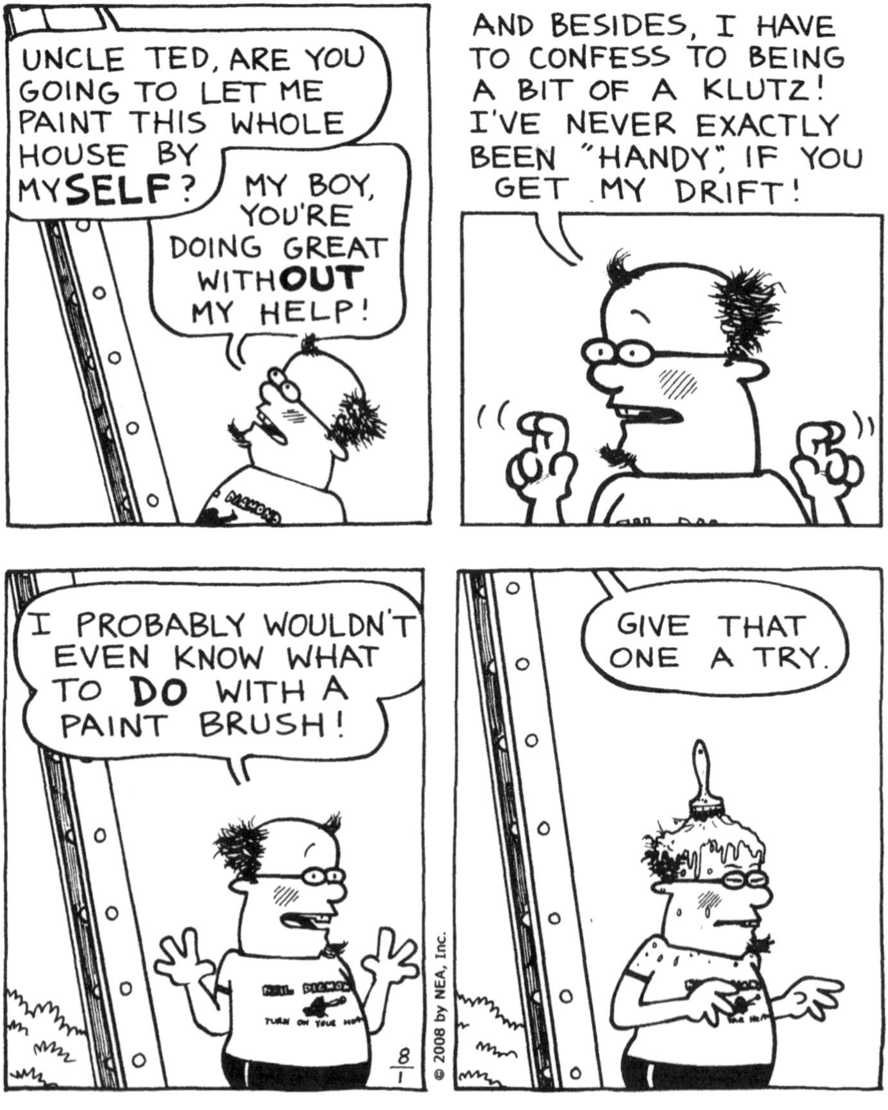
UNCLE TED, ARE YOU GOING TO LET ME PAINT THIS WHOLE HOUSE BY MYSELF?
MY BOY, YOU'RE DOING GREAT WITHOUT MY HELP!
AND BESIDES, I HAVE TO CONFESS TO BEING A BIT OF A KLUTZ! I'VE NEVER EXACTLY BEEN "HANDY," IF YOU GET MY DRIFT!
I PROBABLY WOULDN'T EVEN KNOW WHAT TO DO WITH A PAINT BRUSH!
GIVE THAT ONE A TRY.
8/1

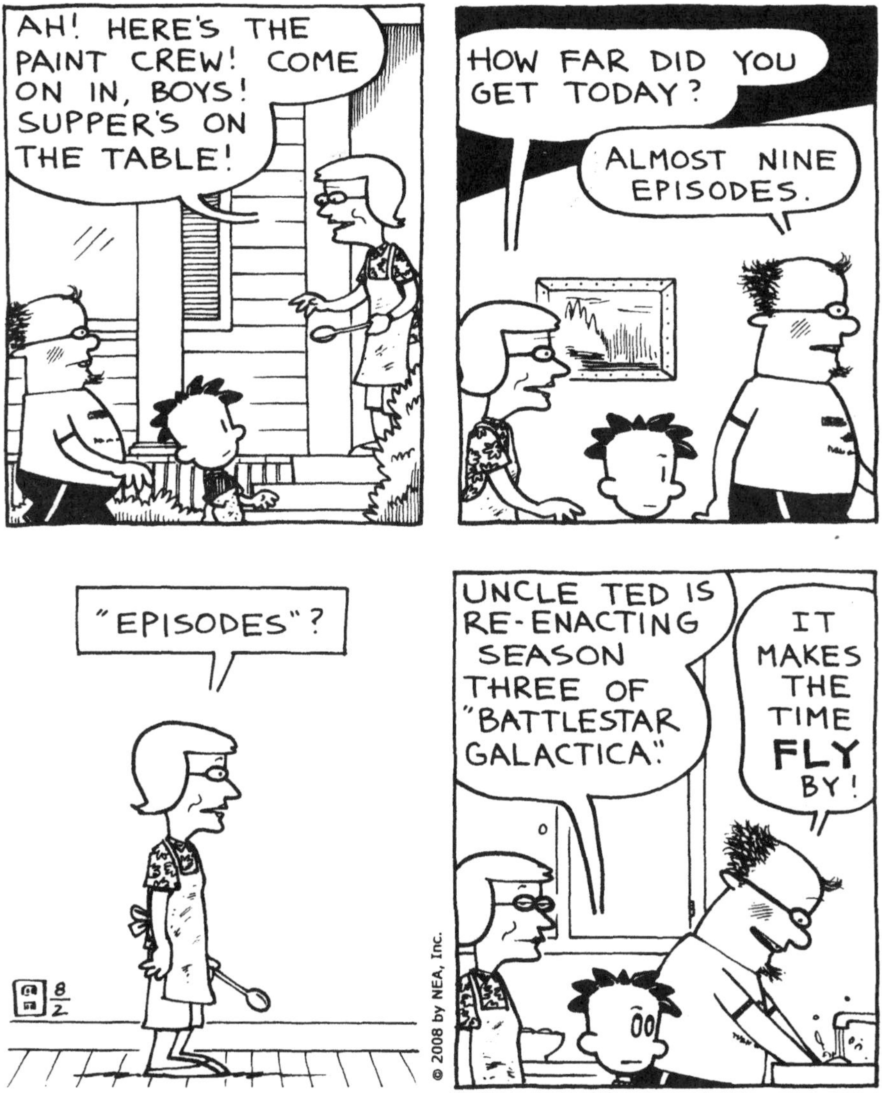
AH! HERE'S THE PAINT CREW! COME ON IN, BOYS! SUPPER'S ON THE TABLE!
HOW FAR DID YOU GET TODAY?
ALMOST NINE EPISODES.
"EPISODES"?
UNCLE TED IS RE-ENACTING SEASON THREE OF "BATTLESTAR GALACTICA."
IT MAKES THE TIME FLY BY!
8/2
© 2008 by NEA, Inc.

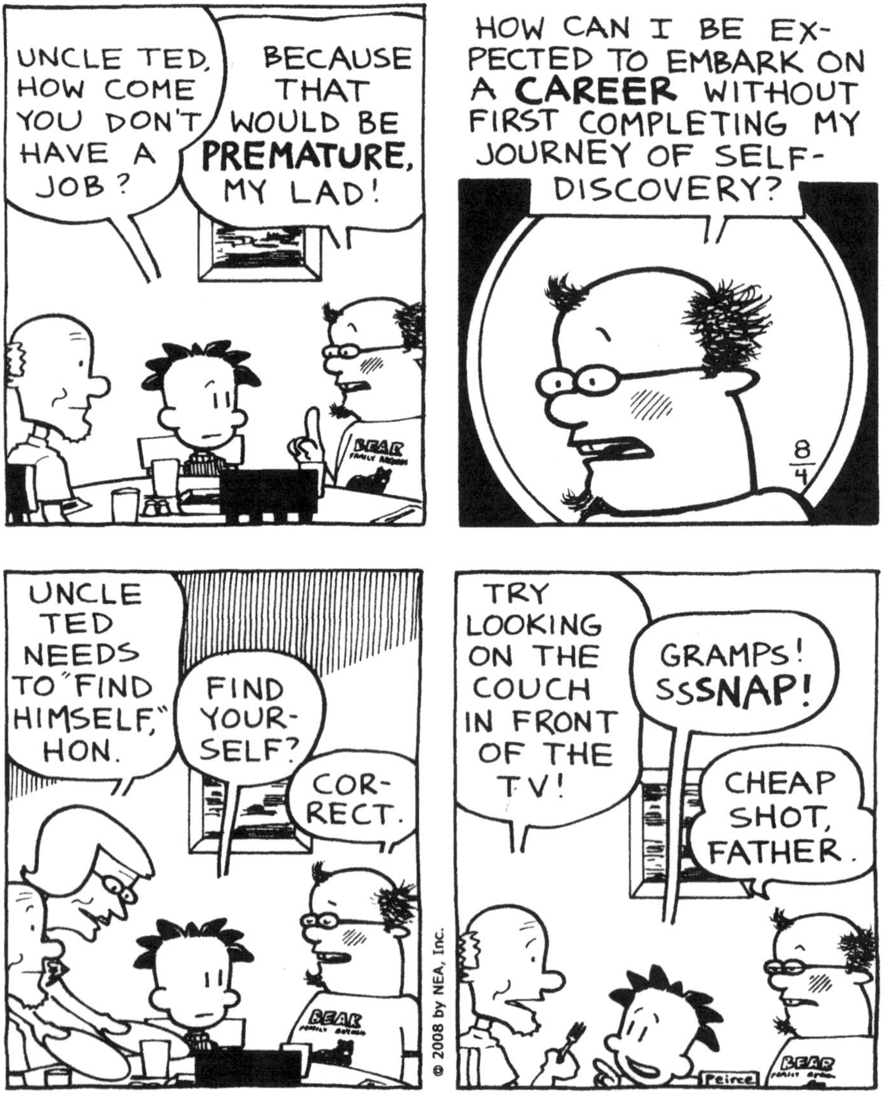
UNCLE TED, HOW COME YOU DON'T HAVE A JOB?
BECAUSE THAT WOULD BE PREMATURE, MY LAD!
HOW CAN I BE EXPECTED TO EMBARK ON A CAREER WITHOUT FIRST COMPLETING MY JOURNEY OF SELF-DISCOVERY?
8/4
UNCLE TED NEEDS TO "FIND HIMSELF," HON.
FIND YOURSELF?
CORRECT.
TRY LOOKING ON THE COUCH IN FRONT OF THE TV!
GRAMPS! SSSNAP!
CHEAP SHOT, FATHER.
Peirce
© 2008 by NEA, Inc.

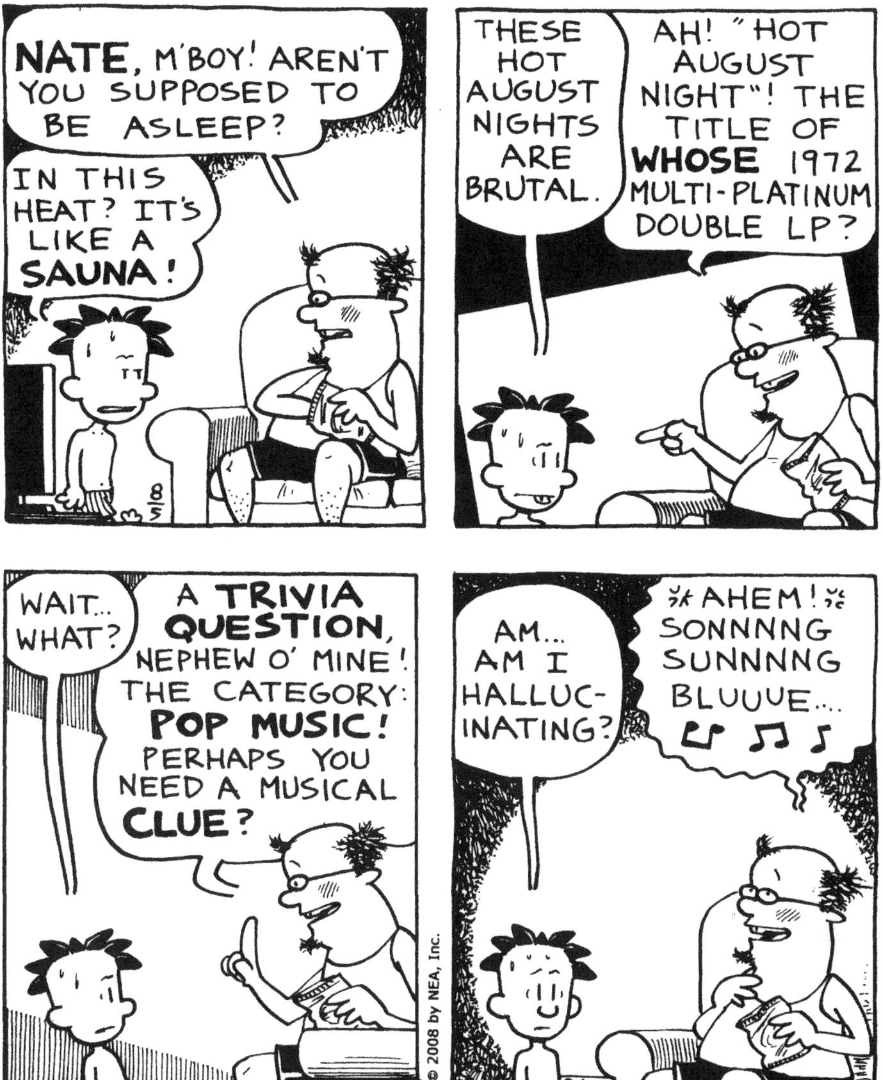
NATE, M'BOY! AREN'T YOU SUPPOSED TO BE ASLEEP?
IN THIS HEAT? IT'S LIKE A SAUNA!
8/5
THESE HOT AUGUST NIGHTS ARE BRUTAL.
AH! "HOT AUGUST NIGHT"! THE TITLE OF WHOSE 1972 MULTI-PLATINUM DOUBLE LP?
WAIT... WHAT?
A TRIVIA QUESTION, NEPHEW O' MINE! THE CATEGORY: POP MUSIC! PERHAPS YOU NEED A MUSICAL CLUE?
© 2008 by NEA, Inc.
AM... AM I HALLUC-INATING?
AHEM! SONNNNG SUNNNNG BLUUUE...
Peirce

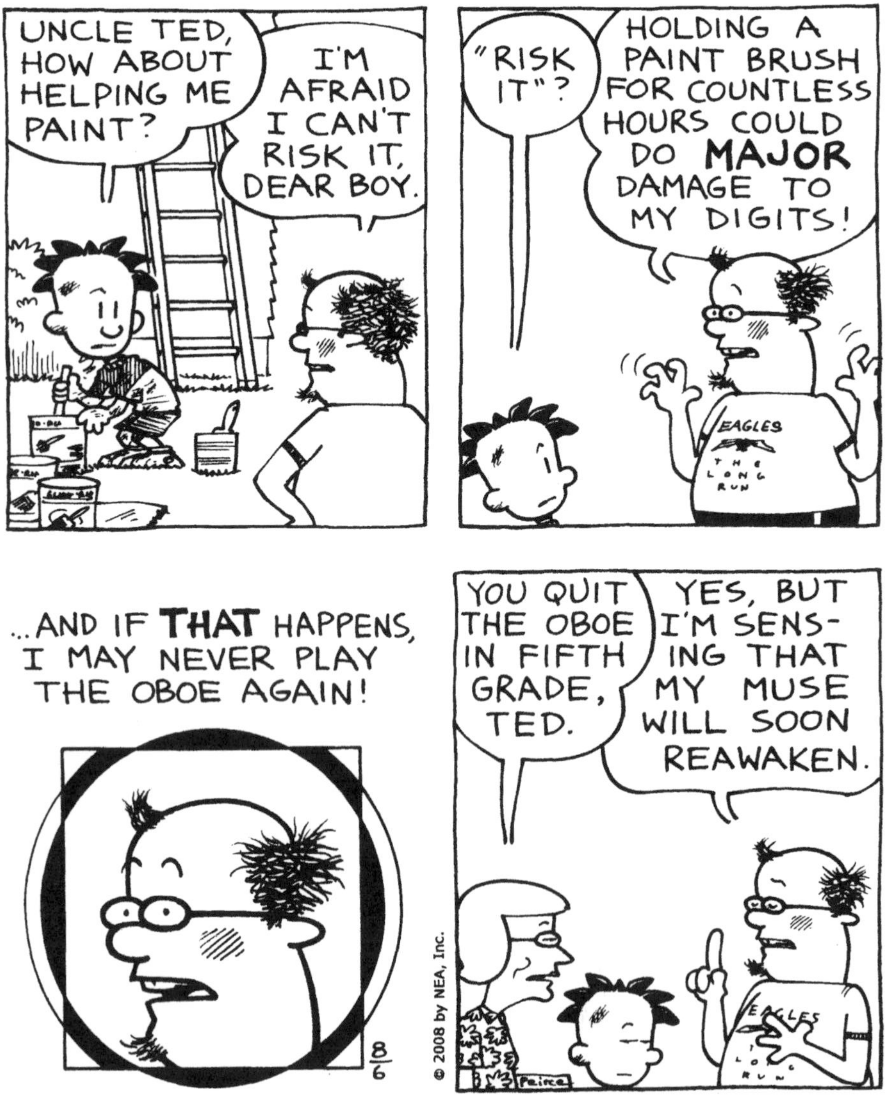
UNCLE TED, HOW ABOUT HELPING ME PAINT?
I'M AFRAID I CAN'T RISK IT, DEAR BOY.
"RISK IT"?
HOLDING A PAINT BRUSH FOR COUNTLESS HOURS COULD DO MAJOR DAMAGE TO MY DIGITS!
EAGLES THE LONG RUN
...AND IF THAT HAPPENS, I MAY NEVER PLAY THE OBOE AGAIN!
8/6
© 2008 by NEA, Inc.
YOU QUIT THE OBOE IN FIFTH GRADE, TED.
YES, BUT I'M SENSING THAT MY MUSE WILL SOON REAWAKEN.
Peirce

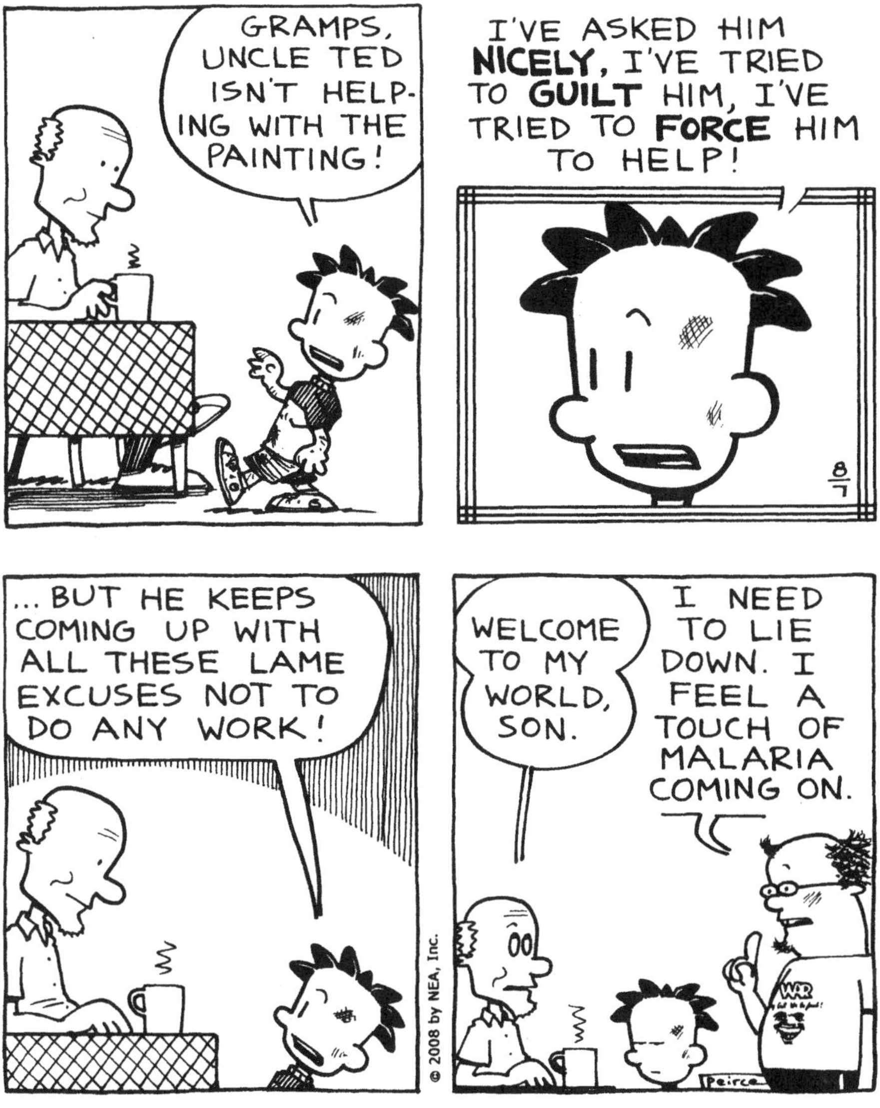
GRAMPS, UNCLE TED ISN'T HELPING WITH THE PAINTING!
I'VE ASKED HIM NICELY, I'VE TRIED TO GUILT HIM, I'VE TRIED TO FORCE HIM TO HELP!
8/7
...BUT HE KEEPS COMING UP WITH ALL THESE LAME EXCUSES NOT TO DO ANY WORK!
© 2008 by NEA, Inc.
WELCOME TO MY WORLD, SON.
I NEED TO LIE DOWN. I FEEL A TOUCH OF MALARIA COMING ON.
Peirce

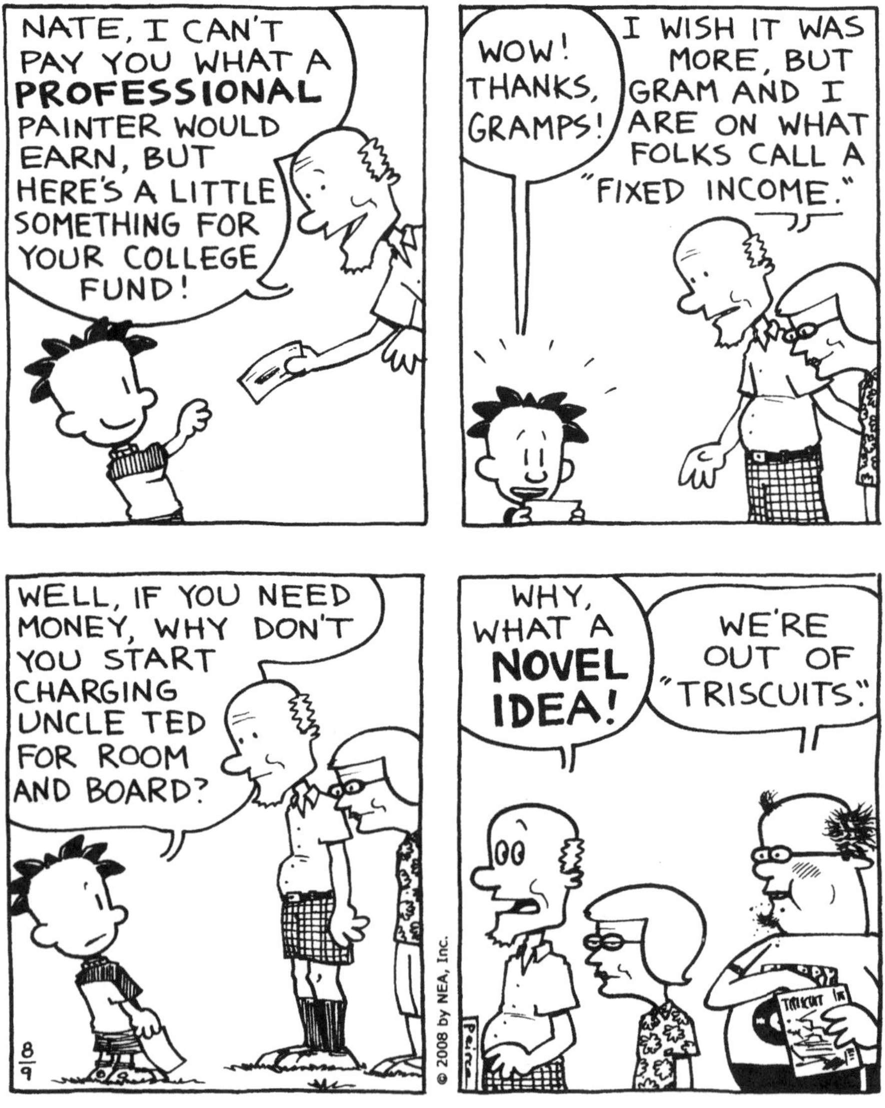
NATE, I CAN'T PAY YOU WHAT A **PROFESSIONAL** PAINTER WOULD EARN, BUT HERE'S A LITTLE SOMETHING FOR YOUR COLLEGE FUND!
WOW! THANKS, GRAMPS!
I WISH IT WAS MORE, BUT GRAM AND I ARE ON WHAT FOLKS CALL A "FIXED INCOME."
WELL, IF YOU NEED MONEY, WHY DON'T YOU START CHARGING UNCLE TED FOR ROOM AND BOARD?
WHY, WHAT A **NOVEL IDEA!**
WE'RE OUT OF "TRISCUITS."
8/9
Peirce
TRISCUIT

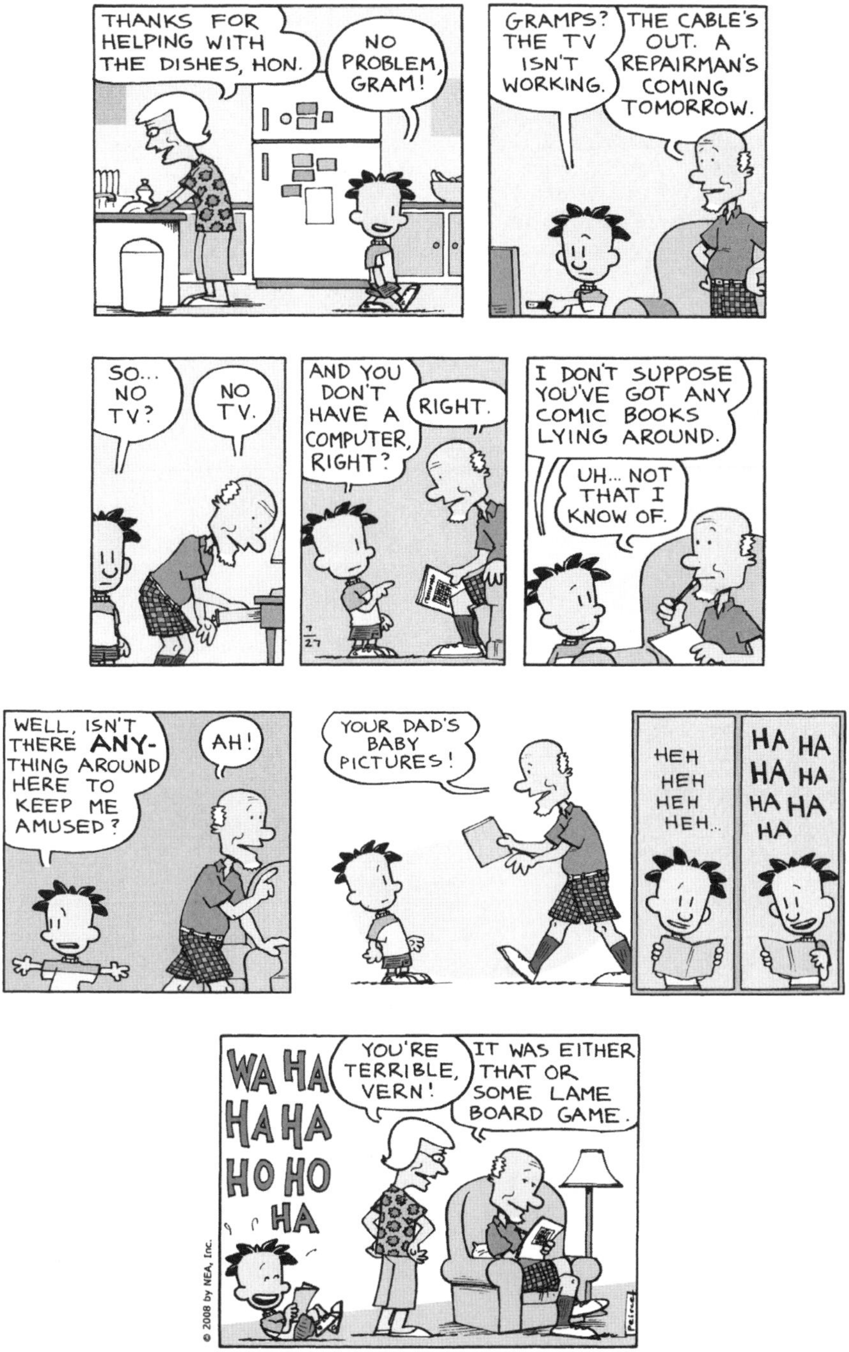

THANKS FOR HELPING WITH THE DISHES, HON.
NO PROBLEM, GRAM!
GRAMPS? THE TV ISN'T WORKING.
THE CABLE'S OUT. A REPAIRMAN'S COMING TOMORROW.
SO... NO TV?
NO TV.
AND YOU DON'T HAVE A COMPUTER, RIGHT?
RIGHT.
I DON'T SUPPOSE YOU'VE GOT ANY COMIC BOOKS LYING AROUND.
UH... NOT THAT I KNOW OF.
WELL, ISN'T THERE **ANY**-THING AROUND HERE TO KEEP ME AMUSED?
AH!
YOUR DAD'S BABY PICTURES!
HEH HEH HEH HEH...
HA HA HA HA HA HA HA HA
WA HA HA HA HA HO HO HA
YOU'RE TERRIBLE, VERN!
IT WAS EITHER THAT OR SOME LAME BOARD GAME.

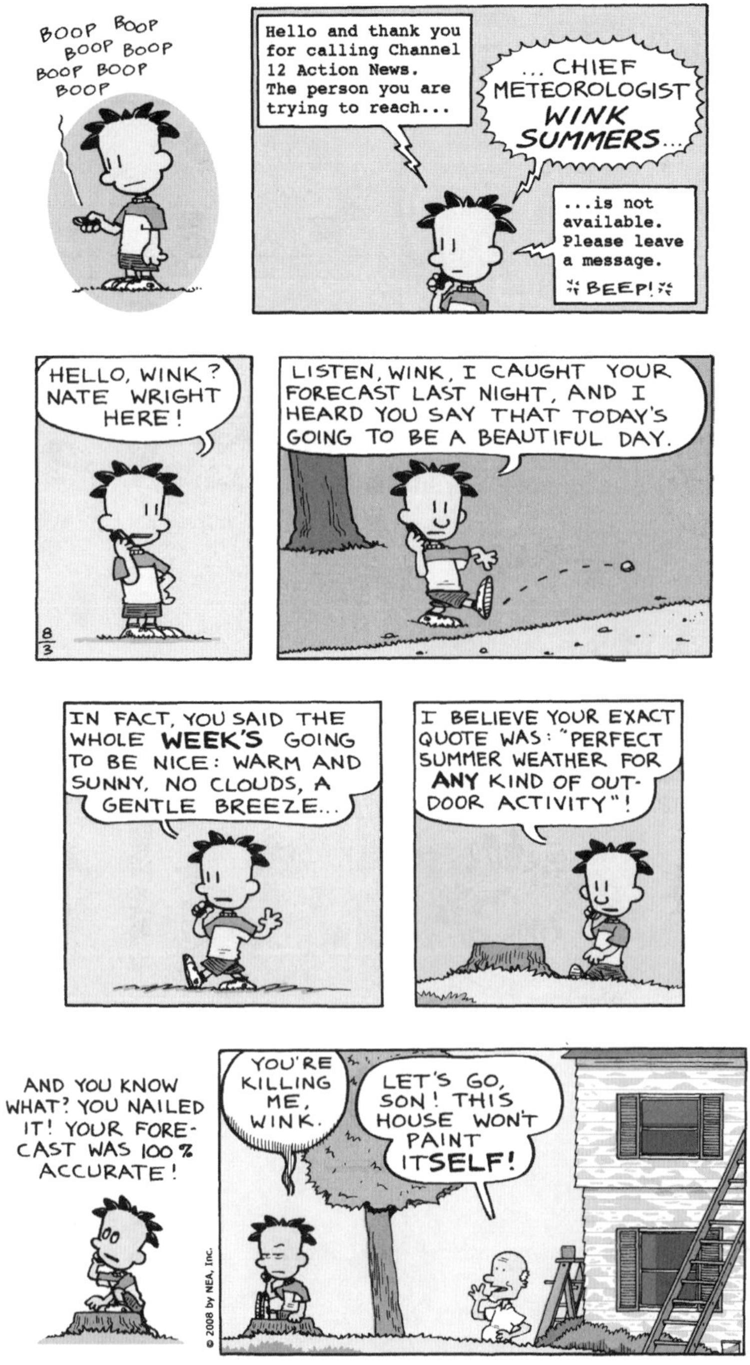
BOOP BOOP BOOP BOOP BOOP BOOP BOOP
Hello and thank you for calling Channel 12 Action News. The person you are trying to reach...
... CHIEF METEOROLOGIST WINK SUMMERS...
...is not available. Please leave a message.
BEEP!
HELLO, WINK? NATE WRIGHT HERE!
8/3
LISTEN, WINK, I CAUGHT YOUR FORECAST LAST NIGHT, AND I HEARD YOU SAY THAT TODAY'S GOING TO BE A BEAUTIFUL DAY.
IN FACT, YOU SAID THE WHOLE WEEK'S GOING TO BE NICE: WARM AND SUNNY, NO CLOUDS, A GENTLE BREEZE...
I BELIEVE YOUR EXACT QUOTE WAS: "PERFECT SUMMER WEATHER FOR ANY KIND OF OUT-DOOR ACTIVITY"!
AND YOU KNOW WHAT? YOU NAILED IT! YOUR FORE-CAST WAS 100% ACCURATE!
YOU'RE KILLING ME, WINK.
LET'S GO, SON! THIS HOUSE WON'T PAINT ITSELF!
© 2008 by NEA, Inc.

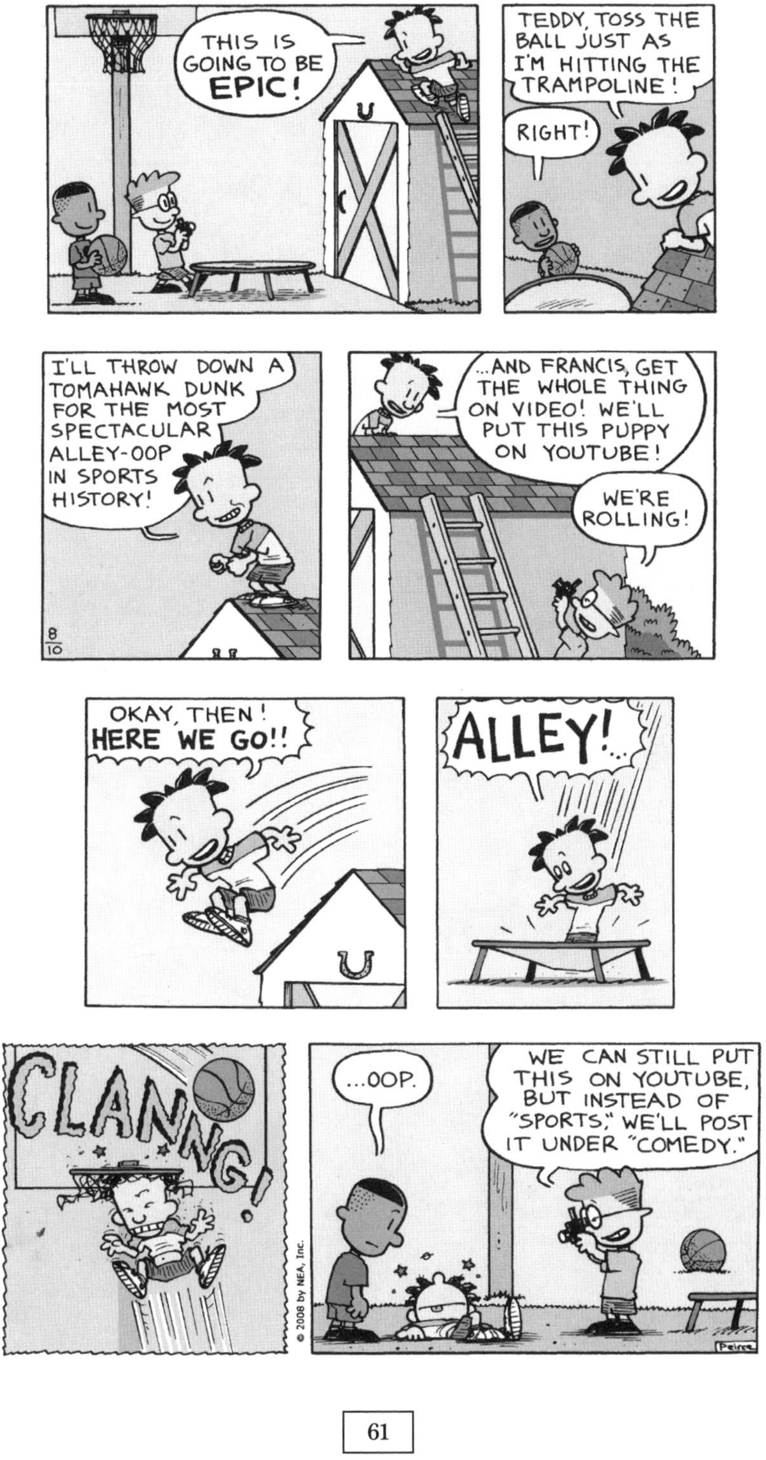
THIS IS GOING TO BE EPIC!
TEDDY, TOSS THE BALL JUST AS I'M HITTING THE TRAMPOLINE!
RIGHT!
I'LL THROW DOWN A TOMAHAWK DUNK FOR THE MOST SPECTACULAR ALLEY-OOP IN SPORTS HISTORY!
8/10
...AND FRANCIS, GET THE WHOLE THING ON VIDEO! WE'LL PUT THIS PUPPY ON YOUTUBE!
WE'RE ROLLING!
OKAY, THEN! HERE WE GO!!
ALLEY!...
CLANNG!
© 2008 by NEA, Inc.
...OOP.
WE CAN STILL PUT THIS ON YOUTUBE, BUT INSTEAD OF "SPORTS," WE'LL POST IT UNDER "COMEDY."
Peirce

WELCOME TO THE REAL WORLD

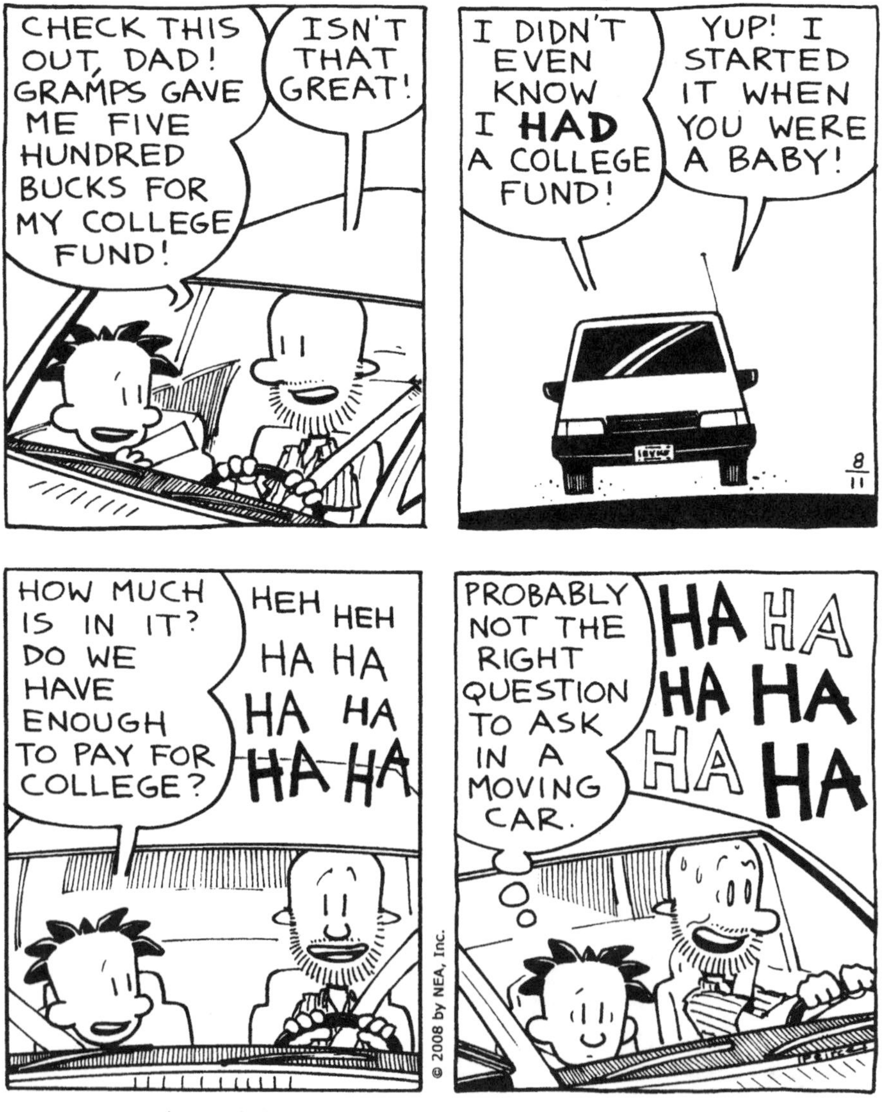
CHECK THIS OUT, DAD! GRAMPS GAVE ME FIVE HUNDRED BUCKS FOR MY COLLEGE FUND!
ISN'T THAT GREAT!
I DIDN'T EVEN KNOW I **HAD** A COLLEGE FUND!
YUP! I STARTED IT WHEN YOU WERE A BABY!
8/11
HOW MUCH IS IN IT? DO WE HAVE ENOUGH TO PAY FOR COLLEGE?
HEH HEH HA HA HA HA HA HA
PROBABLY NOT THE RIGHT QUESTION TO ASK IN A MOVING CAR.
HA HA HA HA HA HA
© 2008 by NEA, Inc.

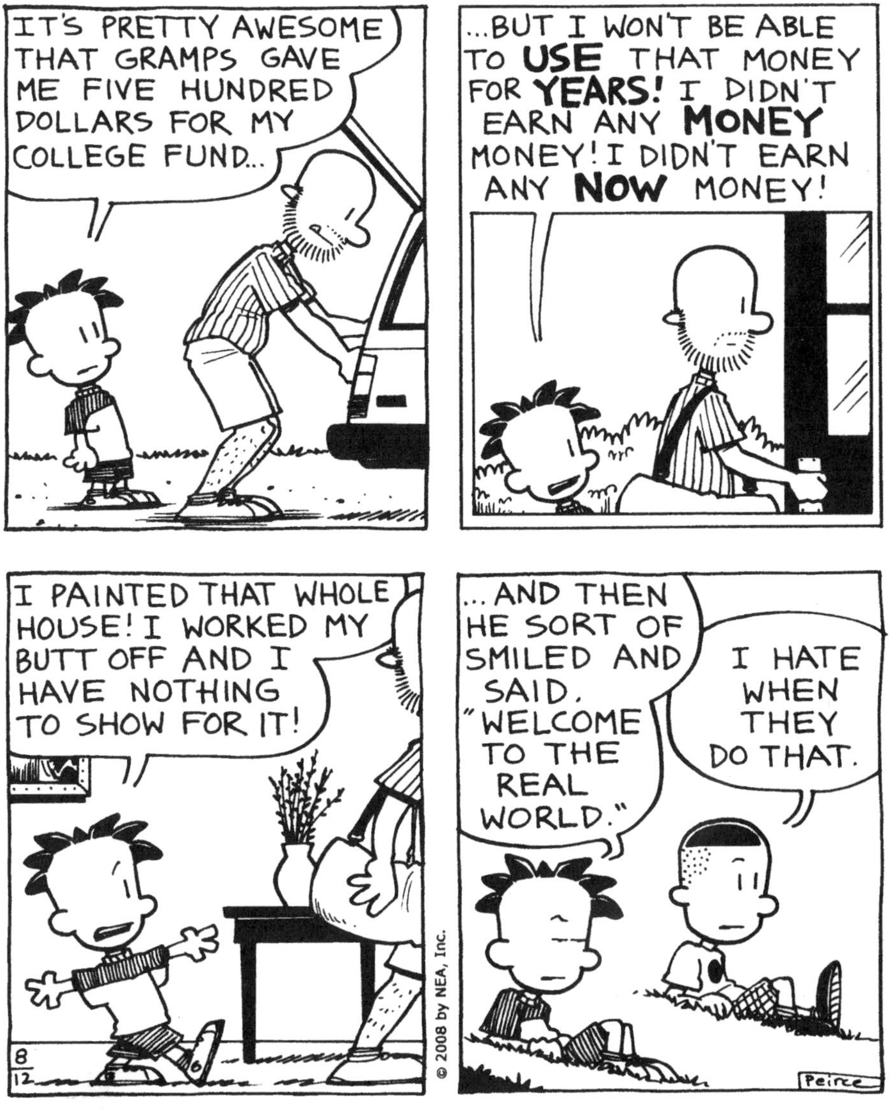
IT'S PRETTY AWESOME THAT GRAMPS GAVE ME FIVE HUNDRED DOLLARS FOR MY COLLEGE FUND...
...BUT I WON'T BE ABLE TO USE THAT MONEY FOR YEARS! I DIDN'T EARN ANY MONEY MONEY! I DIDN'T EARN ANY NOW MONEY!
I PAINTED THAT WHOLE HOUSE! I WORKED MY BUTT OFF AND I HAVE NOTHING TO SHOW FOR IT!
8
12
© 2008 by NEA, Inc.
...AND THEN HE SORT OF SMILED AND SAID, "WELCOME TO THE REAL WORLD."
I HATE WHEN THEY DO THAT.
Peirce

NOTHING TO DO

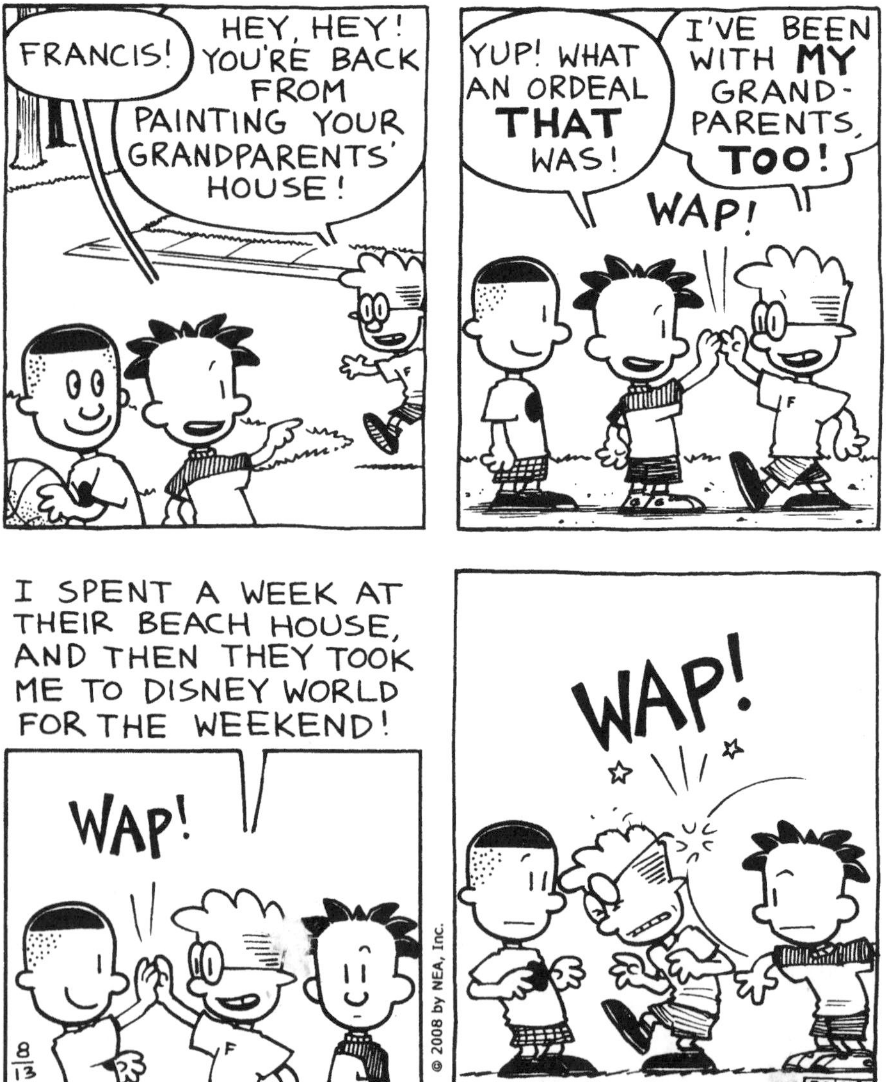
FRANCIS!
HEY, HEY! YOU'RE BACK FROM PAINTING YOUR GRANDPARENTS' HOUSE!
YUP! WHAT AN ORDEAL **THAT** WAS!
I'VE BEEN WITH **MY** GRAND-PARENTS, **TOO!**
WAP!
I SPENT A WEEK AT THEIR BEACH HOUSE, AND THEN THEY TOOK ME TO DISNEY WORLD FOR THE WEEKEND!
WAP!
8/13
© 2008 by NEA, Inc.
WAP!
Peirce

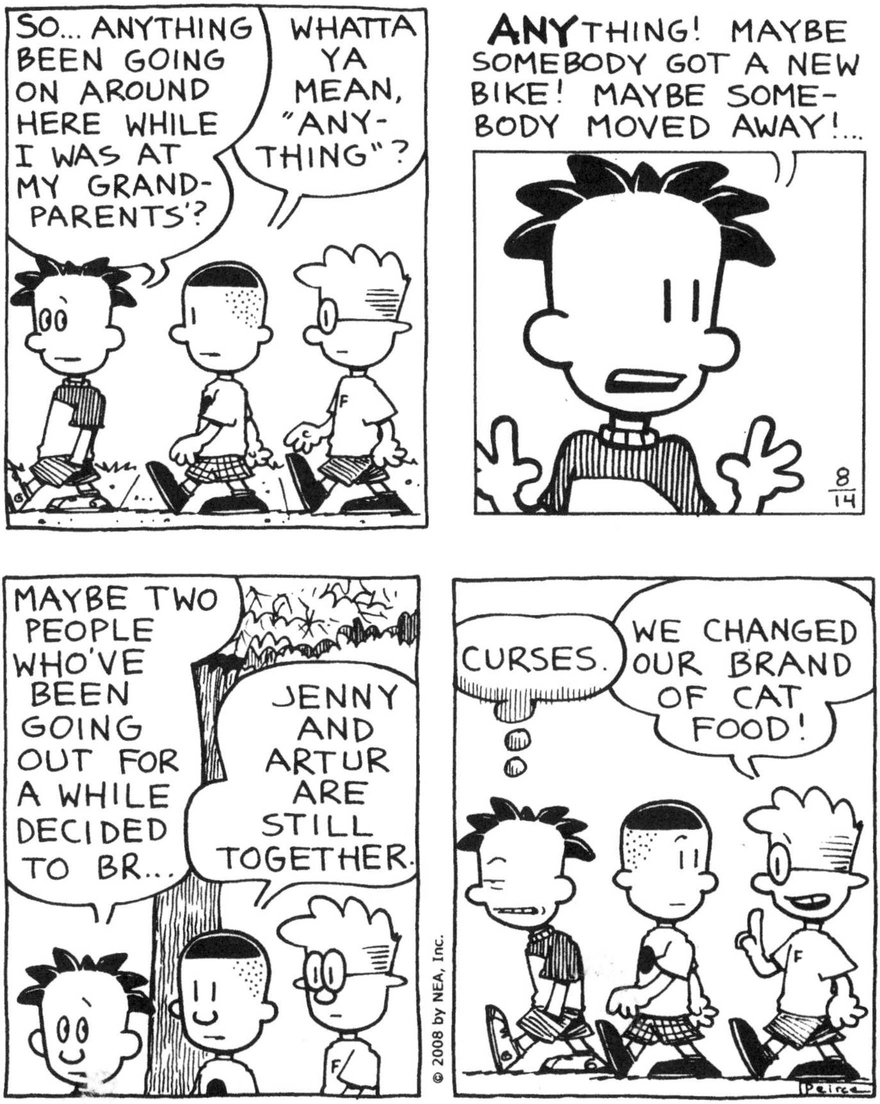
SO... ANYTHING BEEN GOING ON AROUND HERE WHILE I WAS AT MY GRAND-PARENTS'?
WHATTA YA MEAN, "ANY-THING"?
ANYTHING! MAYBE SOMEBODY GOT A NEW BIKE! MAYBE SOME-BODY MOVED AWAY!...
8/14
MAYBE TWO PEOPLE WHO'VE BEEN GOING OUT FOR A WHILE DECIDED TO BR...
JENNY AND ARTUR ARE STILL TOGETHER.
© 2008 by NEA, Inc.
WE CHANGED OUR BRAND OF CAT FOOD!
CURSES.
Peirce

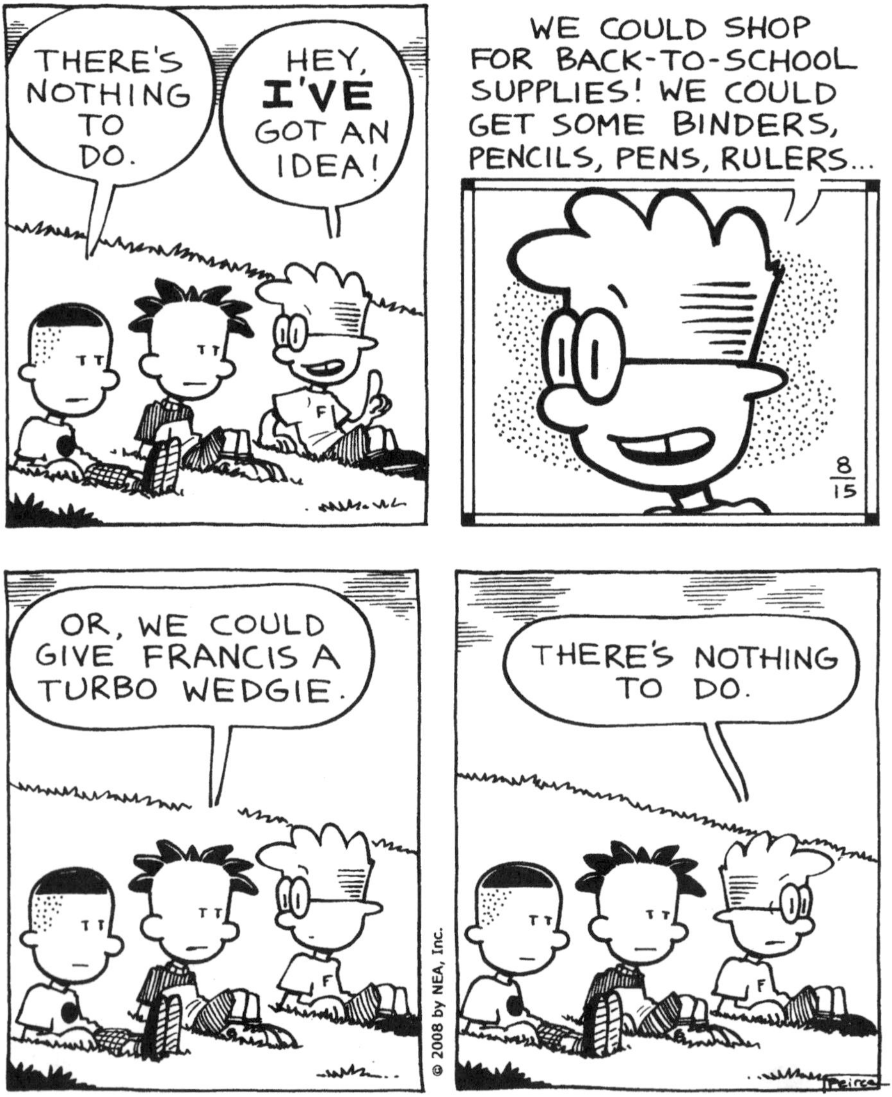
THERE'S NOTHING TO DO.
HEY, **I'VE** GOT AN IDEA!
WE COULD SHOP FOR BACK-TO-SCHOOL SUPPLIES! WE COULD GET SOME BINDERS, PENCILS, PENS, RULERS...
8/15
OR, WE COULD GIVE FRANCIS A TURBO WEDGIE.
THERE'S NOTHING TO DO.
Peirce

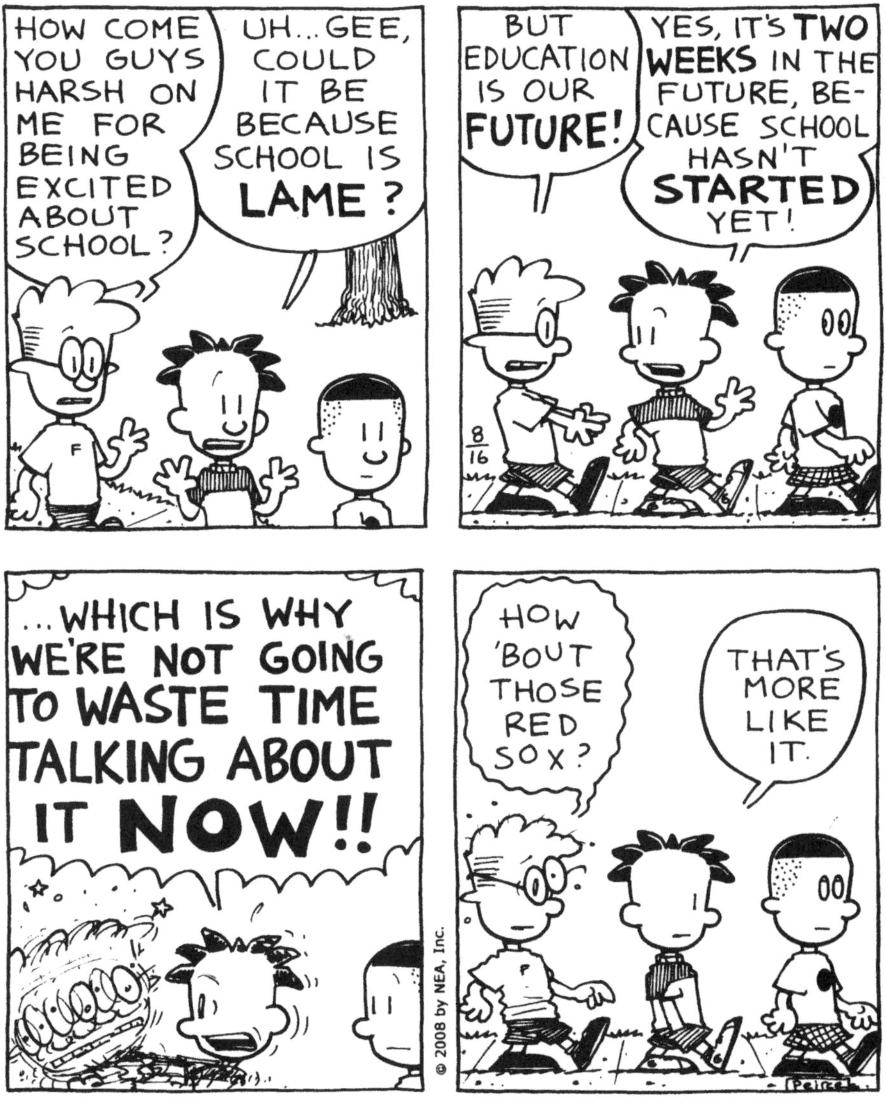
HOW COME YOU GUYS HARSH ON ME FOR BEING EXCITED ABOUT SCHOOL?
UH...GEE, COULD IT BE BECAUSE SCHOOL IS LAME?
BUT EDUCATION IS OUR FUTURE!
YES, IT'S TWO WEEKS IN THE FUTURE, BECAUSE SCHOOL HASN'T STARTED YET!
8/16
...WHICH IS WHY WE'RE NOT GOING TO WASTE TIME TALKING ABOUT IT NOW!!
© 2008 by NEA, Inc.
HOW 'BOUT THOSE RED SOX?
THAT'S MORE LIKE IT.
Peirce

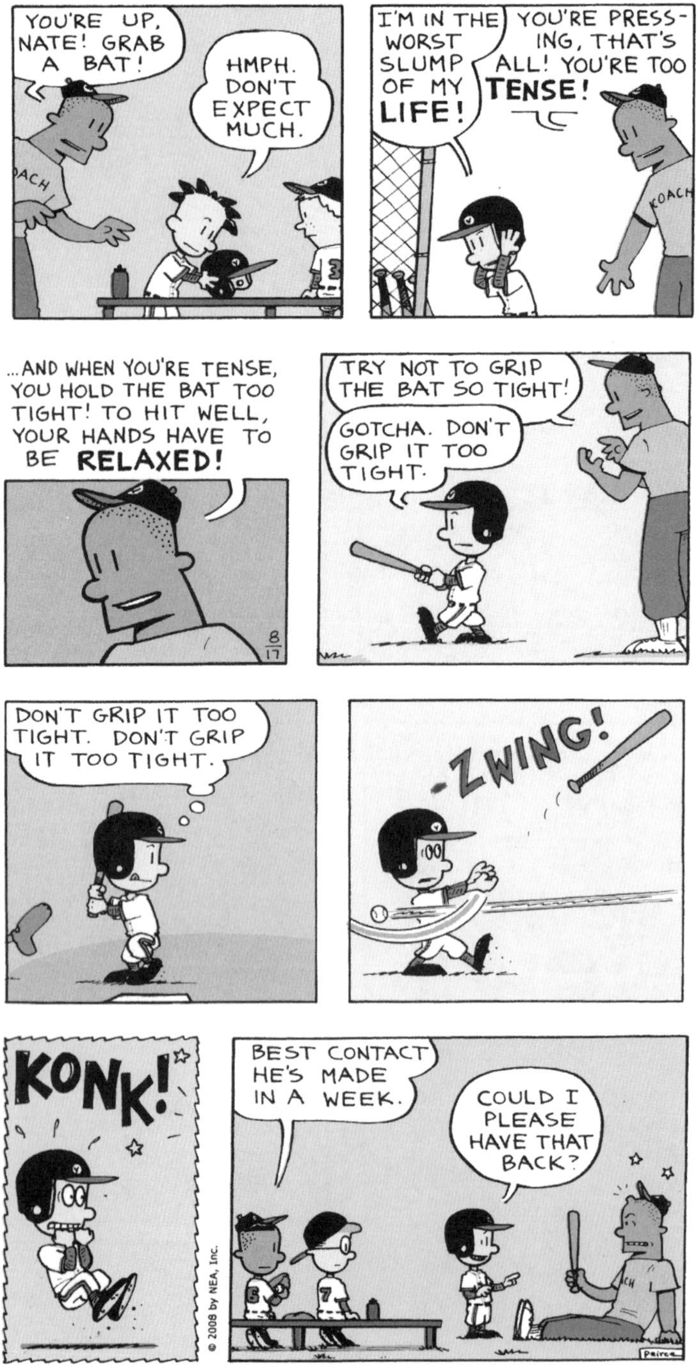
YOU'RE UP, NATE! GRAB A BAT!
HMPH. DON'T EXPECT MUCH.
I'M IN THE WORST SLUMP OF MY LIFE!
YOU'RE PRESSING, THAT'S ALL! YOU'RE TOO TENSE!
...AND WHEN YOU'RE TENSE, YOU HOLD THE BAT TOO TIGHT! TO HIT WELL, YOUR HANDS HAVE TO BE RELAXED!
8/17
TRY NOT TO GRIP THE BAT SO TIGHT!
GOTCHA. DON'T GRIP IT TOO TIGHT.
DON'T GRIP IT TOO TIGHT. DON'T GRIP IT TOO TIGHT.
ZWING!
KONK!
© 2008 by NEA, Inc.
BEST CONTACT HE'S MADE IN A WEEK.
COULD I PLEASE HAVE THAT BACK?
Peirce

MASTER OF DISASTER

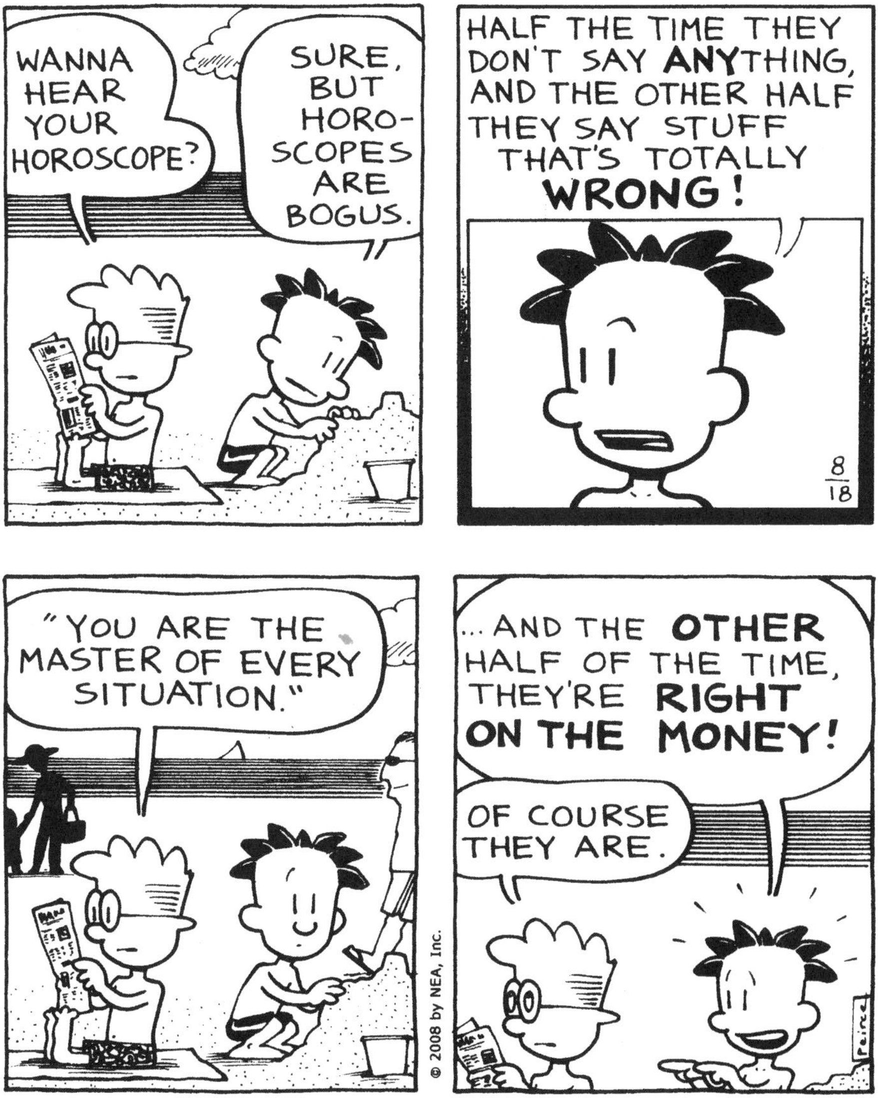

WANNA HEAR YOUR HOROSCOPE?
SURE, BUT HORO-SCOPES ARE BOGUS.
HALF THE TIME THEY DON'T SAY ANYTHING, AND THE OTHER HALF THEY SAY STUFF THAT'S TOTALLY WRONG!
8/18
"YOU ARE THE MASTER OF EVERY SITUATION."
© 2008 by NEA, Inc.
...AND THE OTHER HALF OF THE TIME, THEY'RE RIGHT ON THE MONEY!
OF COURSE THEY ARE.
Peirce

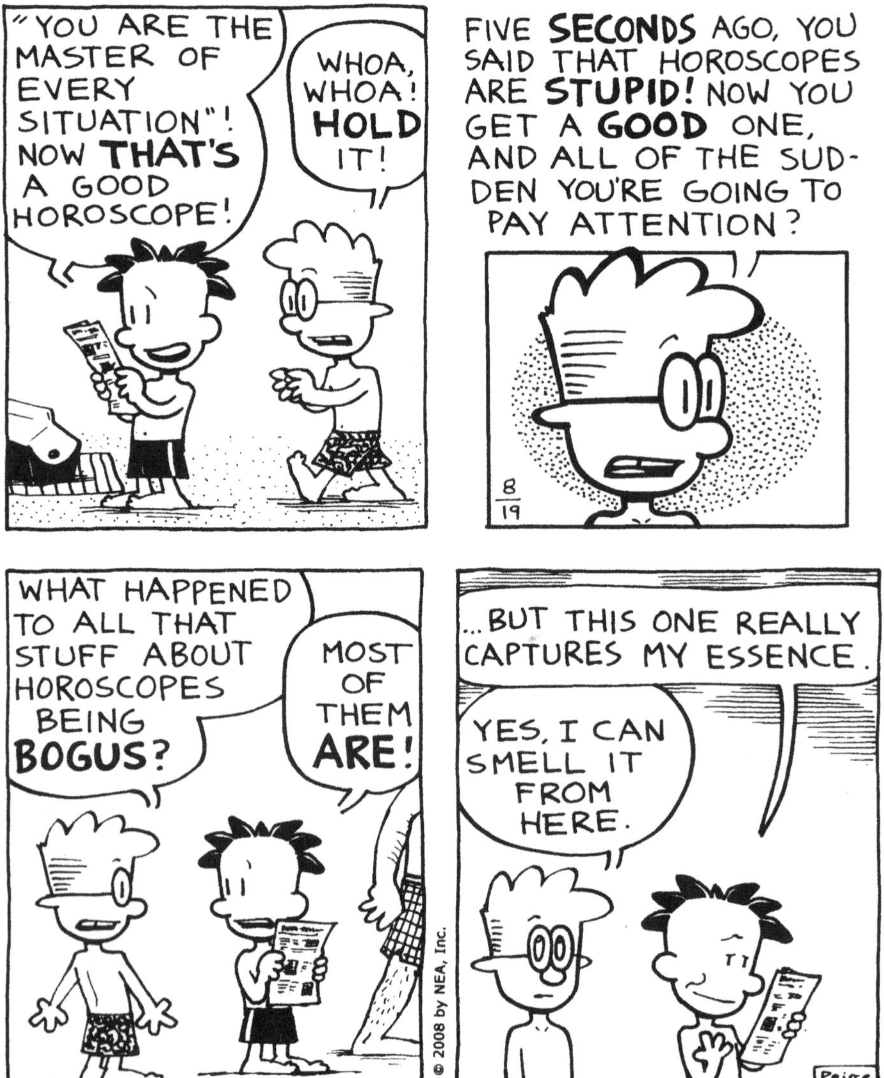
"YOU ARE THE MASTER OF EVERY SITUATION"! NOW THAT'S A GOOD HOROSCOPE!
WHOA, WHOA! HOLD IT!
FIVE SECONDS AGO, YOU SAID THAT HOROSCOPES ARE STUPID! NOW YOU GET A GOOD ONE, AND ALL OF THE SUDDEN YOU'RE GOING TO PAY ATTENTION?
8/19
WHAT HAPPENED TO ALL THAT STUFF ABOUT HOROSCOPES BEING BOGUS?
MOST OF THEM ARE!
© 2008 by NEA, Inc.
...BUT THIS ONE REALLY CAPTURES MY ESSENCE.
YES, I CAN SMELL IT FROM HERE.
Peirce

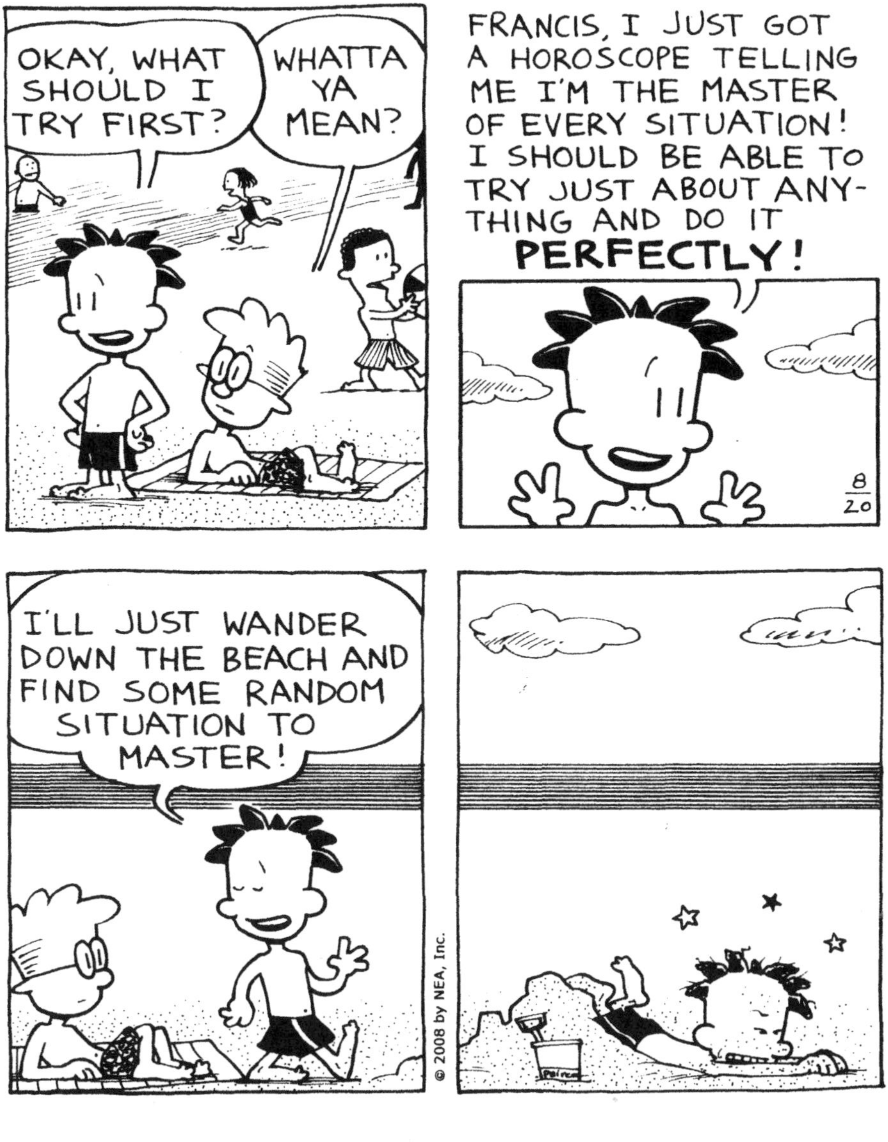
OKAY, WHAT SHOULD I TRY FIRST?
WHATTA YA MEAN?
FRANCIS, I JUST GOT A HOROSCOPE TELLING ME I'M THE MASTER OF EVERY SITUATION! I SHOULD BE ABLE TO TRY JUST ABOUT ANYTHING AND DO IT PERFECTLY!
8/20
I'LL JUST WANDER DOWN THE BEACH AND FIND SOME RANDOM SITUATION TO MASTER!
© 2008 by NEA, Inc.

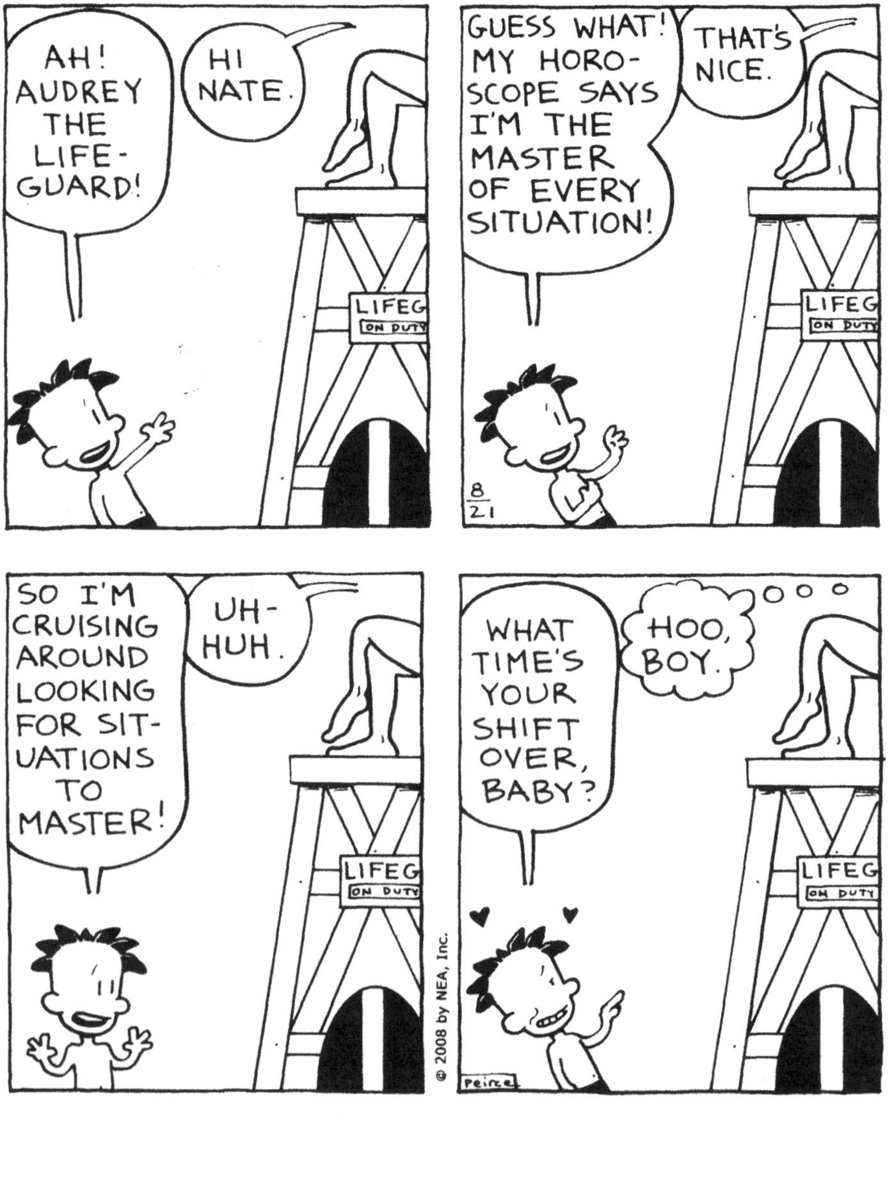

AH! AUDREY THE LIFE-GUARD!
HI NATE.
GUESS WHAT! MY HORO-SCOPE SAYS I'M THE MASTER OF EVERY SITUATION!
THAT'S NICE.
8/21
SO I'M CRUISING AROUND LOOKING FOR SIT-UATIONS TO MASTER!
UH-HUH.
WHAT TIME'S YOUR SHIFT OVER, BABY?
HOO, BOY.
LIFEG
ON DUTY
© 2008 by NEA, Inc.
Peirce

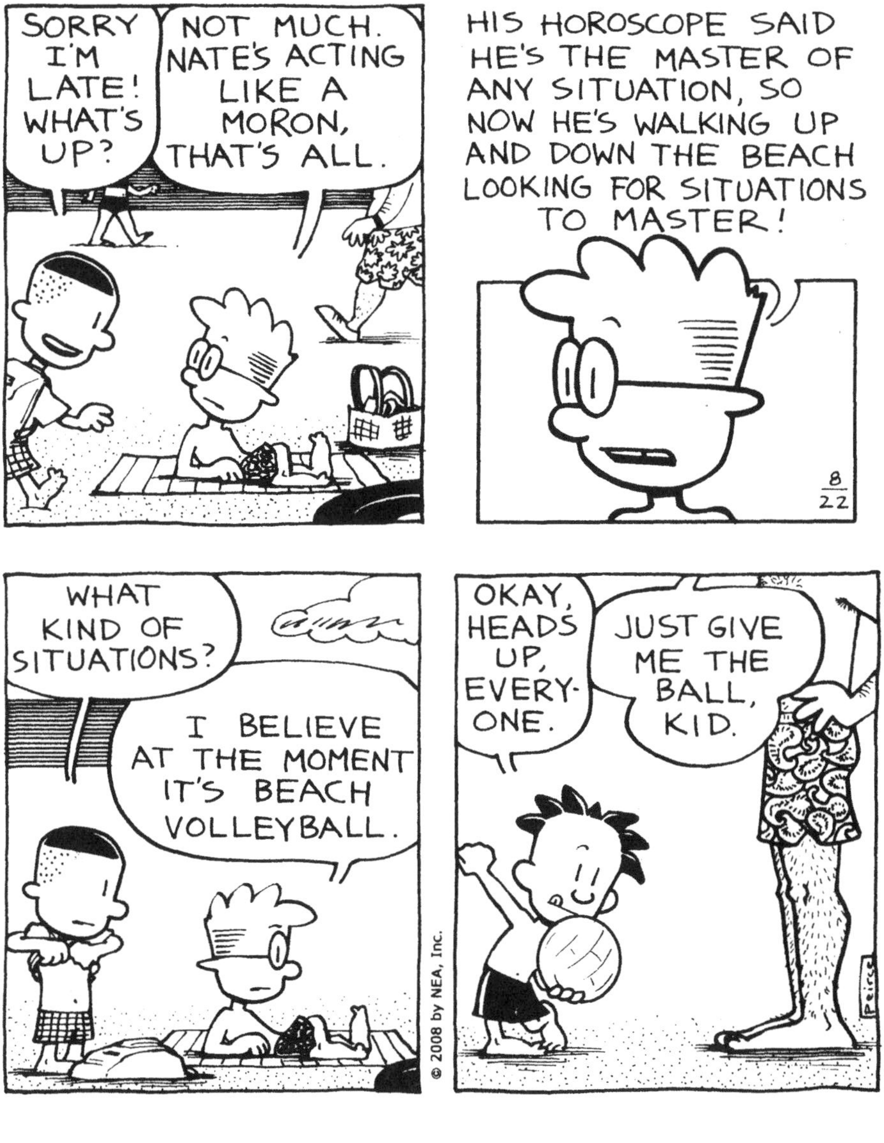

SORRY I'M LATE! WHAT'S UP?
NOT MUCH. NATE'S ACTING LIKE A MORON, THAT'S ALL.
HIS HOROSCOPE SAID HE'S THE MASTER OF ANY SITUATION, SO NOW HE'S WALKING UP AND DOWN THE BEACH LOOKING FOR SITUATIONS TO MASTER!
8/22
WHAT KIND OF SITUATIONS?
I BELIEVE AT THE MOMENT IT'S BEACH VOLLEYBALL.
© 2008 by NEA, Inc.
OKAY, HEADS UP, EVERY-ONE.
JUST GIVE ME THE BALL, KID.
Peirse

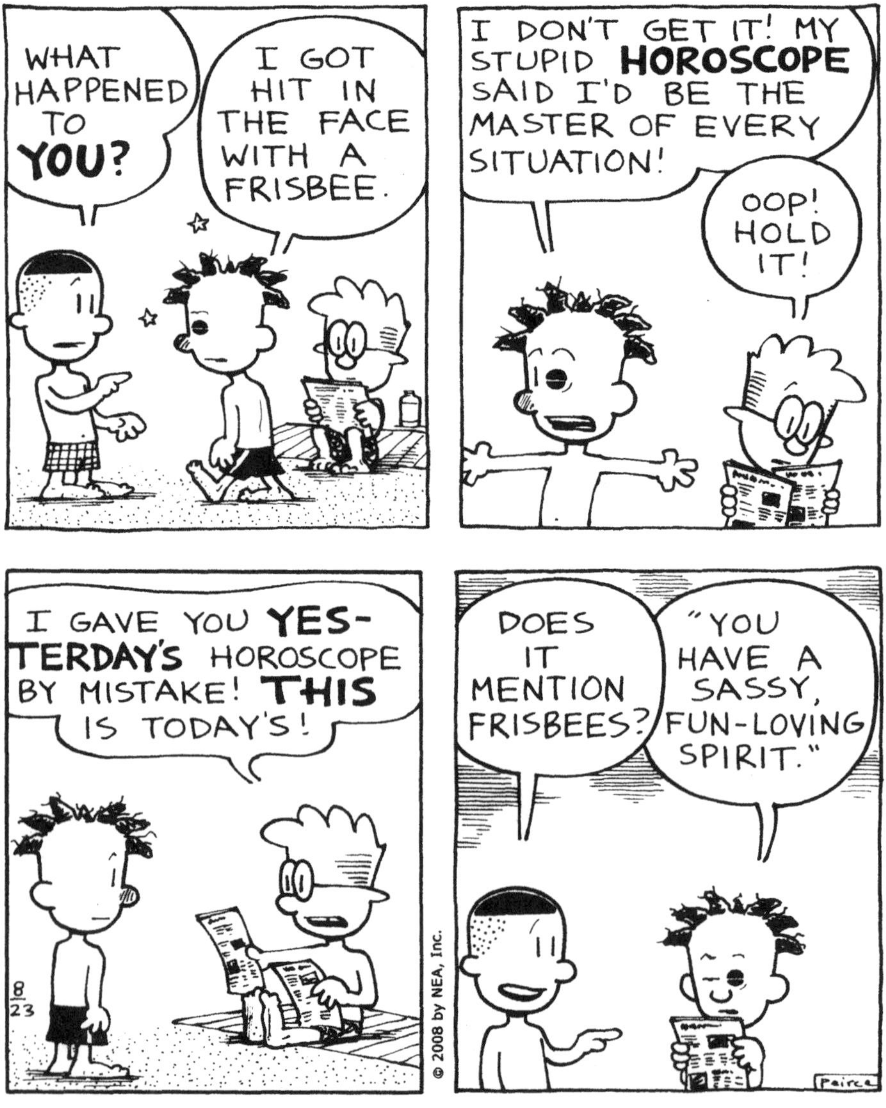
WHAT HAPPENED TO YOU?
I GOT HIT IN THE FACE WITH A FRISBEE.
I DON'T GET IT! MY STUPID HOROSCOPE SAID I'D BE THE MASTER OF EVERY SITUATION!
OOP! HOLD IT!
I GAVE YOU YES-TERDAY'S HOROSCOPE BY MISTAKE! THIS IS TODAY'S!
8/23
© 2008 by NEA, Inc.
DOES IT MENTION FRISBEES?
"YOU HAVE A SASSY, FUN-LOVING SPIRIT."
Peirce

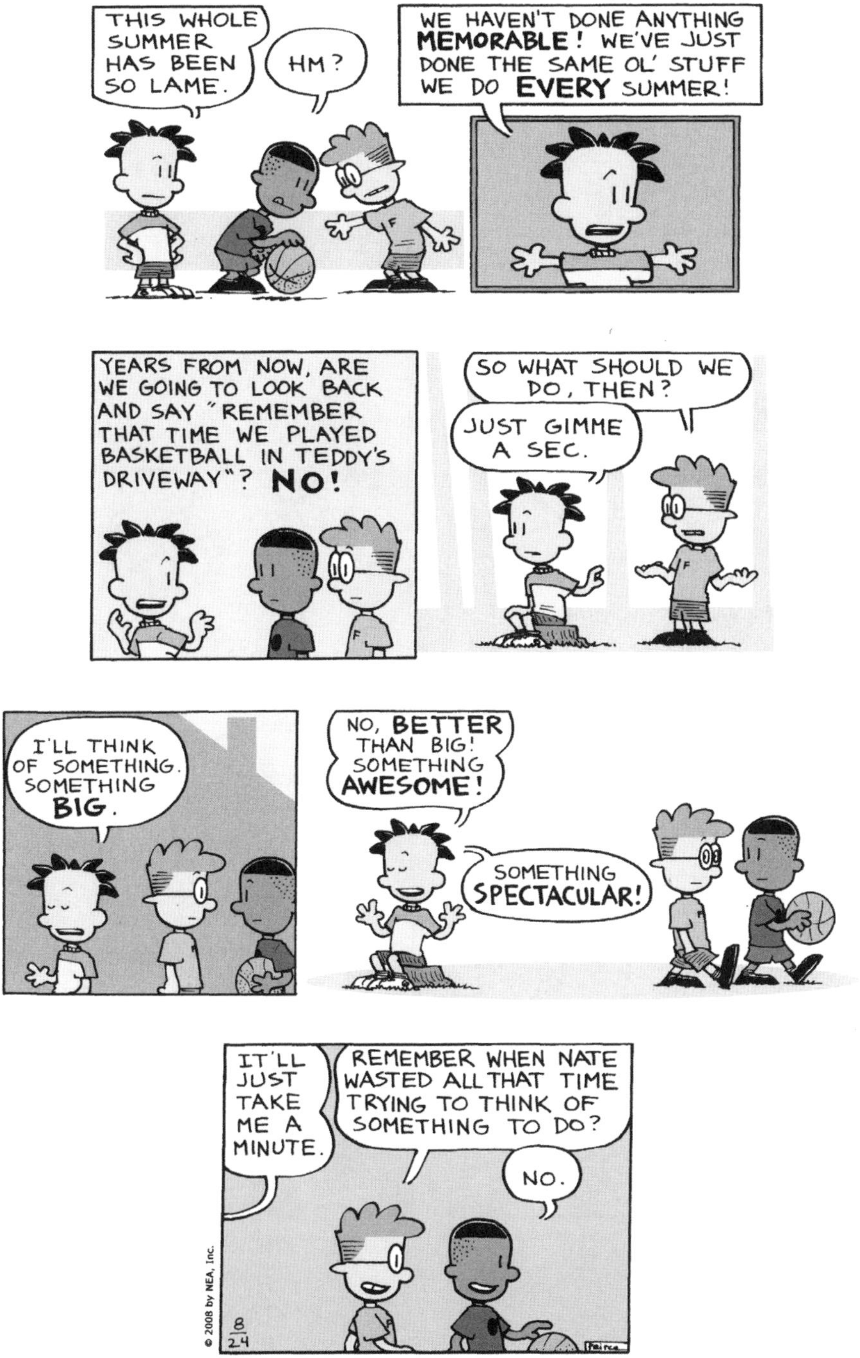
THIS WHOLE SUMMER HAS BEEN SO LAME.
HM?
WE HAVEN'T DONE ANYTHING MEMORABLE! WE'VE JUST DONE THE SAME OL' STUFF WE DO EVERY SUMMER!
YEARS FROM NOW, ARE WE GOING TO LOOK BACK AND SAY "REMEMBER THAT TIME WE PLAYED BASKETBALL IN TEDDY'S DRIVEWAY"? NO!
SO WHAT SHOULD WE DO, THEN?
JUST GIMME A SEC.
I'LL THINK OF SOMETHING. SOMETHING BIG.
NO, BETTER THAN BIG! SOMETHING AWESOME!
SOMETHING SPECTACULAR!
IT'LL JUST TAKE ME A MINUTE.
REMEMBER WHEN NATE WASTED ALL THAT TIME TRYING TO THINK OF SOMETHING TO DO?
NO.
8 24
© 2008 by NEA, Inc.

BUY BYE

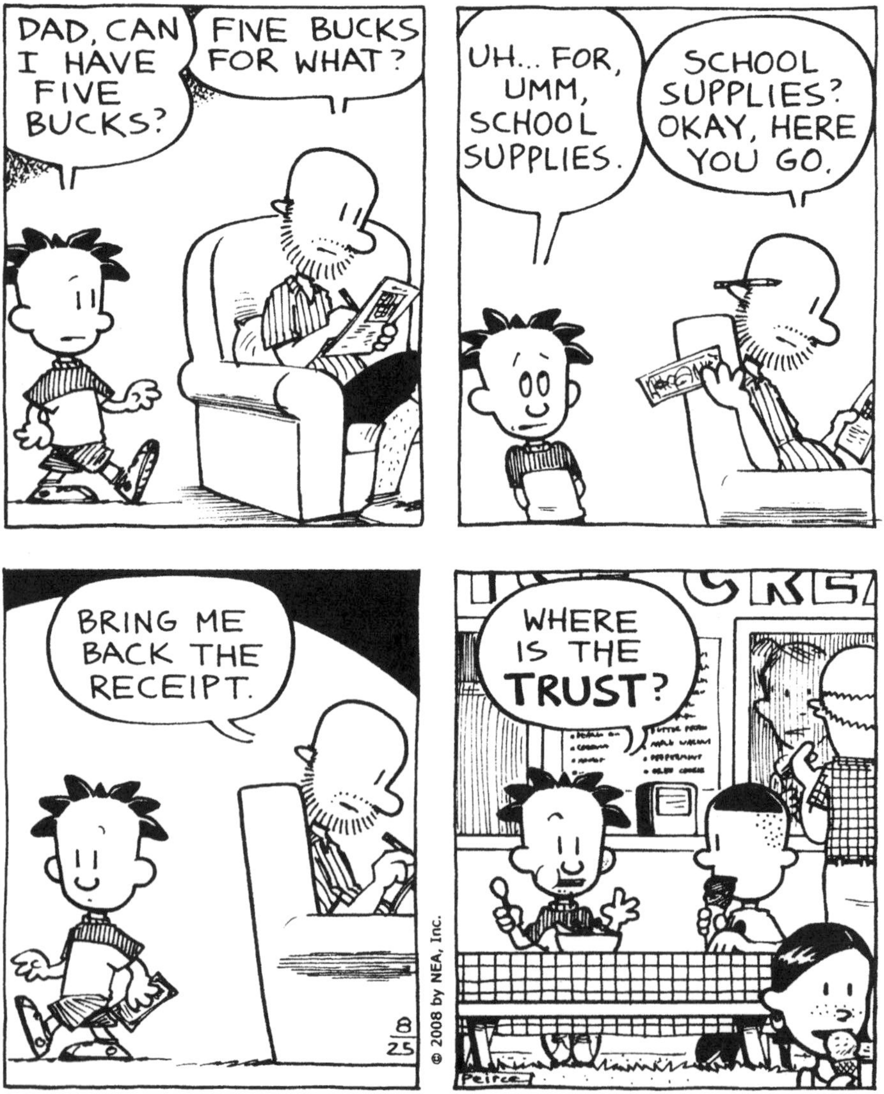
DAD, CAN I HAVE FIVE BUCKS?
FIVE BUCKS FOR WHAT?
UH... FOR, UMM, SCHOOL SUPPLIES.
SCHOOL SUPPLIES? OKAY, HERE YOU GO.
BRING ME BACK THE RECEIPT.
© 2008 by NEA, Inc.
8 25
WHERE IS THE **TRUST**?
Peirce

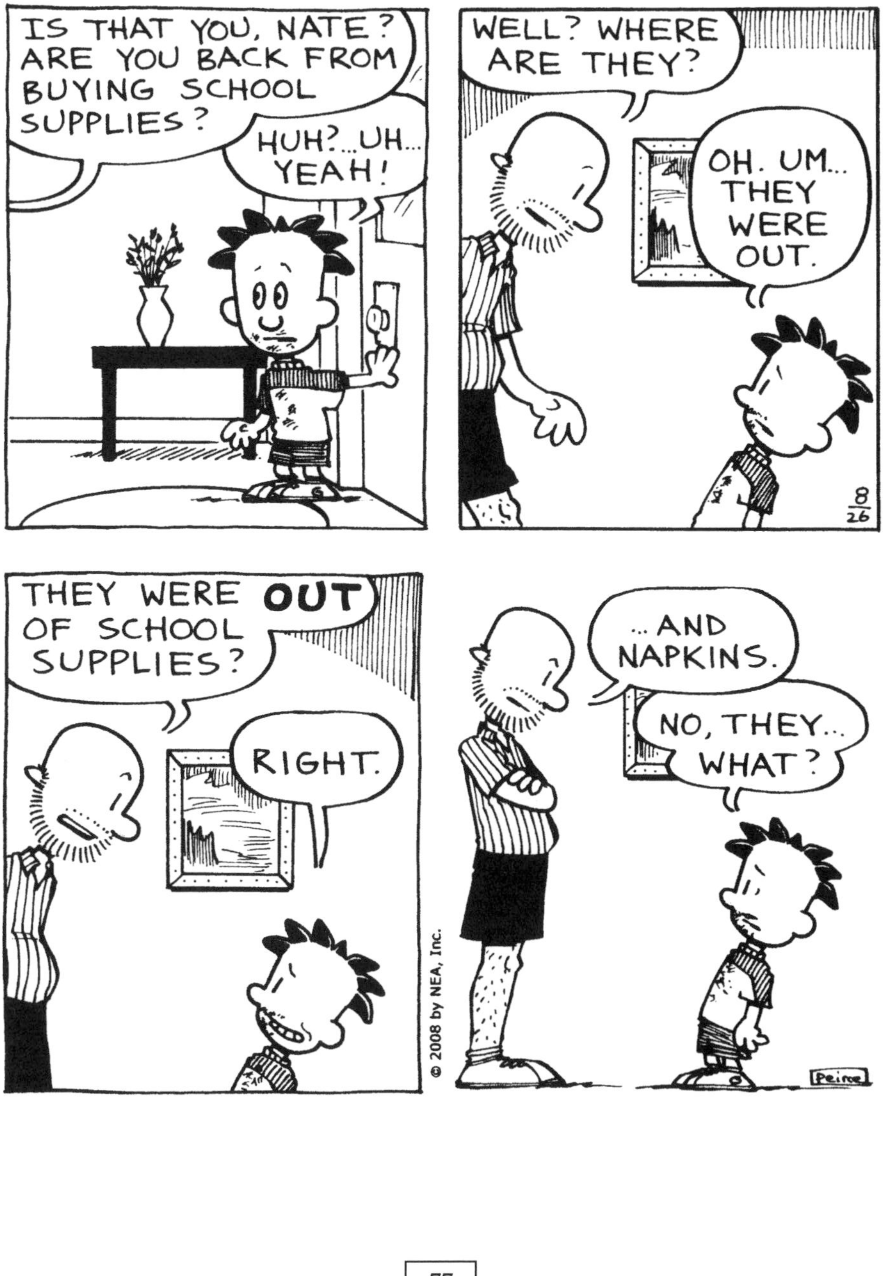
IS THAT YOU, NATE? ARE YOU BACK FROM BUYING SCHOOL SUPPLIES?
HUH?...UH... YEAH!
WELL? WHERE ARE THEY?
OH. UM... THEY WERE OUT.
8/26
THEY WERE **OUT** OF SCHOOL SUPPLIES?
RIGHT.
© 2008 by NEA, Inc.
...AND NAPKINS.
NO, THEY... WHAT?
Peirce

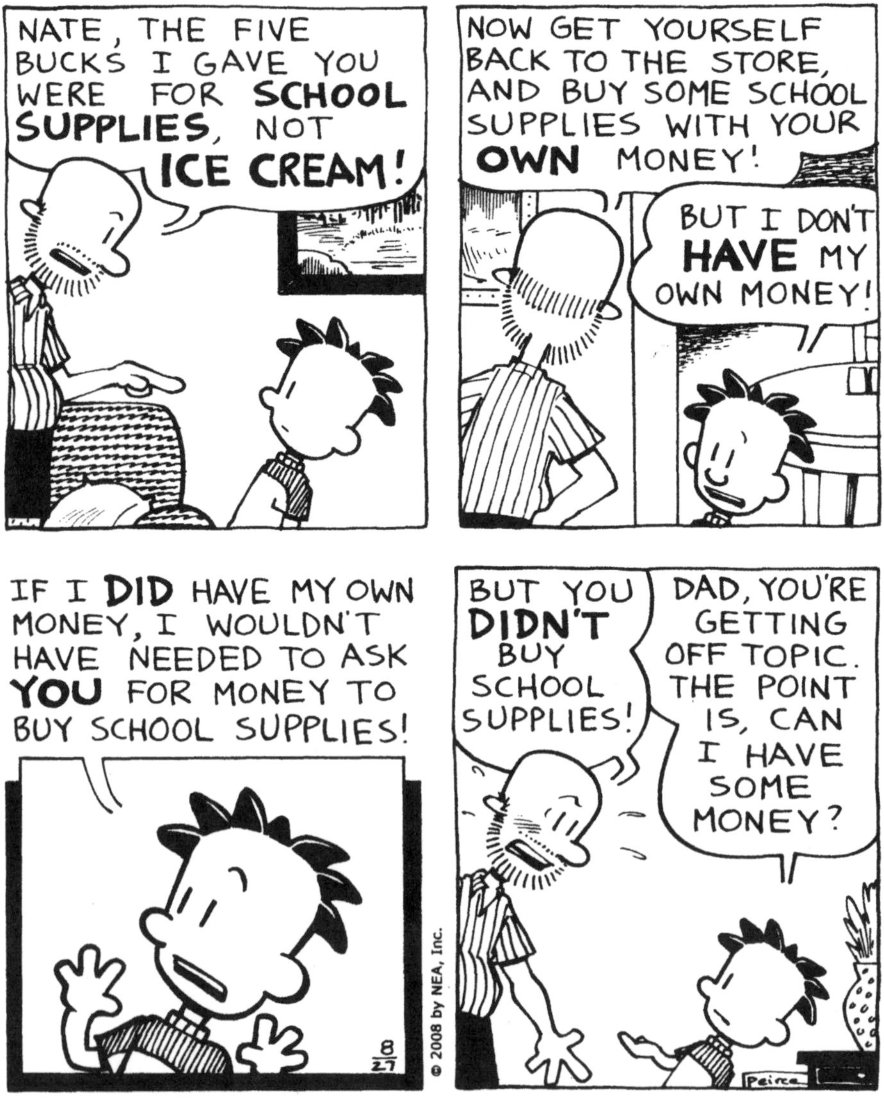
NATE, THE FIVE BUCKS I GAVE YOU WERE FOR SCHOOL SUPPLIES, NOT ICE CREAM!
NOW GET YOURSELF BACK TO THE STORE, AND BUY SOME SCHOOL SUPPLIES WITH YOUR OWN MONEY!
BUT I DON'T HAVE MY OWN MONEY!
IF I DID HAVE MY OWN MONEY, I WOULDN'T HAVE NEEDED TO ASK YOU FOR MONEY TO BUY SCHOOL SUPPLIES!
8
27
© 2008 by NEA, Inc.
BUT YOU DIDN'T BUY SCHOOL SUPPLIES!
DAD, YOU'RE GETTING OFF TOPIC. THE POINT IS, CAN I HAVE SOME MONEY?
Peirce

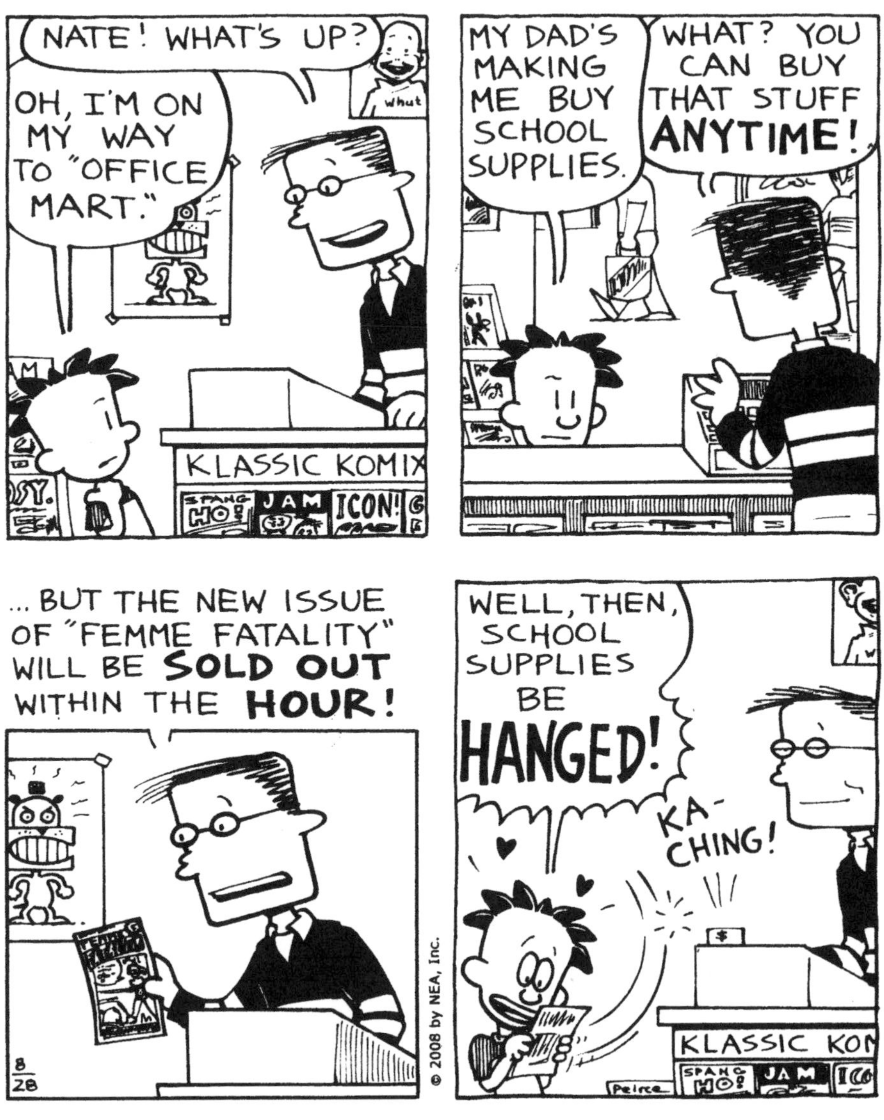
NATE! WHAT'S UP?
OH, I'M ON MY WAY TO "OFFICE MART."
KLASSIC KOMIX
MY DAD'S MAKING ME BUY SCHOOL SUPPLIES.
WHAT? YOU CAN BUY THAT STUFF ANYTIME!
... BUT THE NEW ISSUE OF "FEMME FATALITY" WILL BE SOLD OUT WITHIN THE HOUR!
8/28
© 2008 by NEA, Inc.
WELL, THEN, SCHOOL SUPPLIES BE HANGED!
KA-CHING!
KLASSIC KOM
Peirce

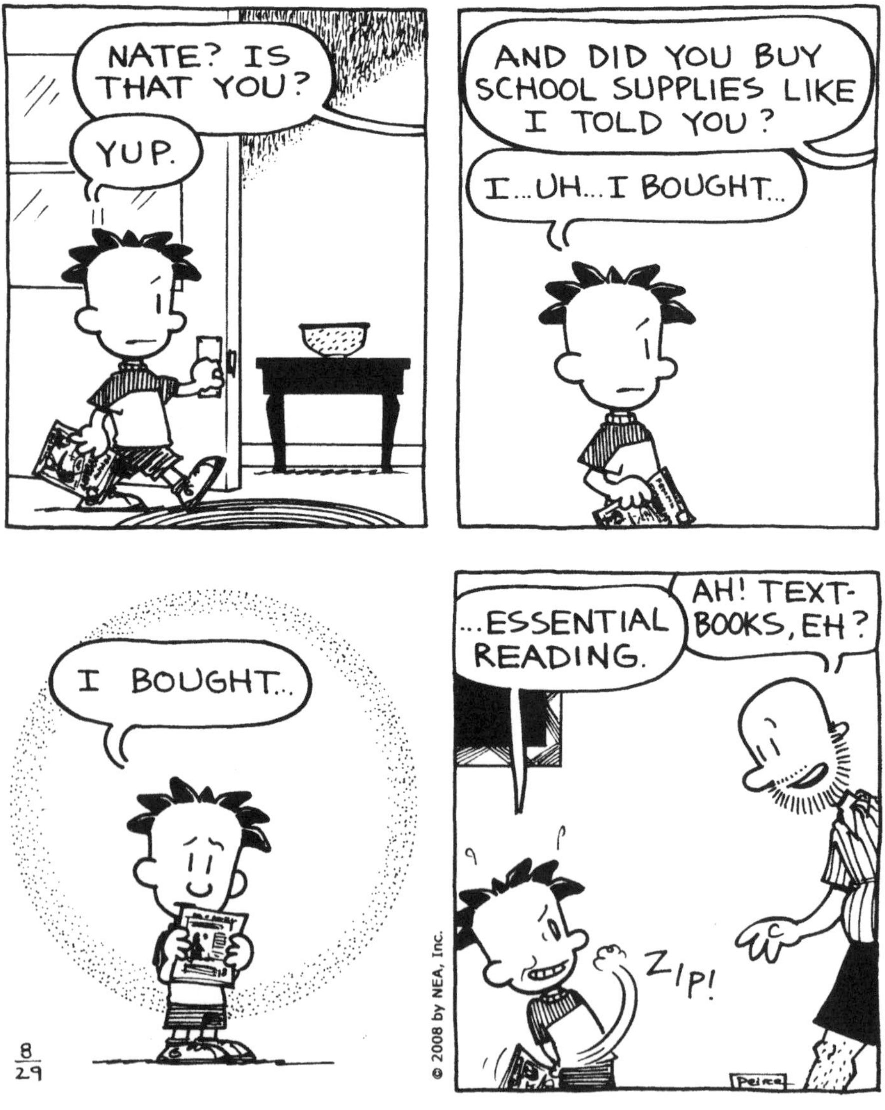
NATE? IS THAT YOU?
YUP.
AND DID YOU BUY SCHOOL SUPPLIES LIKE I TOLD YOU?
I...UH...I BOUGHT...
I BOUGHT...
8/29
...ESSENTIAL READING.
AH! TEXT-BOOKS, EH?
ZIP!
© 2008 by NEA, Inc.
Peirce

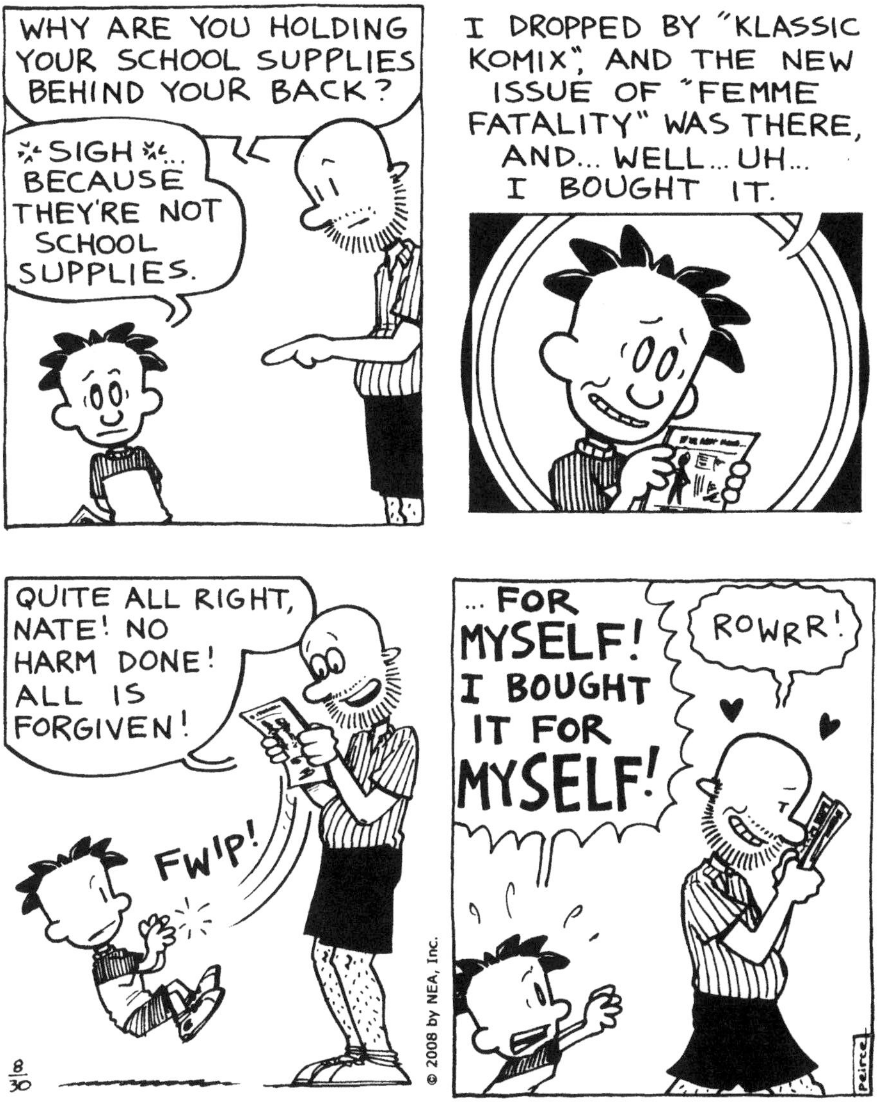
WHY ARE YOU HOLDING YOUR SCHOOL SUPPLIES BEHIND YOUR BACK?
SIGH... BECAUSE THEY'RE NOT SCHOOL SUPPLIES.
I DROPPED BY "KLASSIC KOMIX", AND THE NEW ISSUE OF "FEMME FATALITY" WAS THERE, AND... WELL... UH... I BOUGHT IT.
QUITE ALL RIGHT, NATE! NO HARM DONE! ALL IS FORGIVEN!
FWIP!
8/30
© 2008 by NEA, Inc.
... FOR MYSELF! I BOUGHT IT FOR MYSELF!
ROWRR!
peirce

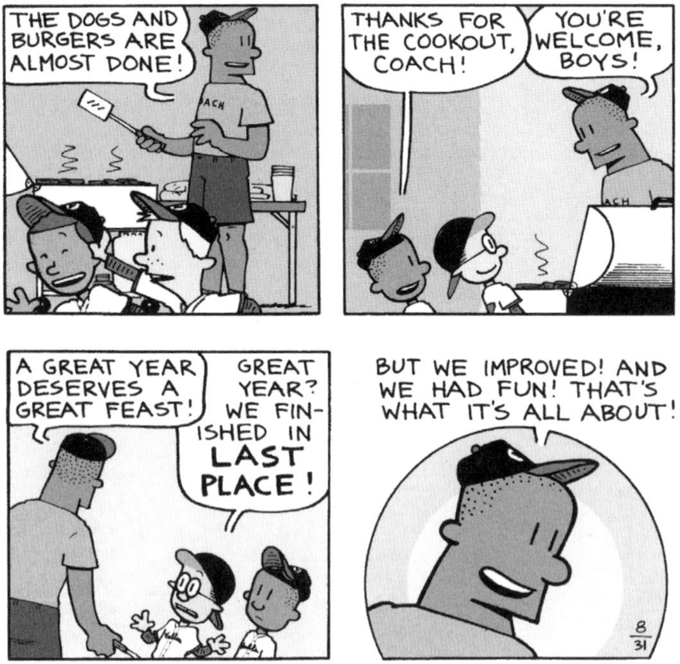
THE DOGS AND BURGERS ARE ALMOST DONE!
THANKS FOR THE COOKOUT, COACH!
YOU'RE WELCOME, BOYS!
A GREAT YEAR DESERVES A GREAT FEAST!
GREAT YEAR? WE FIN-ISHED IN LAST PLACE!
BUT WE IMPROVED! AND WE HAD FUN! THAT'S WHAT IT'S ALL ABOUT!
8/31

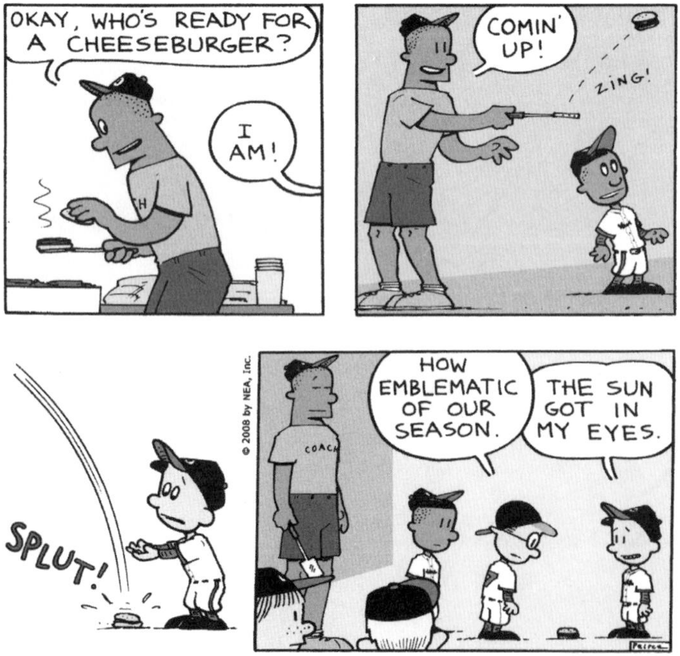
OKAY, WHO'S READY FOR A CHEESEBURGER?
I AM!
COMIN' UP!
ZING!
SPLUT!
© 2008 by NEA, Inc.
HOW EMBLEMATIC OF OUR SEASON.
THE SUN GOT IN MY EYES.

MOLD!

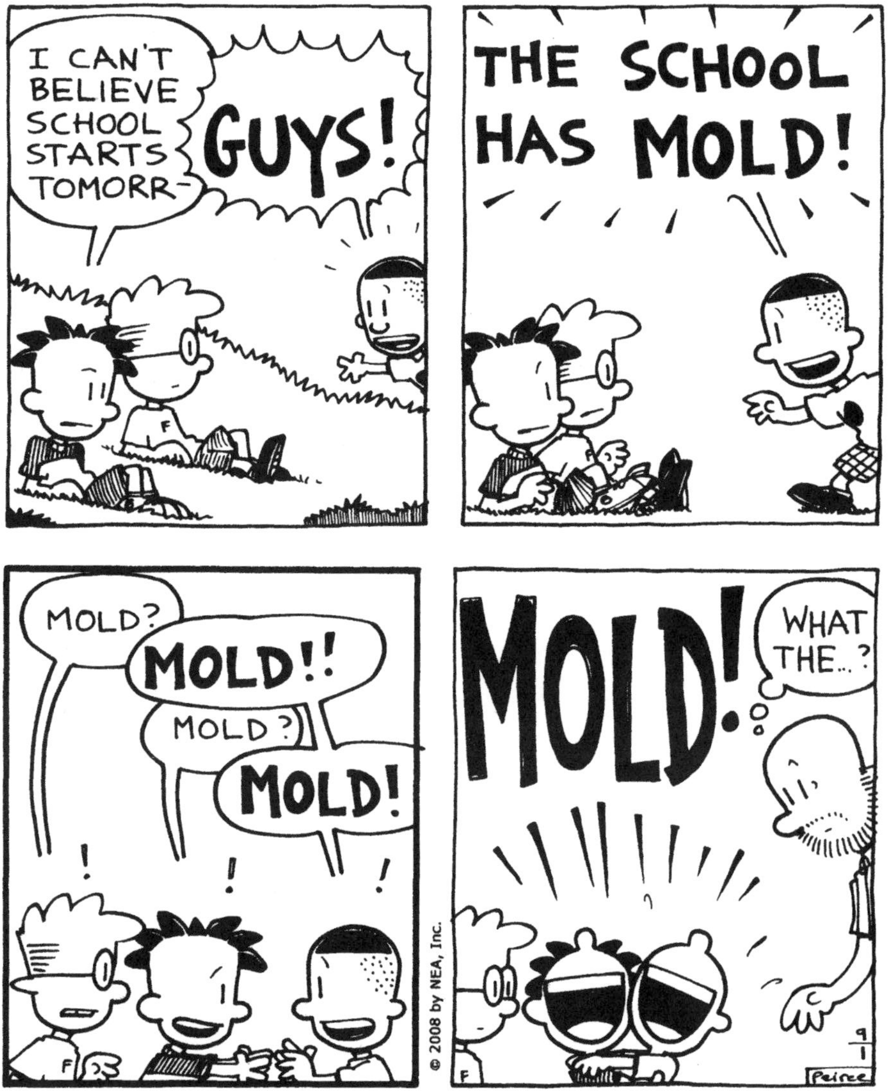
I CAN'T BELIEVE SCHOOL STARTS TOMORR-
GUYS!
THE SCHOOL HAS MOLD!
MOLD?
MOLD!!
MOLD?
MOLD!
!
!
!
© 2008 by NEA, Inc.
MOLD!
WHAT THE...?
9/1
Peirce

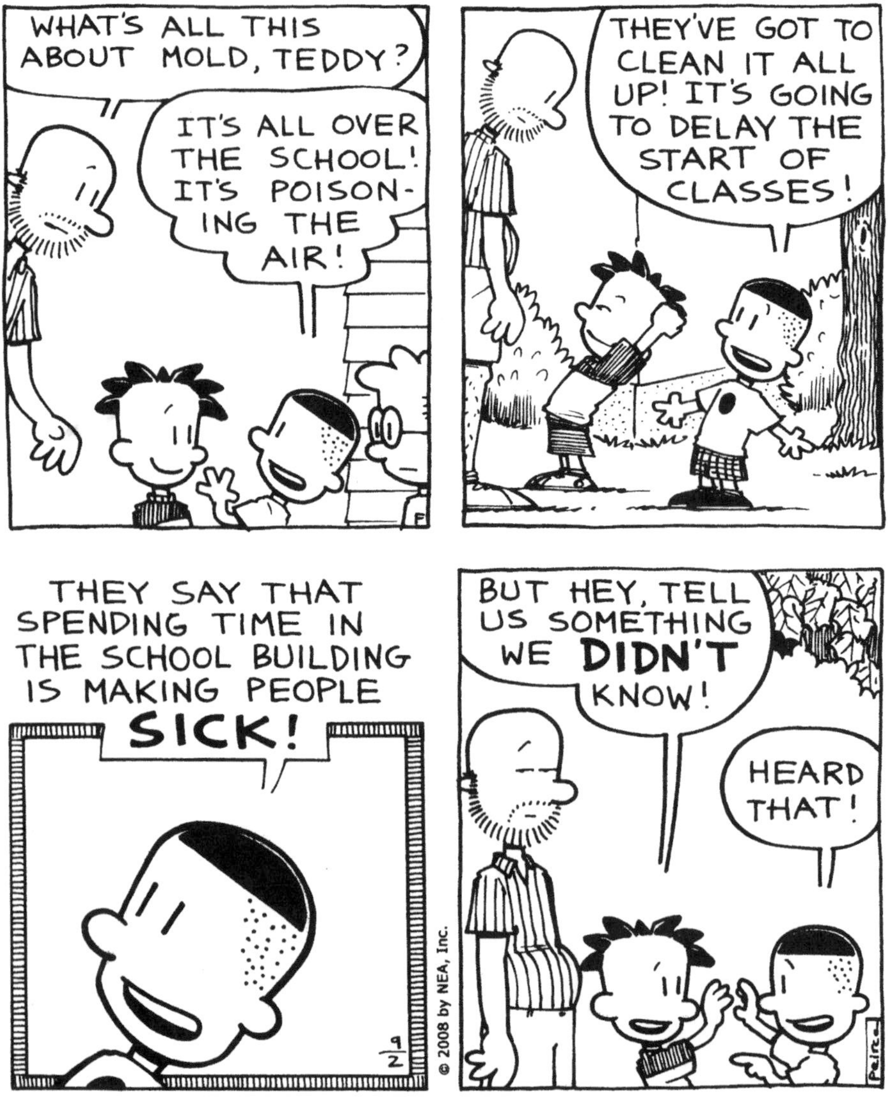
WHAT'S ALL THIS ABOUT MOLD, TEDDY?
IT'S ALL OVER THE SCHOOL! IT'S POISONING THE AIR!
THEY'VE GOT TO CLEAN IT ALL UP! IT'S GOING TO DELAY THE START OF CLASSES!
THEY SAY THAT SPENDING TIME IN THE SCHOOL BUILDING IS MAKING PEOPLE SICK!
© 2008 by NEA, Inc.
BUT HEY, TELL US SOMETHING WE DIDN'T KNOW!
HEARD THAT!
Peirce

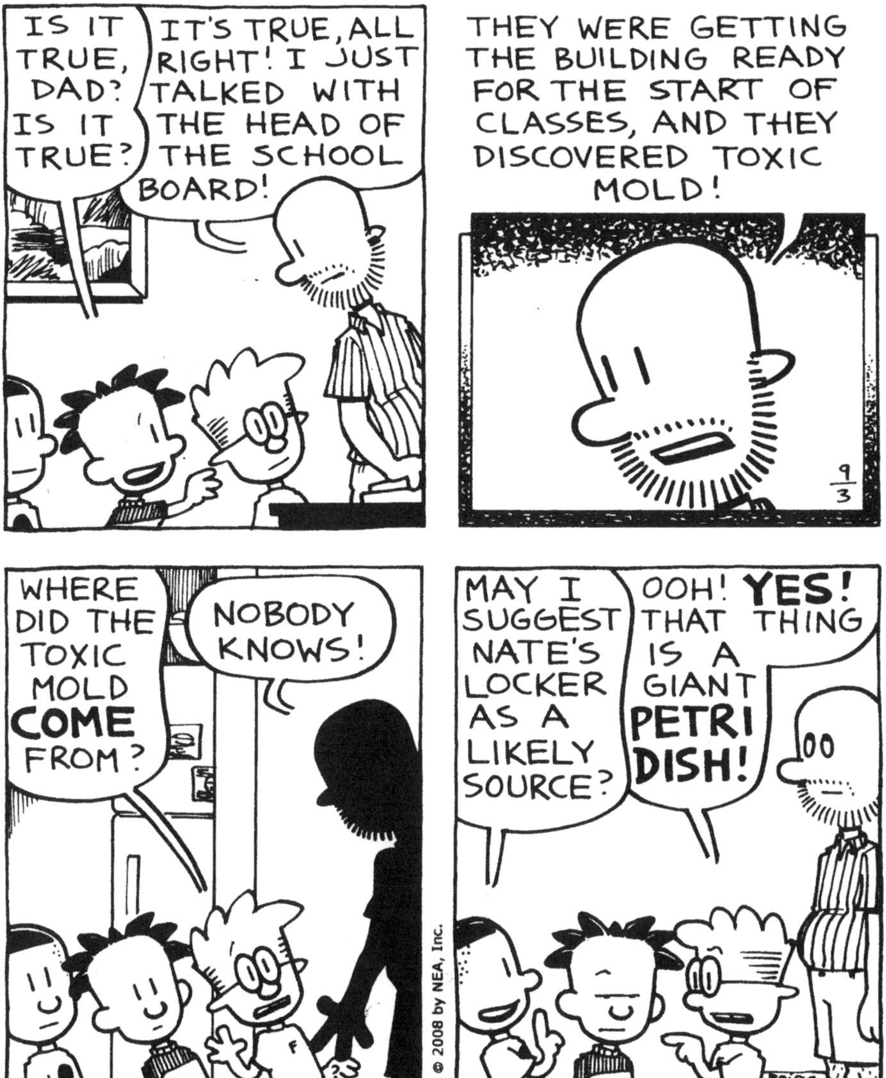
IS IT TRUE, DAD? IS IT TRUE?
IT'S TRUE, ALL RIGHT! I JUST TALKED WITH THE HEAD OF THE SCHOOL BOARD!
THEY WERE GETTING THE BUILDING READY FOR THE START OF CLASSES, AND THEY DISCOVERED TOXIC MOLD!
9/3
WHERE DID THE TOXIC MOLD **COME** FROM?
NOBODY KNOWS!
© 2008 by NEA, Inc.
MAY I SUGGEST NATE'S LOCKER AS A LIKELY SOURCE?
OOH! **YES!** THAT THING IS A GIANT **PETRI DISH!**
PEIRCE

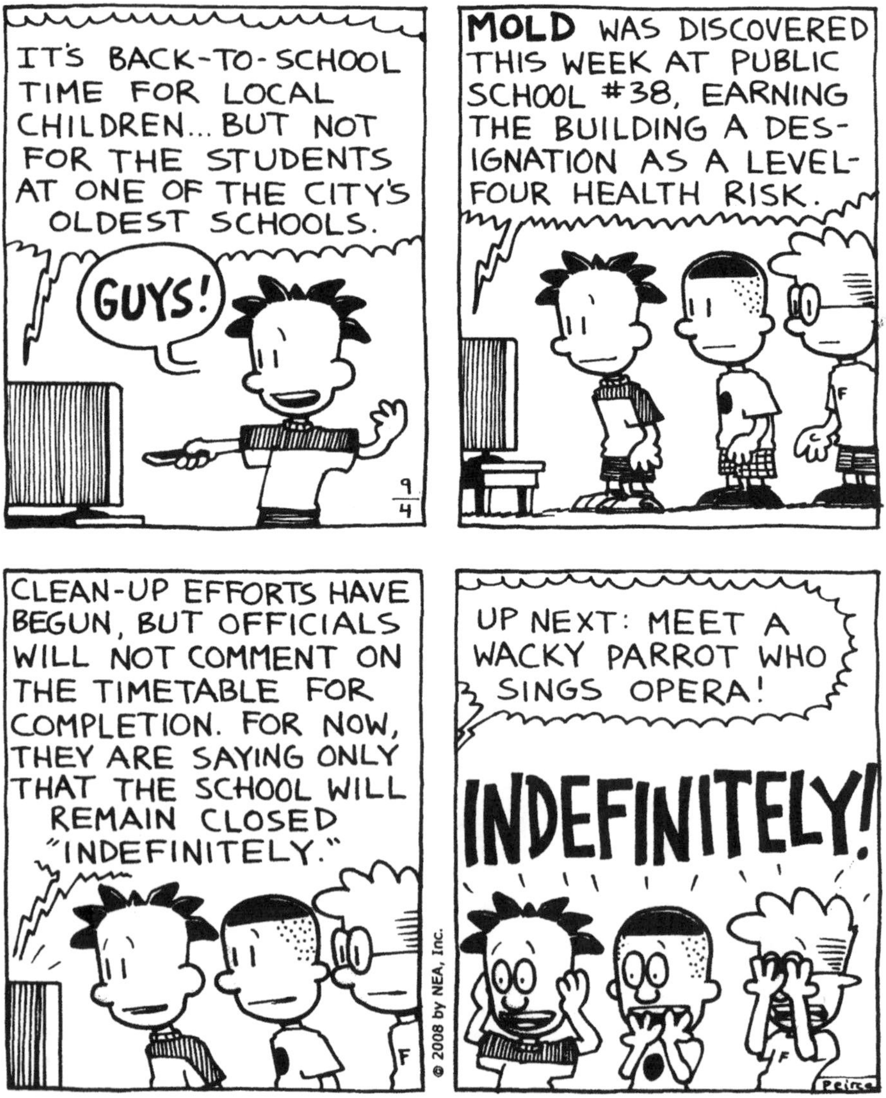
IT'S BACK-TO-SCHOOL TIME FOR LOCAL CHILDREN... BUT NOT FOR THE STUDENTS AT ONE OF THE CITY'S OLDEST SCHOOLS.
GUYS!
9/4
MOLD WAS DISCOVERED THIS WEEK AT PUBLIC SCHOOL #38, EARNING THE BUILDING A DESIGNATION AS A LEVEL-FOUR HEALTH RISK.
CLEAN-UP EFFORTS HAVE BEGUN, BUT OFFICIALS WILL NOT COMMENT ON THE TIMETABLE FOR COMPLETION. FOR NOW, THEY ARE SAYING ONLY THAT THE SCHOOL WILL REMAIN CLOSED "INDEFINITELY."
© 2008 by NEA, Inc.
UP NEXT: MEET A WACKY PARROT WHO SINGS OPERA!
INDEFINITELY!
Peirce

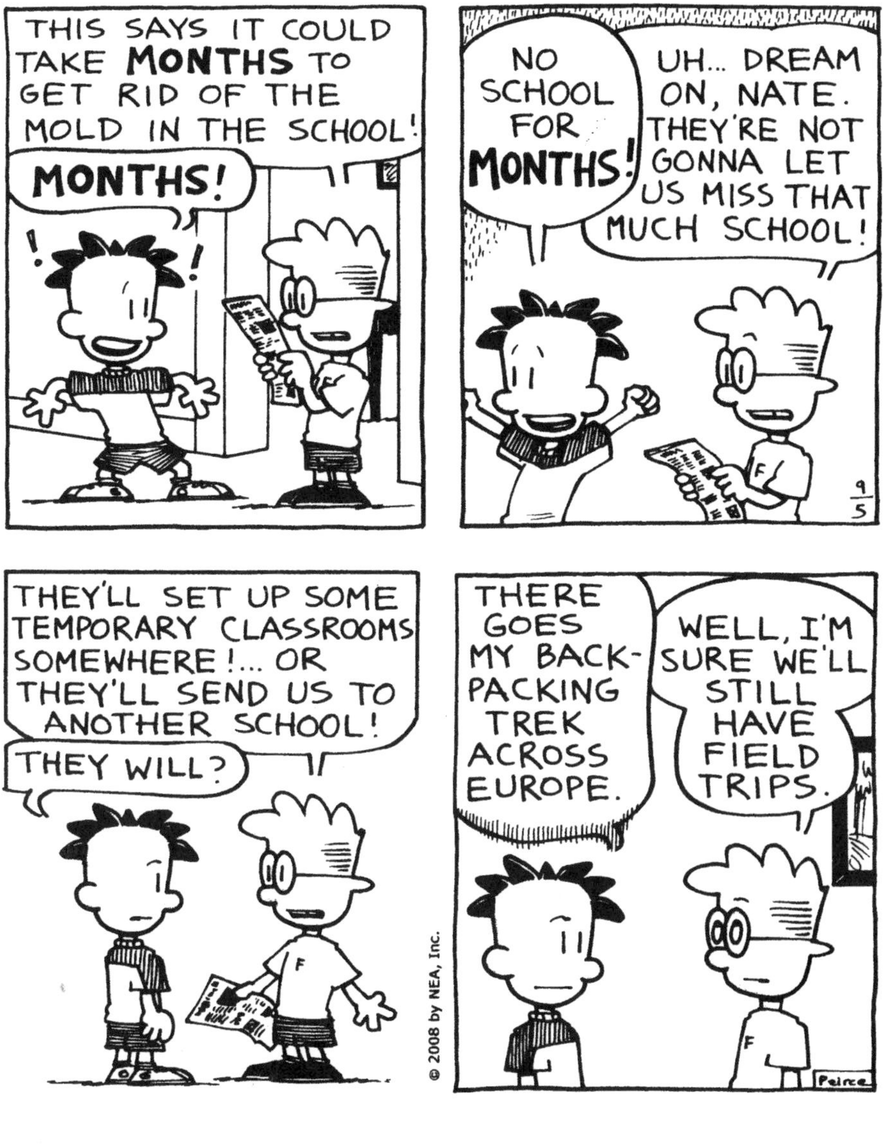
THIS SAYS IT COULD TAKE **MONTHS** TO GET RID OF THE MOLD IN THE SCHOOL!
MONTHS!
NO SCHOOL FOR MONTHS!
UH... DREAM ON, NATE. THEY'RE NOT GONNA LET US MISS THAT MUCH SCHOOL!
9/5
THEY'LL SET UP SOME TEMPORARY CLASSROOMS SOMEWHERE!... OR THEY'LL SEND US TO ANOTHER SCHOOL!
THEY WILL?
© 2008 by NEA, Inc.
THERE GOES MY BACK-PACKING TREK ACROSS EUROPE.
WELL, I'M SURE WE'LL STILL HAVE FIELD TRIPS.
Peirce

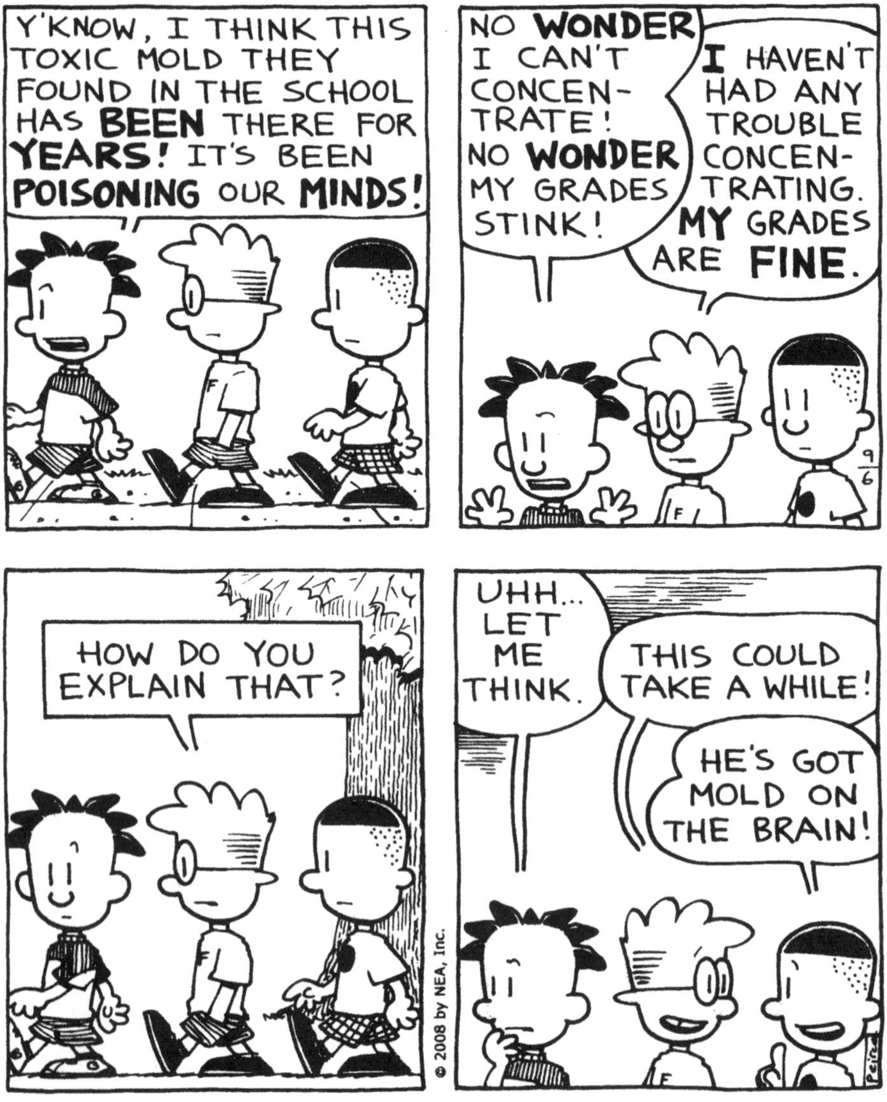

Y'KNOW, I THINK THIS TOXIC MOLD THEY FOUND IN THE SCHOOL HAS **BEEN** THERE FOR **YEARS!** IT'S BEEN **POISONING** OUR **MINDS!**
NO **WONDER** I CAN'T CONCENTRATE! NO **WONDER** MY GRADES STINK!
I HAVEN'T HAD ANY TROUBLE CONCENTRATING. **MY** GRADES ARE **FINE**.
9/6
HOW DO YOU EXPLAIN THAT?
UHH... LET ME THINK.
THIS COULD TAKE A WHILE!
HE'S GOT MOLD ON THE BRAIN!

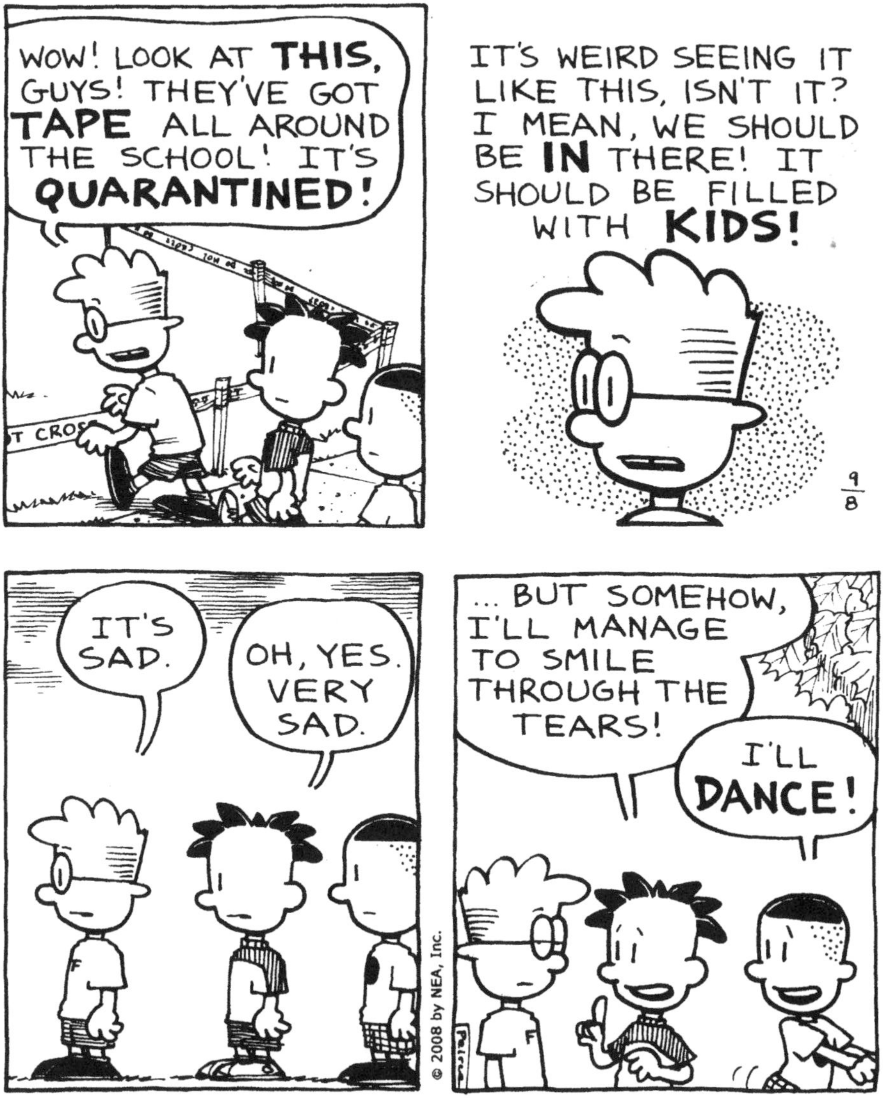
WOW! LOOK AT THIS, GUYS! THEY'VE GOT TAPE ALL AROUND THE SCHOOL! IT'S QUARANTINED!
IT'S WEIRD SEEING IT LIKE THIS, ISN'T IT? I MEAN, WE SHOULD BE IN THERE! IT SHOULD BE FILLED WITH KIDS!
9/8
IT'S SAD.
OH, YES. VERY SAD.
... BUT SOMEHOW, I'LL MANAGE TO SMILE THROUGH THE TEARS!
I'LL DANCE!
© 2008 by NEA, Inc.

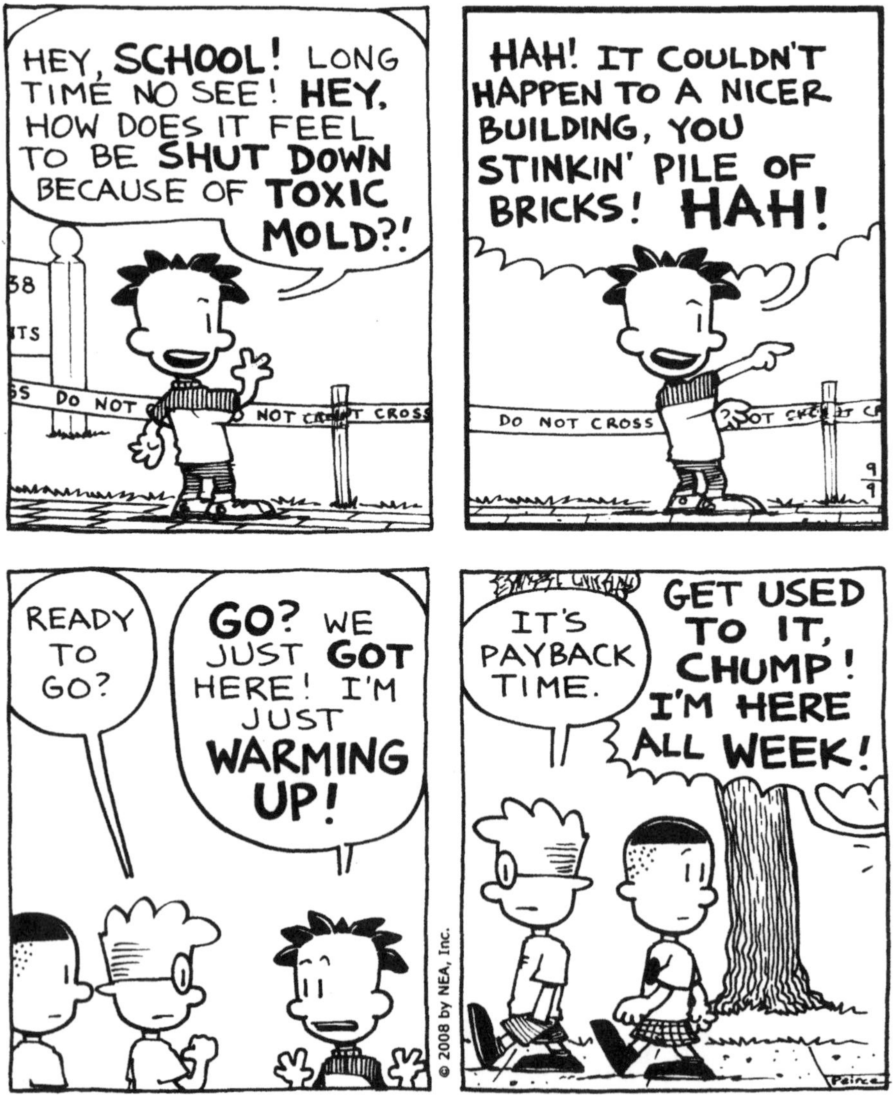
HEY, SCHOOL! LONG TIME NO SEE! HEY, HOW DOES IT FEEL TO BE SHUT DOWN BECAUSE OF TOXIC MOLD?!
DO NOT CROSS
HAH! IT COULDN'T HAPPEN TO A NICER BUILDING, YOU STINKIN' PILE OF BRICKS! HAH!
DO NOT CROSS
READY TO GO?
GO? WE JUST GOT HERE! I'M JUST WARMING UP!
© 2008 by NEA, Inc.
IT'S PAYBACK TIME.
GET USED TO IT, CHUMP! I'M HERE ALL WEEK!
Peirce

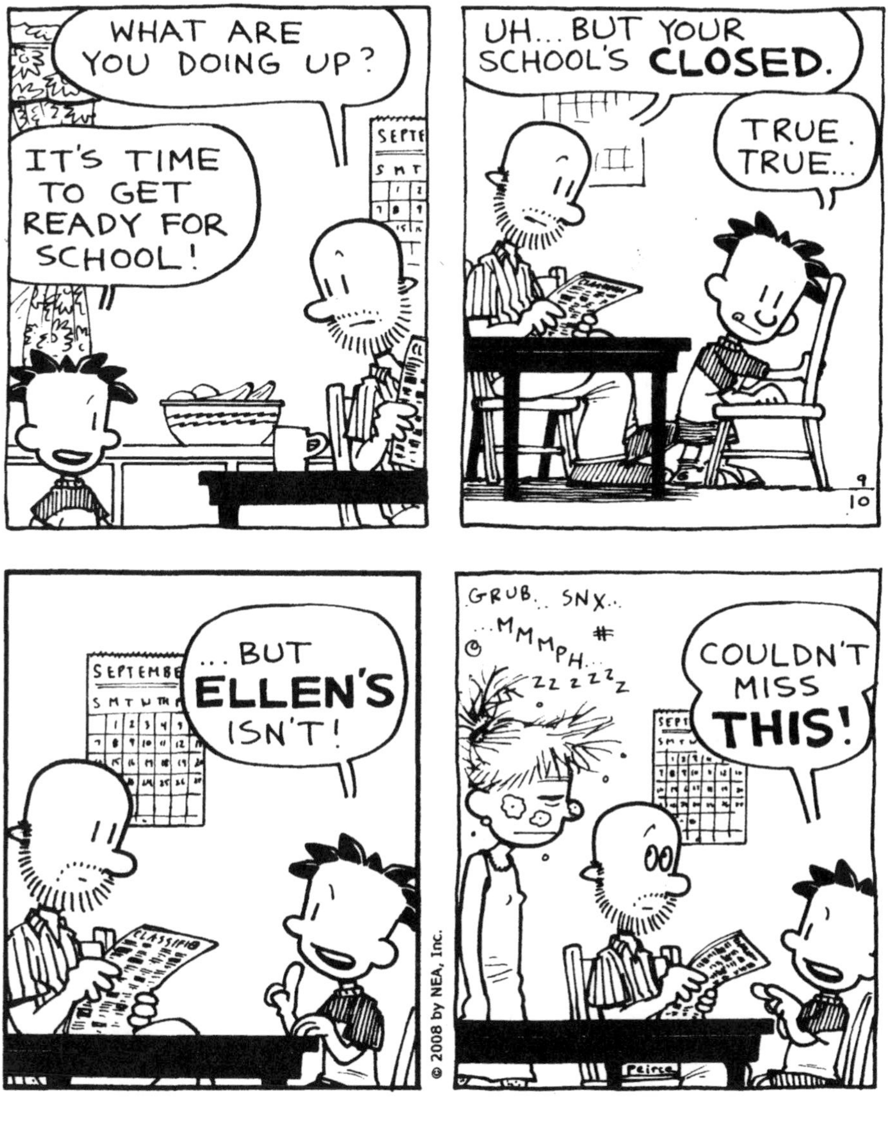

WHAT ARE YOU DOING UP?
IT'S TIME TO GET READY FOR SCHOOL!
UH... BUT YOUR SCHOOL'S **CLOSED.**
TRUE. TRUE...
...BUT **ELLEN'S** ISN'T!
GRUB.. SNX..
...MMMPH...
ZZZZZZ
COULDN'T MISS **THIS!**

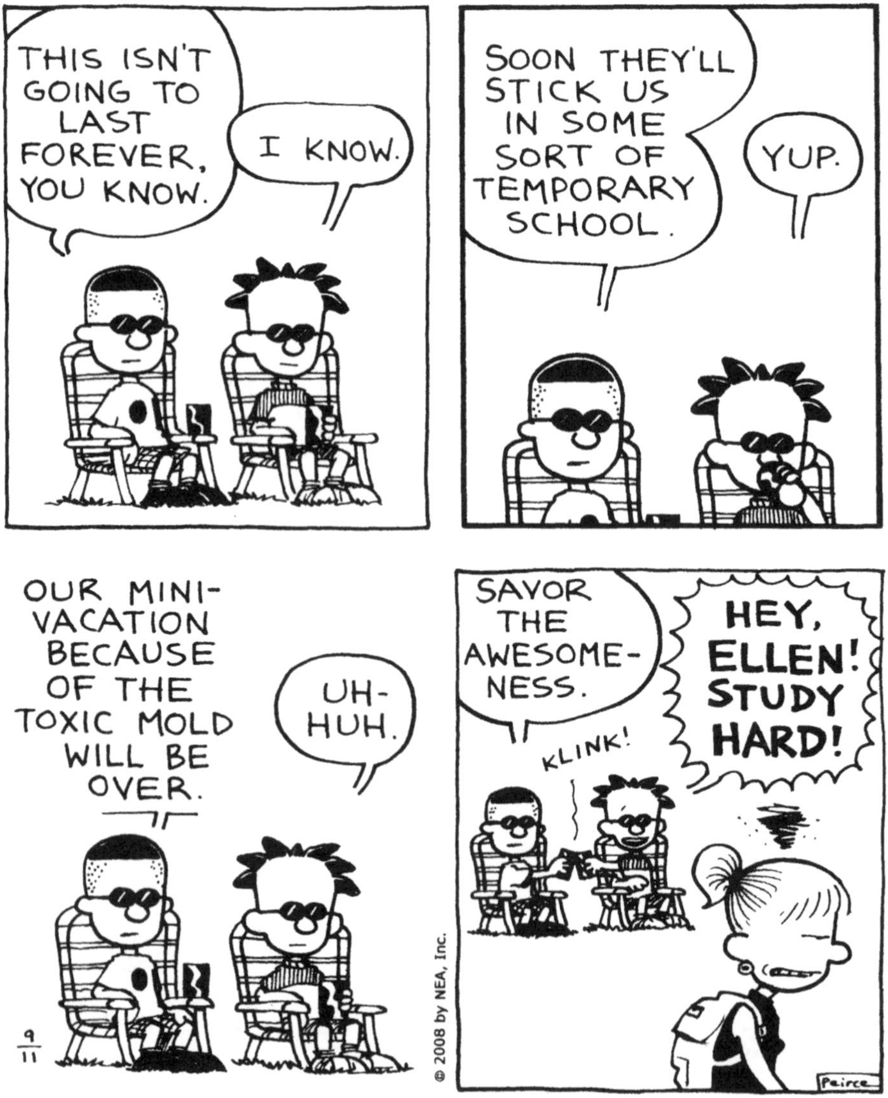
THIS ISN'T GOING TO LAST FOREVER, YOU KNOW.
I KNOW.
SOON THEY'LL STICK US IN SOME SORT OF TEMPORARY SCHOOL.
YUP.
OUR MINI-VACATION BECAUSE OF THE TOXIC MOLD WILL BE OVER.
UH-HUH.
SAVOR THE AWESOME-NESS.
KLINK!
HEY, ELLEN! STUDY HARD!
9/11
© 2008 by NEA, Inc.
Peirce

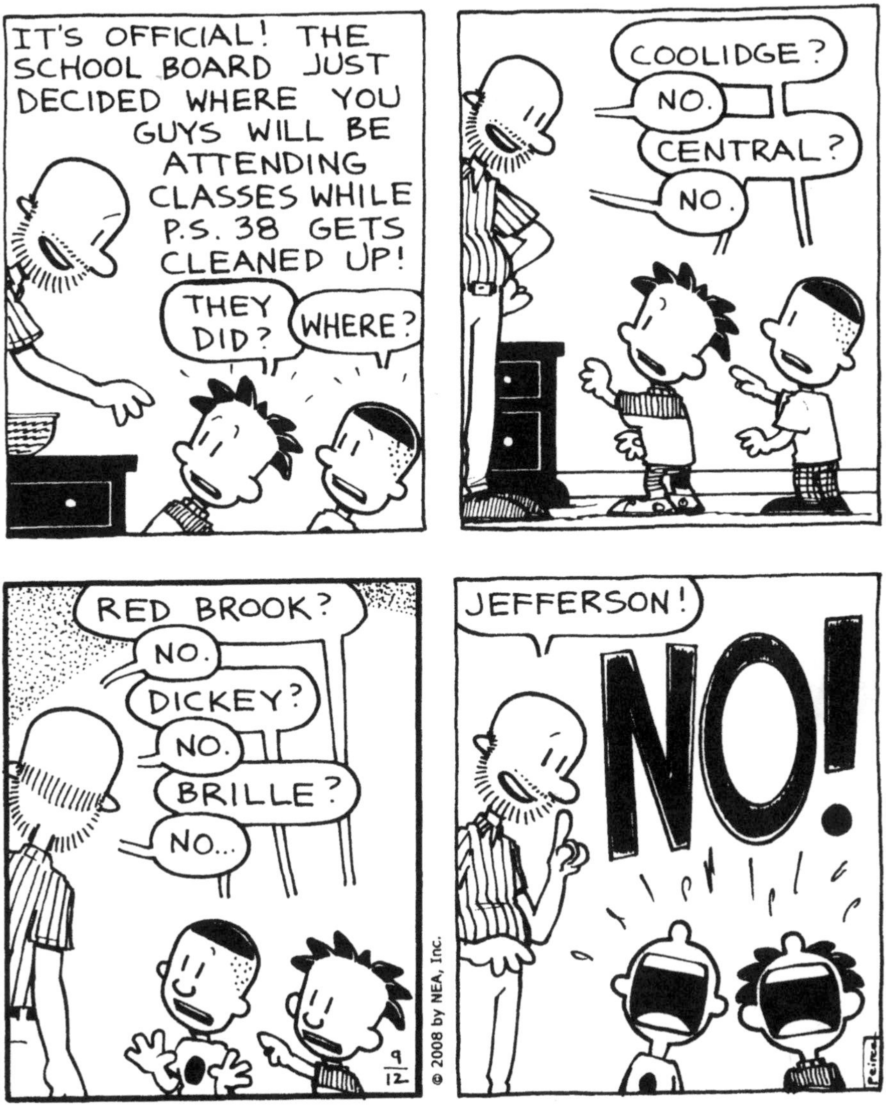
IT'S OFFICIAL! THE SCHOOL BOARD JUST DECIDED WHERE YOU GUYS WILL BE ATTENDING CLASSES WHILE P.S. 38 GETS CLEANED UP!
THEY DID?
WHERE?
COOLIDGE?
NO.
CENTRAL?
NO.
RED BROOK?
NO.
DICKEY?
NO.
BRILLE?
NO...
9/12
© 2008 by NEA, Inc.
JEFFERSON!
NO!
Peirce

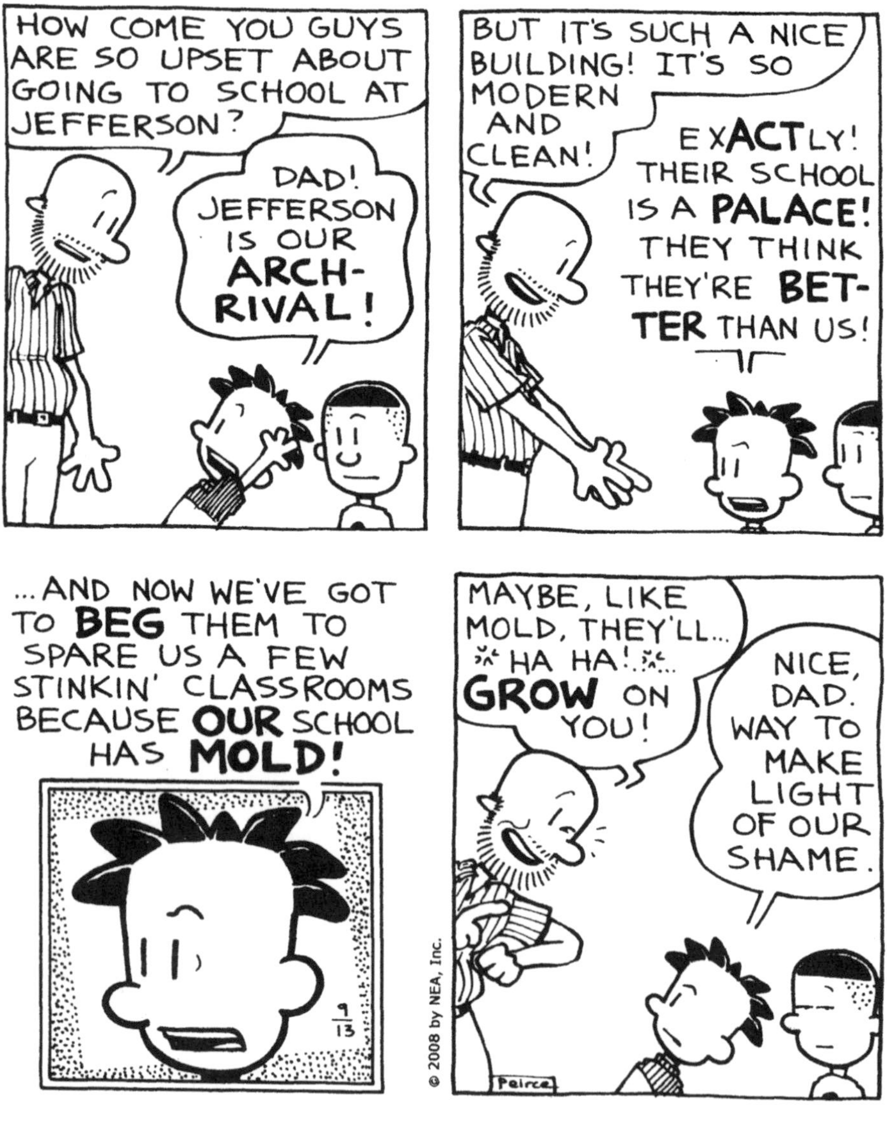
HOW COME YOU GUYS ARE SO UPSET ABOUT GOING TO SCHOOL AT JEFFERSON?
DAD! JEFFERSON IS OUR ARCH-RIVAL!
BUT IT'S SUCH A NICE BUILDING! IT'S SO MODERN AND CLEAN!
EXACTLY! THEIR SCHOOL IS A PALACE! THEY THINK THEY'RE BETTER THAN US!
...AND NOW WE'VE GOT TO BEG THEM TO SPARE US A FEW STINKIN' CLASSROOMS BECAUSE OUR SCHOOL HAS MOLD!
9/13
MAYBE, LIKE MOLD, THEY'LL... HA HA! GROW ON YOU!
NICE, DAD. WAY TO MAKE LIGHT OF OUR SHAME.
Peirce

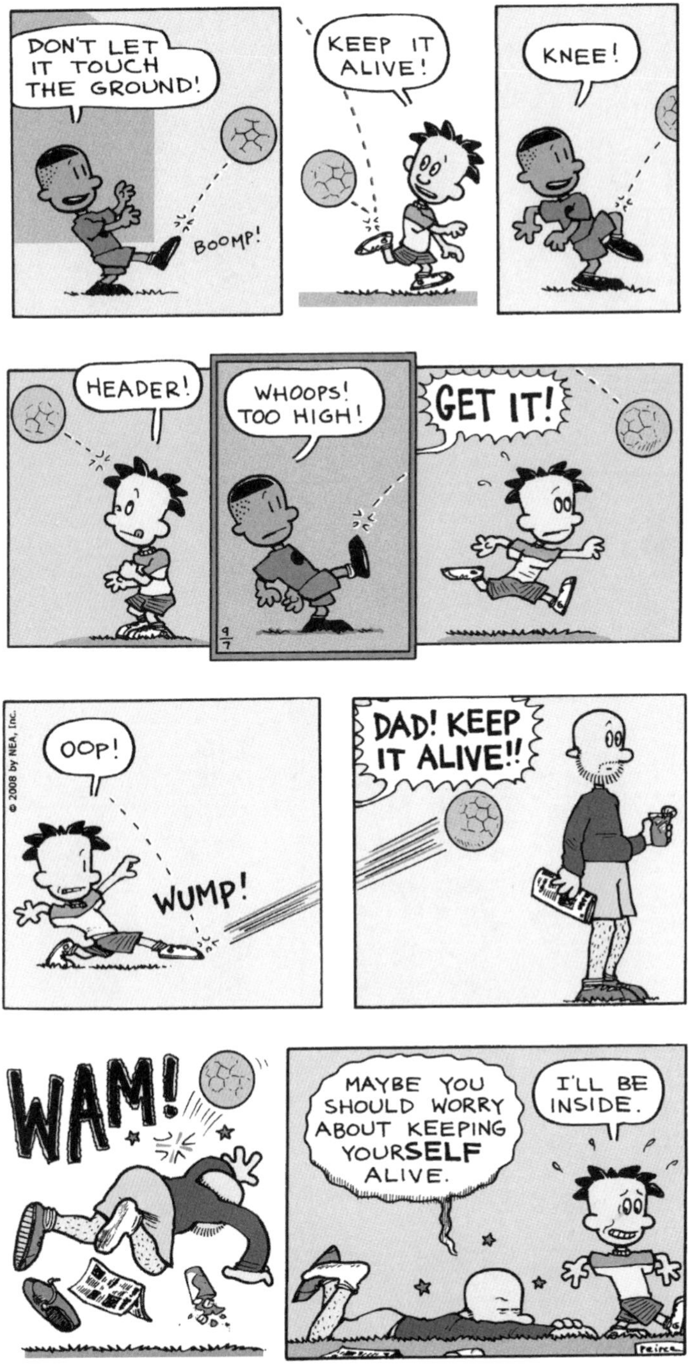
DON'T LET IT TOUCH THE GROUND!
BOOMP!
KEEP IT ALIVE!
KNEE!
HEADER!
WHOOPS! TOO HIGH!
GET IT!
OOP!
WUMP!
DAD! KEEP IT ALIVE!!
WAM!
MAYBE YOU SHOULD WORRY ABOUT KEEPING YOURSELF ALIVE.
I'LL BE INSIDE.

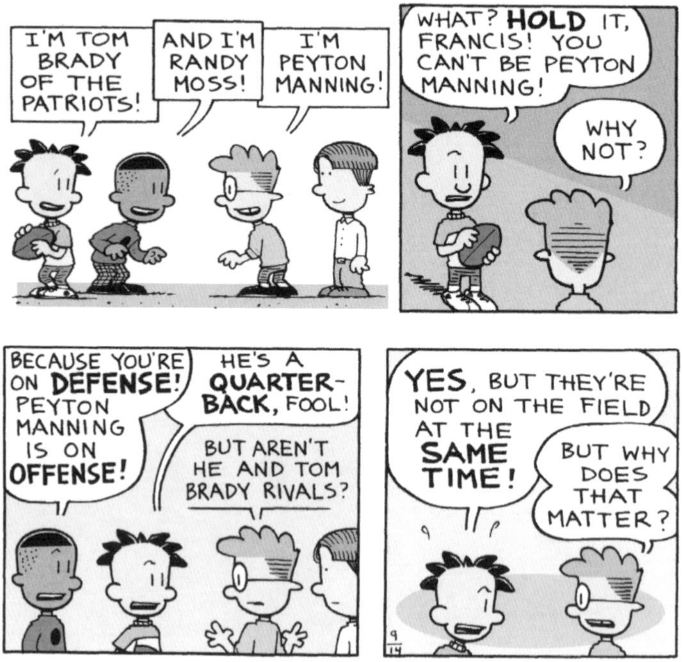
I'M TOM BRADY OF THE PATRIOTS!
AND I'M RANDY MOSS!
I'M PEYTON MANNING!
WHAT? **HOLD** IT, FRANCIS! YOU CAN'T BE PEYTON MANNING!
WHY NOT?
BECAUSE YOU'RE ON **DEFENSE**! PEYTON MANNING IS ON **OFFENSE**!
HE'S A **QUARTER-BACK,** FOOL!
BUT AREN'T HE AND TOM BRADY RIVALS?
YES, BUT THEY'RE NOT ON THE FIELD AT THE **SAME TIME**!
BUT WHY DOES THAT MATTER?
9/14

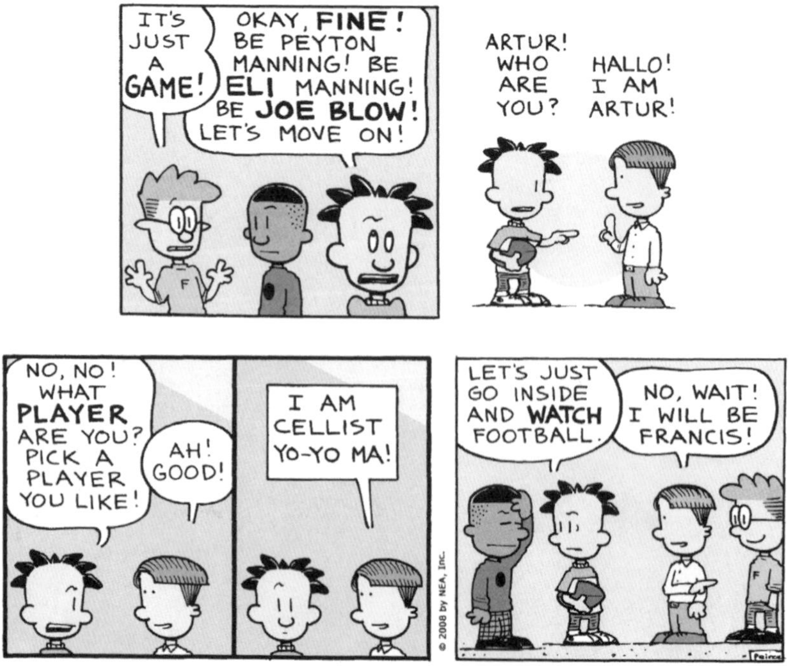
IT'S JUST A **GAME**!
OKAY, **FINE**! BE PEYTON MANNING! BE **ELI** MANNING! BE **JOE BLOW**! LET'S MOVE ON!
ARTUR! WHO ARE YOU?
HALLO! I AM ARTUR!
NO, NO! WHAT **PLAYER** ARE YOU? PICK A PLAYER YOU LIKE!
AH! GOOD!
I AM CELLIST YO-YO MA!
LET'S JUST GO INSIDE AND **WATCH** FOOTBALL.
NO, WAIT! I WILL BE FRANCIS!
Peirce

WHAT A DUMP

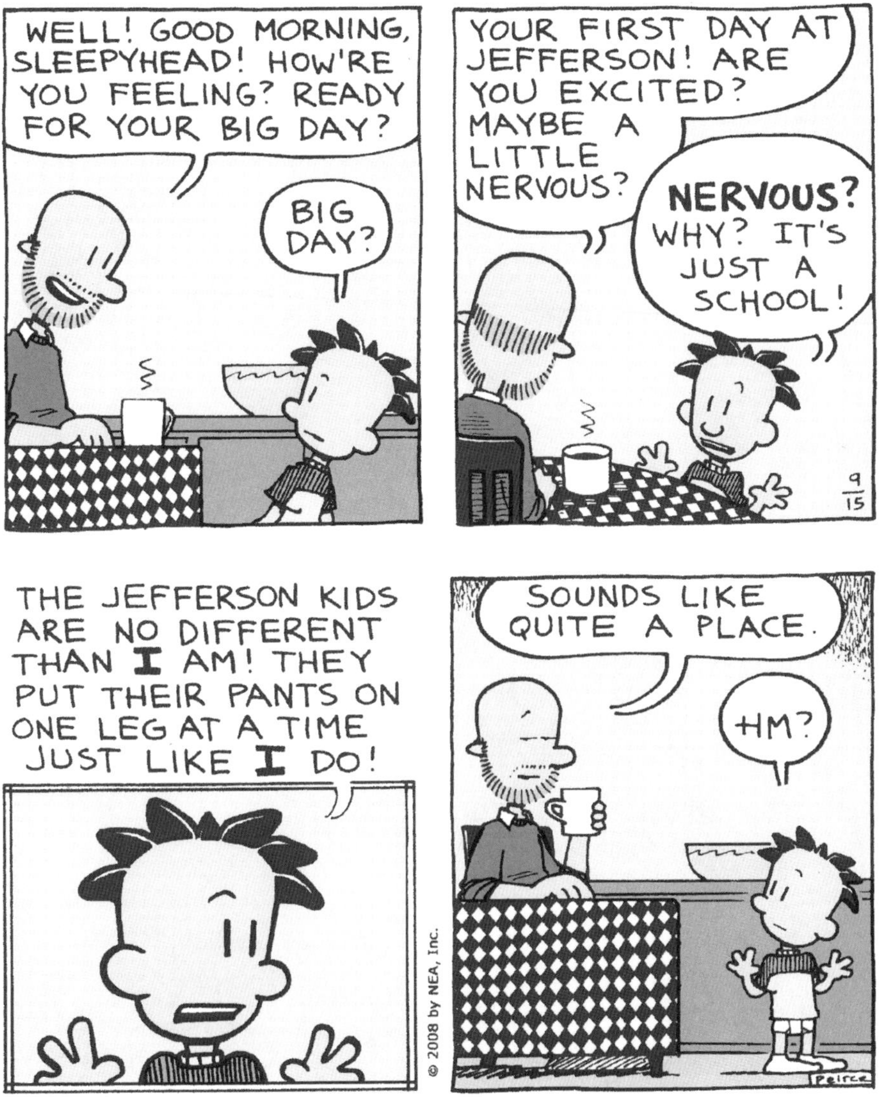
WELL! GOOD MORNING, SLEEPYHEAD! HOW'RE YOU FEELING? READY FOR YOUR BIG DAY?
BIG DAY?
YOUR FIRST DAY AT JEFFERSON! ARE YOU EXCITED? MAYBE A LITTLE NERVOUS?
NERVOUS? WHY? IT'S JUST A SCHOOL!
9/15
THE JEFFERSON KIDS ARE NO DIFFERENT THAN I AM! THEY PUT THEIR PANTS ON ONE LEG AT A TIME JUST LIKE I DO!
© 2008 by NEA, Inc.
SOUNDS LIKE QUITE A PLACE.
HM?
Peirce

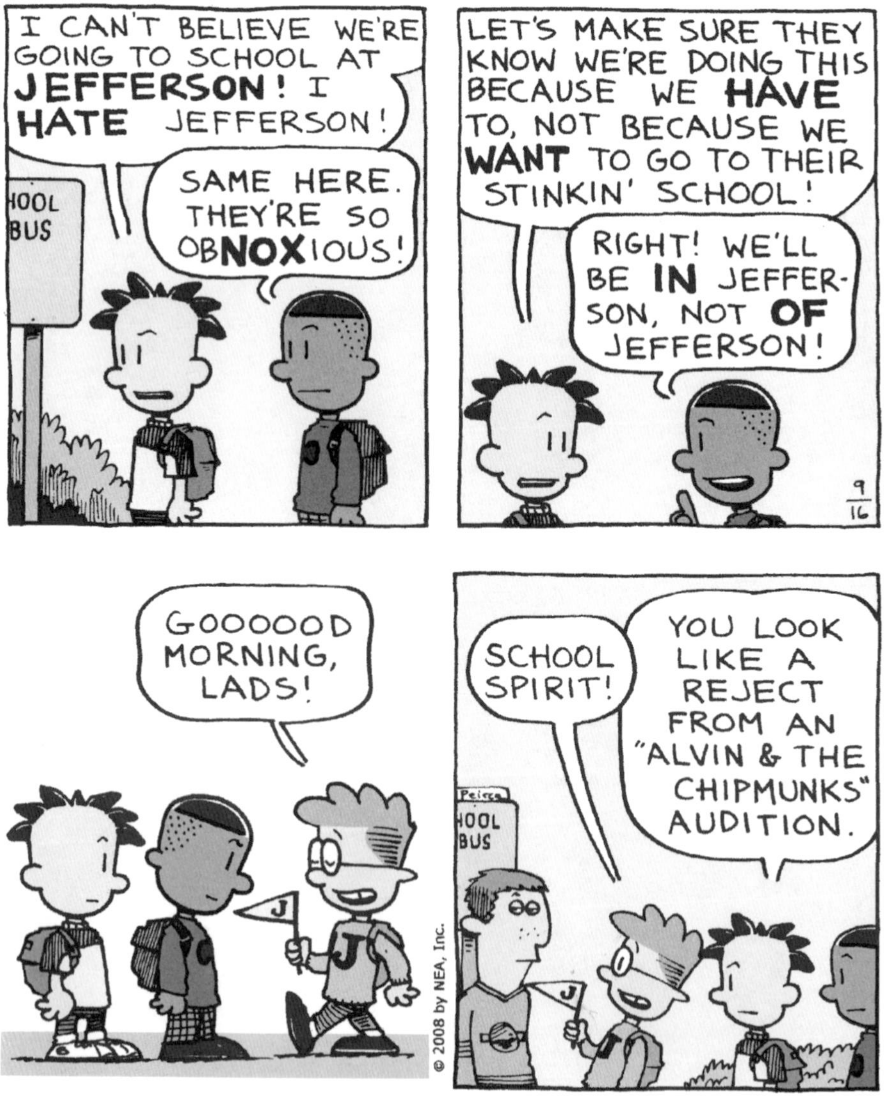
I CAN'T BELIEVE WE'RE GOING TO SCHOOL AT **JEFFERSON**! I **HATE** JEFFERSON!
SAME HERE. THEY'RE SO OB**NOX**IOUS!
LET'S MAKE SURE THEY KNOW WE'RE DOING THIS BECAUSE WE **HAVE** TO, NOT BECAUSE WE **WANT** TO GO TO THEIR STINKIN' SCHOOL!
RIGHT! WE'LL BE **IN** JEFFERSON, NOT **OF** JEFFERSON!
GOOOOOD MORNING, LADS!
SCHOOL SPIRIT!
YOU LOOK LIKE A REJECT FROM AN "ALVIN & THE CHIPMUNKS" AUDITION.

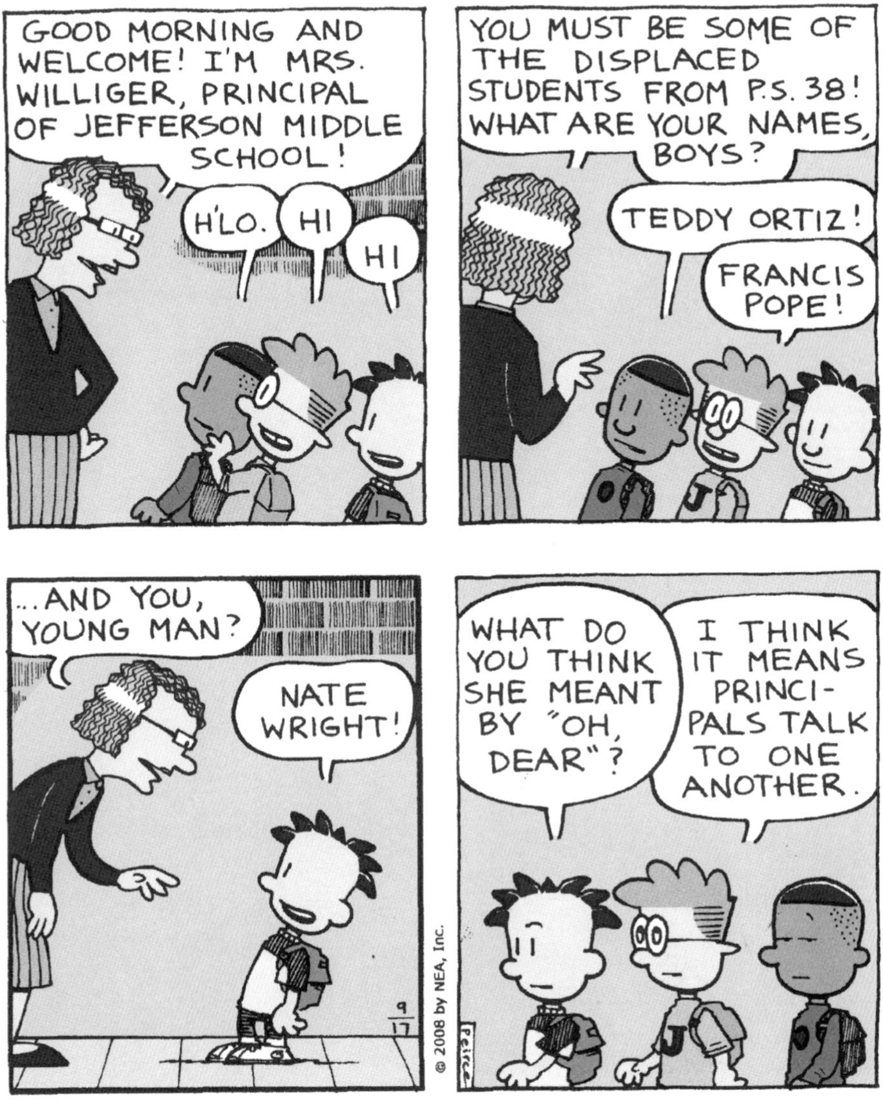
GOOD MORNING AND WELCOME! I'M MRS. WILLIGER, PRINCIPAL OF JEFFERSON MIDDLE SCHOOL!
H'LO.
HI
HI
YOU MUST BE SOME OF THE DISPLACED STUDENTS FROM P.S. 38! WHAT ARE YOUR NAMES, BOYS?
TEDDY ORTIZ!
FRANCIS POPE!
...AND YOU, YOUNG MAN?
NATE WRIGHT!
9/17
© 2008 by NEA, Inc.
Peirce
WHAT DO YOU THINK SHE MEANT BY "OH, DEAR"?
I THINK IT MEANS PRINCI-PALS TALK TO ONE ANOTHER.

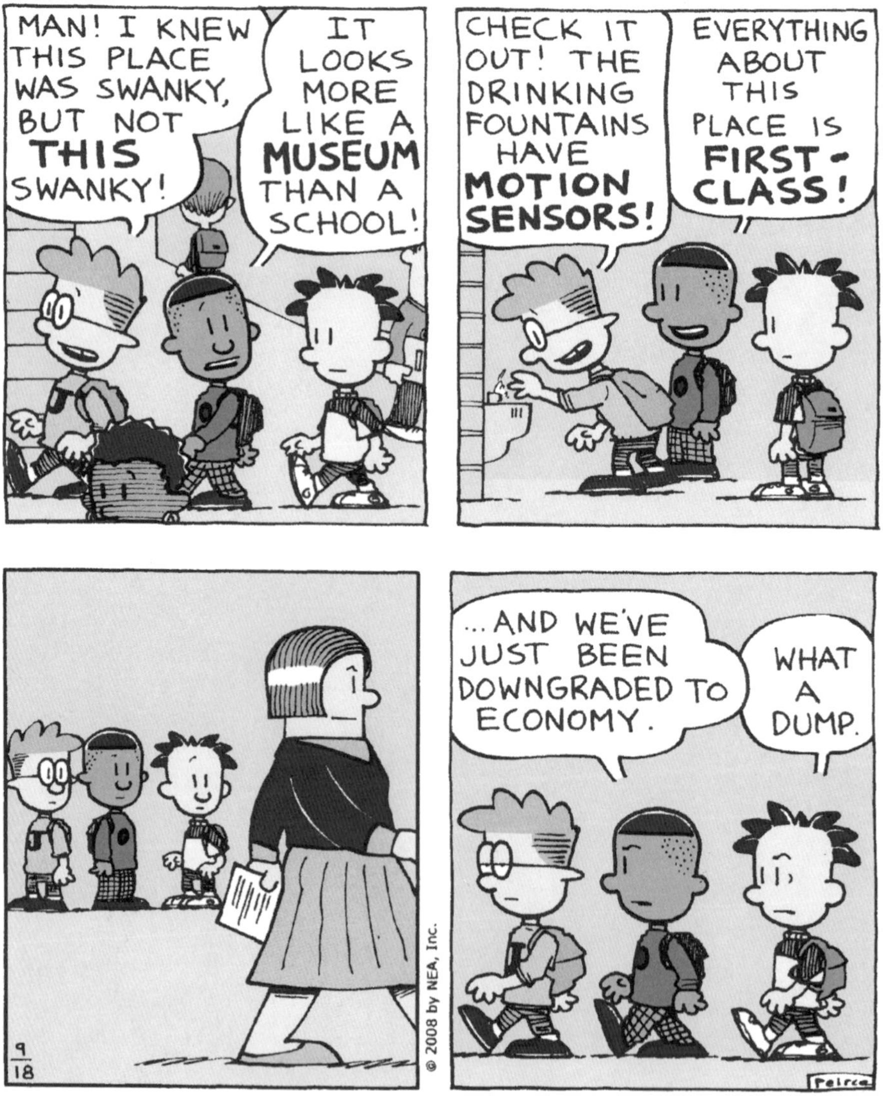

MAN! I KNEW THIS PLACE WAS SWANKY, BUT NOT **THIS** SWANKY!
IT LOOKS MORE LIKE A **MUSEUM** THAN A SCHOOL!
CHECK IT OUT! THE DRINKING FOUNTAINS HAVE **MOTION SENSORS!**
EVERYTHING ABOUT THIS PLACE IS **FIRST-CLASS!**
9/18
© 2008 by NEA, Inc.
...AND WE'VE JUST BEEN DOWNGRADED TO ECONOMY.
WHAT A DUMP.
Peirce

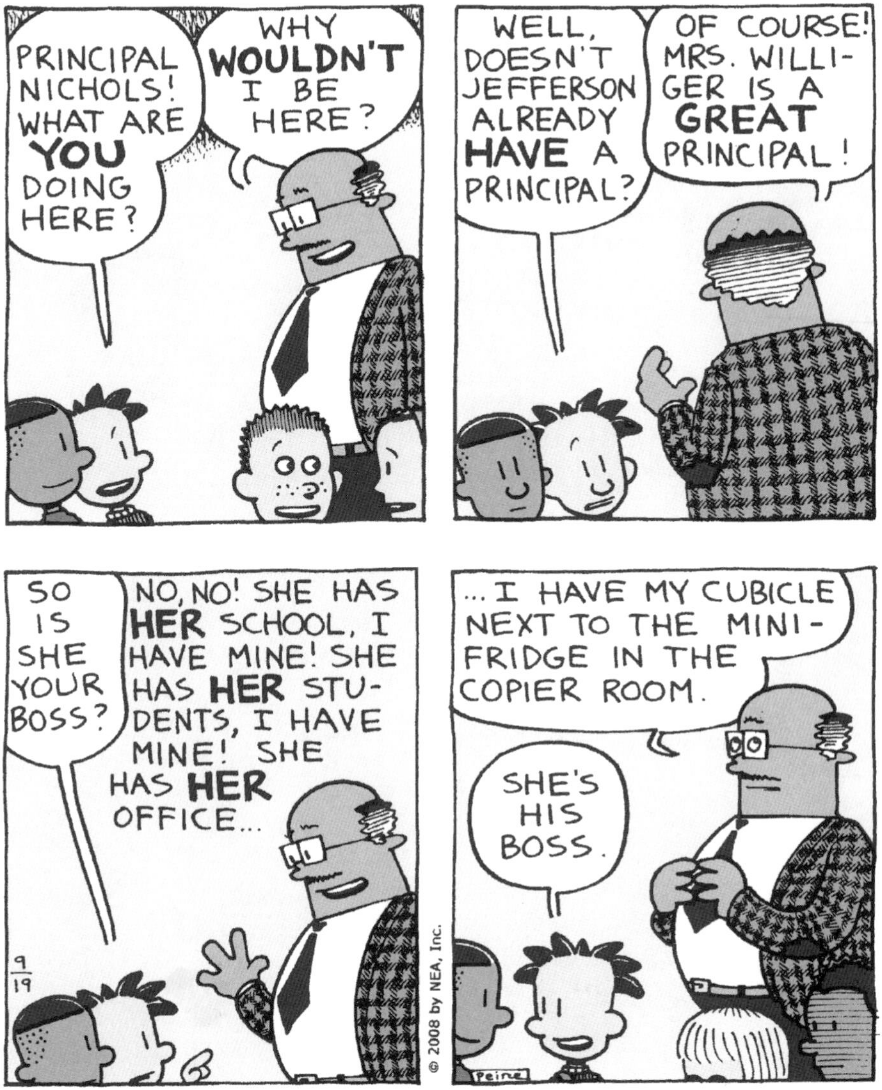
PRINCIPAL NICHOLS! WHAT ARE **YOU** DOING HERE?
WHY **WOULDN'T** I BE HERE?
WELL, DOESN'T JEFFERSON ALREADY **HAVE** A PRINCIPAL?
OF COURSE! MRS. WILLIGER IS A **GREAT** PRINCIPAL!
SO IS SHE YOUR BOSS?
NO, NO! SHE HAS **HER** SCHOOL, I HAVE MINE! SHE HAS **HER** STUDENTS, I HAVE MINE! SHE HAS **HER** OFFICE...
9/19
© 2008 by NEA, Inc.
...I HAVE MY CUBICLE NEXT TO THE MINI-FRIDGE IN THE COPIER ROOM.
SHE'S HIS BOSS.
Peirce

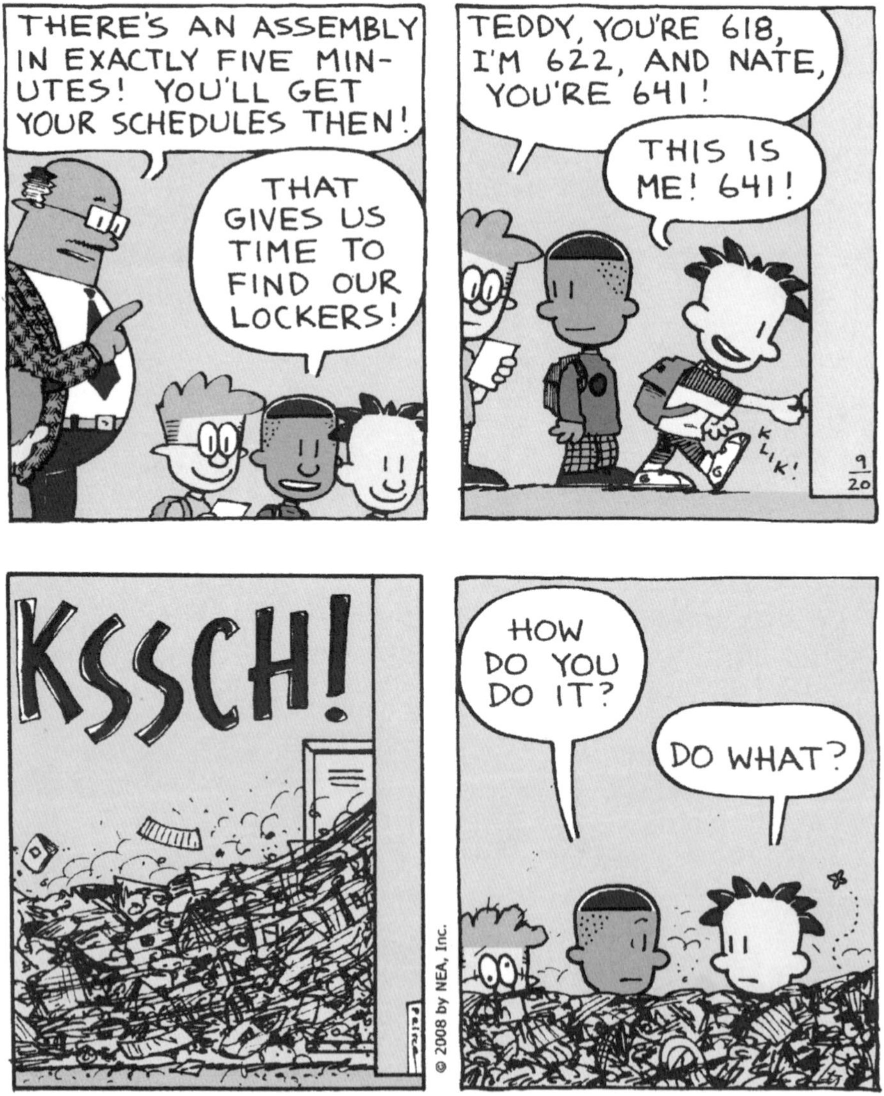
THERE'S AN ASSEMBLY IN EXACTLY FIVE MIN- UTES! YOU'LL GET YOUR SCHEDULES THEN!
THAT GIVES US TIME TO FIND OUR LOCKERS!
TEDDY, YOU'RE 618, I'M 622, AND NATE, YOU'RE 641!
THIS IS ME! 641!
KLIK!
9/20
KSSCH!
HOW DO YOU DO IT?
DO WHAT?
© 2008 by NEA, Inc.

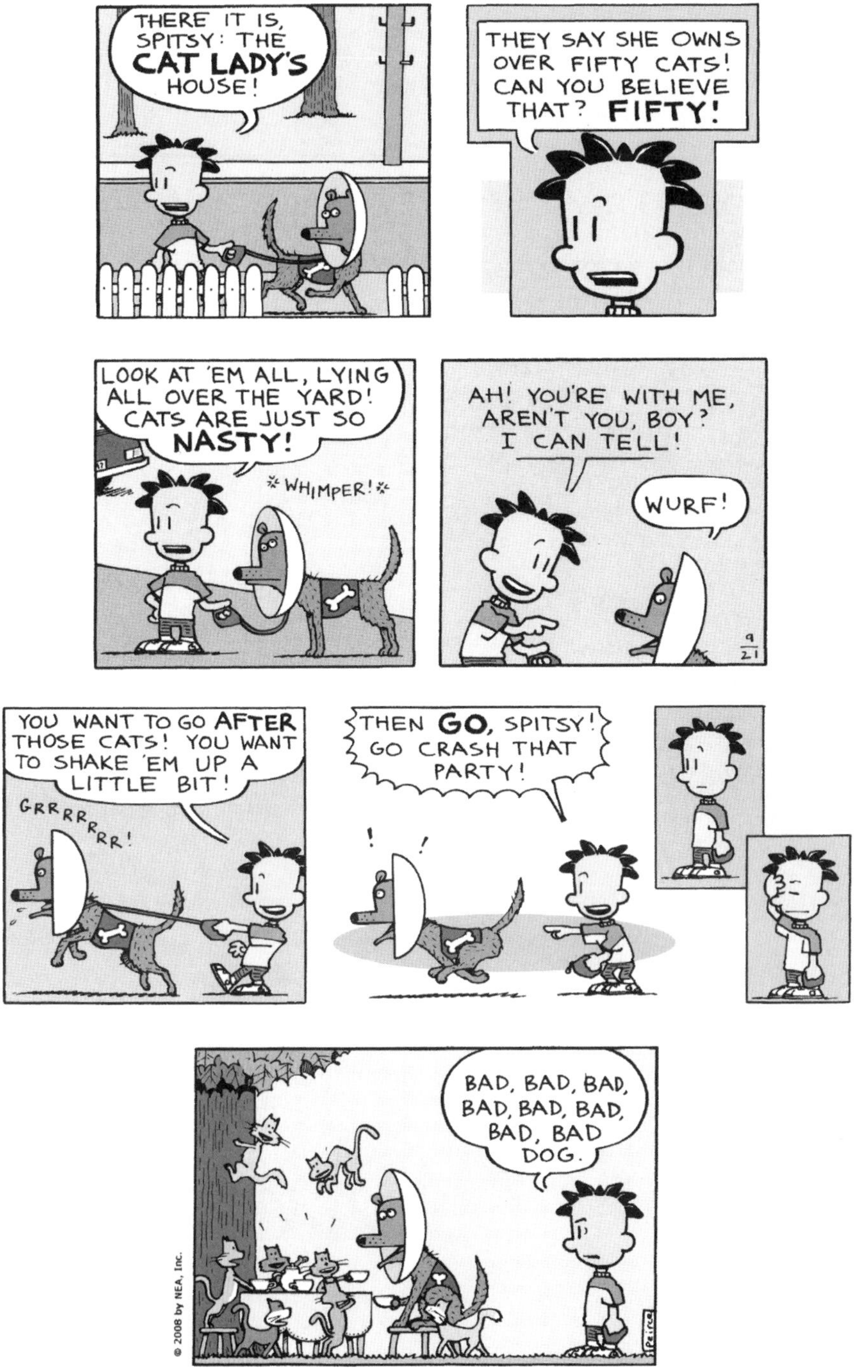
THERE IT IS, SPITSY: THE CAT LADY'S HOUSE!
THEY SAY SHE OWNS OVER FIFTY CATS! CAN YOU BELIEVE THAT? FIFTY!
LOOK AT 'EM ALL, LYING ALL OVER THE YARD! CATS ARE JUST SO NASTY!
WHIMPER!
AH! YOU'RE WITH ME, AREN'T YOU, BOY? I CAN TELL!
WURF!
9/21
YOU WANT TO GO AFTER THOSE CATS! YOU WANT TO SHAKE 'EM UP A LITTLE BIT!
GRRRRRRRR!
THEN GO, SPITSY! GO CRASH THAT PARTY!
! !
BAD, BAD, BAD, BAD, BAD, BAD, BAD, BAD DOG.
© 2008 by NEA, Inc.
Peirce

LUCKY, LUCKIER, LUCKIEST

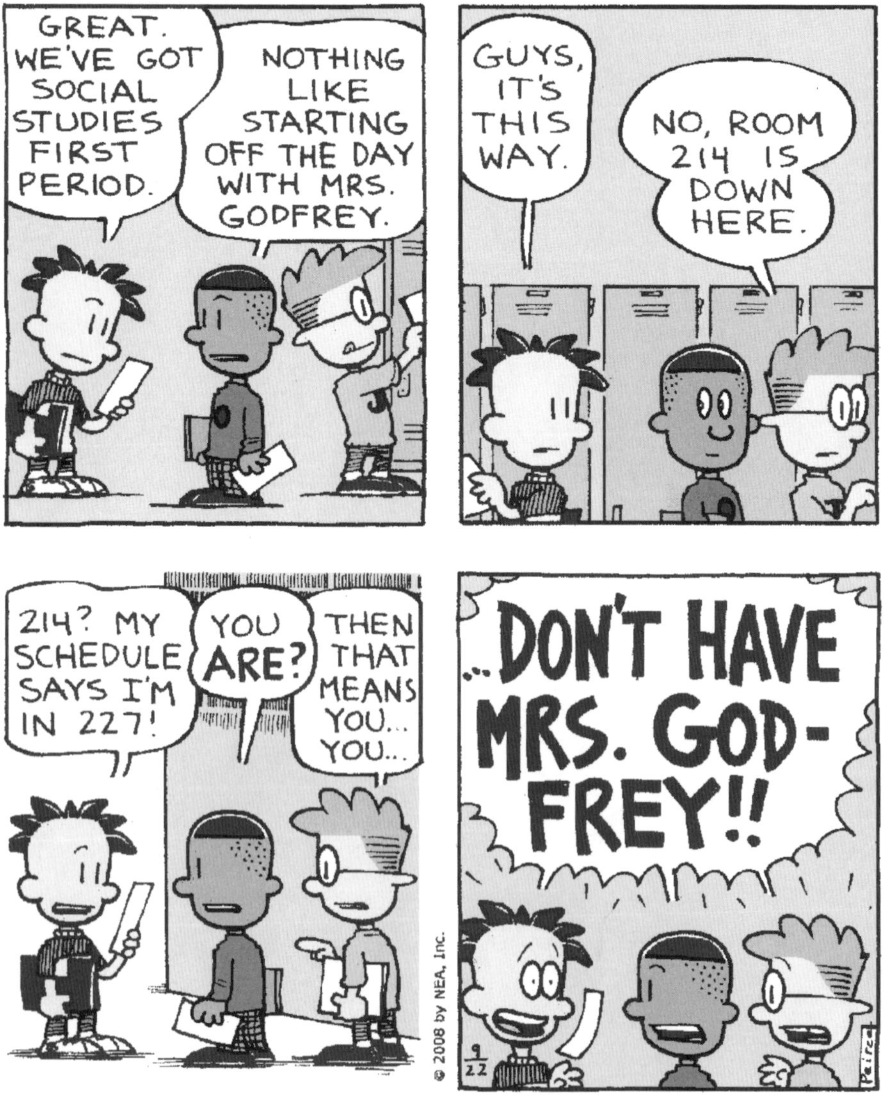
GREAT. WE'VE GOT SOCIAL STUDIES FIRST PERIOD.
NOTHING LIKE STARTING OFF THE DAY WITH MRS. GODFREY.
GUYS, IT'S THIS WAY.
NO, ROOM 214 IS DOWN HERE.
214? MY SCHEDULE SAYS I'M IN 227!
YOU ARE?
THEN THAT MEANS YOU... YOU...
...DON'T HAVE MRS. GOD-FREY!!
© 2008 by NEA, Inc.
9/22
Peirce

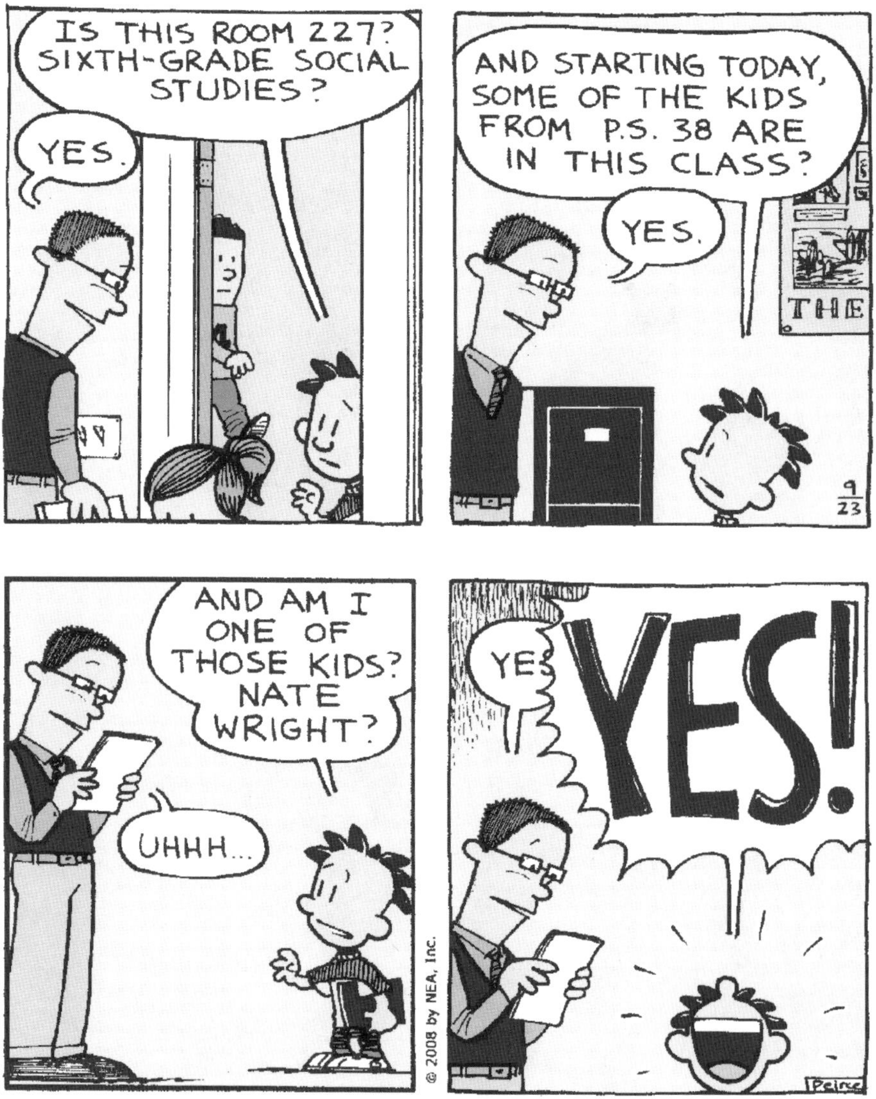
IS THIS ROOM 227? SIXTH-GRADE SOCIAL STUDIES?
YES.
AND STARTING TODAY, SOME OF THE KIDS FROM P.S. 38 ARE IN THIS CLASS?
YES.
THE
9/23
AND AM I ONE OF THOSE KIDS? NATE WRIGHT?
UHHH...
YES
YES!
Peirce

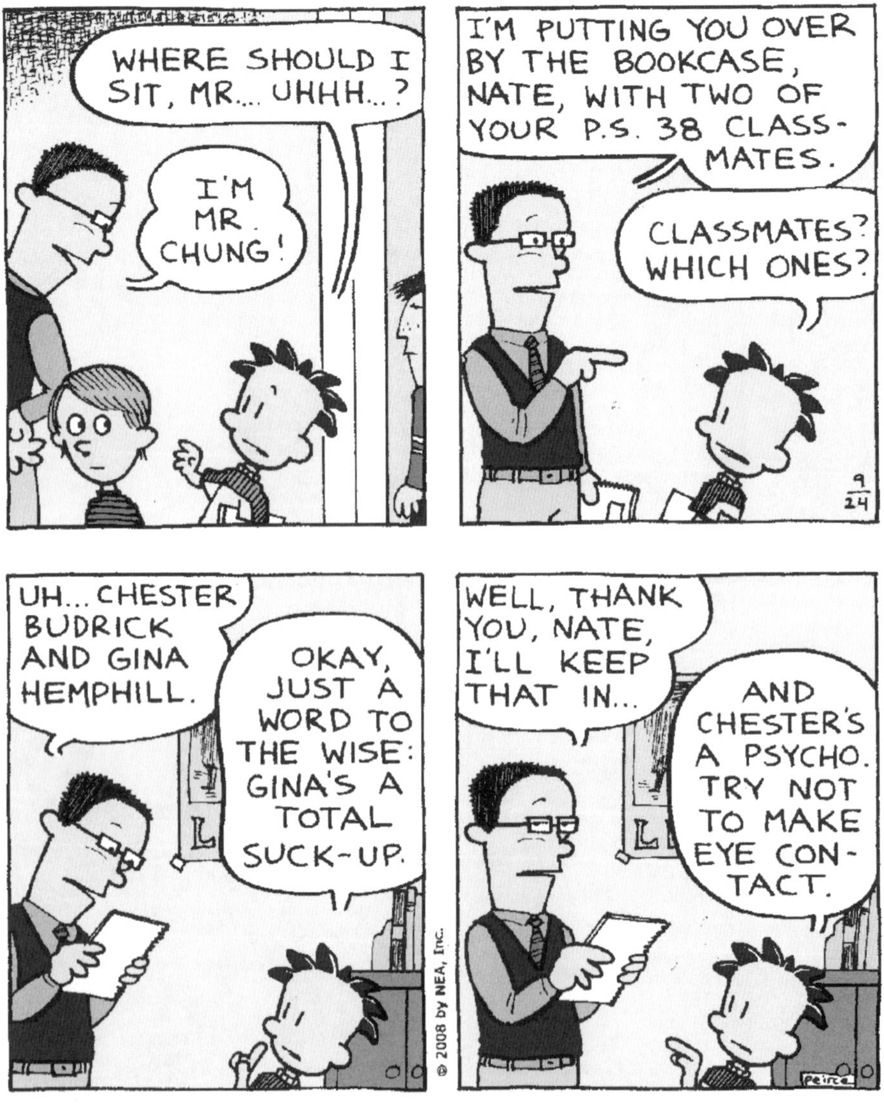
WHERE SHOULD I SIT, MR.... UHHH...?
I'M MR. CHUNG!
I'M PUTTING YOU OVER BY THE BOOKCASE, NATE, WITH TWO OF YOUR P.S. 38 CLASS-MATES.
CLASSMATES? WHICH ONES?
9
24
UH... CHESTER BUDRICK AND GINA HEMPHILL.
OKAY, JUST A WORD TO THE WISE: GINA'S A TOTAL SUCK-UP.
© 2008 by NEA, Inc.
WELL, THANK YOU, NATE, I'LL KEEP THAT IN...
AND CHESTER'S A PSYCHO. TRY NOT TO MAKE EYE CON-TACT.
peirce

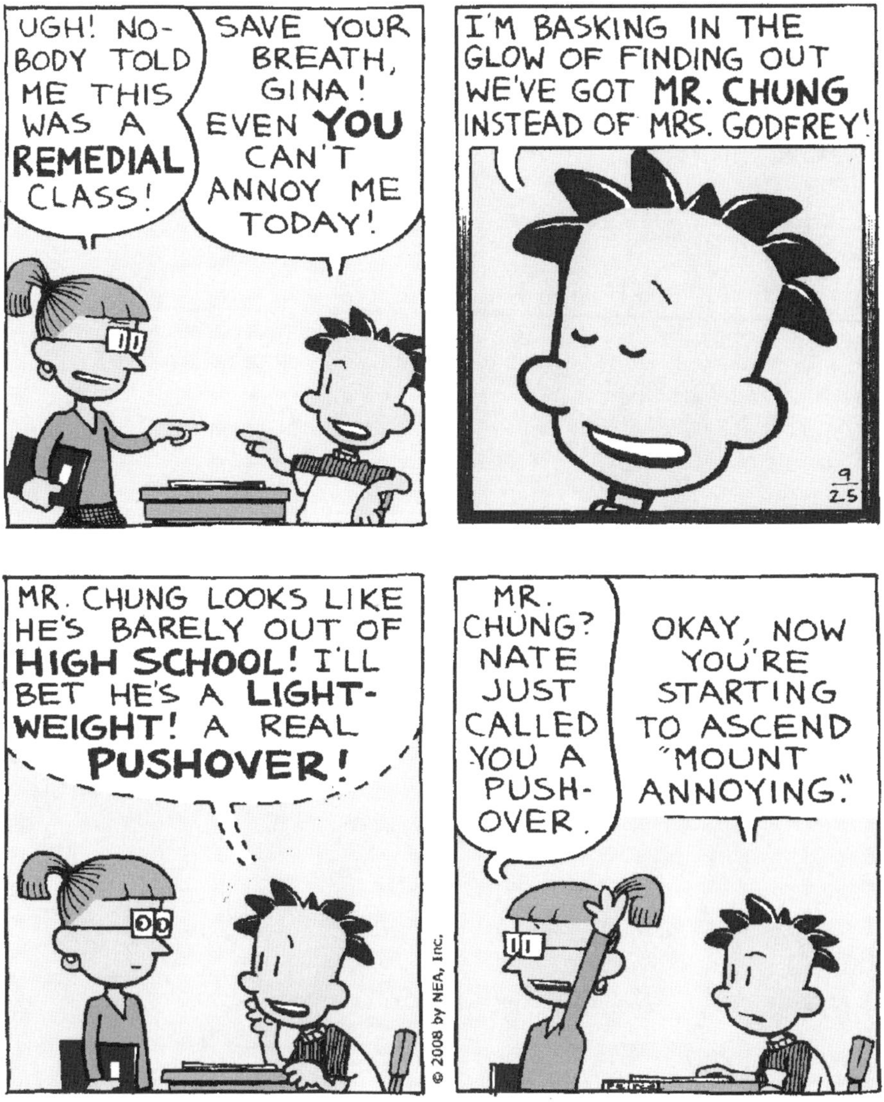
UGH! NOBODY TOLD ME THIS WAS A **REMEDIAL** CLASS!
SAVE YOUR BREATH, GINA! EVEN **YOU** CAN'T ANNOY ME TODAY!
I'M BASKING IN THE GLOW OF FINDING OUT WE'VE GOT **MR. CHUNG** INSTEAD OF MRS. GODFREY!
9/25
MR. CHUNG LOOKS LIKE HE'S BARELY OUT OF **HIGH SCHOOL!** I'LL BET HE'S A **LIGHTWEIGHT!** A REAL **PUSHOVER!**
© 2008 by NEA, Inc.
MR. CHUNG? NATE JUST CALLED YOU A PUSHOVER.
OKAY, NOW YOU'RE STARTING TO ASCEND "MOUNT ANNOYING."

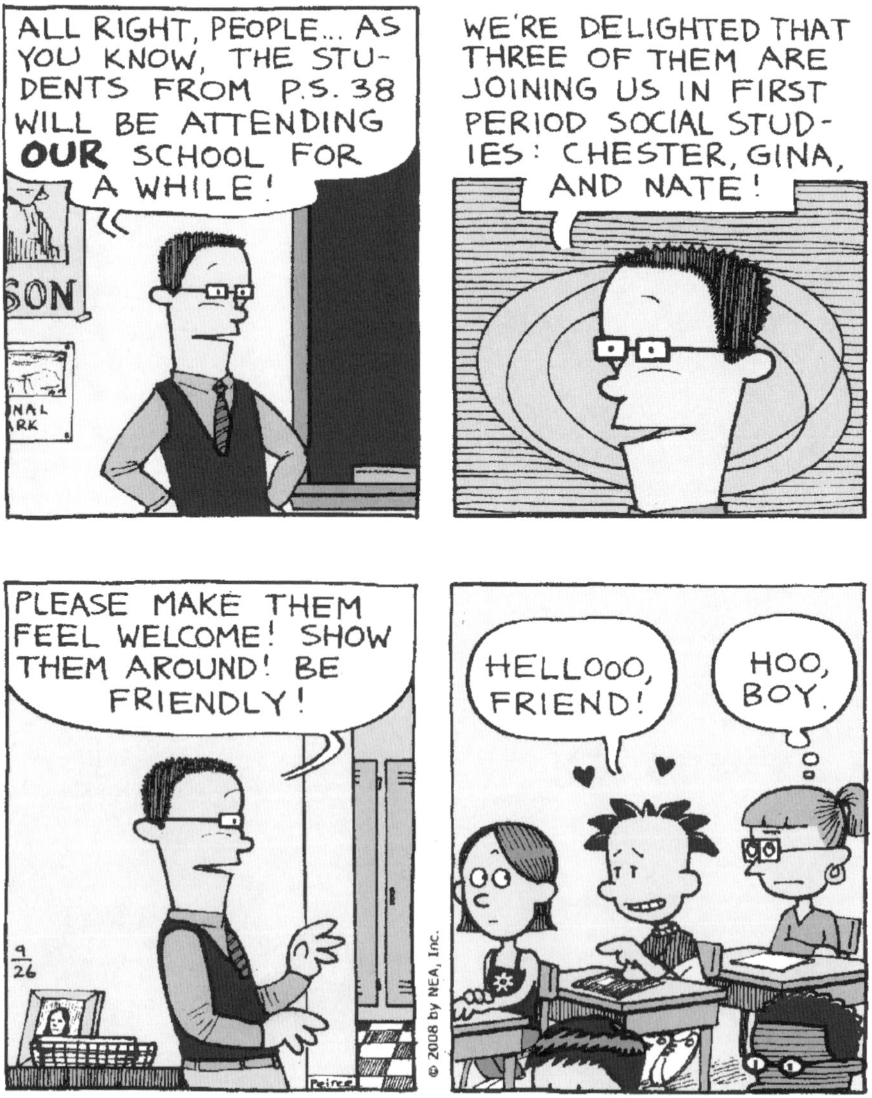
ALL RIGHT, PEOPLE... AS YOU KNOW, THE STUDENTS FROM P.S. 38 WILL BE ATTENDING **OUR** SCHOOL FOR A WHILE!
SON
WE'RE DELIGHTED THAT THREE OF THEM ARE JOINING US IN FIRST PERIOD SOCIAL STUDIES: CHESTER, GINA, AND NATE!
PLEASE MAKE THEM FEEL WELCOME! SHOW THEM AROUND! BE FRIENDLY!
9/26
Peirce
© 2008 by NEA, Inc.
HELLOOO, FRIEND!
HOO, BOY.

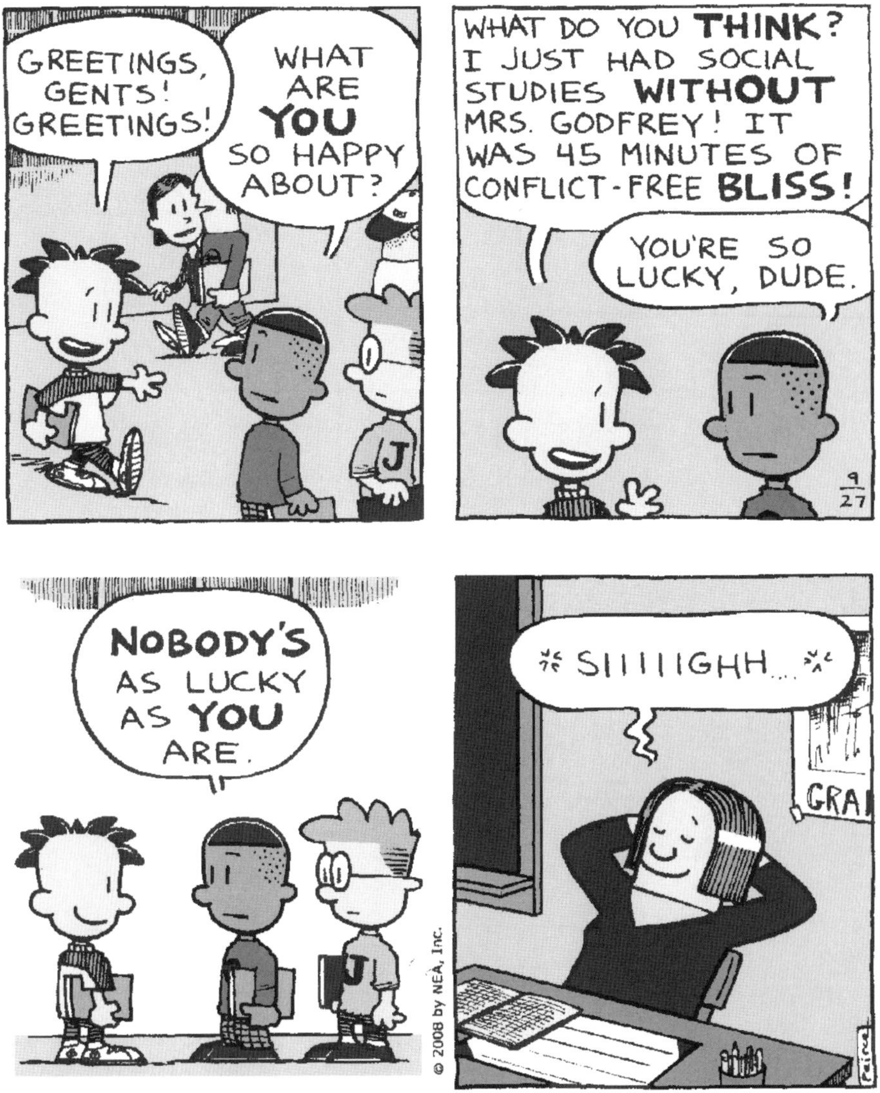
GREETINGS, GENTS! GREETINGS!
WHAT ARE YOU SO HAPPY ABOUT?
J
WHAT DO YOU THINK? I JUST HAD SOCIAL STUDIES WITHOUT MRS. GODFREY! IT WAS 45 MINUTES OF CONFLICT-FREE BLISS!
YOU'RE SO LUCKY, DUDE.
9/27
NOBODY'S AS LUCKY AS YOU ARE.
J
© 2008 by NEA, Inc.
SIIIIIGHH...
GRA
Peirce

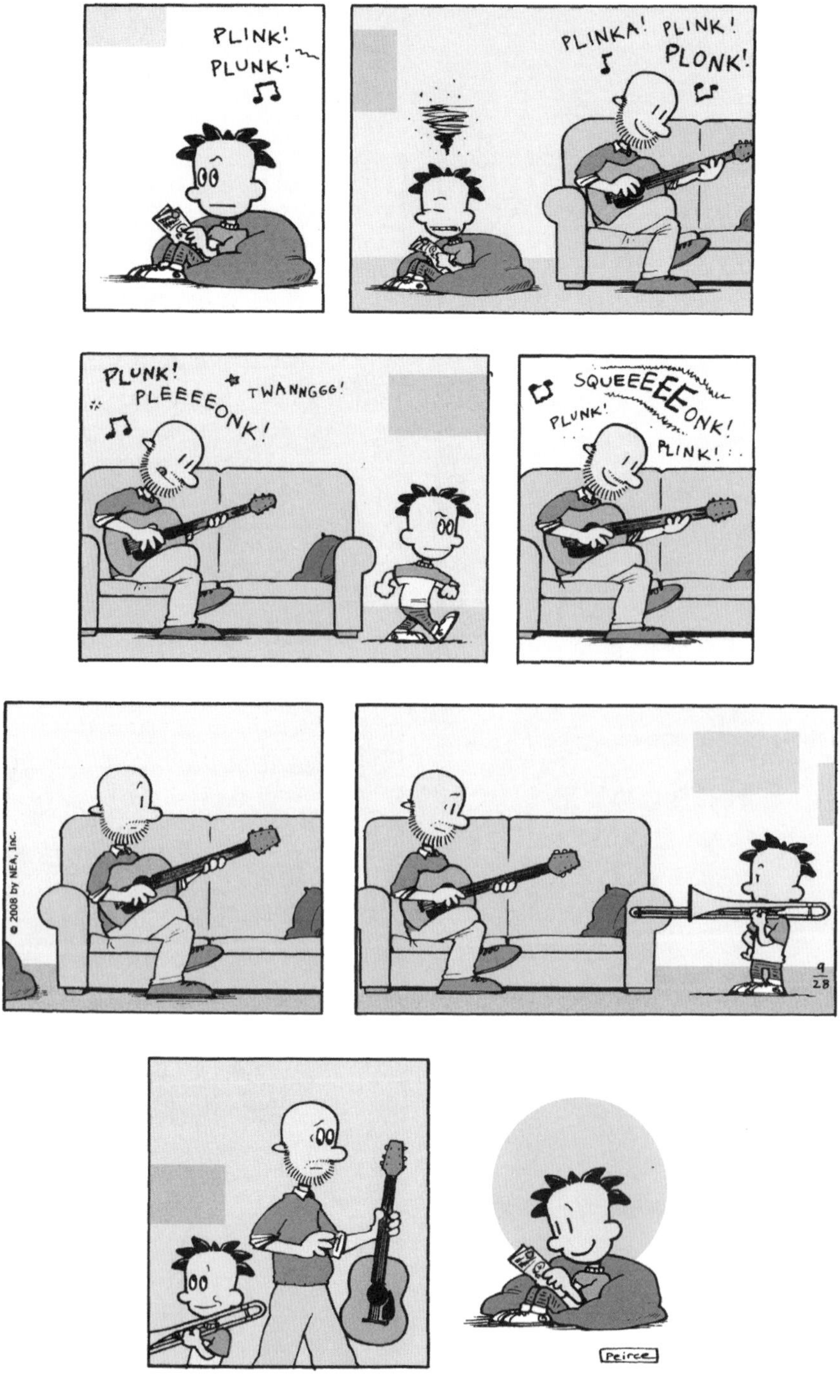
PLINK!
PLUNK!
PLINKA! PLINK!
PLONK!
PLUNK!
PLEEEEEONK!
TWANNGGG!
SQUEEEEEEONK!
PLUNK!
PLINK!
© 2008 by NEA, Inc.
9/28
Peirce

GET REAL

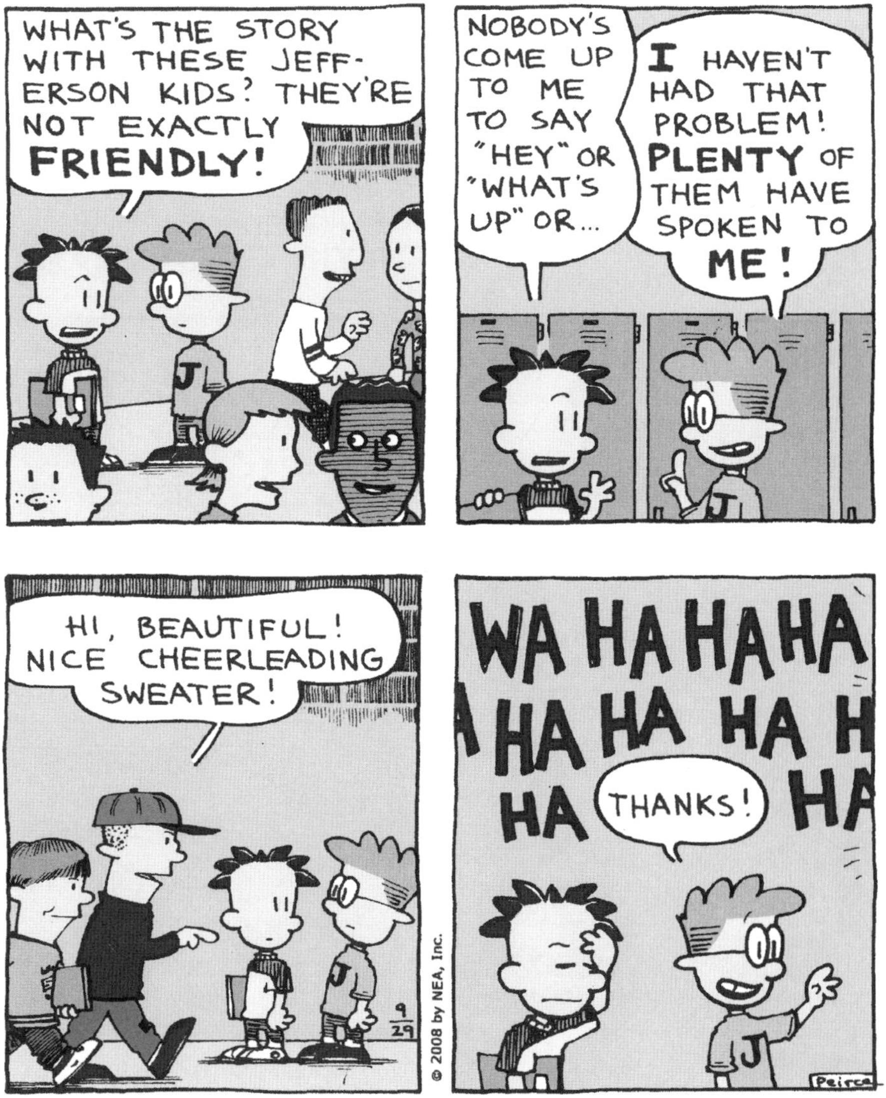
WHAT'S THE STORY WITH THESE JEFF-ERSON KIDS? THEY'RE NOT EXACTLY **FRIENDLY**!
NOBODY'S COME UP TO ME TO SAY "HEY" OR "WHAT'S UP" OR...
I HAVEN'T HAD THAT PROBLEM! **PLENTY** OF THEM HAVE SPOKEN TO **ME**!
HI, BEAUTIFUL! NICE CHEERLEADING SWEATER!
9/29
© 2008 by NEA, Inc.
WA HA HA HA HA HA HA HA HA HA HA
THANKS!
Peirce

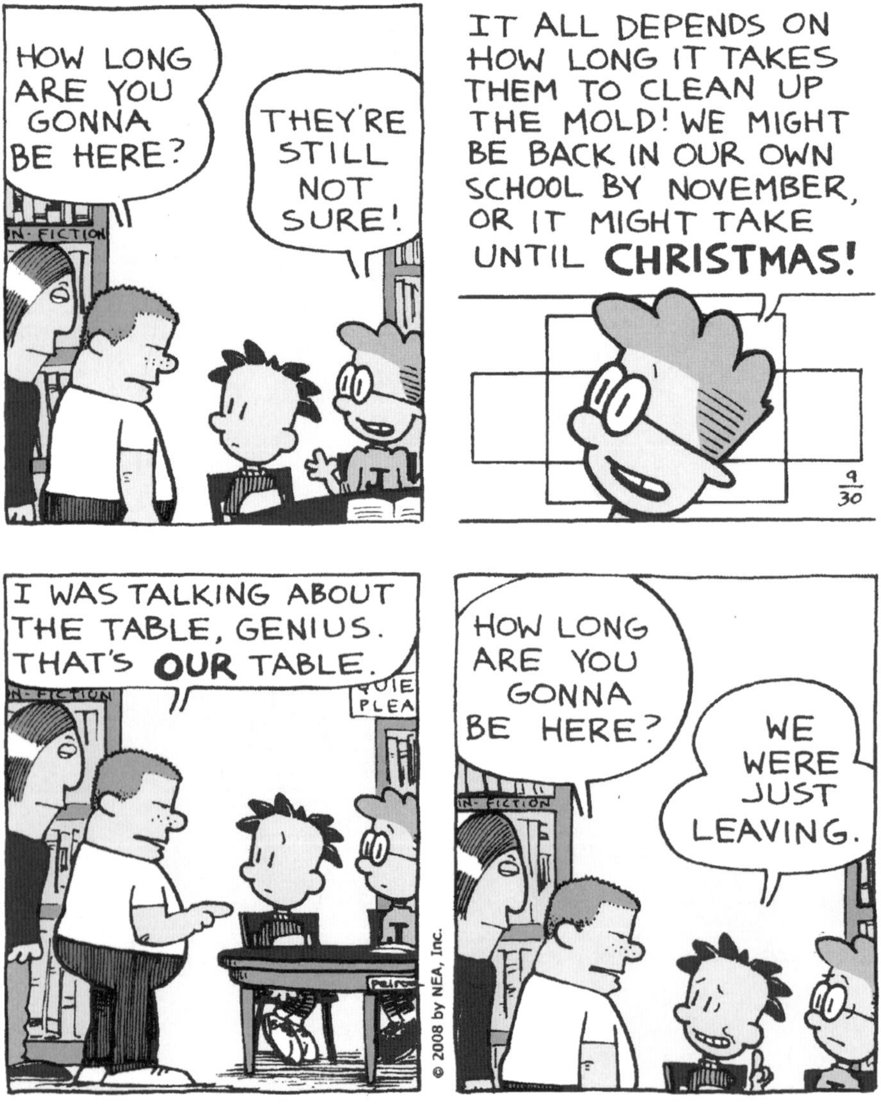
HOW LONG ARE YOU GONNA BE HERE?
THEY'RE STILL NOT SURE!
IT ALL DEPENDS ON HOW LONG IT TAKES THEM TO CLEAN UP THE MOLD! WE MIGHT BE BACK IN OUR OWN SCHOOL BY NOVEMBER, OR IT MIGHT TAKE UNTIL **CHRISTMAS!**
9/30
I WAS TALKING ABOUT THE TABLE, GENIUS. THAT'S **OUR** TABLE.
© 2008 by NEA, Inc.
HOW LONG ARE YOU GONNA BE HERE?
WE WERE JUST LEAVING.

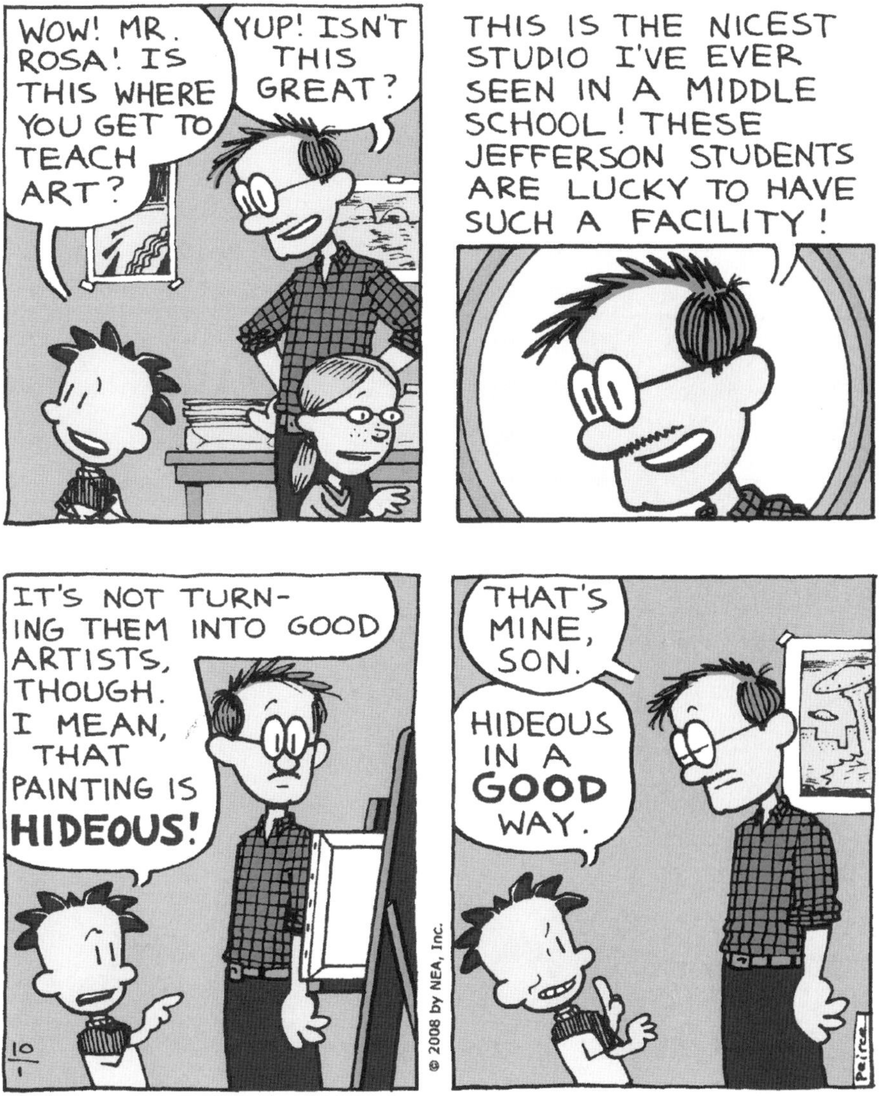
WOW! MR. ROSA! IS THIS WHERE YOU GET TO TEACH ART?
YUP! ISN'T THIS GREAT?
THIS IS THE NICEST STUDIO I'VE EVER SEEN IN A MIDDLE SCHOOL! THESE JEFFERSON STUDENTS ARE LUCKY TO HAVE SUCH A FACILITY!
IT'S NOT TURNING THEM INTO GOOD ARTISTS, THOUGH. I MEAN, THAT PAINTING IS **HIDEOUS!**
10/1
© 2008 by NEA, Inc.
THAT'S MINE, SON.
HIDEOUS IN A **GOOD** WAY.
Peirce

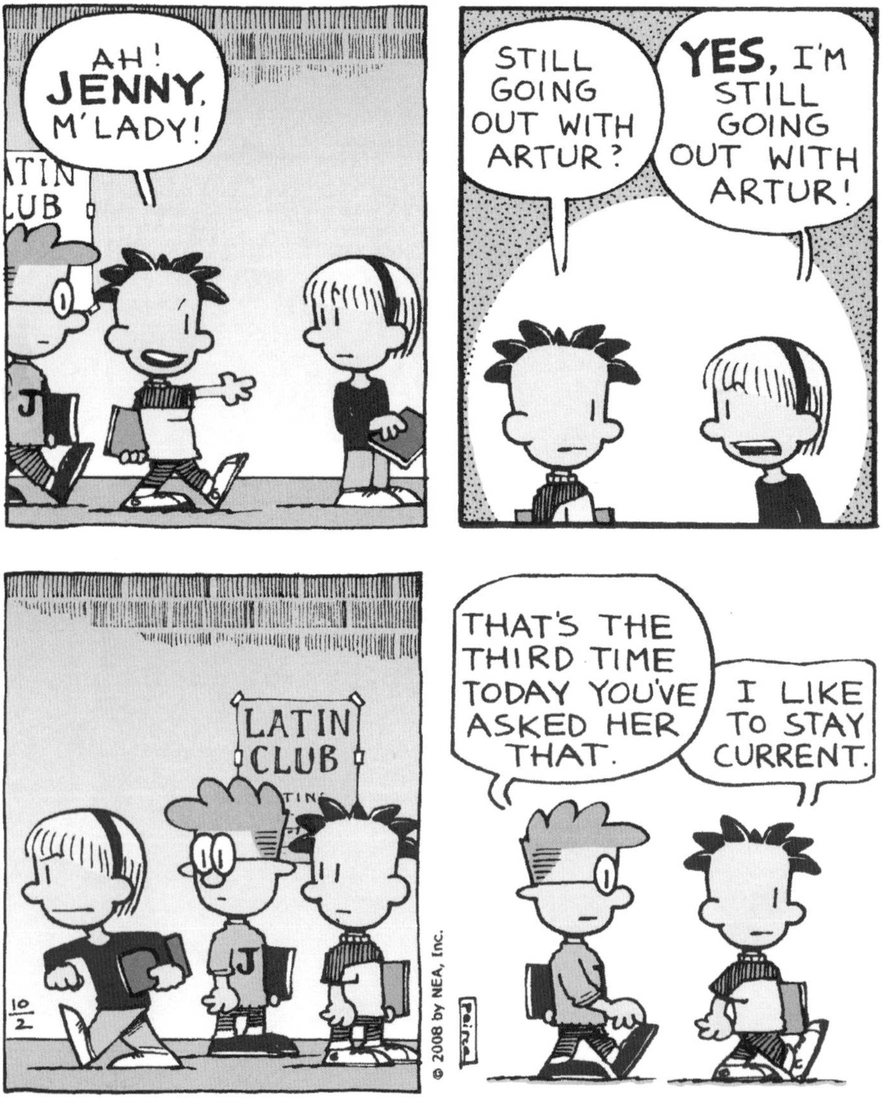
LATIN CLUB
AH! JENNY, M'LADY!
STILL GOING OUT WITH ARTUR?
YES, I'M STILL GOING OUT WITH ARTUR!
LATIN CLUB
10/2
© 2008 by NEA, Inc.
Peirce
THAT'S THE THIRD TIME TODAY YOU'VE ASKED HER THAT.
I LIKE TO STAY CURRENT.

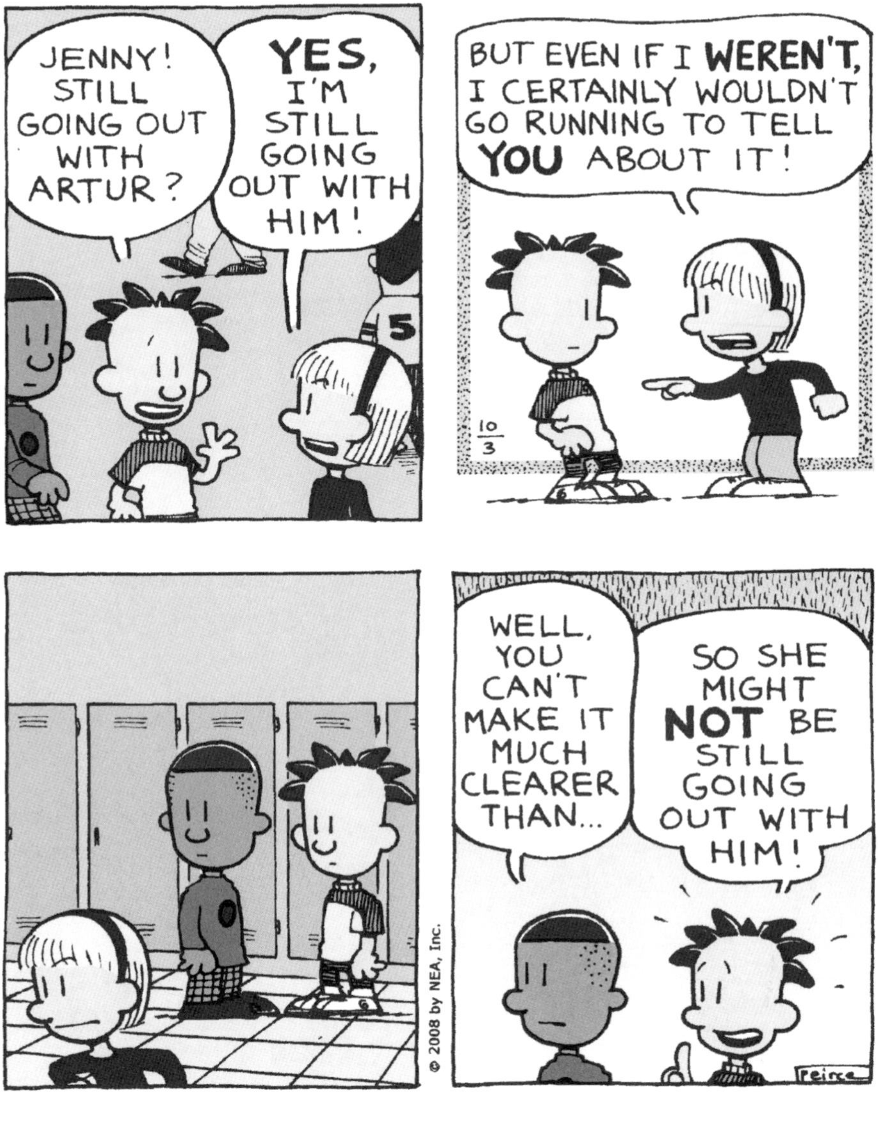
JENNY! STILL GOING OUT WITH ARTUR?
YES, I'M STILL GOING OUT WITH HIM!
BUT EVEN IF I WEREN'T, I CERTAINLY WOULDN'T GO RUNNING TO TELL YOU ABOUT IT!
10/3
© 2008 by NEA, Inc.
WELL, YOU CAN'T MAKE IT MUCH CLEARER THAN...
SO SHE MIGHT NOT BE STILL GOING OUT WITH HIM!
Peirce

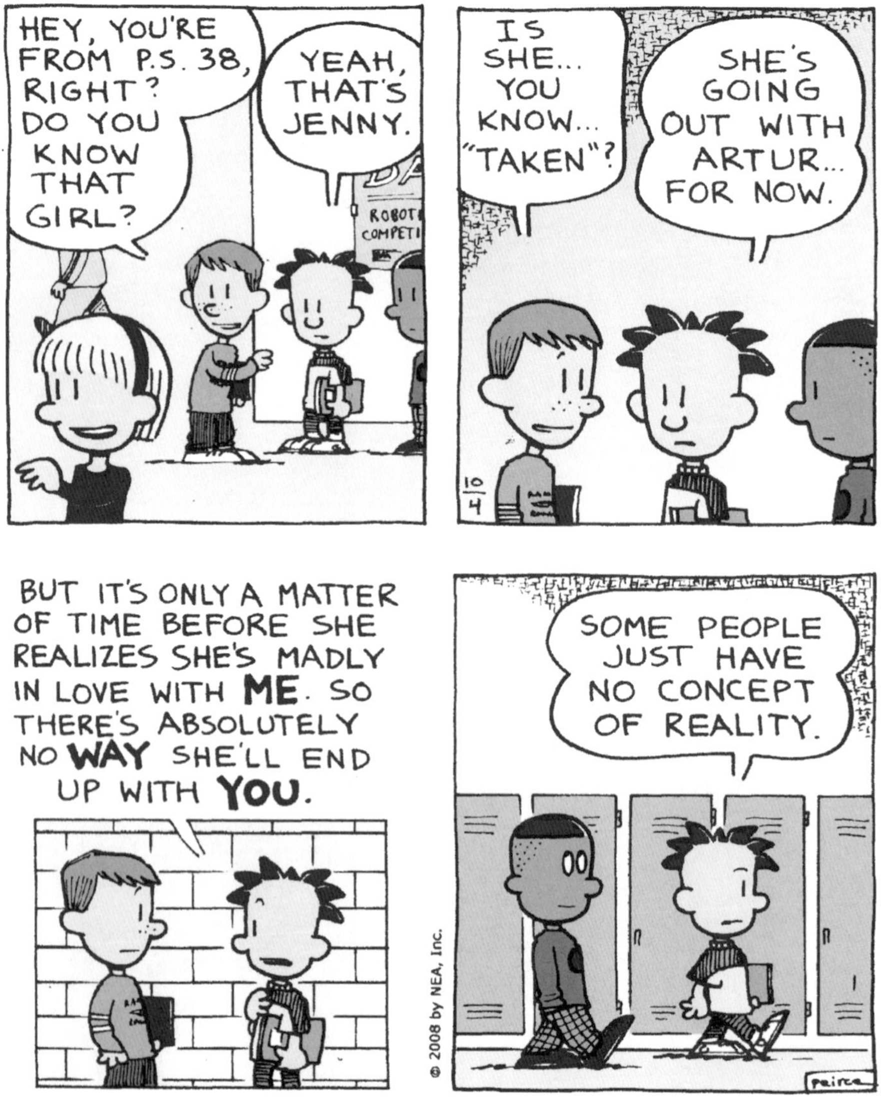
HEY, YOU'RE FROM P.S. 38, RIGHT? DO YOU KNOW THAT GIRL?
YEAH, THAT'S JENNY.
ROBOT COMPETI
IS SHE... YOU KNOW... "TAKEN"?
SHE'S GOING OUT WITH ARTUR... FOR NOW.
10/4
BUT IT'S ONLY A MATTER OF TIME BEFORE SHE REALIZES SHE'S MADLY IN LOVE WITH ME. SO THERE'S ABSOLUTELY NO WAY SHE'LL END UP WITH YOU.
© 2008 by NEA, Inc.
SOME PEOPLE JUST HAVE NO CONCEPT OF REALITY.
peirce

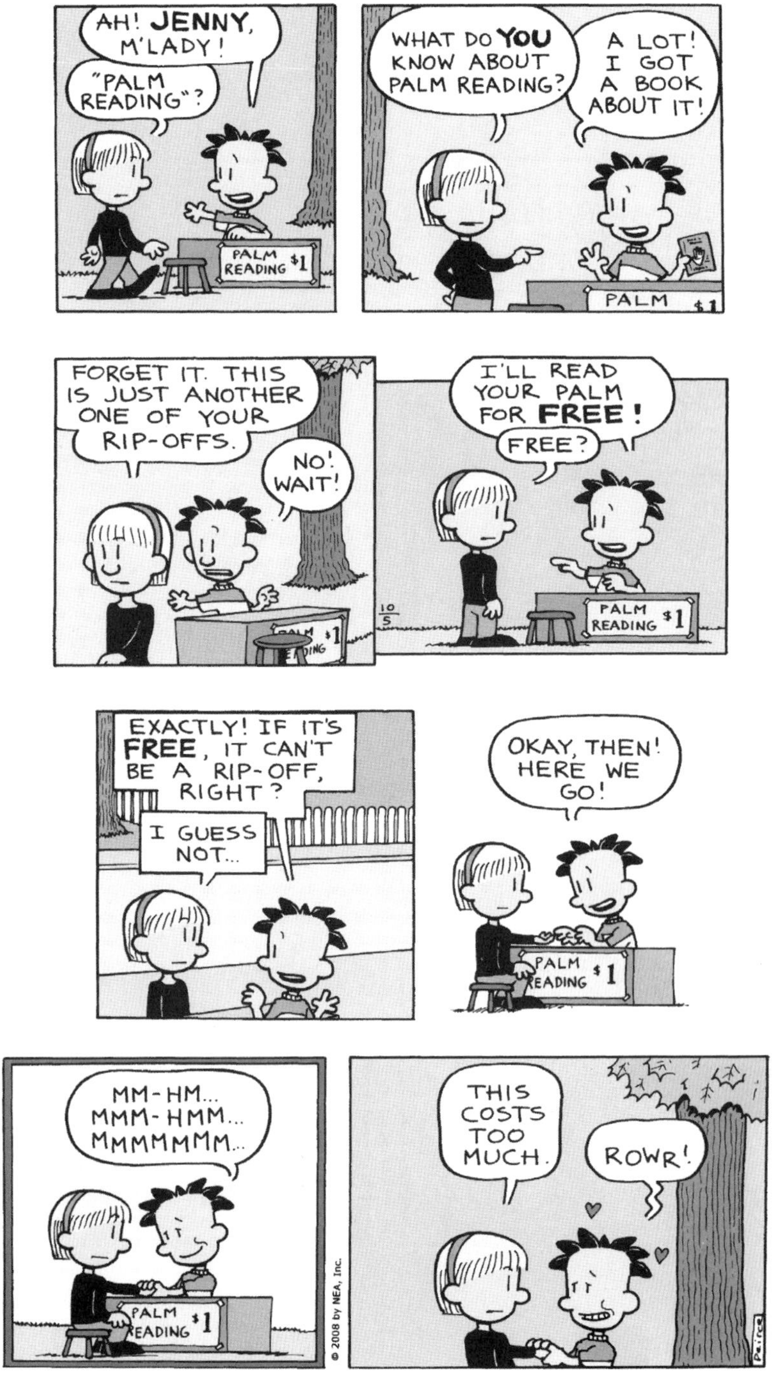
AH! JENNY, M'LADY!
"PALM READING"?
PALM READING $1
WHAT DO YOU KNOW ABOUT PALM READING?
A LOT! I GOT A BOOK ABOUT IT!
PALM $1
FORGET IT. THIS IS JUST ANOTHER ONE OF YOUR RIP-OFFS.
NO! WAIT!
I'LL READ YOUR PALM FOR FREE!
FREE?
10/5
PALM READING $1
EXACTLY! IF IT'S FREE, IT CAN'T BE A RIP-OFF, RIGHT?
I GUESS NOT...
OKAY, THEN! HERE WE GO!
PALM READING $1
MM-HM... MMM-HMM... MMMMMMM...
PALM READING $1
© 2008 by NEA, Inc.
THIS COSTS TOO MUCH.
ROWR!
PEIRCE

HERE GOES NOTHING

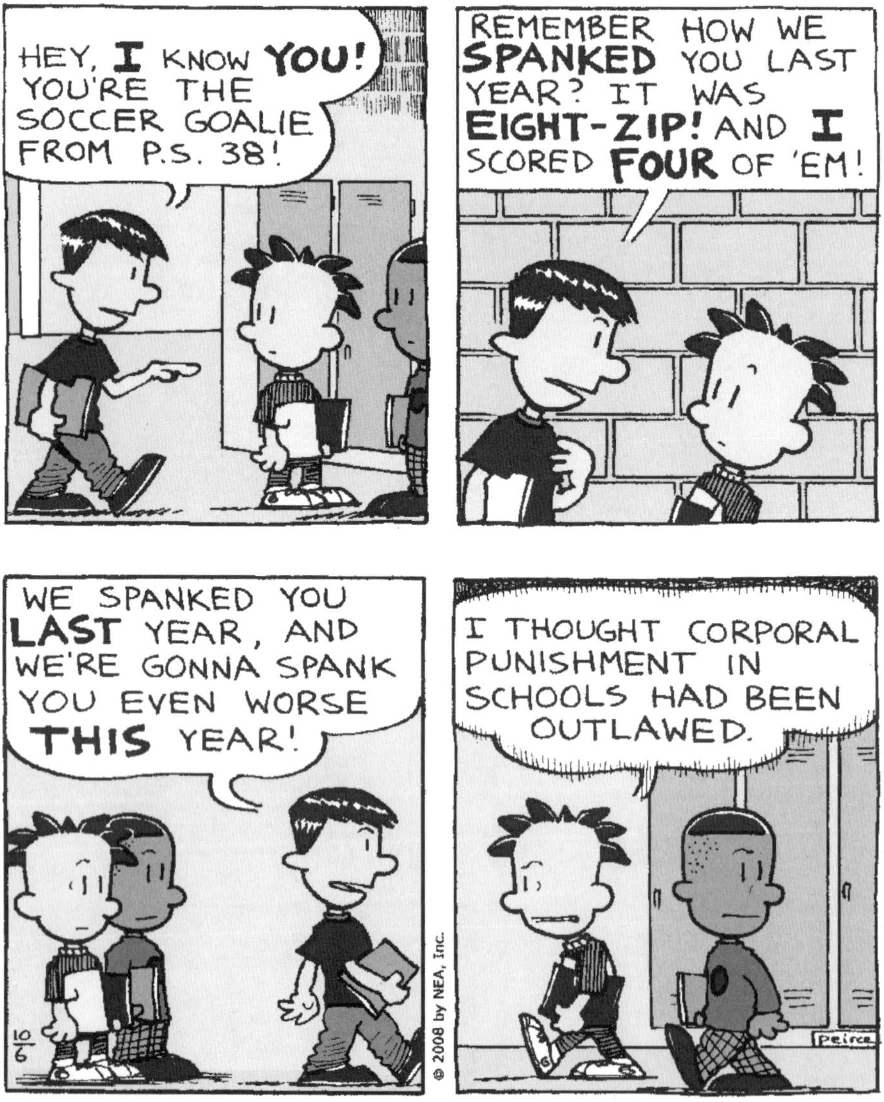
HEY, **I** KNOW **YOU!** YOU'RE THE SOCCER GOALIE FROM P.S. 38!
REMEMBER HOW WE **SPANKED** YOU LAST YEAR? IT WAS **EIGHT-ZIP!** AND **I** SCORED **FOUR** OF 'EM!
WE SPANKED YOU **LAST** YEAR, AND WE'RE GONNA SPANK YOU EVEN WORSE **THIS** YEAR!
10/6
I THOUGHT CORPORAL PUNISHMENT IN SCHOOLS HAD BEEN OUTLAWED.
peirce

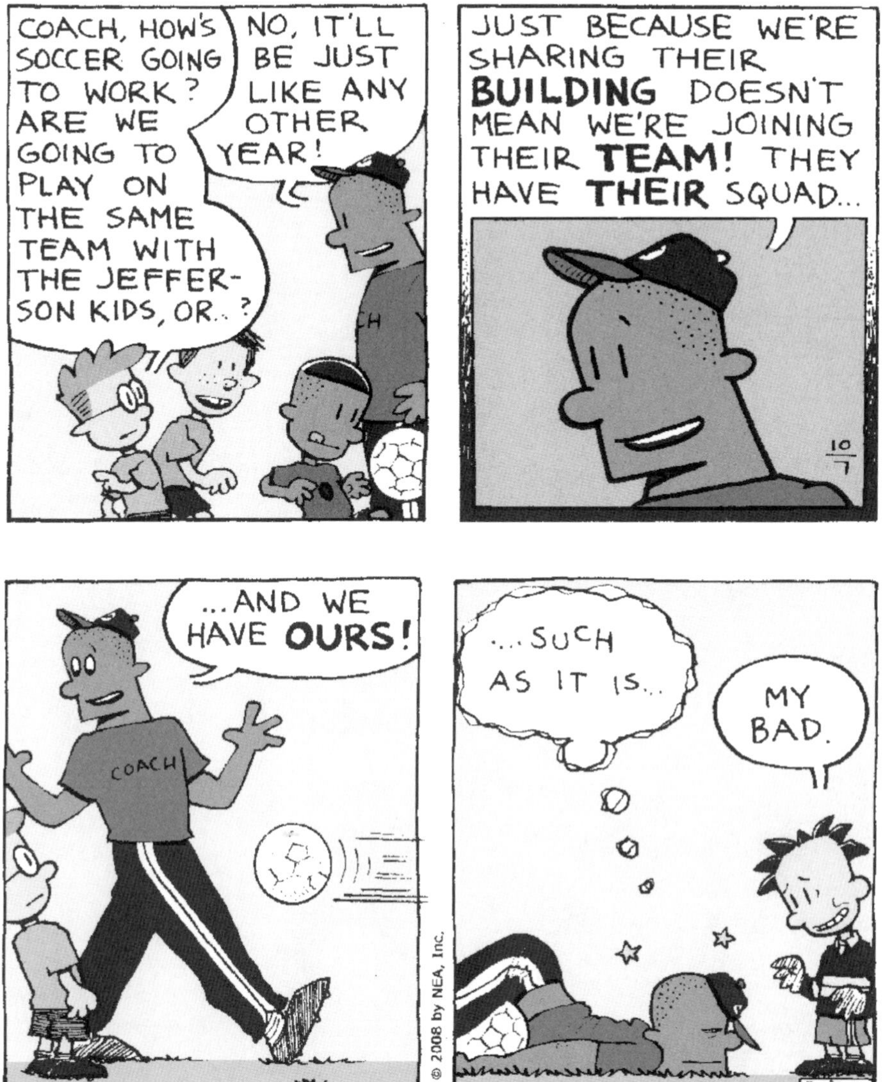
COACH, HOW'S SOCCER GOING TO WORK? ARE WE GOING TO PLAY ON THE SAME TEAM WITH THE JEFFERSON KIDS, OR..?
NO, IT'LL BE JUST LIKE ANY OTHER YEAR!
JUST BECAUSE WE'RE SHARING THEIR **BUILDING** DOESN'T MEAN WE'RE JOINING THEIR **TEAM!** THEY HAVE **THEIR** SQUAD...
10/7
...AND WE HAVE **OURS!**
COACH
© 2008 by NEA, Inc.
...SUCH AS IT IS...
MY BAD.
Peirce

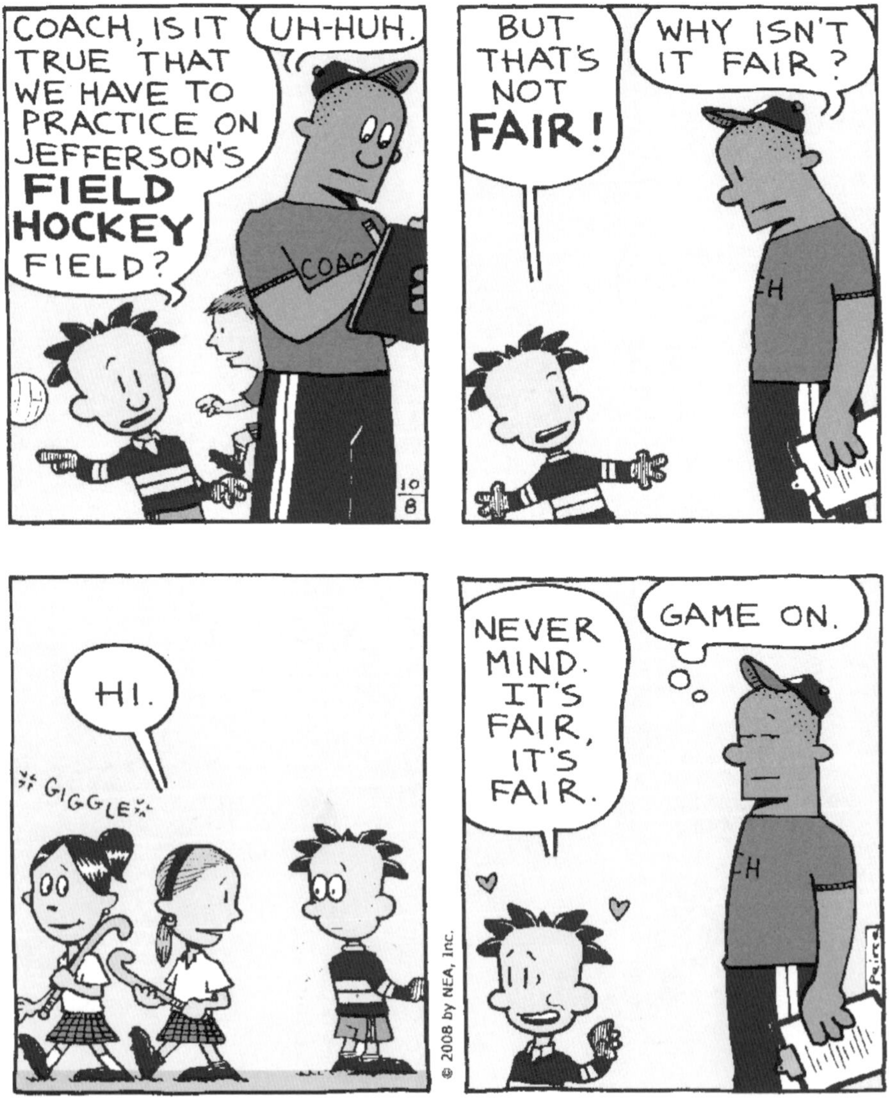
COACH, IS IT TRUE THAT WE HAVE TO PRACTICE ON JEFFERSON'S FIELD HOCKEY FIELD?
UH-HUH.
COACH
10
8
BUT THAT'S NOT FAIR!
WHY ISN'T IT FAIR?
HI.
GIGGLE
NEVER MIND. IT'S FAIR, IT'S FAIR.
GAME ON.
Peirce
© 2008 by NEA, Inc.

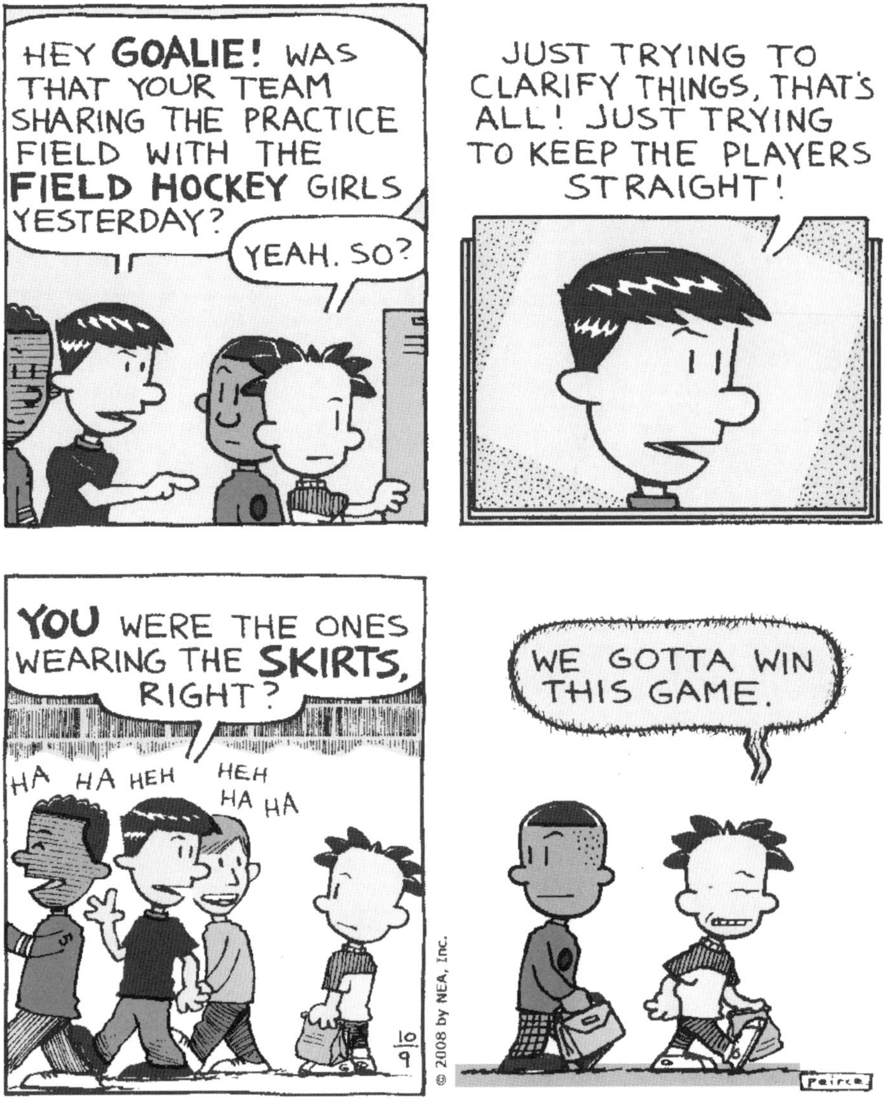
HEY GOALIE! WAS THAT YOUR TEAM SHARING THE PRACTICE FIELD WITH THE FIELD HOCKEY GIRLS YESTERDAY?
YEAH. SO?
JUST TRYING TO CLARIFY THINGS, THAT'S ALL! JUST TRYING TO KEEP THE PLAYERS STRAIGHT!
YOU WERE THE ONES WEARING THE SKIRTS, RIGHT?
HA HA HEH
HEH HA HA
10 9
© 2008 by NEA, Inc.
WE GOTTA WIN THIS GAME.
peirce

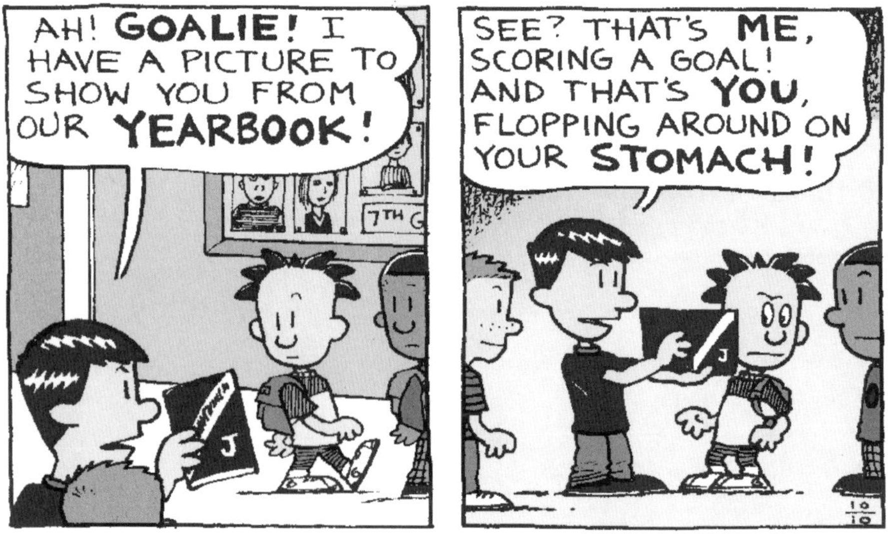
AH! **GOALIE!** I HAVE A PICTURE TO SHOW YOU FROM OUR **YEARBOOK!**
7TH G
J
SEE? THAT'S **ME**, SCORING A GOAL! AND THAT'S **YOU**, FLOPPING AROUND ON YOUR **STOMACH!**
J
10/10

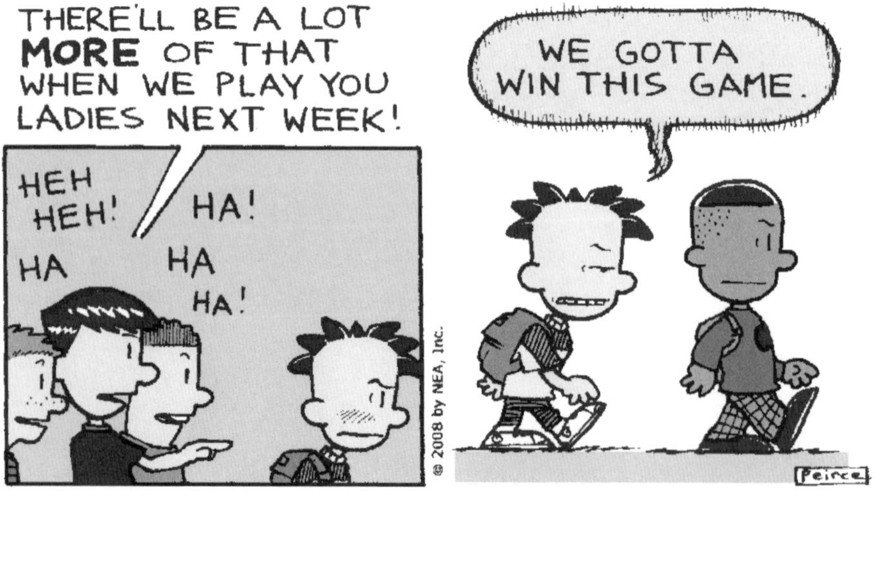
THERE'LL BE A LOT **MORE** OF THAT WHEN WE PLAY YOU LADIES NEXT WEEK!
HEH HEH!
HA!
HA
HA
HA!
© 2008 by NEA, Inc.
WE GOTTA WIN THIS GAME.
Peirce

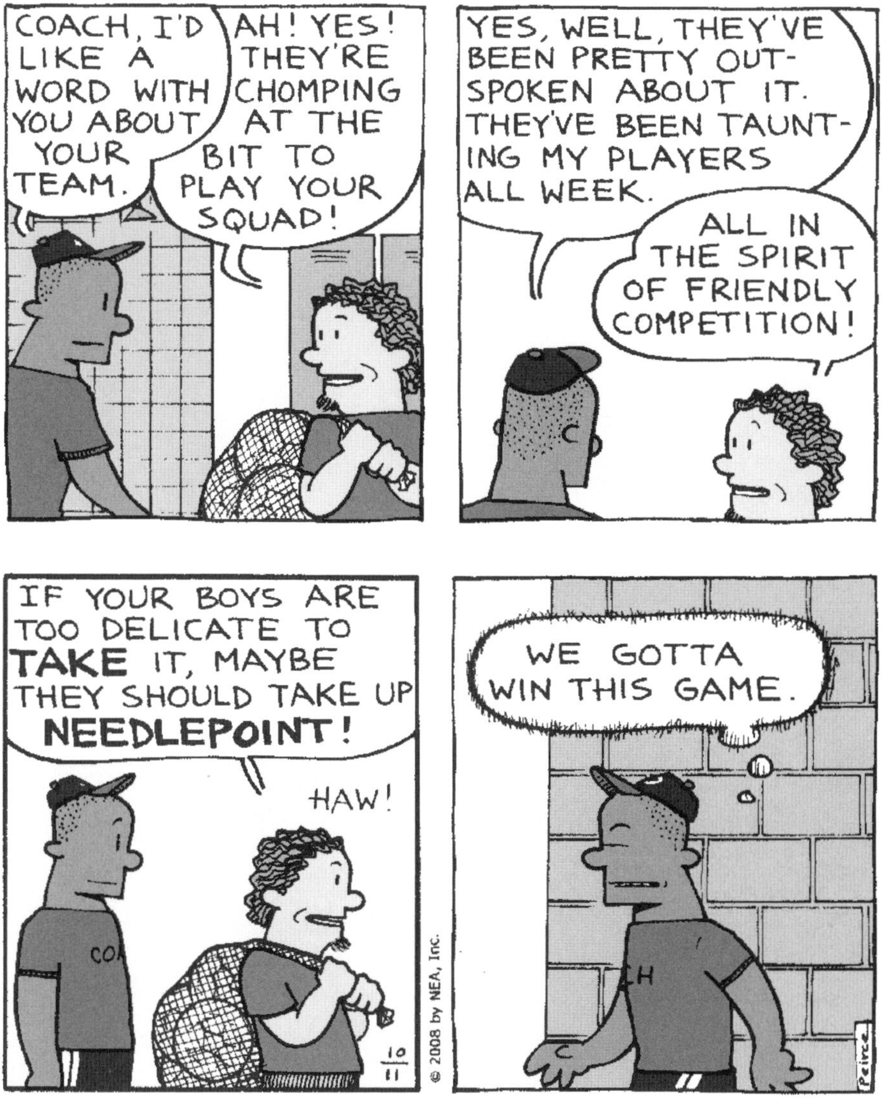
COACH, I'D LIKE A WORD WITH YOU ABOUT YOUR TEAM.
AH! YES! THEY'RE CHOMPING AT THE BIT TO PLAY YOUR SQUAD!
YES, WELL, THEY'VE BEEN PRETTY OUT-SPOKEN ABOUT IT. THEY'VE BEEN TAUNT-ING MY PLAYERS ALL WEEK.
ALL IN THE SPIRIT OF FRIENDLY COMPETITION!
IF YOUR BOYS ARE TOO DELICATE TO TAKE IT, MAYBE THEY SHOULD TAKE UP NEEDLEPOINT!
HAW!
WE GOTTA WIN THIS GAME.
© 2008 by NEA, Inc.
Peirce

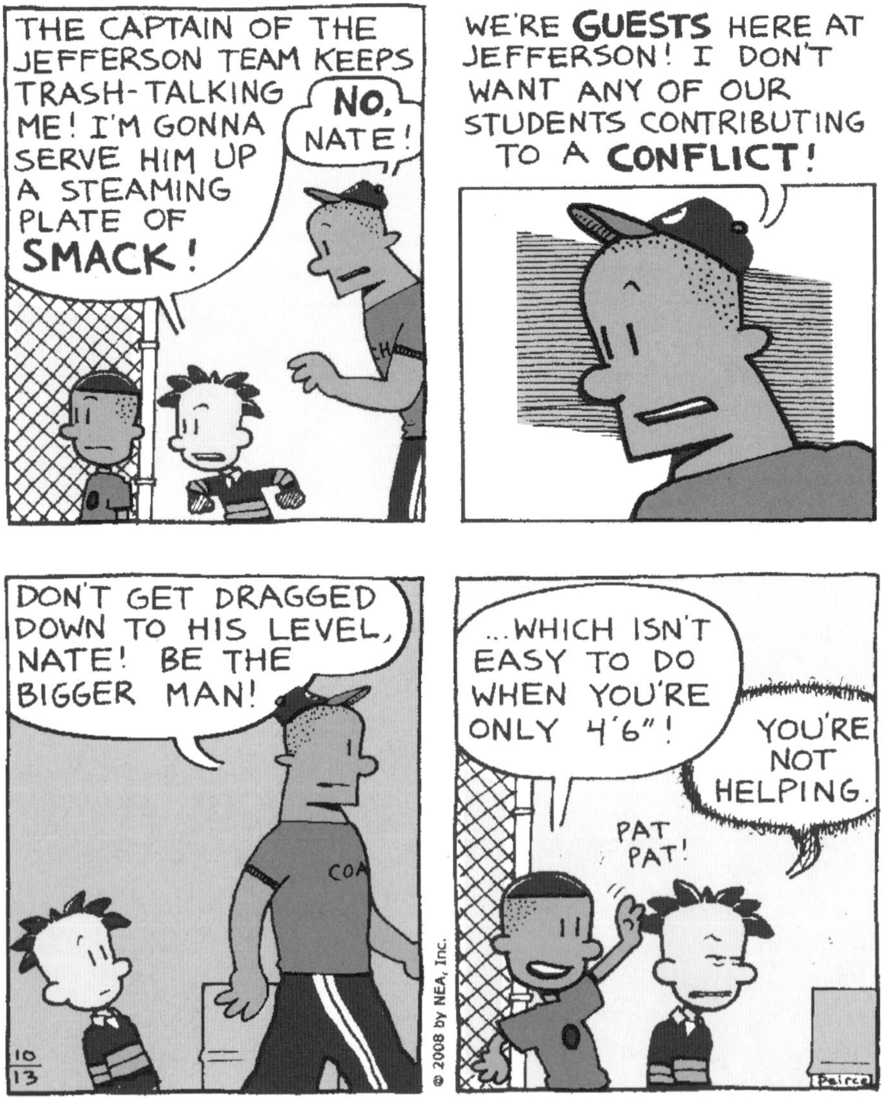
THE CAPTAIN OF THE JEFFERSON TEAM KEEPS TRASH-TALKING ME! I'M GONNA SERVE HIM UP A STEAMING PLATE OF SMACK!
NO, NATE!
WE'RE GUESTS HERE AT JEFFERSON! I DON'T WANT ANY OF OUR STUDENTS CONTRIBUTING TO A CONFLICT!
DON'T GET DRAGGED DOWN TO HIS LEVEL, NATE! BE THE BIGGER MAN!
...WHICH ISN'T EASY TO DO WHEN YOU'RE ONLY 4'6"!
YOU'RE NOT HELPING.
PAT PAT!
10/13
© 2008 by NEA, Inc.

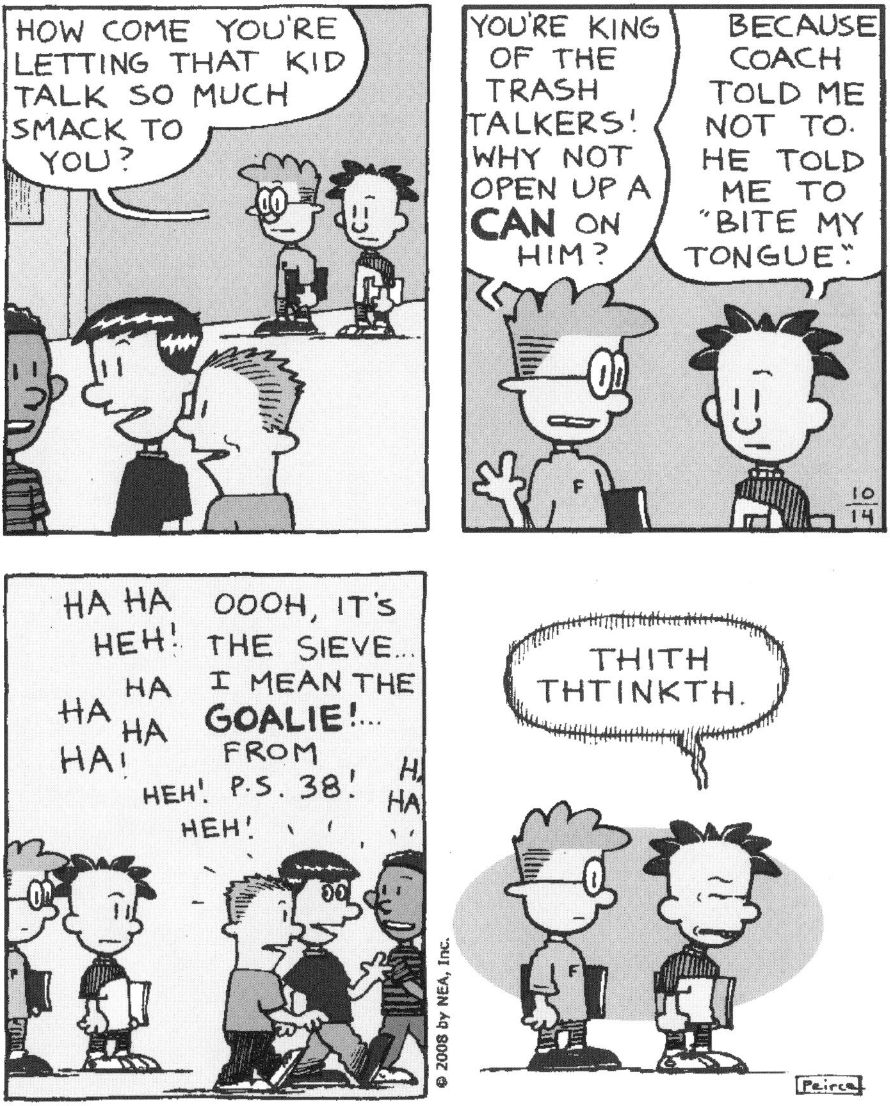
HOW COME YOU'RE LETTING THAT KID TALK SO MUCH SMACK TO YOU?
YOU'RE KING OF THE TRASH TALKERS! WHY NOT OPEN UP A **CAN** ON HIM?
BECAUSE COACH TOLD ME NOT TO. HE TOLD ME TO "BITE MY TONGUE."
10/14
HA HA HEH! HA HA HA HA HA!
OOOH, IT'S THE SIEVE... I MEAN THE **GOALIE**!... FROM P.S. 38!
HEH! HEH!
THITH THTINKTH.
© 2008 by NEA, Inc.
Peirce

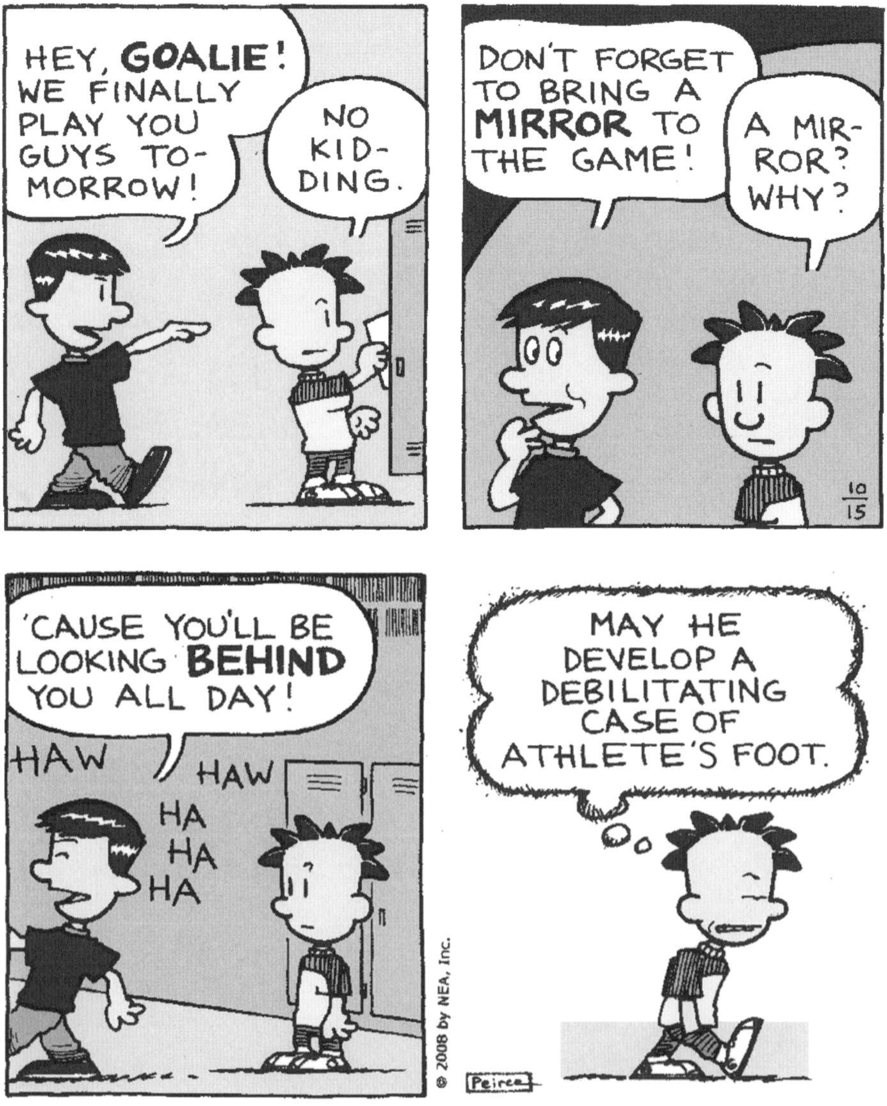
HEY, **GOALIE**! WE FINALLY PLAY YOU GUYS TO-MORROW!
NO KID-DING.
DON'T FORGET TO BRING A **MIRROR** TO THE GAME!
A MIR-ROR? WHY?
10/15
'CAUSE YOU'LL BE LOOKING **BEHIND** YOU ALL DAY!
HAW
HAW
HA HA HA
© 2008 by NEA, Inc.
Peirce
MAY HE DEVELOP A DEBILITATING CASE OF ATHLETE'S FOOT.

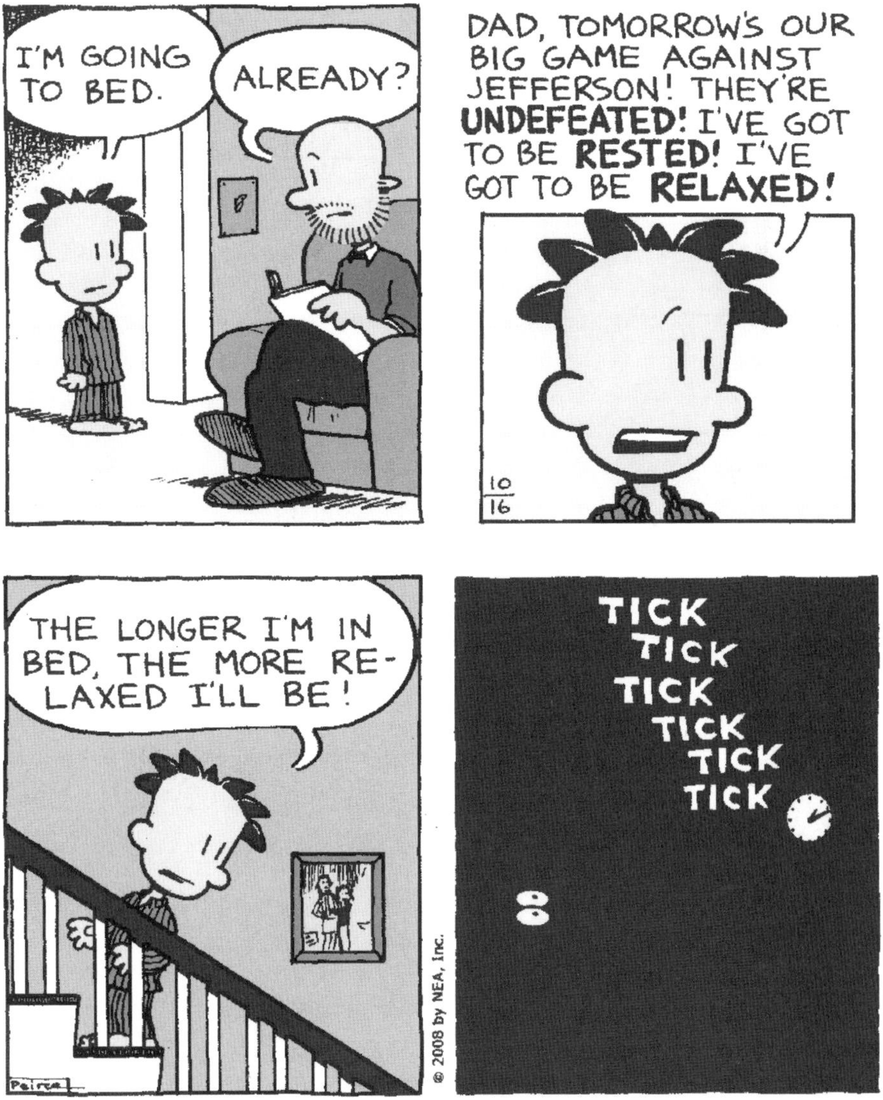
I'M GOING TO BED.
ALREADY?
DAD, TOMORROW'S OUR BIG GAME AGAINST JEFFERSON! THEY'RE UNDEFEATED! I'VE GOT TO BE RESTED! I'VE GOT TO BE RELAXED!
10/16
THE LONGER I'M IN BED, THE MORE RE-LAXED I'LL BE!
TICK
TICK
TICK
TICK
TICK
TICK

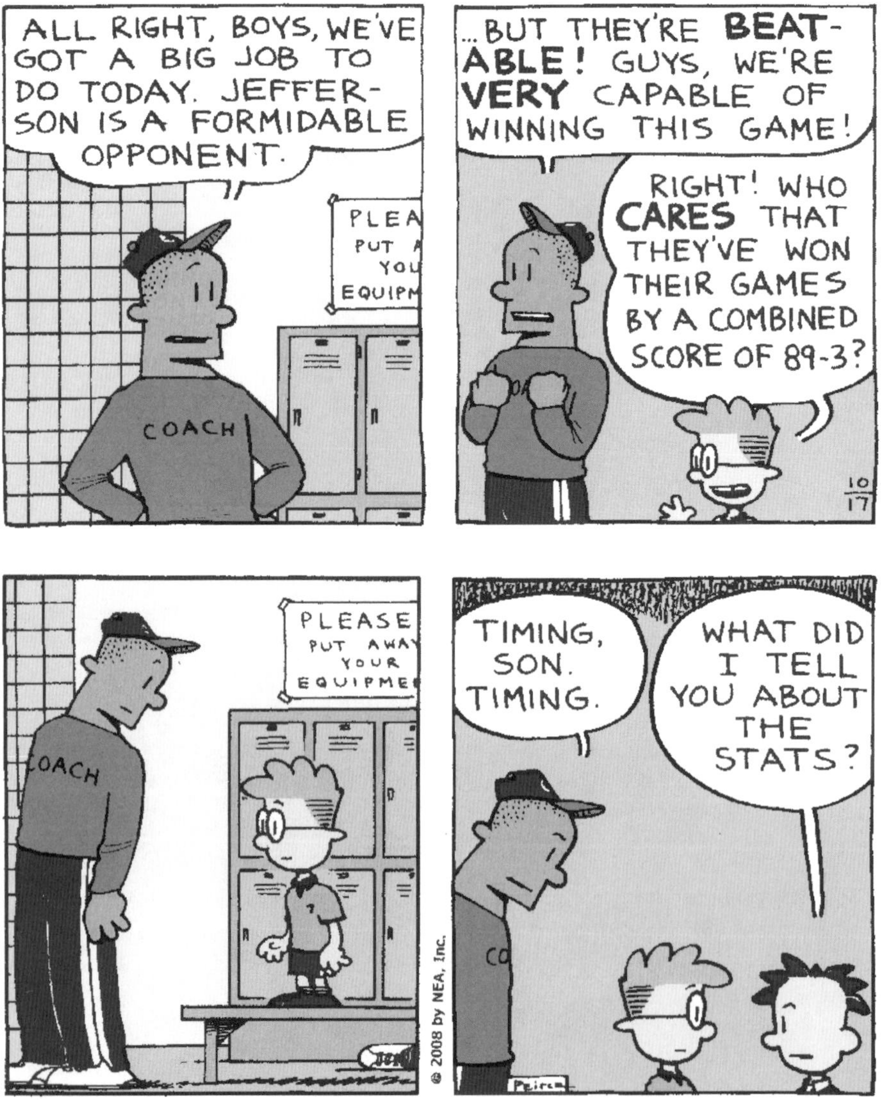
ALL RIGHT, BOYS, WE'VE GOT A BIG JOB TO DO TODAY. JEFFERSON IS A FORMIDABLE OPPONENT.
PLEA PUT A YOU EQUIPM
COACH
...BUT THEY'RE **BEAT-ABLE!** GUYS, WE'RE **VERY** CAPABLE OF WINNING THIS GAME!
RIGHT! WHO **CARES** THAT THEY'VE WON THEIR GAMES BY A COMBINED SCORE OF 89-3?
10/17
PLEASE PUT AWAY YOUR EQUIPME
OACH
© 2008 by NEA, Inc.
TIMING, SON. TIMING.
WHAT DID I TELL YOU ABOUT THE STATS?
Peirce

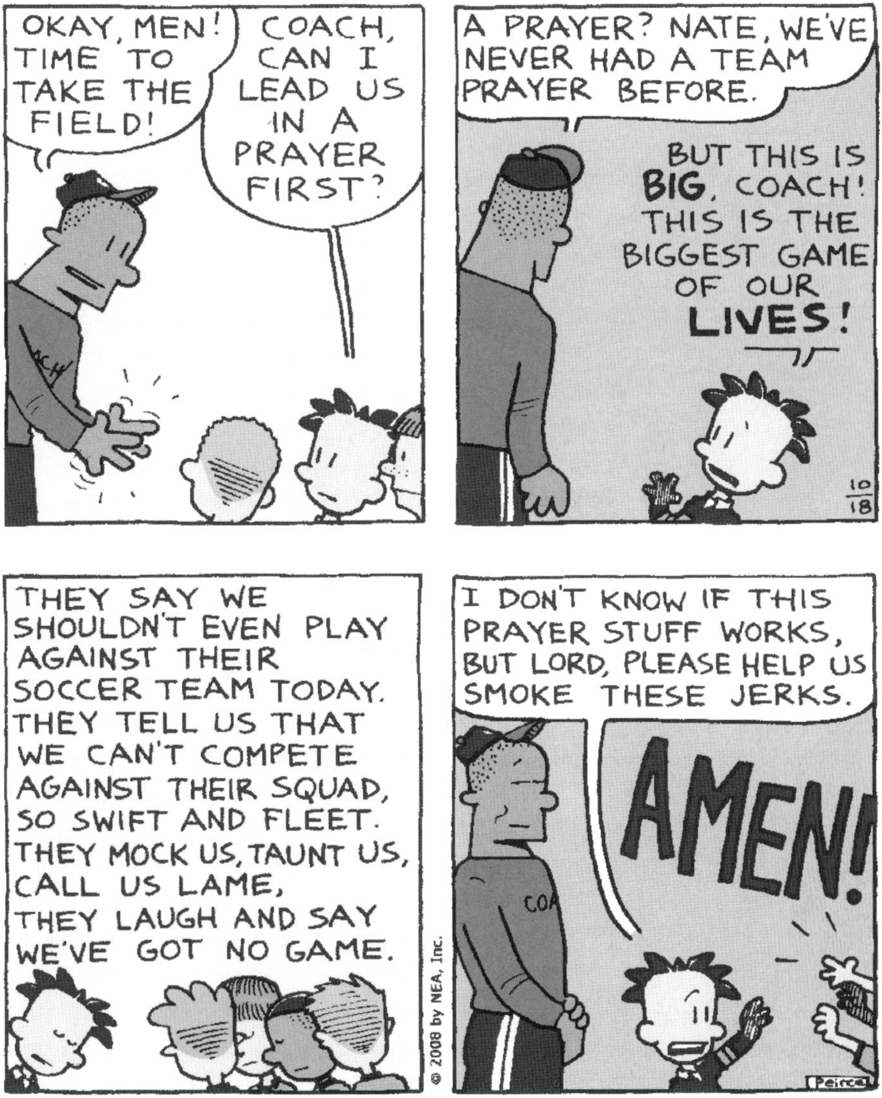
OKAY, MEN! TIME TO TAKE THE FIELD!
COACH, CAN I LEAD US IN A PRAYER FIRST?
A PRAYER? NATE, WE'VE NEVER HAD A TEAM PRAYER BEFORE.
BUT THIS IS BIG, COACH! THIS IS THE BIGGEST GAME OF OUR LIVES!
10/18
THEY SAY WE SHOULDN'T EVEN PLAY AGAINST THEIR SOCCER TEAM TODAY. THEY TELL US THAT WE CAN'T COMPETE AGAINST THEIR SQUAD, SO SWIFT AND FLEET. THEY MOCK US, TAUNT US, CALL US LAME, THEY LAUGH AND SAY WE'VE GOT NO GAME.
© 2008 by NEA, Inc.
I DON'T KNOW IF THIS PRAYER STUFF WORKS, BUT LORD, PLEASE HELP US SMOKE THESE JERKS.
AMEN!
COA
Peirce

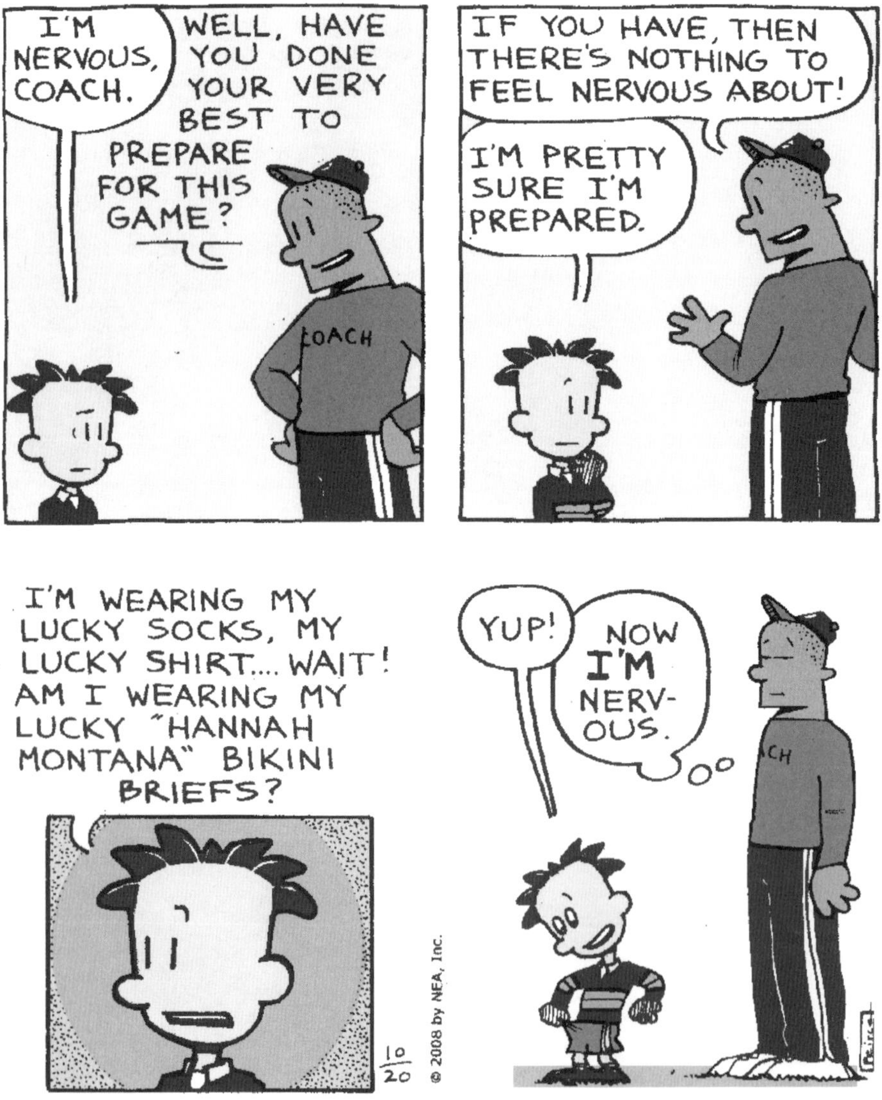
I'M NERVOUS, COACH.
WELL, HAVE YOU DONE YOUR VERY BEST TO PREPARE FOR THIS GAME?
COACH
IF YOU HAVE, THEN THERE'S NOTHING TO FEEL NERVOUS ABOUT!
I'M PRETTY SURE I'M PREPARED.
I'M WEARING MY LUCKY SOCKS, MY LUCKY SHIRT.... WAIT! AM I WEARING MY LUCKY "HANNAH MONTANA" BIKINI BRIEFS?
10/20
YUP!
NOW **I'M** NERVOUS.
Peirce

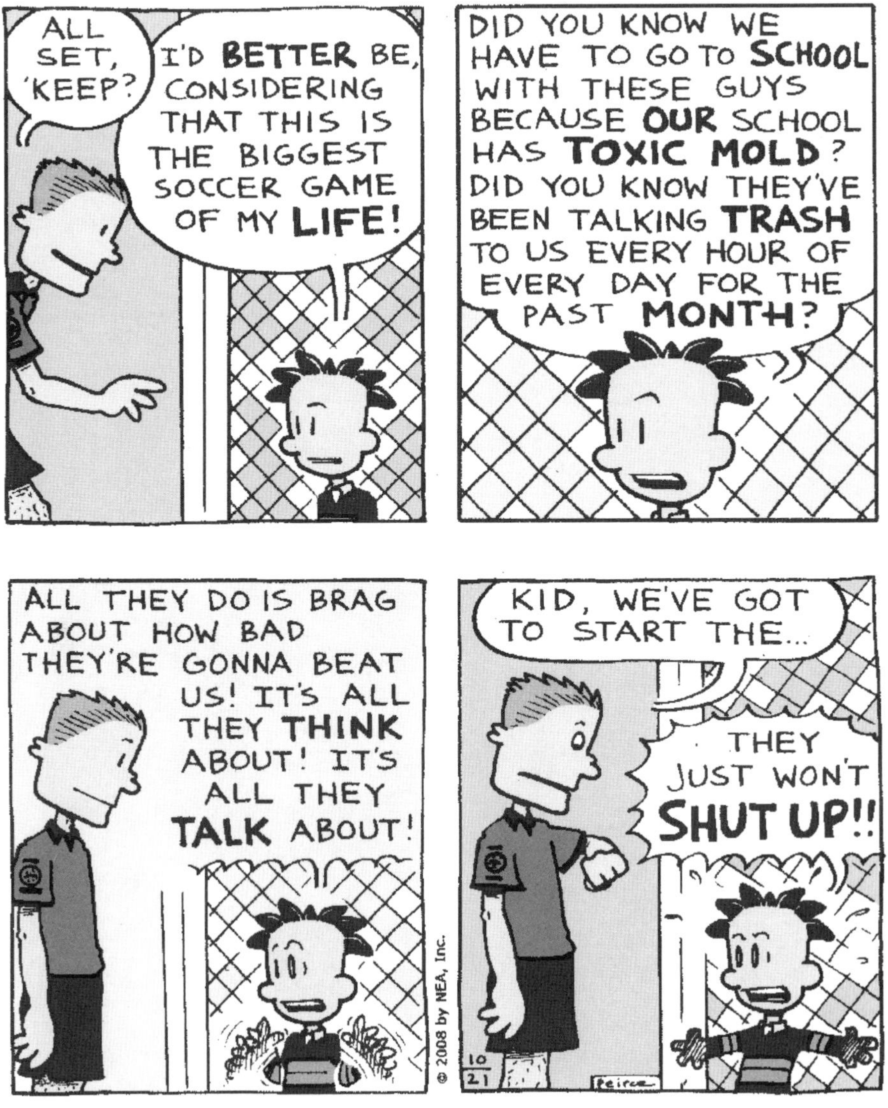
ALL SET, 'KEEP?
I'D **BETTER** BE, CONSIDERING THAT THIS IS THE BIGGEST SOCCER GAME OF MY **LIFE**!
DID YOU KNOW WE HAVE TO GO TO **SCHOOL** WITH THESE GUYS BECAUSE **OUR** SCHOOL HAS **TOXIC MOLD**? DID YOU KNOW THEY'VE BEEN TALKING **TRASH** TO US EVERY HOUR OF EVERY DAY FOR THE PAST **MONTH**?
ALL THEY DO IS BRAG ABOUT HOW BAD THEY'RE GONNA BEAT US! IT'S ALL THEY **THINK** ABOUT! IT'S ALL THEY **TALK** ABOUT!
© 2008 by NEA, Inc.
KID, WE'VE GOT TO START THE...
THEY JUST WON'T **SHUT UP!!**
10 21
Peirce

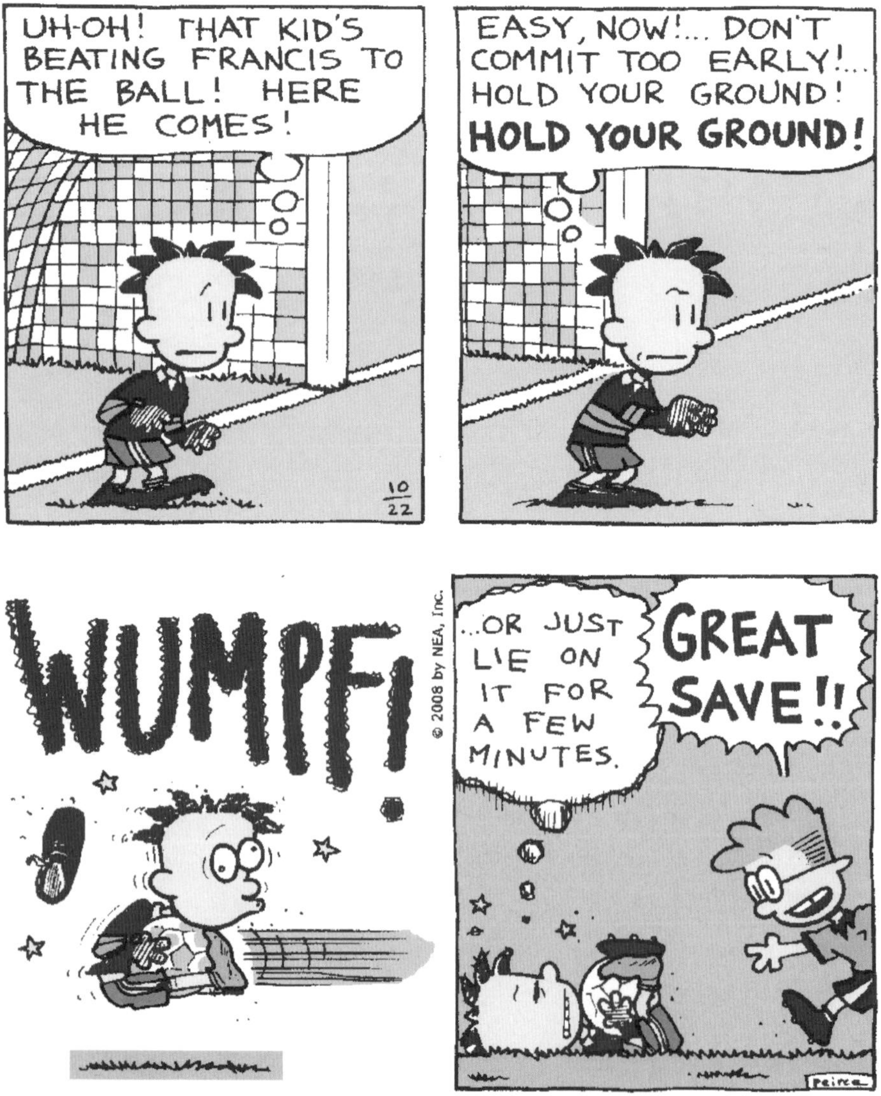
UH-OH! THAT KID'S BEATING FRANCIS TO THE BALL! HERE HE COMES!
10/22
EASY, NOW!... DON'T COMMIT TOO EARLY!... HOLD YOUR GROUND! HOLD YOUR GROUND!
WUMPF!
© 2008 by NEA, Inc.
...OR JUST LIE ON IT FOR A FEW MINUTES.
GREAT SAVE!!
peirce

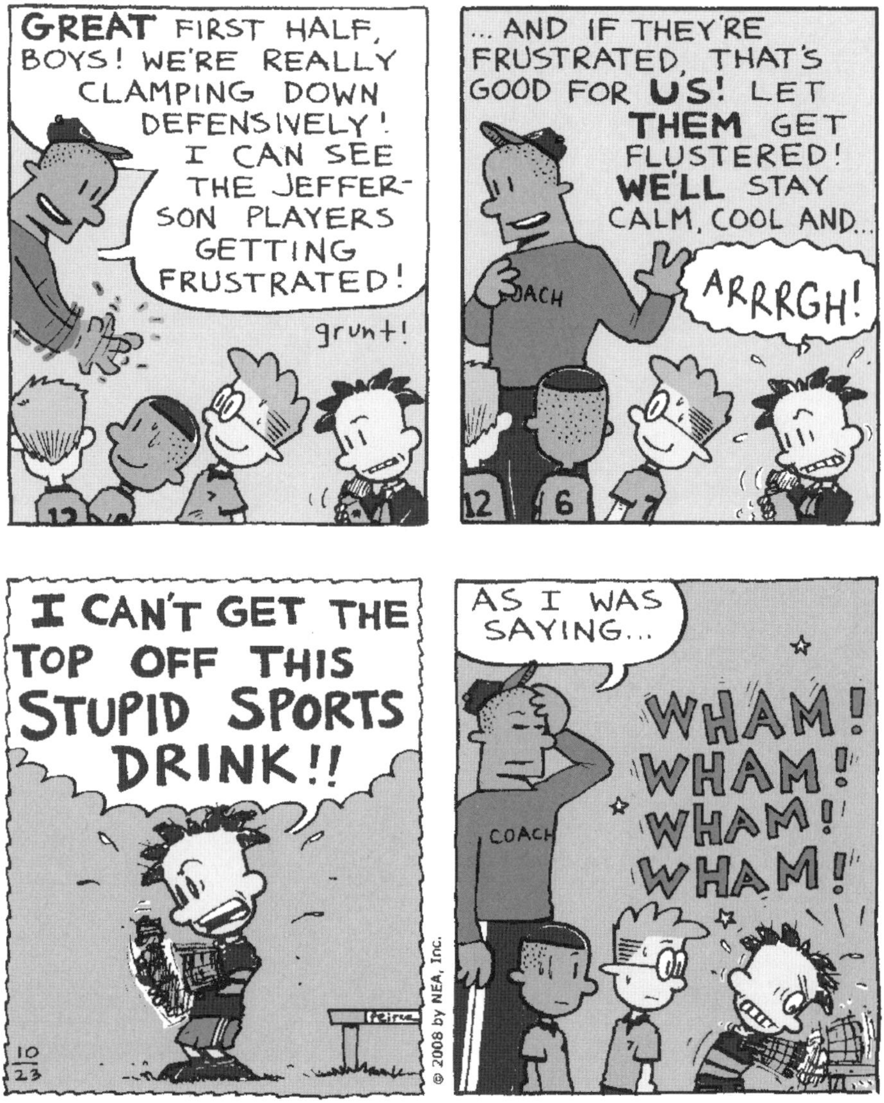
GREAT FIRST HALF, BOYS! WE'RE REALLY CLAMPING DOWN DEFENSIVELY! I CAN SEE THE JEFFERSON PLAYERS GETTING FRUSTRATED!
grunt!
... AND IF THEY'RE FRUSTRATED, THAT'S GOOD FOR US! LET THEM GET FLUSTERED! WE'LL STAY CALM, COOL AND...
ARRRGH!
I CAN'T GET THE TOP OFF THIS STUPID SPORTS DRINK!!
10
23
© 2008 by NEA, Inc.
AS I WAS SAYING...
WHAM! WHAM! WHAM! WHAM!

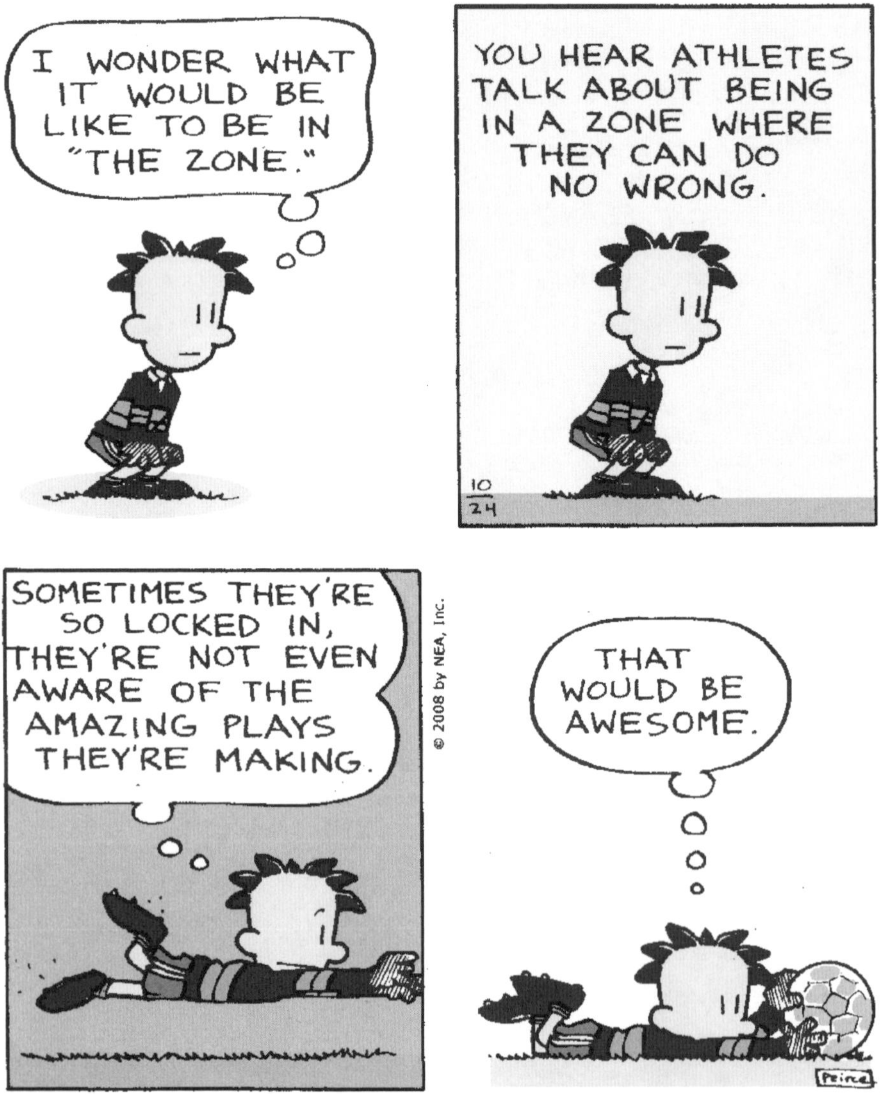
I WONDER WHAT IT WOULD BE LIKE TO BE IN "THE ZONE."
YOU HEAR ATHLETES TALK ABOUT BEING IN A ZONE WHERE THEY CAN DO NO WRONG.
10/24
SOMETIMES THEY'RE SO LOCKED IN, THEY'RE NOT EVEN AWARE OF THE AMAZING PLAYS THEY'RE MAKING.
© 2008 by NEA, Inc.
THAT WOULD BE AWESOME.
Peirce

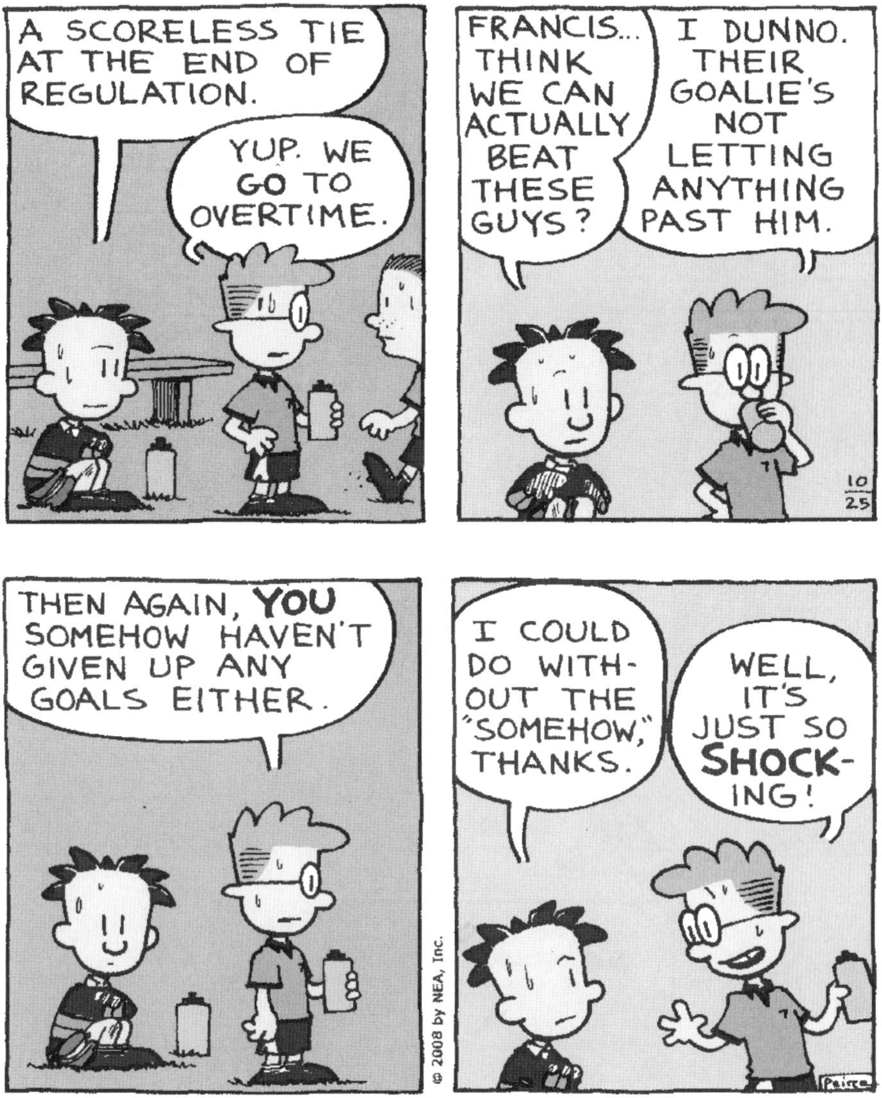
A SCORELESS TIE AT THE END OF REGULATION.
YUP. WE GO TO OVERTIME.
FRANCIS... THINK WE CAN ACTUALLY BEAT THESE GUYS?
I DUNNO. THEIR GOALIE'S NOT LETTING ANYTHING PAST HIM.
10/25
THEN AGAIN, **YOU** SOMEHOW HAVEN'T GIVEN UP ANY GOALS EITHER.
© 2008 by NEA, Inc.
I COULD DO WITHOUT THE "SOMEHOW," THANKS.
WELL, IT'S JUST SO **SHOCKING**!
Peirce

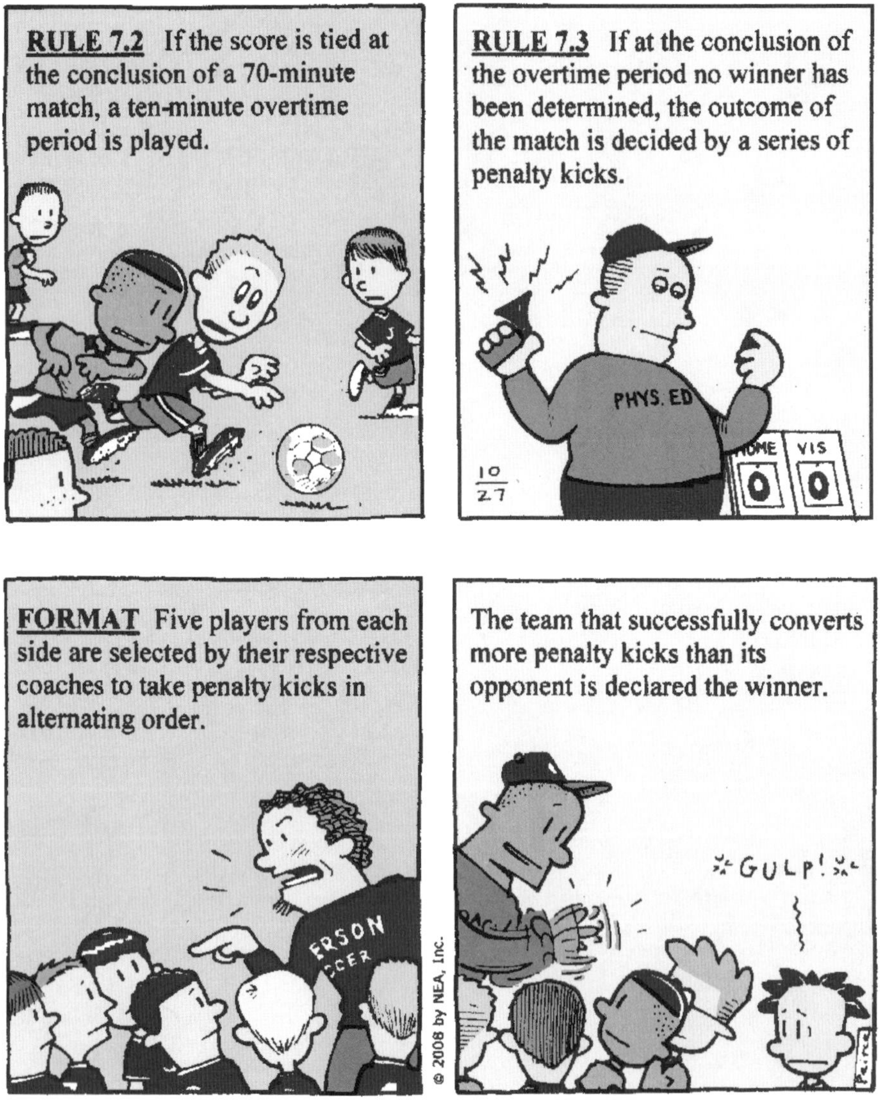
RULE 7.2 If the score is tied at the conclusion of a 70-minute match, a ten-minute overtime period is played.
RULE 7.3 If at the conclusion of the overtime period no winner has been determined, the outcome of the match is decided by a series of penalty kicks.
PHYS. ED
HOME VIS
0 0
10/27
FORMAT Five players from each side are selected by their respective coaches to take penalty kicks in alternating order.
© 2008 by NEA, Inc.
The team that successfully converts more penalty kicks than its opponent is declared the winner.
GULP!

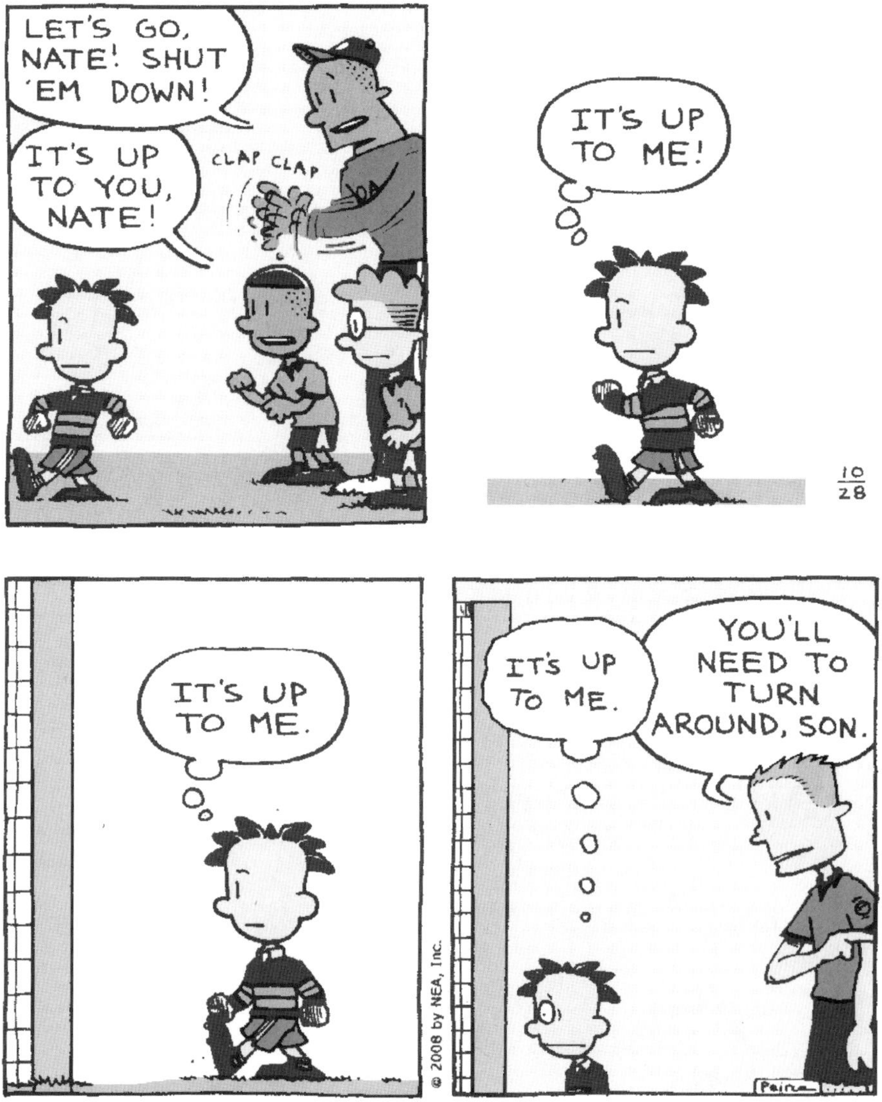
LET'S GO, NATE! SHUT 'EM DOWN!
IT'S UP TO YOU, NATE!
CLAP CLAP
IT'S UP TO ME!
10/28
IT'S UP TO ME.
IT'S UP TO ME.
YOU'LL NEED TO TURN AROUND, SON.
Peirce

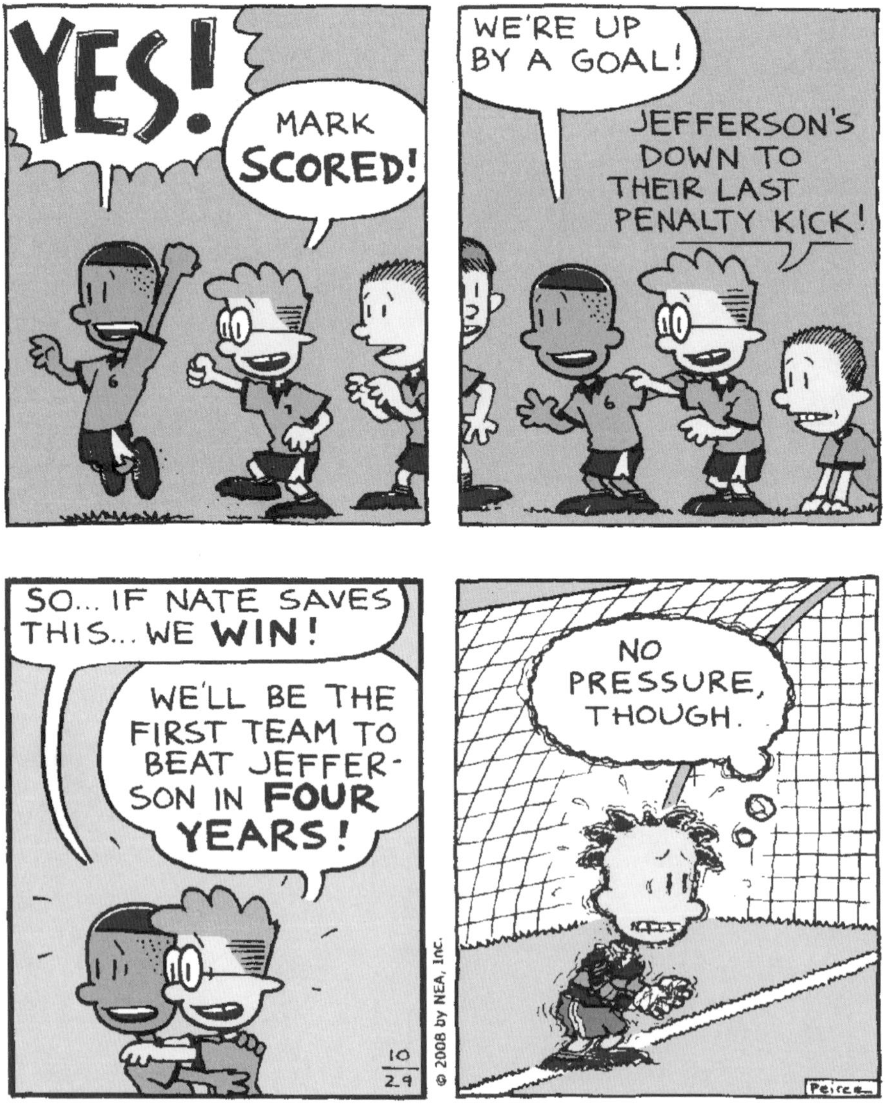
YES!
MARK SCORED!
WE'RE UP BY A GOAL!
JEFFERSON'S DOWN TO THEIR LAST PENALTY KICK!
SO... IF NATE SAVES THIS... WE WIN!
WE'LL BE THE FIRST TEAM TO BEAT JEFFERSON IN FOUR YEARS!
10 2-9
© 2008 by NEA, Inc.
NO PRESSURE, THOUGH.
Peirce

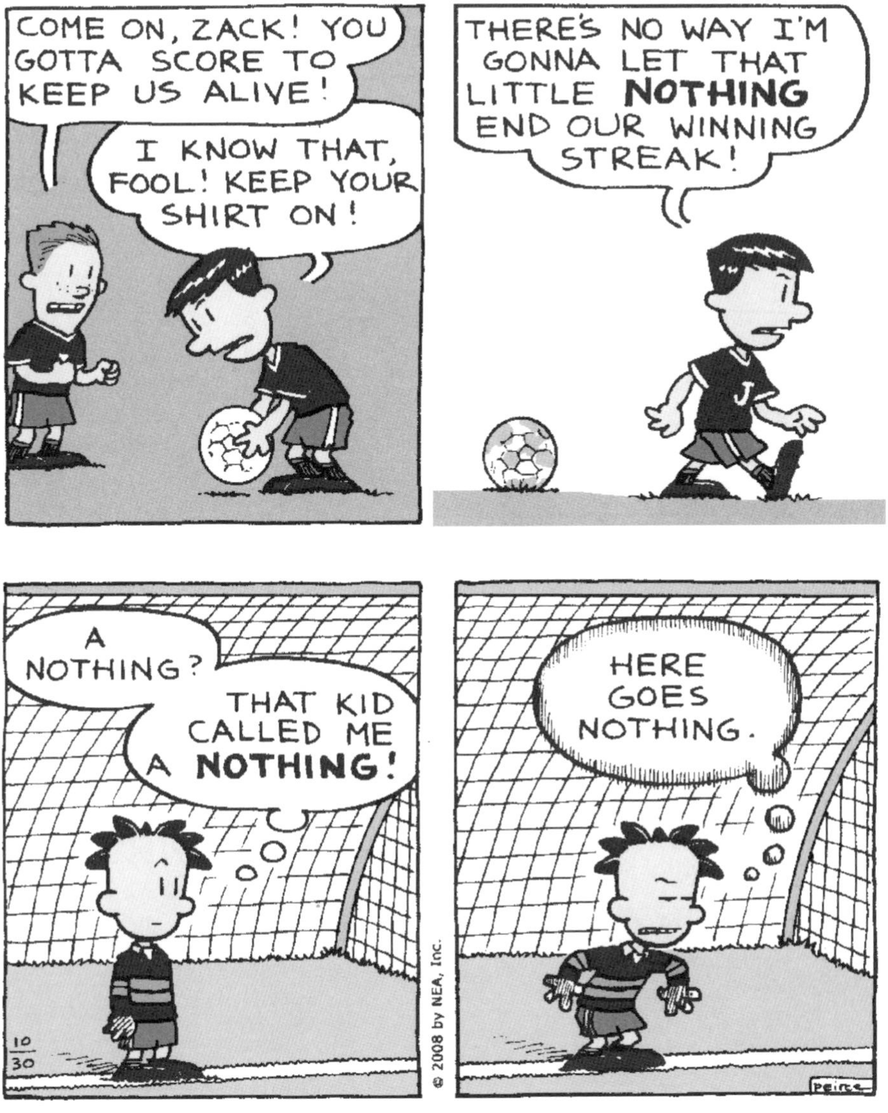
COME ON, ZACK! YOU GOTTA SCORE TO KEEP US ALIVE!
I KNOW THAT, FOOL! KEEP YOUR SHIRT ON!
THERE'S NO WAY I'M GONNA LET THAT LITTLE **NOTHING** END OUR WINNING STREAK!
A NOTHING?
THAT KID CALLED ME A **NOTHING!**
HERE GOES NOTHING.
10/30
© 2008 by NEA, Inc.
PEIRCE

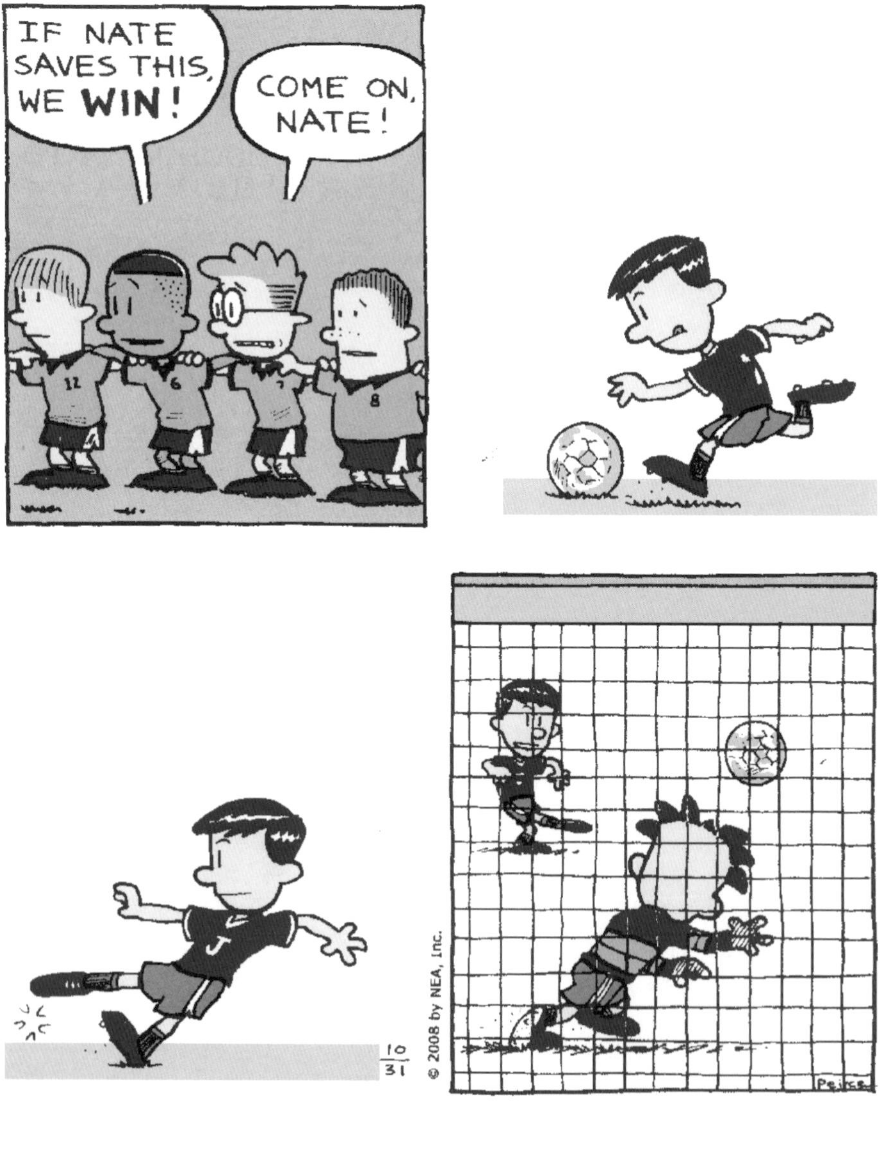
IF NATE SAVES THIS, WE **WIN**!
COME ON, NATE!
10
31
© 2008 by NEA, Inc.
Peirce

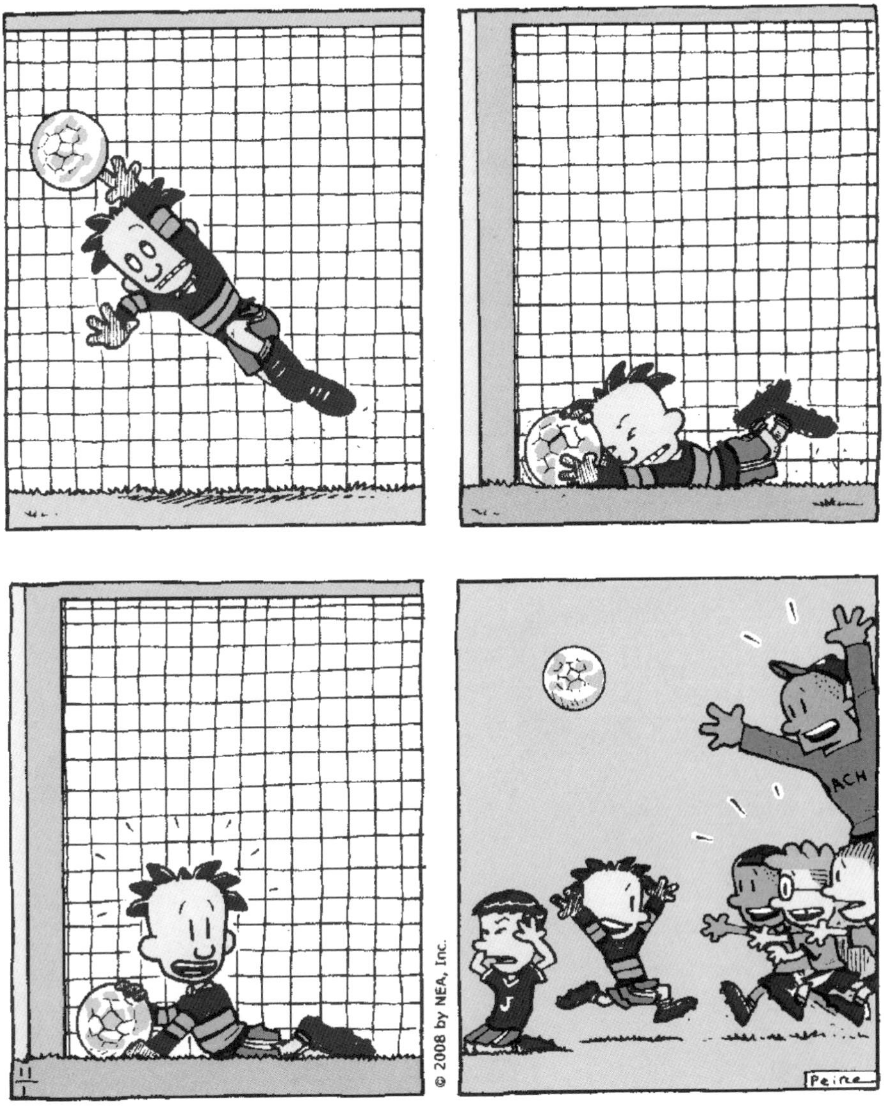
Peirce

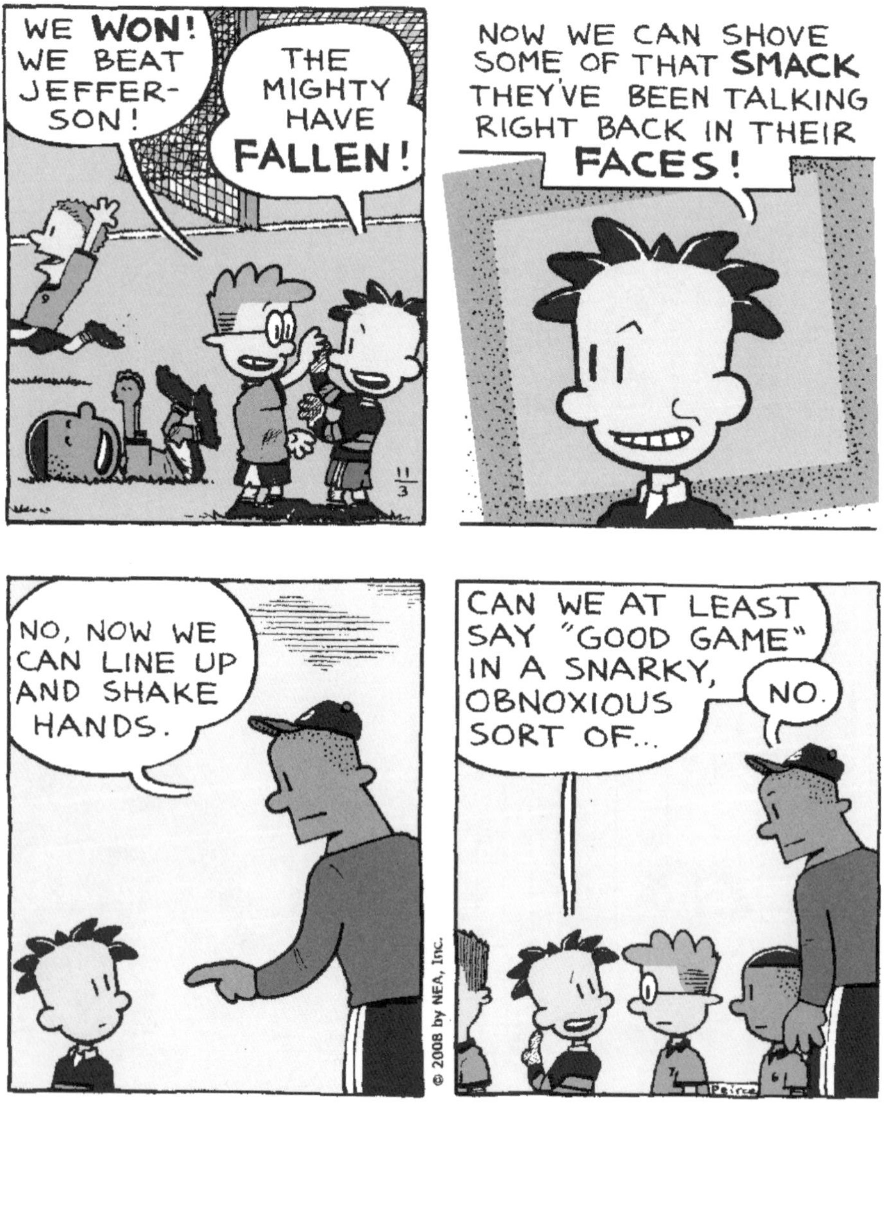
WE WON! WE BEAT JEFFER-SON!
THE MIGHTY HAVE FALLEN!
11/3
NOW WE CAN SHOVE SOME OF THAT SMACK THEY'VE BEEN TALKING RIGHT BACK IN THEIR FACES!
NO, NOW WE CAN LINE UP AND SHAKE HANDS.
© 2008 by NEA, Inc.
CAN WE AT LEAST SAY "GOOD GAME" IN A SNARKY, OBNOXIOUS SORT OF...
NO.
Peirce

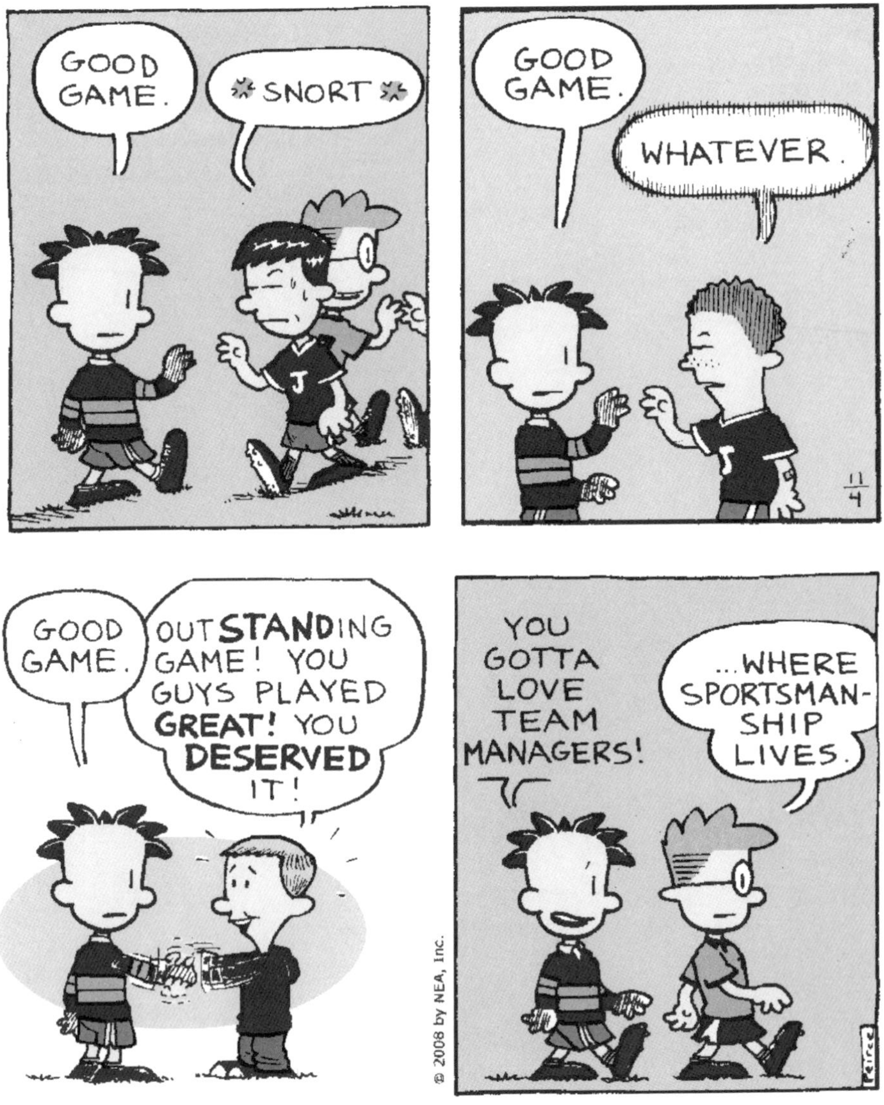
GOOD GAME.
SNORT
GOOD GAME.
WHATEVER.
11/4
GOOD GAME.
OUTSTANDING GAME! YOU GUYS PLAYED GREAT! YOU DESERVED IT!
YOU GOTTA LOVE TEAM MANAGERS!
...WHERE SPORTSMANSHIP LIVES.
Peirce

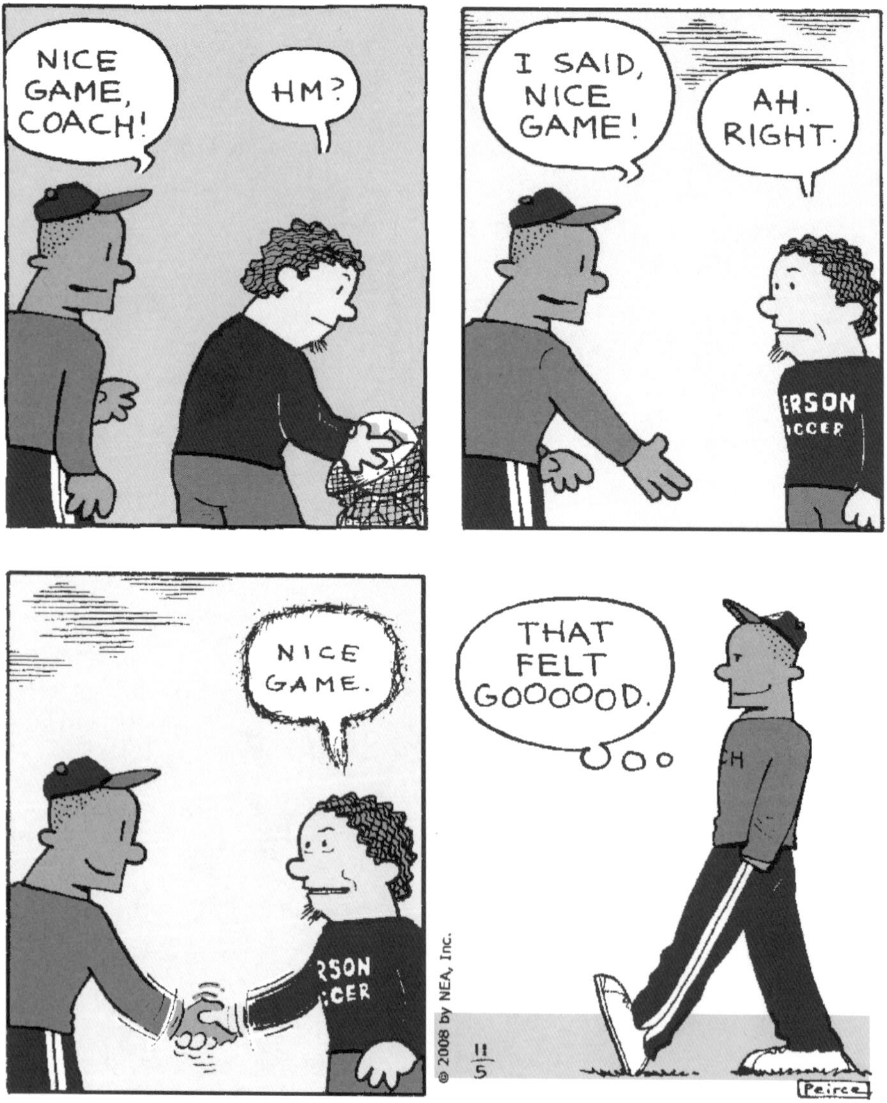
NICE GAME, COACH!
HM?
I SAID, NICE GAME!
AH. RIGHT.
RSON
CCER
NICE GAME.
THAT FELT GOOOOOD.
© 2008 by NEA, Inc.
11/5
Peirce

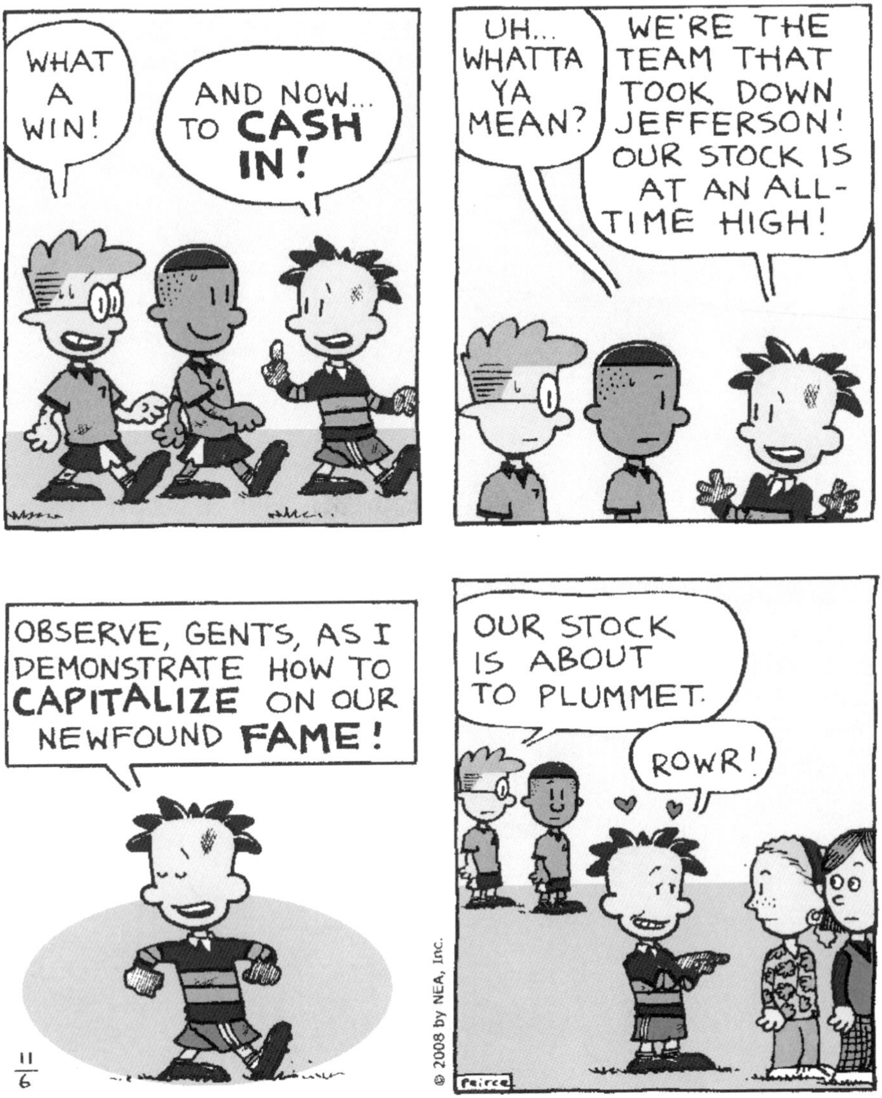
WHAT A WIN!
AND NOW... TO CASH IN!
UH... WHATTA YA MEAN?
WE'RE THE TEAM THAT TOOK DOWN JEFFERSON! OUR STOCK IS AT AN ALL-TIME HIGH!
OBSERVE, GENTS, AS I DEMONSTRATE HOW TO CAPITALIZE ON OUR NEWFOUND FAME!
11/6
OUR STOCK IS ABOUT TO PLUMMET.
ROWR!
Peirce
© 2008 by NEA, Inc.

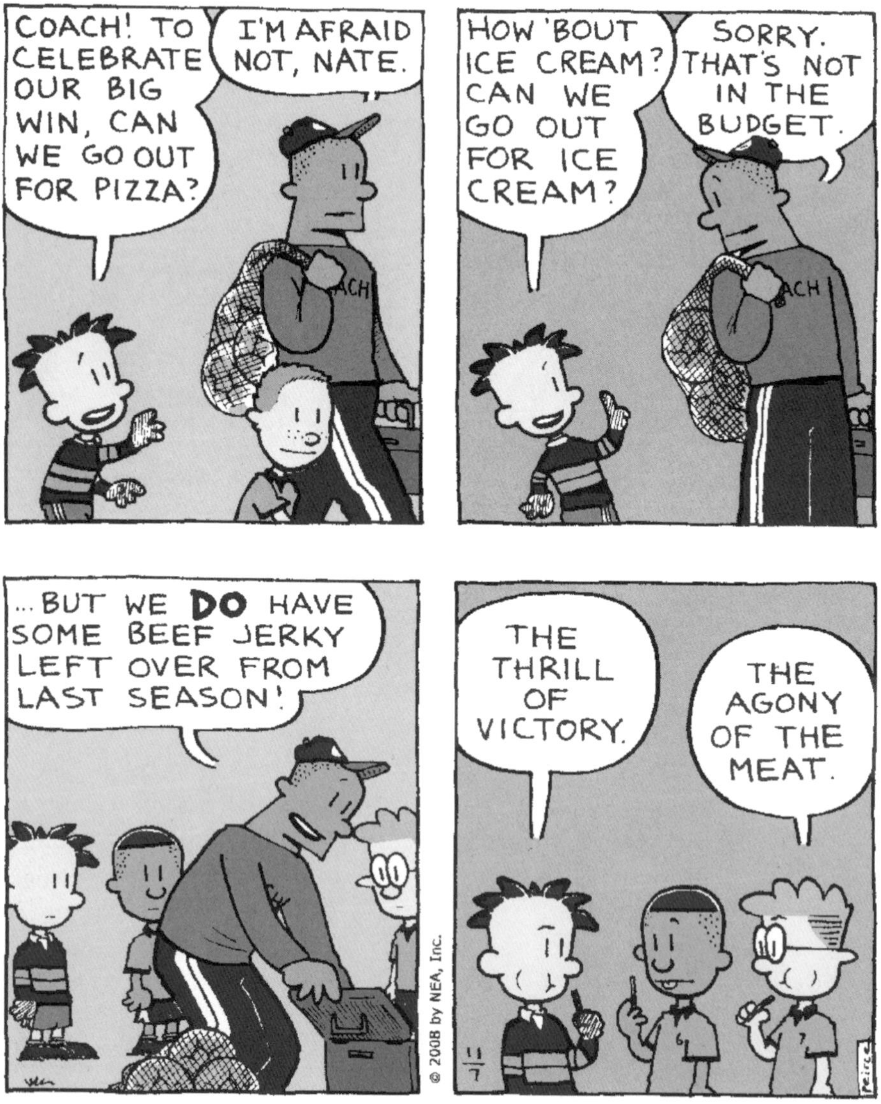
COACH! TO CELEBRATE OUR BIG WIN, CAN WE GO OUT FOR PIZZA?
I'M AFRAID NOT, NATE.
HOW 'BOUT ICE CREAM? CAN WE GO OUT FOR ICE CREAM?
SORRY. THAT'S NOT IN THE BUDGET.
...BUT WE DO HAVE SOME BEEF JERKY LEFT OVER FROM LAST SEASON!
THE THRILL OF VICTORY.
THE AGONY OF THE MEAT.
© 2008 by NEA, Inc.
11/7
Peirce

CHECK IT OUT, NATE! FRONT PAGE OF THE SPORTS SECTION! "P.S. 38 SHOCKS JEFFERSON"!

OOH! READ IT!

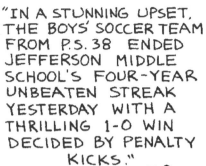

"IN A STUNNING UPSET, THE BOYS' SOCCER TEAM FROM P.S. 38 ENDED JEFFERSON MIDDLE SCHOOL'S FOUR-YEAR UNBEATEN STREAK YESTERDAY WITH A THRILLING 1-0 WIN DECIDED BY PENALTY KICKS."

"THE OUTCOME WAS IN DOUBT UNTIL JEFFERSON'S FINAL SHOOTER, STAR STRIKER ZACK BELFOUR, WAS ROBBED ON A SPECTACULAR SAVE BY P.S. 38 GOAL-KEEPER MATE WRIGHT."

"MATE WRIGHT"?

THAT SOUNDS DIRTY.

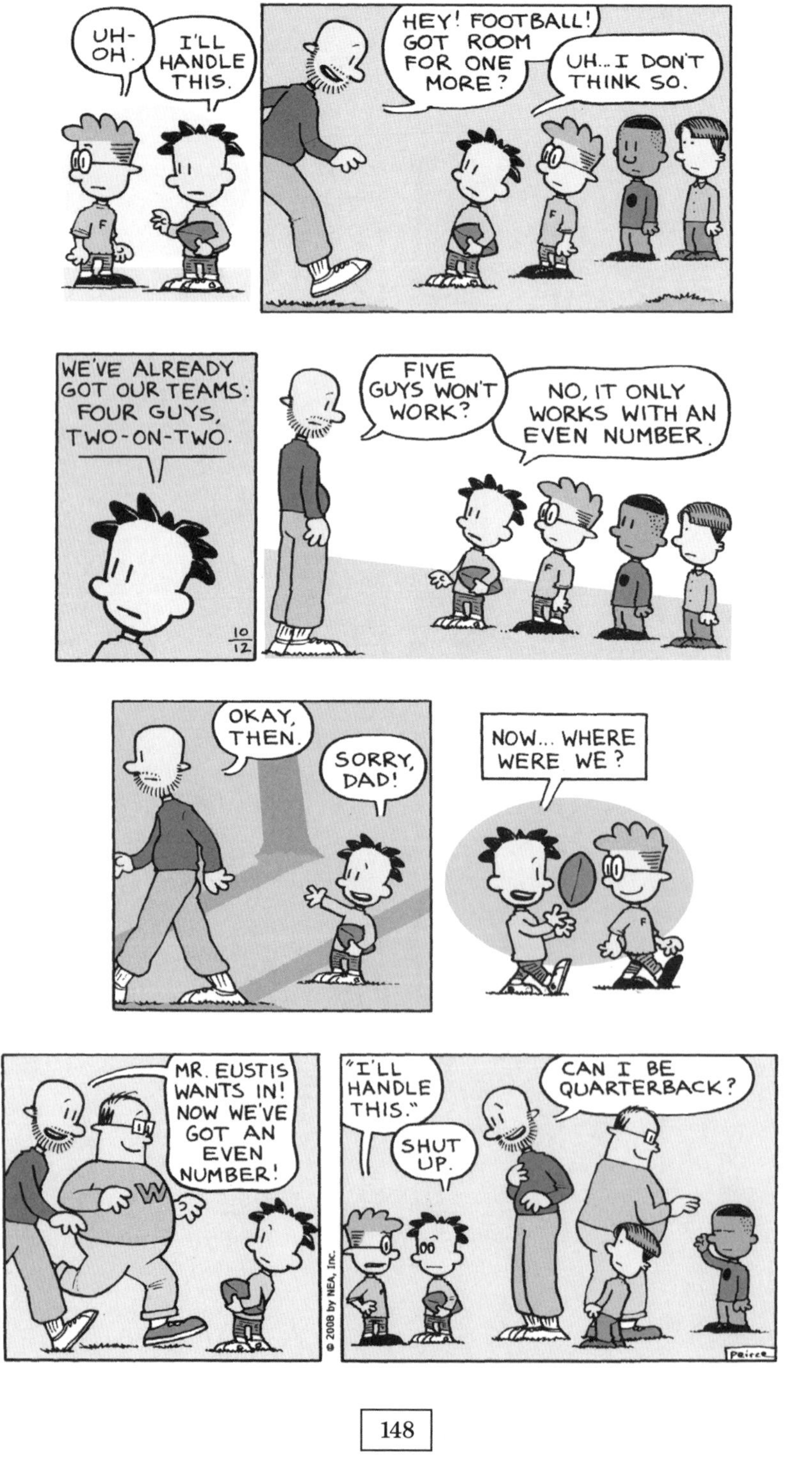

UH-OH.
I'LL HANDLE THIS.
HEY! FOOTBALL! GOT ROOM FOR ONE MORE?
UH... I DON'T THINK SO.
WE'VE ALREADY GOT OUR TEAMS: FOUR GUYS, TWO-ON-TWO.
10/12
FIVE GUYS WON'T WORK?
NO, IT ONLY WORKS WITH AN EVEN NUMBER.
OKAY, THEN.
SORRY, DAD!
NOW... WHERE WERE WE?
MR. EUSTIS WANTS IN! NOW WE'VE GOT AN EVEN NUMBER!
© 2008 by NEA, Inc.
"I'LL HANDLE THIS."
SHUT UP.
CAN I BE QUARTERBACK?
peirce

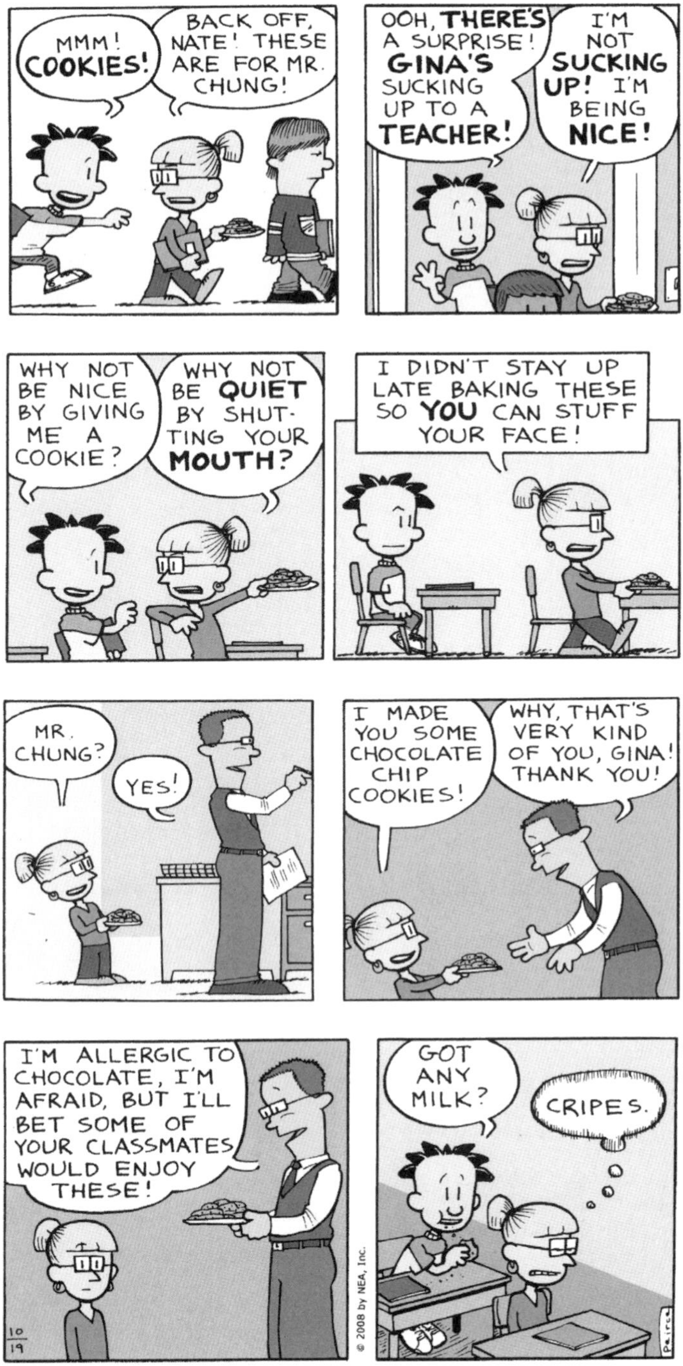
MMM! COOKIES!
BACK OFF, NATE! THESE ARE FOR MR. CHUNG!
OOH, THERE'S A SURPRISE! GINA'S SUCKING UP TO A TEACHER!
I'M NOT SUCKING UP! I'M BEING NICE!
WHY NOT BE NICE BY GIVING ME A COOKIE?
WHY NOT BE QUIET BY SHUTTING YOUR MOUTH?
I DIDN'T STAY UP LATE BAKING THESE SO YOU CAN STUFF YOUR FACE!
MR. CHUNG?
YES!
I MADE YOU SOME CHOCOLATE CHIP COOKIES!
WHY, THAT'S VERY KIND OF YOU, GINA! THANK YOU!
I'M ALLERGIC TO CHOCOLATE, I'M AFRAID, BUT I'LL BET SOME OF YOUR CLASSMATES WOULD ENJOY THESE!
10 19
© 2008 by NEA, Inc.
GOT ANY MILK?
CRIPES.
Peirce

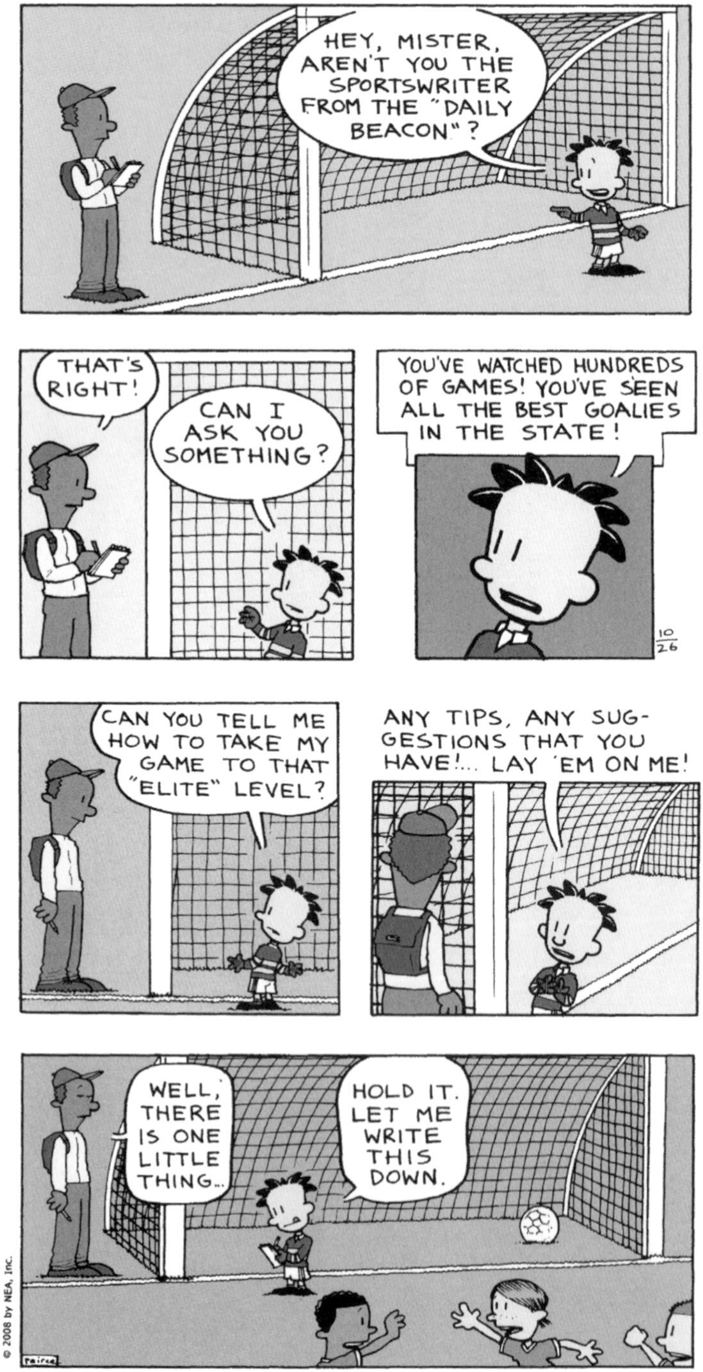
HEY, MISTER, AREN'T YOU THE SPORTSWRITER FROM THE "DAILY BEACON"?
THAT'S RIGHT!
CAN I ASK YOU SOMETHING?
YOU'VE WATCHED HUNDREDS OF GAMES! YOU'VE SEEN ALL THE BEST GOALIES IN THE STATE!
10/26
CAN YOU TELL ME HOW TO TAKE MY GAME TO THAT "ELITE" LEVEL?
ANY TIPS, ANY SUGGESTIONS THAT YOU HAVE!... LAY 'EM ON ME!
WELL, THERE IS ONE LITTLE THING...
HOLD IT. LET ME WRITE THIS DOWN.
© 2008 by NEA, Inc.
peirce

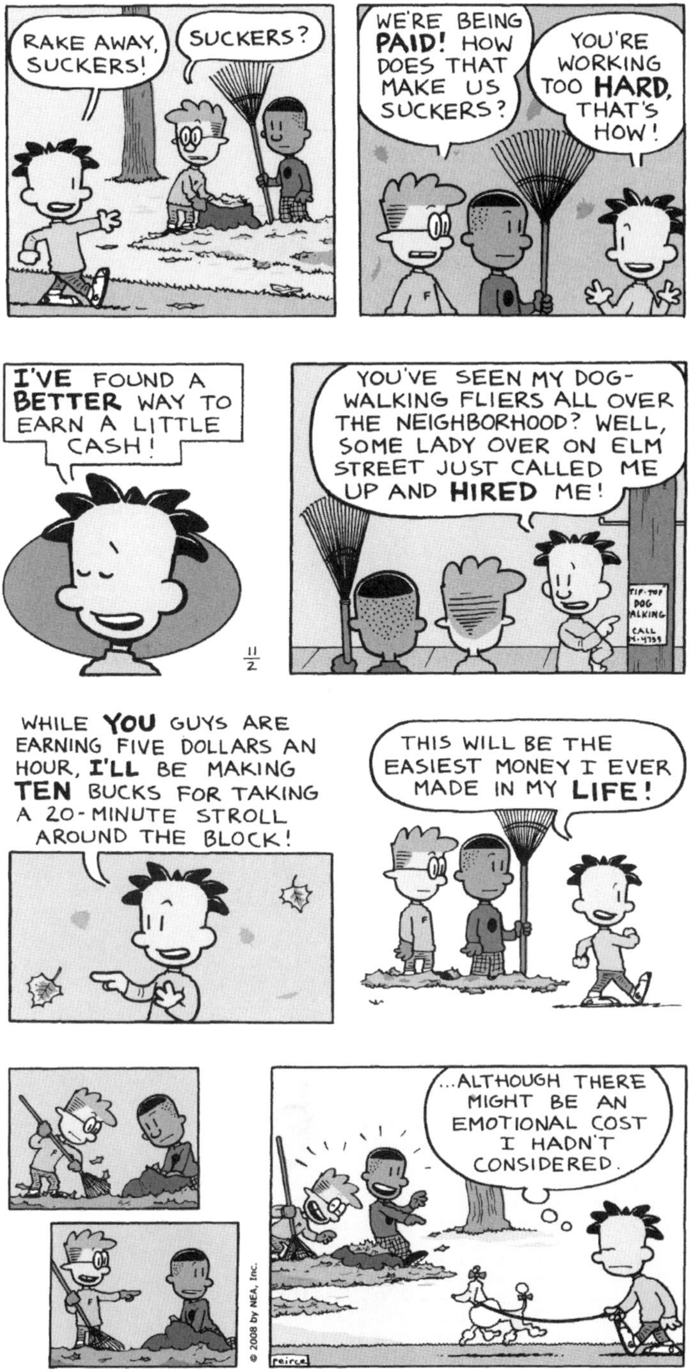
RAKE AWAY, SUCKERS!
SUCKERS?
WE'RE BEING PAID! HOW DOES THAT MAKE US SUCKERS?
YOU'RE WORKING TOO HARD, THAT'S HOW!
I'VE FOUND A BETTER WAY TO EARN A LITTLE CASH!
11/2
YOU'VE SEEN MY DOG-WALKING FLIERS ALL OVER THE NEIGHBORHOOD? WELL, SOME LADY OVER ON ELM STREET JUST CALLED ME UP AND HIRED ME!
WHILE YOU GUYS ARE EARNING FIVE DOLLARS AN HOUR, I'LL BE MAKING TEN BUCKS FOR TAKING A 20-MINUTE STROLL AROUND THE BLOCK!
THIS WILL BE THE EASIEST MONEY I EVER MADE IN MY LIFE!
© 2008 by NEA, Inc.
...ALTHOUGH THERE MIGHT BE AN EMOTIONAL COST I HADN'T CONSIDERED.
peirce

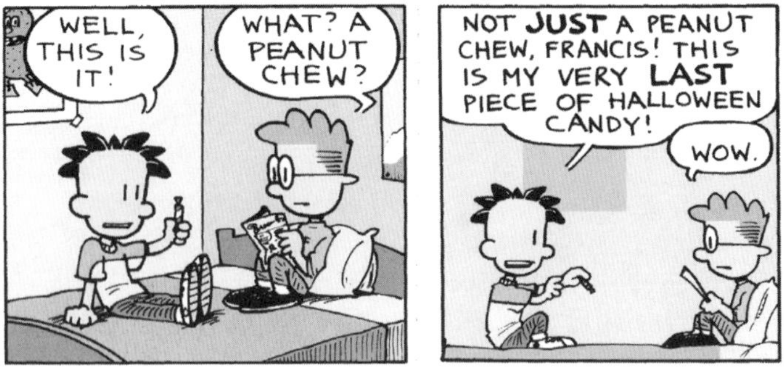
WELL, THIS IS IT!
WHAT? A PEANUT CHEW?
NOT **JUST** A PEANUT CHEW, FRANCIS! THIS IS MY VERY **LAST** PIECE OF HALLOWEEN CANDY!
WOW.

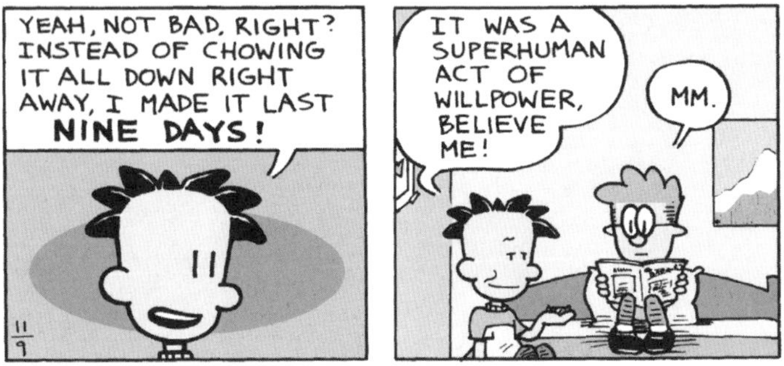
YEAH, NOT BAD, RIGHT? INSTEAD OF CHOWING IT ALL DOWN RIGHT AWAY, I MADE IT LAST **NINE DAYS**!
11/9
IT WAS A SUPERHUMAN ACT OF WILLPOWER, BELIEVE ME!
MM.

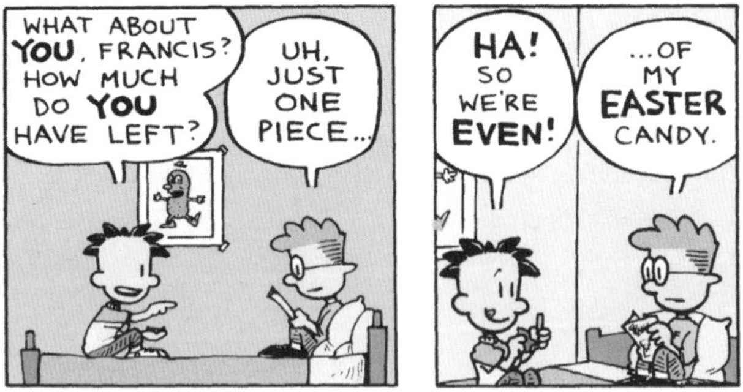
WHAT ABOUT **YOU**, FRANCIS? HOW MUCH DO **YOU** HAVE LEFT?
UH, JUST ONE PIECE...
HA! SO WE'RE **EVEN**!
...OF MY **EASTER** CANDY.

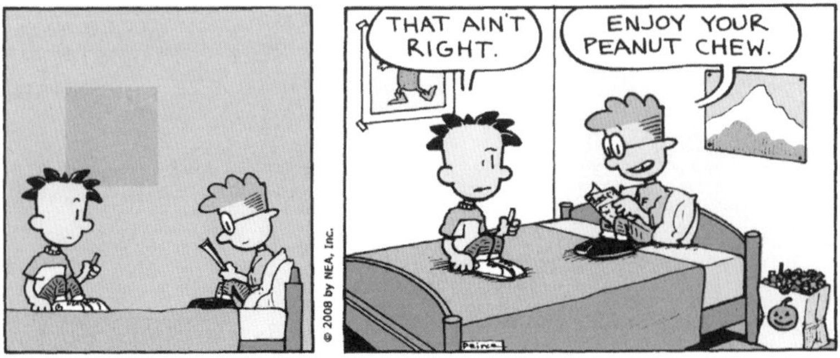
THAT AIN'T RIGHT.
ENJOY YOUR PEANUT CHEW.

CATFIGHT!

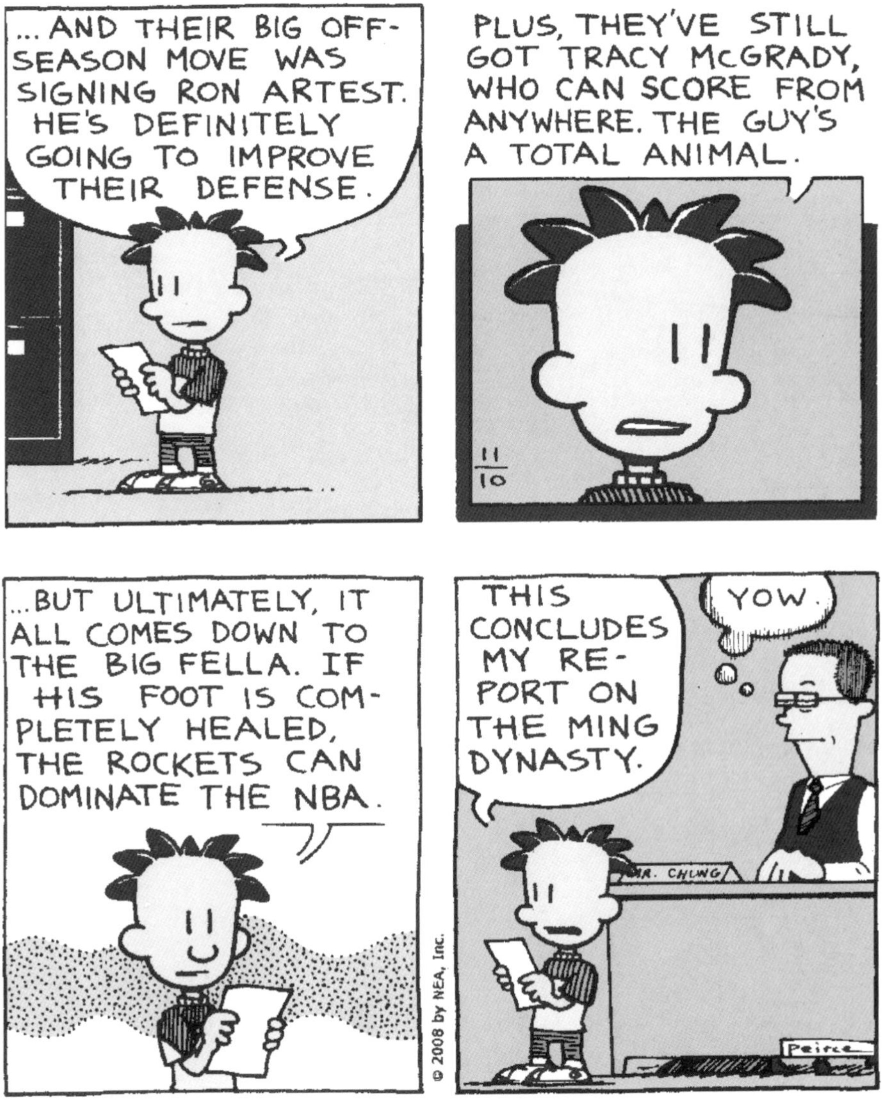
...AND THEIR BIG OFF-SEASON MOVE WAS SIGNING RON ARTEST. HE'S DEFINITELY GOING TO IMPROVE THEIR DEFENSE.
PLUS, THEY'VE STILL GOT TRACY McGRADY, WHO CAN SCORE FROM ANYWHERE. THE GUY'S A TOTAL ANIMAL.
11/10
...BUT ULTIMATELY, IT ALL COMES DOWN TO THE BIG FELLA. IF HIS FOOT IS COMPLETELY HEALED, THE ROCKETS CAN DOMINATE THE NBA.
THIS CONCLUDES MY REPORT ON THE MING DYNASTY.
YOW.
MR. CHUNG
© 2008 by NEA, Inc.
Peirce

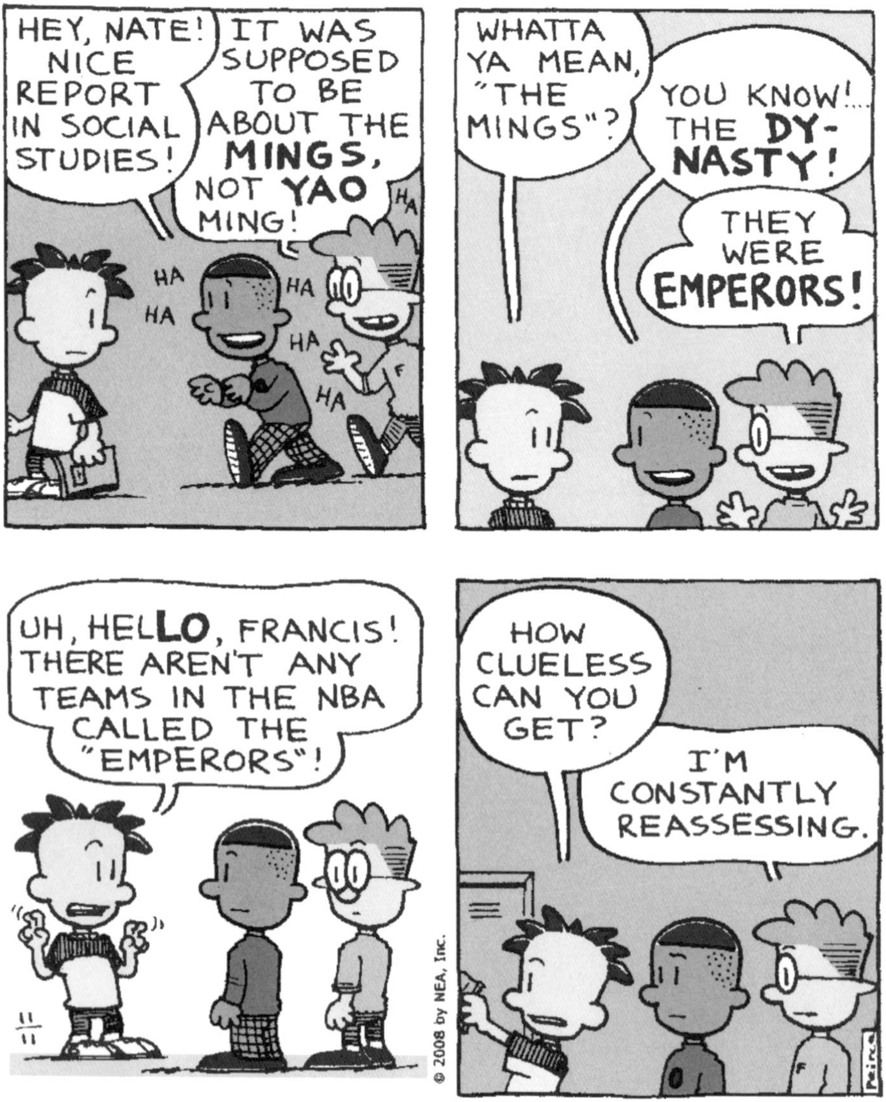
HEY, NATE! NICE REPORT IN SOCIAL STUDIES!
IT WAS SUPPOSED TO BE ABOUT THE MINGS, NOT YAO MING!
HA HA HA HA HA HA
WHATTA YA MEAN, "THE MINGS"?
YOU KNOW!... THE DY-NASTY!
THEY WERE EMPERORS!
UH, HELLO, FRANCIS! THERE AREN'T ANY TEAMS IN THE NBA CALLED THE "EMPERORS"!
HOW CLUELESS CAN YOU GET?
I'M CONSTANTLY REASSESSING.
Peirce

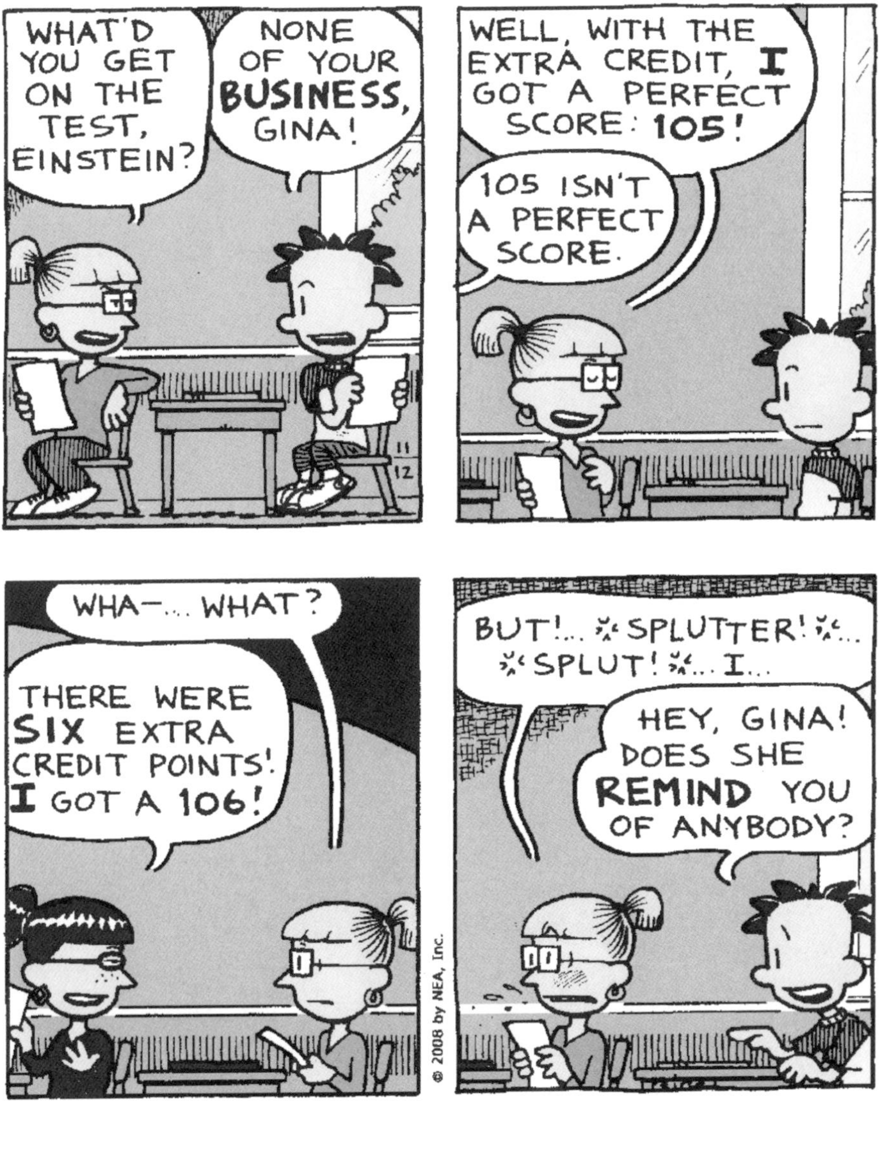
WHAT'D YOU GET ON THE TEST, EINSTEIN?
NONE OF YOUR **BUSINESS**, GINA!
WELL, WITH THE EXTRA CREDIT, **I** GOT A PERFECT SCORE: **105**!
105 ISN'T A PERFECT SCORE.
WHA-... WHAT?
THERE WERE **SIX** EXTRA CREDIT POINTS! **I** GOT A **106**!
BUT!... SPLUTTER!... SPLUT!... I...
HEY, GINA! DOES SHE **REMIND** YOU OF ANYBODY?
© 2008 by NEA, Inc.

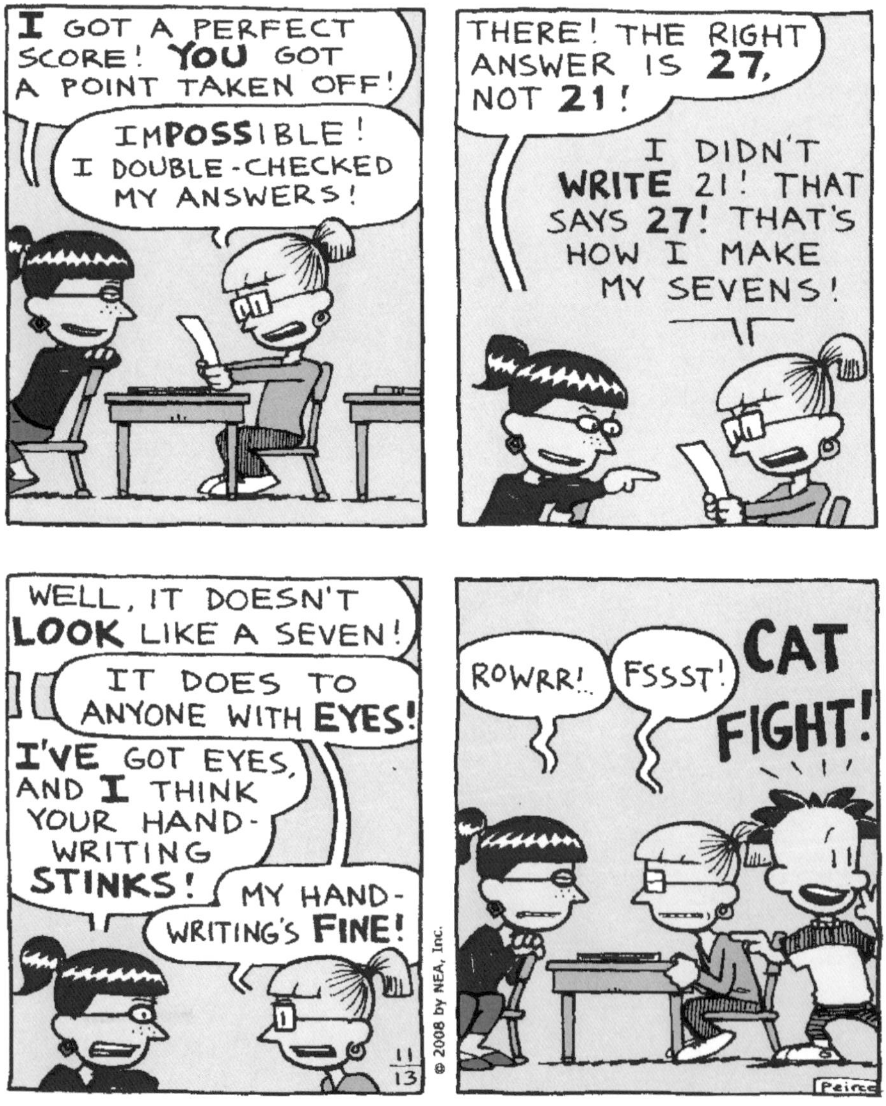
I GOT A PERFECT SCORE! YOU GOT A POINT TAKEN OFF!
IMPOSSIBLE! I DOUBLE-CHECKED MY ANSWERS!
THERE! THE RIGHT ANSWER IS 27, NOT 21!
I DIDN'T WRITE 21! THAT SAYS 27! THAT'S HOW I MAKE MY SEVENS!
WELL, IT DOESN'T LOOK LIKE A SEVEN!
IT DOES TO ANYONE WITH EYES!
I'VE GOT EYES, AND I THINK YOUR HAND-WRITING STINKS!
MY HAND-WRITING'S FINE!
11/13
© 2008 by NEA, Inc.
ROWRR!..
FSSST!
CAT FIGHT!
Peirce

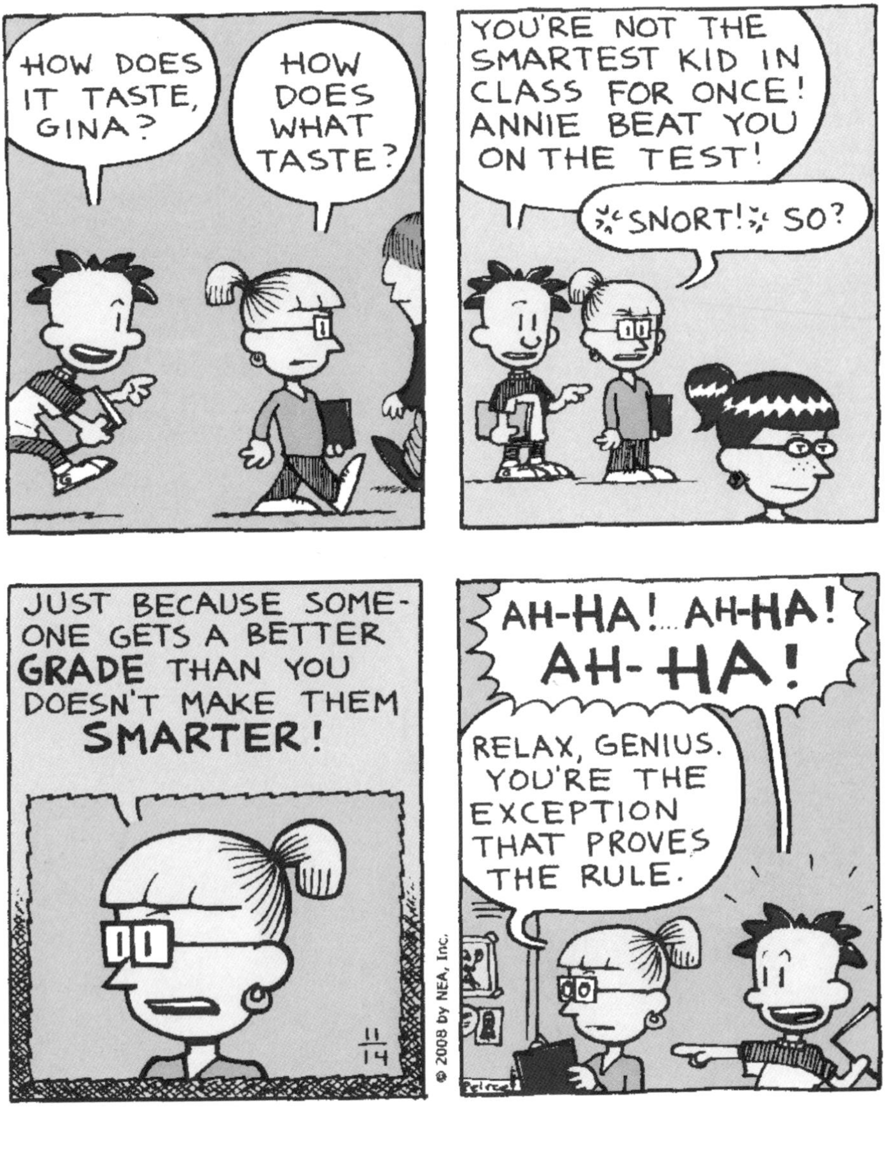
HOW DOES IT TASTE, GINA?
HOW DOES WHAT TASTE?
YOU'RE NOT THE SMARTEST KID IN CLASS FOR ONCE! ANNIE BEAT YOU ON THE TEST!
SNORT! SO?
JUST BECAUSE SOME-ONE GETS A BETTER GRADE THAN YOU DOESN'T MAKE THEM SMARTER!
11 14
© 2008 by NEA, Inc.
AH-HA!... AH-HA! AH-HA!
RELAX, GENIUS. YOU'RE THE EXCEPTION THAT PROVES THE RULE.
Peirce

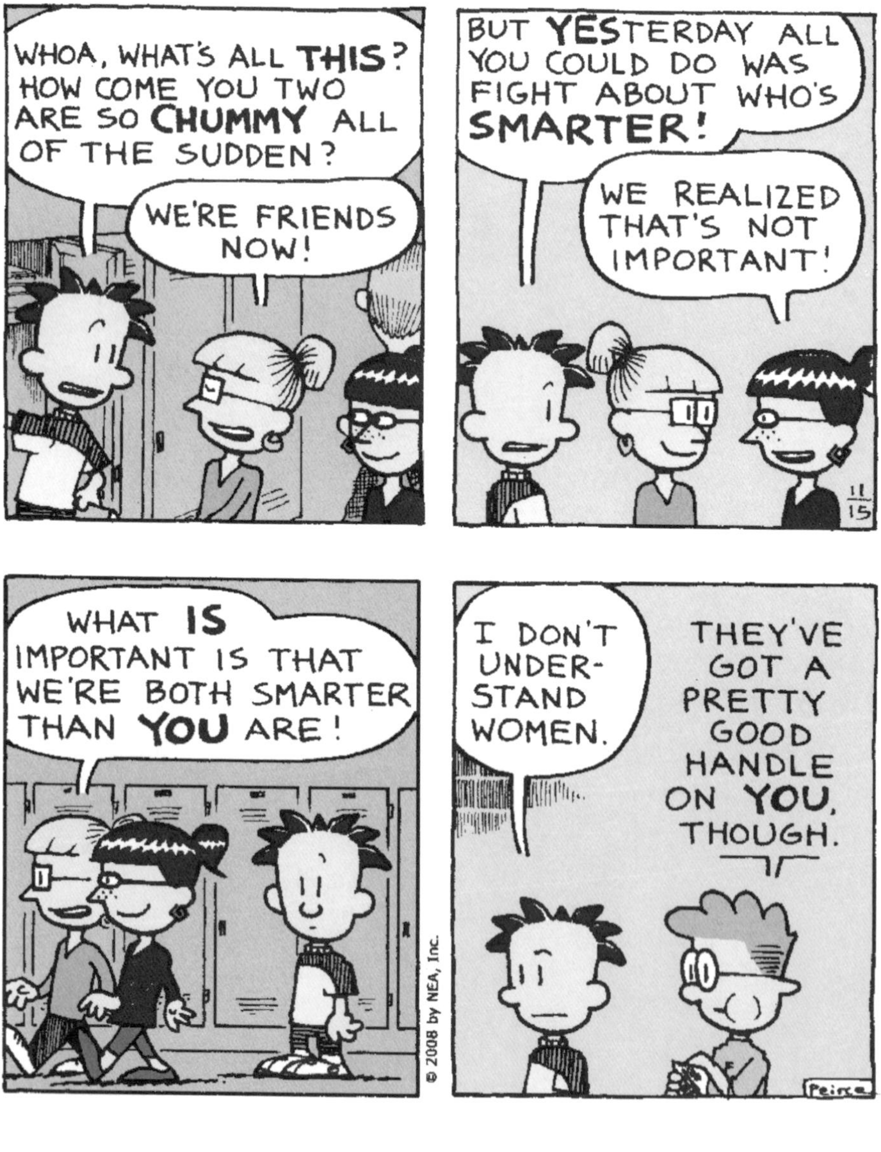
WHOA, WHAT'S ALL **THIS**? HOW COME YOU TWO ARE SO **CHUMMY** ALL OF THE SUDDEN?
WE'RE FRIENDS NOW!
BUT **YES**TERDAY ALL YOU COULD DO WAS FIGHT ABOUT WHO'S **SMARTER**!
WE REALIZED THAT'S NOT IMPORTANT!
11/15
WHAT **IS** IMPORTANT IS THAT WE'RE BOTH SMARTER THAN **YOU** ARE!
© 2008 by NEA, Inc.
I DON'T UNDER-STAND WOMEN.
THEY'VE GOT A PRETTY GOOD HANDLE ON **YOU**, THOUGH.
Peirce

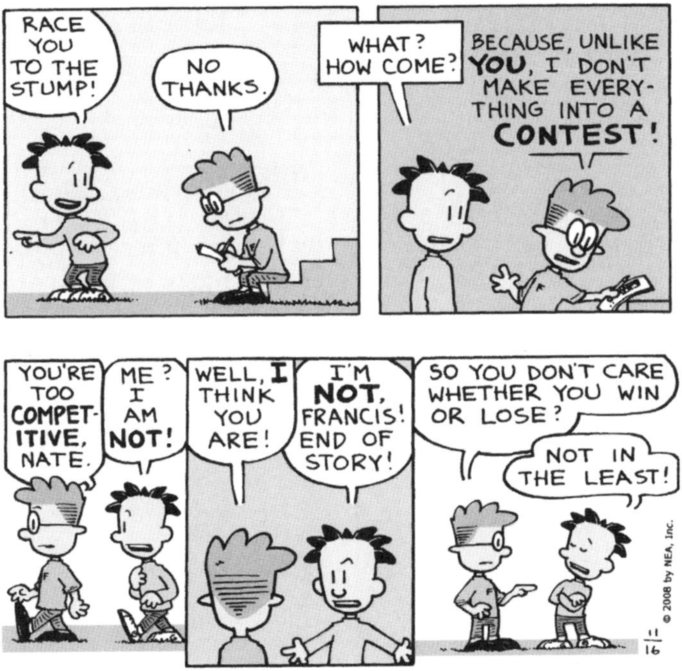
RACE YOU TO THE STUMP!
NO THANKS.
WHAT? HOW COME?
BECAUSE, UNLIKE YOU, I DON'T MAKE EVERY-THING INTO A CONTEST!
YOU'RE TOO COMPET-ITIVE, NATE.
ME? I AM NOT!
WELL, I THINK YOU ARE!
I'M NOT, FRANCIS! END OF STORY!
SO YOU DON'T CARE WHETHER YOU WIN OR LOSE?
NOT IN THE LEAST!
11/16
© 2008 by NEA, Inc.

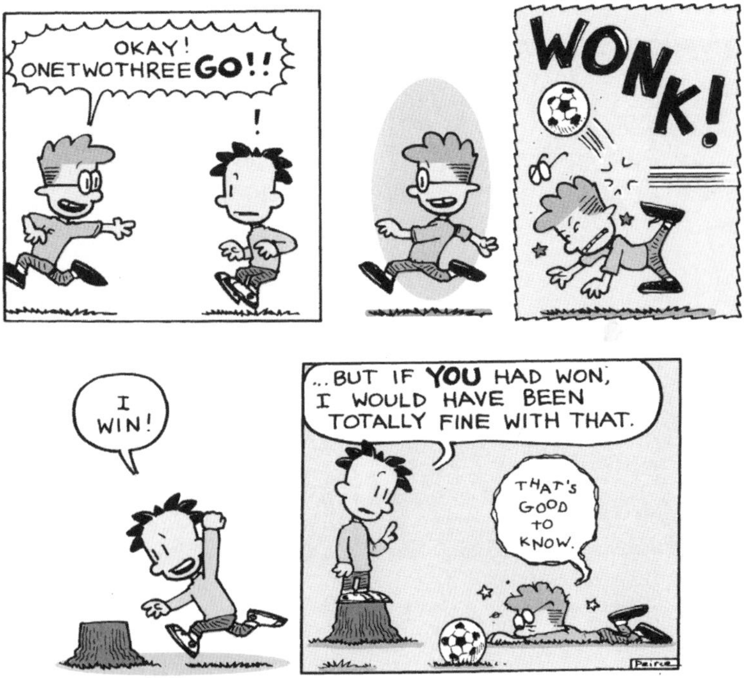
OKAY! ONETWOTHREEGO!!
!
WONK!
I WIN!
...BUT IF YOU HAD WON, I WOULD HAVE BEEN TOTALLY FINE WITH THAT.
THAT'S GOOD TO KNOW.
PEIRCE

NATE WRIGHT, SUPERBLOGGER

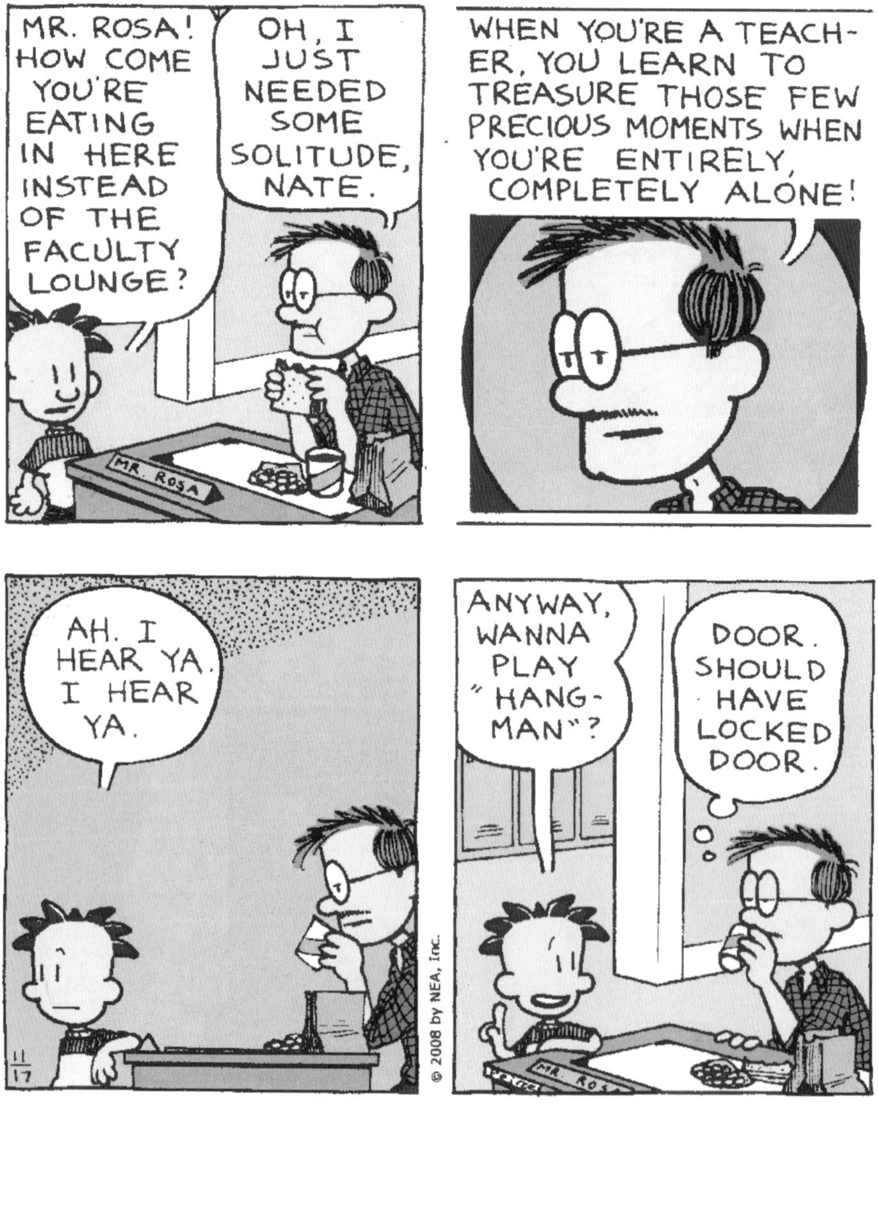
MR. ROSA! HOW COME YOU'RE EATING IN HERE INSTEAD OF THE FACULTY LOUNGE?
OH, I JUST NEEDED SOME SOLITUDE, NATE.
MR. ROSA
WHEN YOU'RE A TEACHER, YOU LEARN TO TREASURE THOSE FEW PRECIOUS MOMENTS WHEN YOU'RE ENTIRELY, COMPLETELY ALONE!
AH. I HEAR YA. I HEAR YA.
11/17
© 2008 by NEA, Inc.
ANYWAY, WANNA PLAY "HANG-MAN"?
DOOR. SHOULD HAVE LOCKED DOOR.
MR. ROSA

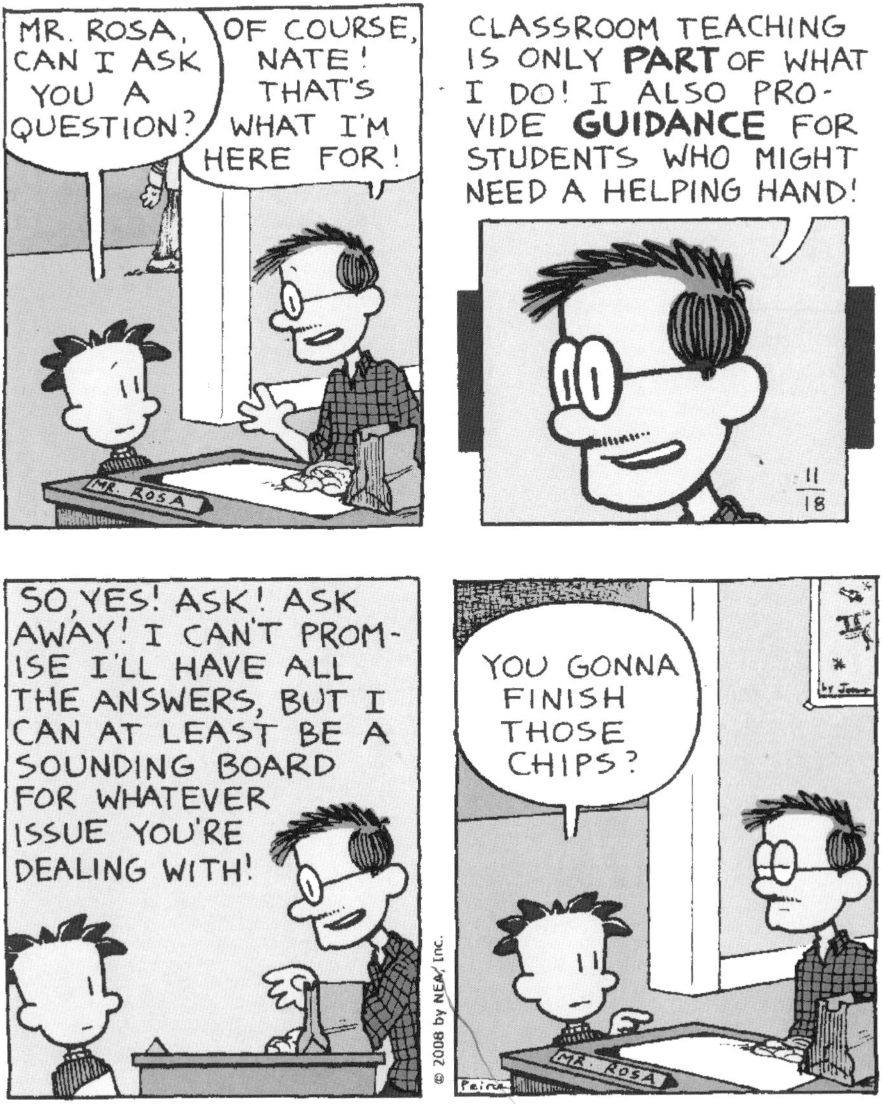
MR. ROSA, CAN I ASK YOU A QUESTION?
OF COURSE, NATE! THAT'S WHAT I'M HERE FOR!
MR. ROSA
CLASSROOM TEACHING IS ONLY **PART** OF WHAT I DO! I ALSO PROVIDE **GUIDANCE** FOR STUDENTS WHO MIGHT NEED A HELPING HAND!
11 18
SO, YES! ASK! ASK AWAY! I CAN'T PROMISE I'LL HAVE ALL THE ANSWERS, BUT I CAN AT LEAST BE A SOUNDING BOARD FOR WHATEVER ISSUE YOU'RE DEALING WITH!
© 2008 by NEA, Inc.
YOU GONNA FINISH THOSE CHIPS?
MR. ROSA
Peirce

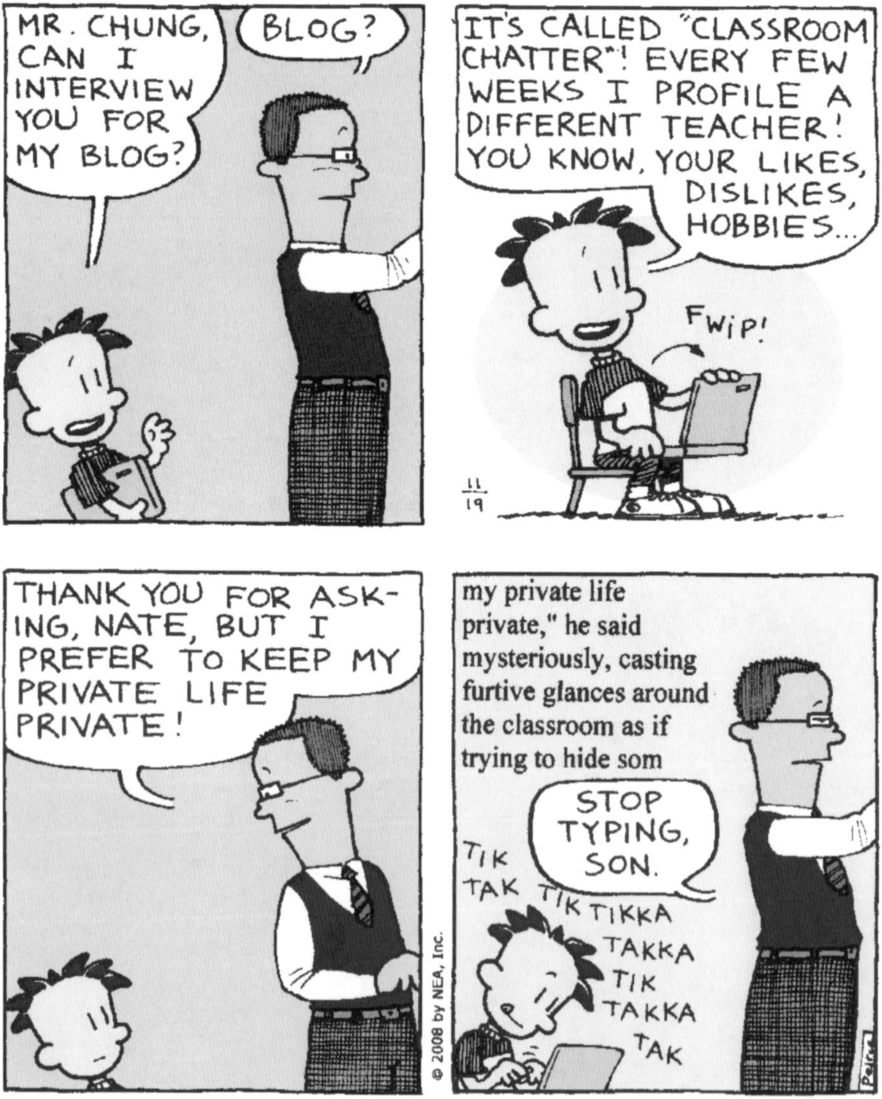
MR. CHUNG, CAN I INTERVIEW YOU FOR MY BLOG?
BLOG?
IT'S CALLED "CLASSROOM CHATTER"! EVERY FEW WEEKS I PROFILE A DIFFERENT TEACHER! YOU KNOW, YOUR LIKES, DISLIKES, HOBBIES...
FWIP!
11/19
THANK YOU FOR ASKING, NATE, BUT I PREFER TO KEEP MY PRIVATE LIFE PRIVATE!
© 2008 by NEA, Inc.
my private life private," he said mysteriously, casting furtive glances around the classroom as if trying to hide som
STOP TYPING, SON.
TIK TAK TIK TIKKA TAKKA TIK TAKKA TAK
Peirce

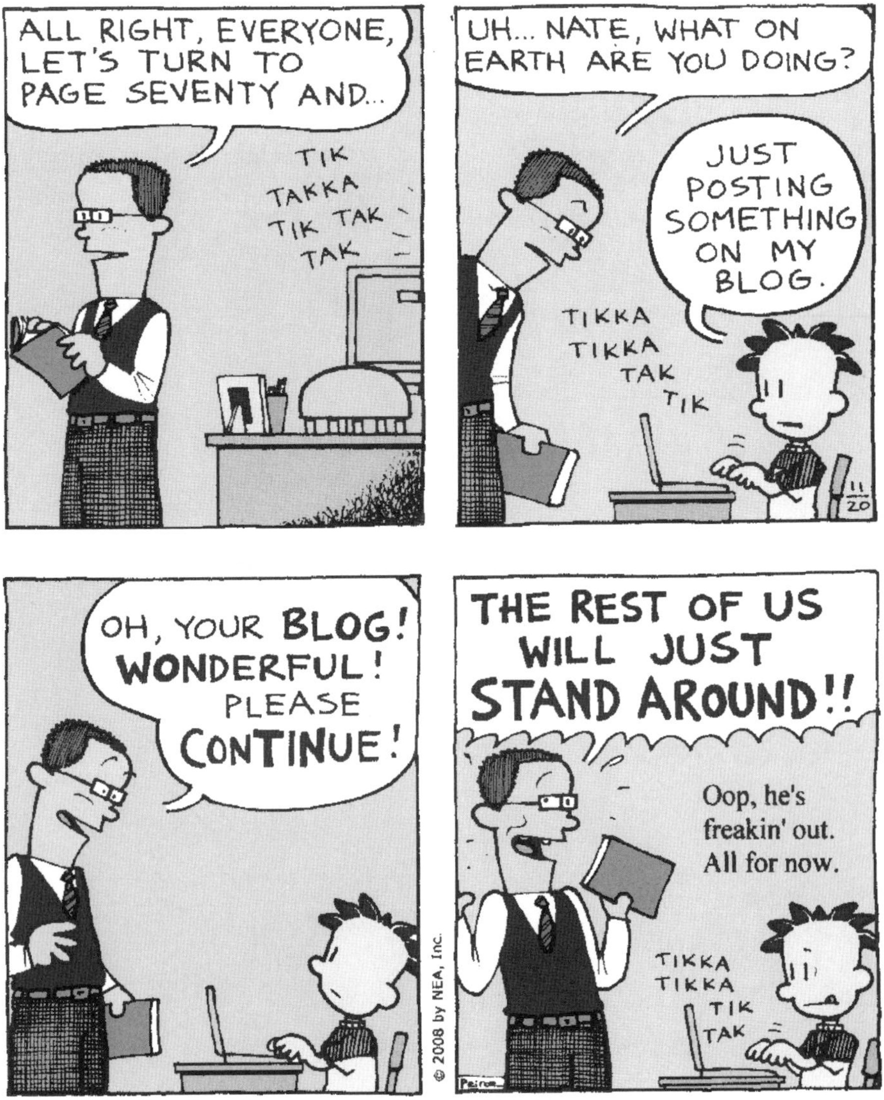

ALL RIGHT, EVERYONE, LET'S TURN TO PAGE SEVENTY AND...
TIK TAKKA TIK TAK TAK
UH... NATE, WHAT ON EARTH ARE YOU DOING?
JUST POSTING SOMETHING ON MY BLOG.
TIKKA TIKKA TAK TIK
OH, YOUR BLOG! WONDERFUL! PLEASE CONTINUE!
THE REST OF US WILL JUST STAND AROUND!!
Oop, he's freakin' out. All for now.
TIKKA TIKKA TIK TAK

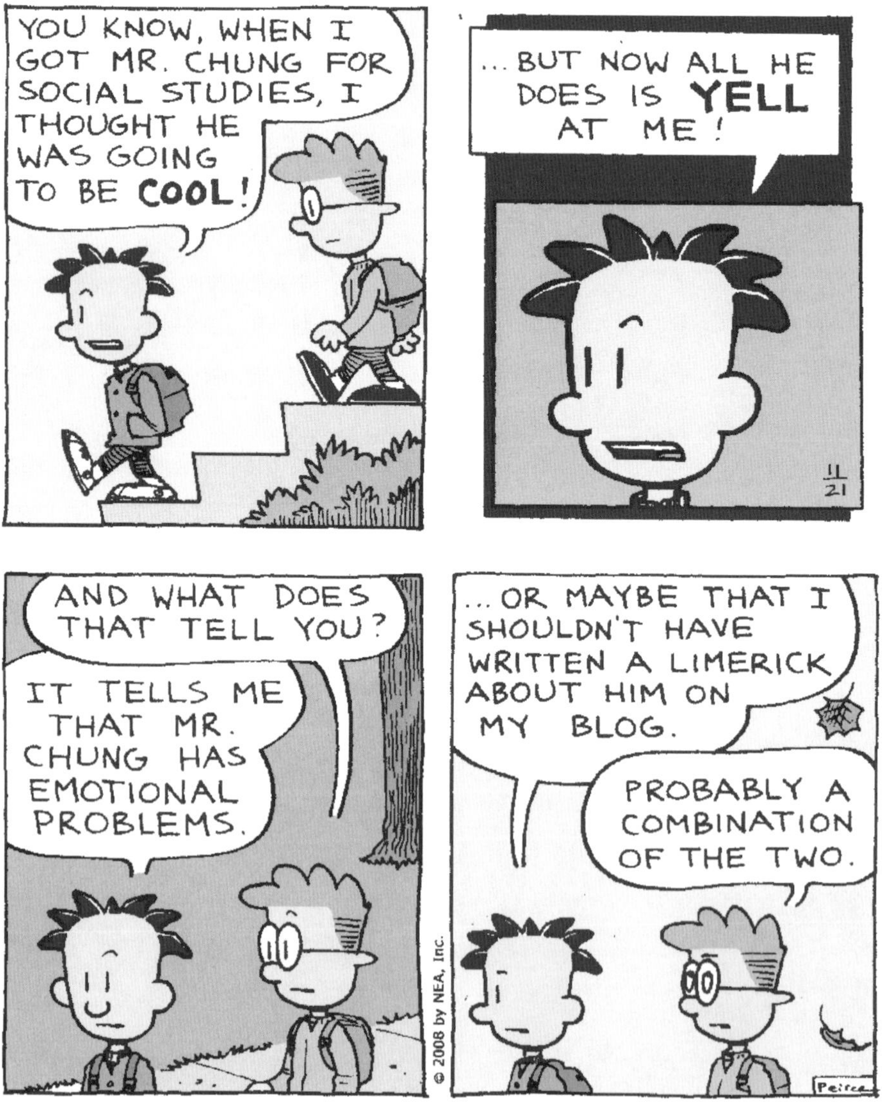
YOU KNOW, WHEN I GOT MR. CHUNG FOR SOCIAL STUDIES, I THOUGHT HE WAS GOING TO BE COOL!
...BUT NOW ALL HE DOES IS YELL AT ME!
11 21
AND WHAT DOES THAT TELL YOU?
IT TELLS ME THAT MR. CHUNG HAS EMOTIONAL PROBLEMS.
© 2008 by NEA, Inc.
...OR MAYBE THAT I SHOULDN'T HAVE WRITTEN A LIMERICK ABOUT HIM ON MY BLOG.
PROBABLY A COMBINATION OF THE TWO.
Peirce

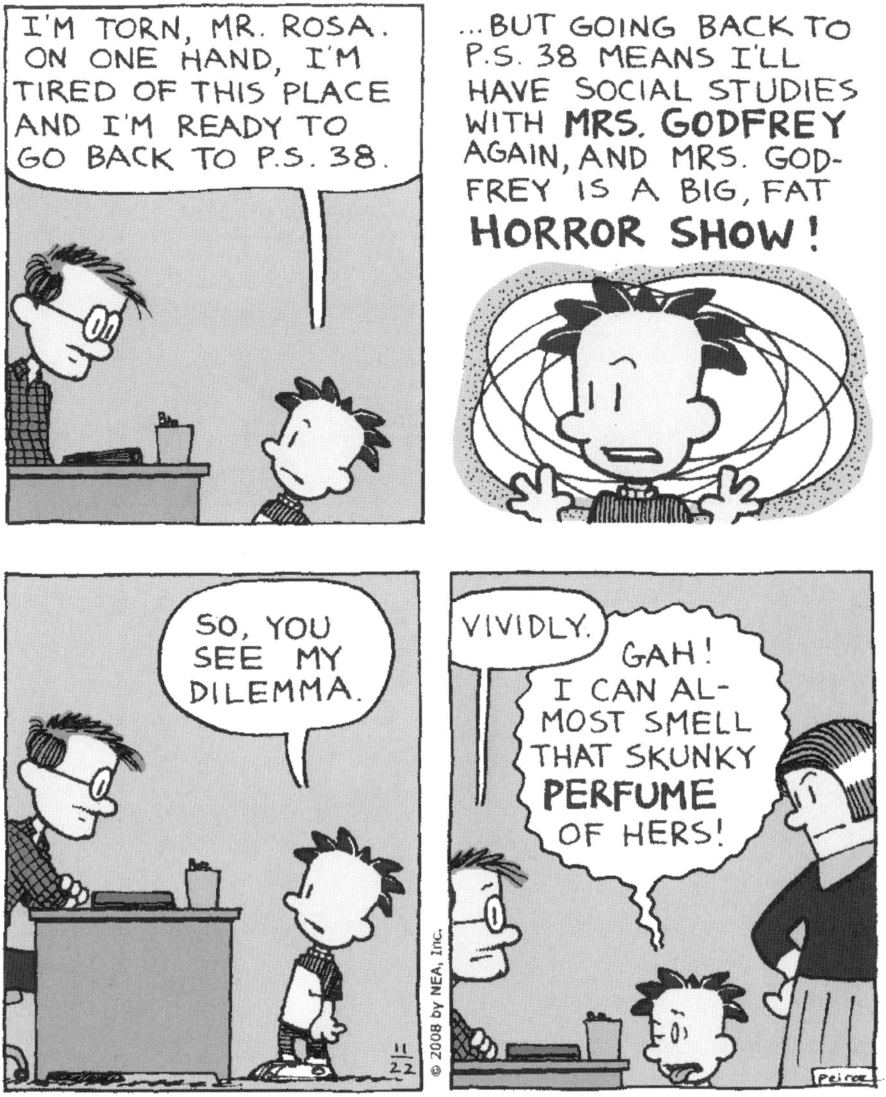
I'M TORN, MR. ROSA. ON ONE HAND, I'M TIRED OF THIS PLACE AND I'M READY TO GO BACK TO P.S. 38.
...BUT GOING BACK TO P.S. 38 MEANS I'LL HAVE SOCIAL STUDIES WITH MRS. GODFREY AGAIN, AND MRS. GODFREY IS A BIG, FAT HORROR SHOW!
SO, YOU SEE MY DILEMMA.
11 22
© 2008 by NEA, Inc.
VIVIDLY.
GAH! I CAN ALMOST SMELL THAT SKUNKY PERFUME OF HERS!
Peirce

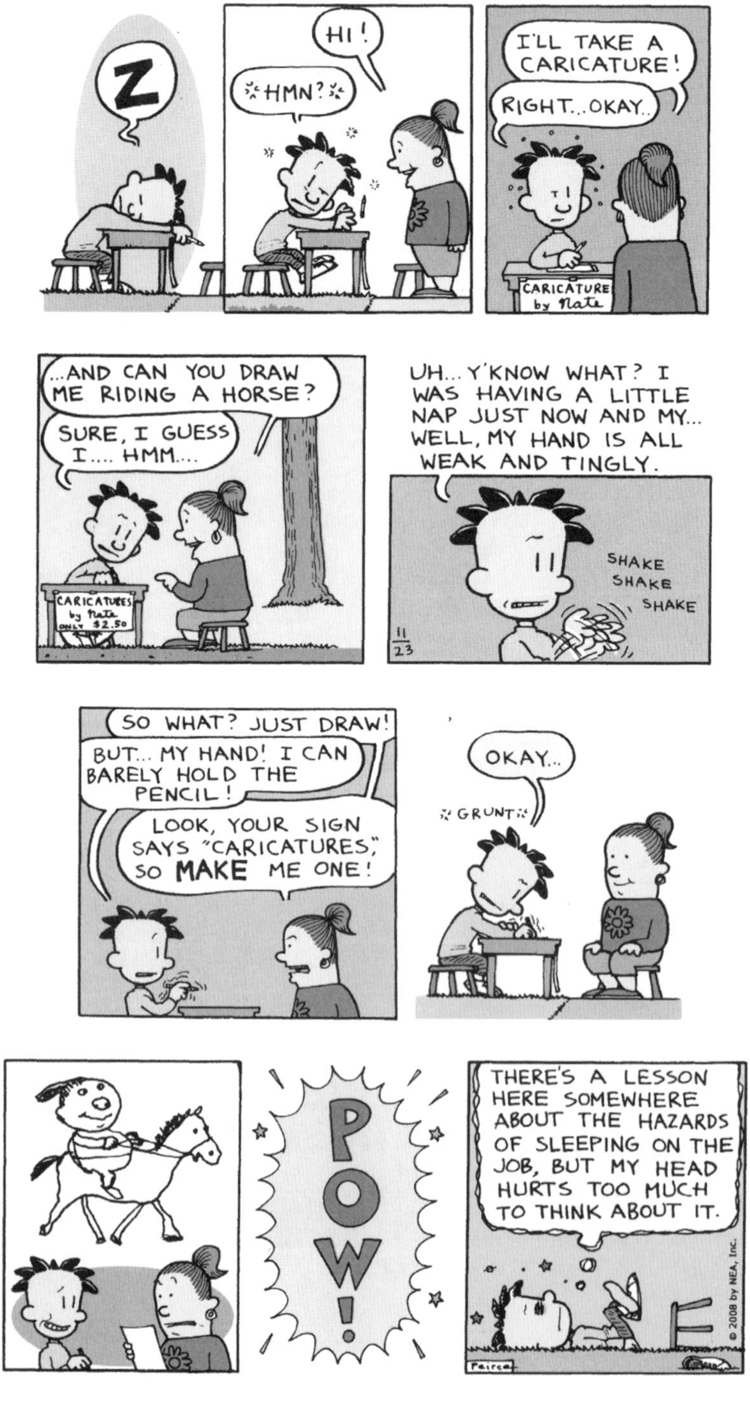
Z
HI!
HMN?
I'LL TAKE A CARICATURE!
RIGHT... OKAY...
CARICATURES by Nate
...AND CAN YOU DRAW ME RIDING A HORSE?
SURE, I GUESS I.... HMM....
CARICATURES by Nate ONLY $2.50
UH... Y'KNOW WHAT? I WAS HAVING A LITTLE NAP JUST NOW AND MY... WELL, MY HAND IS ALL WEAK AND TINGLY.
SHAKE
SHAKE
SHAKE
11/23
SO WHAT? JUST DRAW!
BUT... MY HAND! I CAN BARELY HOLD THE PENCIL!
LOOK, YOUR SIGN SAYS "CARICATURES," SO MAKE ME ONE!
GRUNT
OKAY...
POW!
THERE'S A LESSON HERE SOMEWHERE ABOUT THE HAZARDS OF SLEEPING ON THE JOB, BUT MY HEAD HURTS TOO MUCH TO THINK ABOUT IT.
Peirce
© 2008 by NEA, Inc.

NATE'S "FIRST" THANKSGIVING

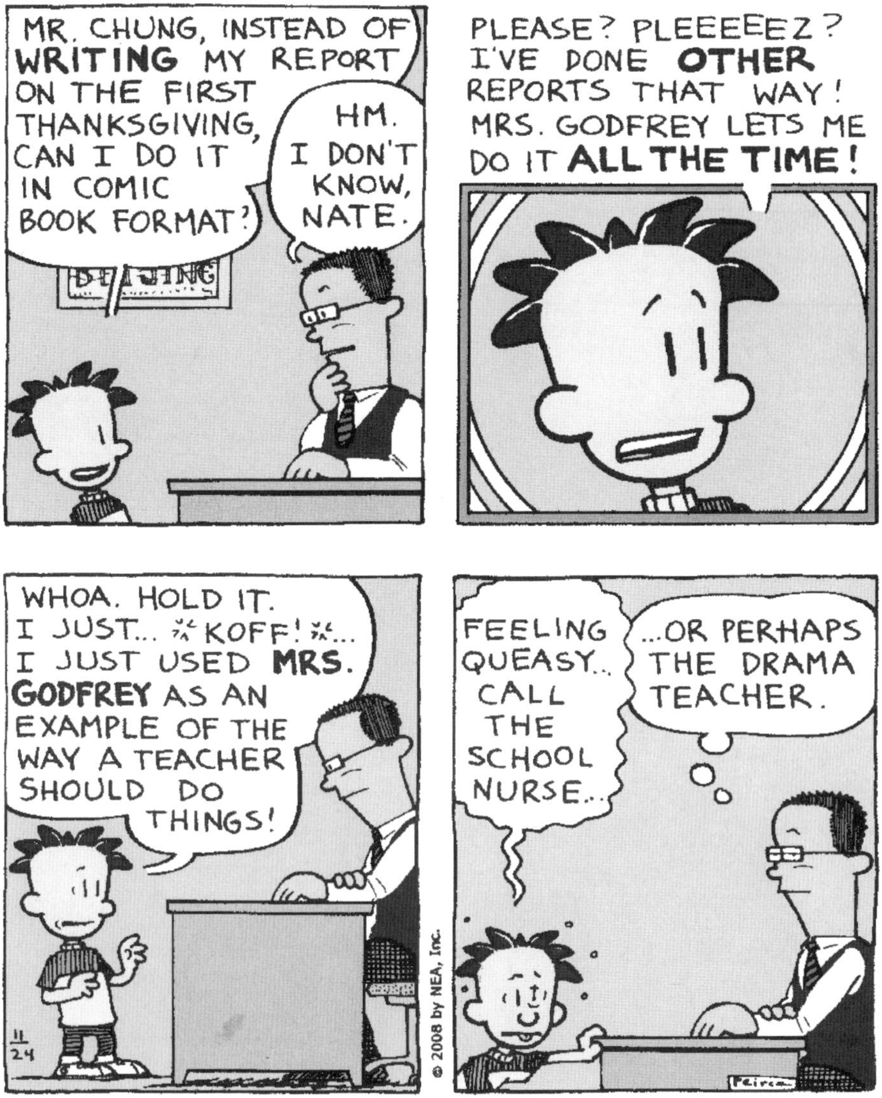
MR. CHUNG, INSTEAD OF WRITING MY REPORT ON THE FIRST THANKSGIVING, CAN I DO IT IN COMIC BOOK FORMAT?
HM. I DON'T KNOW, NATE.
PLEASE? PLEEEEEEZ? I'VE DONE OTHER REPORTS THAT WAY! MRS. GODFREY LETS ME DO IT ALL THE TIME!
WHOA. HOLD IT. I JUST... KOFF!... I JUST USED MRS. GODFREY AS AN EXAMPLE OF THE WAY A TEACHER SHOULD DO THINGS!
11/24
© 2008 by NEA, Inc.
FEELING QUEASY... CALL THE SCHOOL NURSE...
...OR PERHAPS THE DRAMA TEACHER.
Peirce

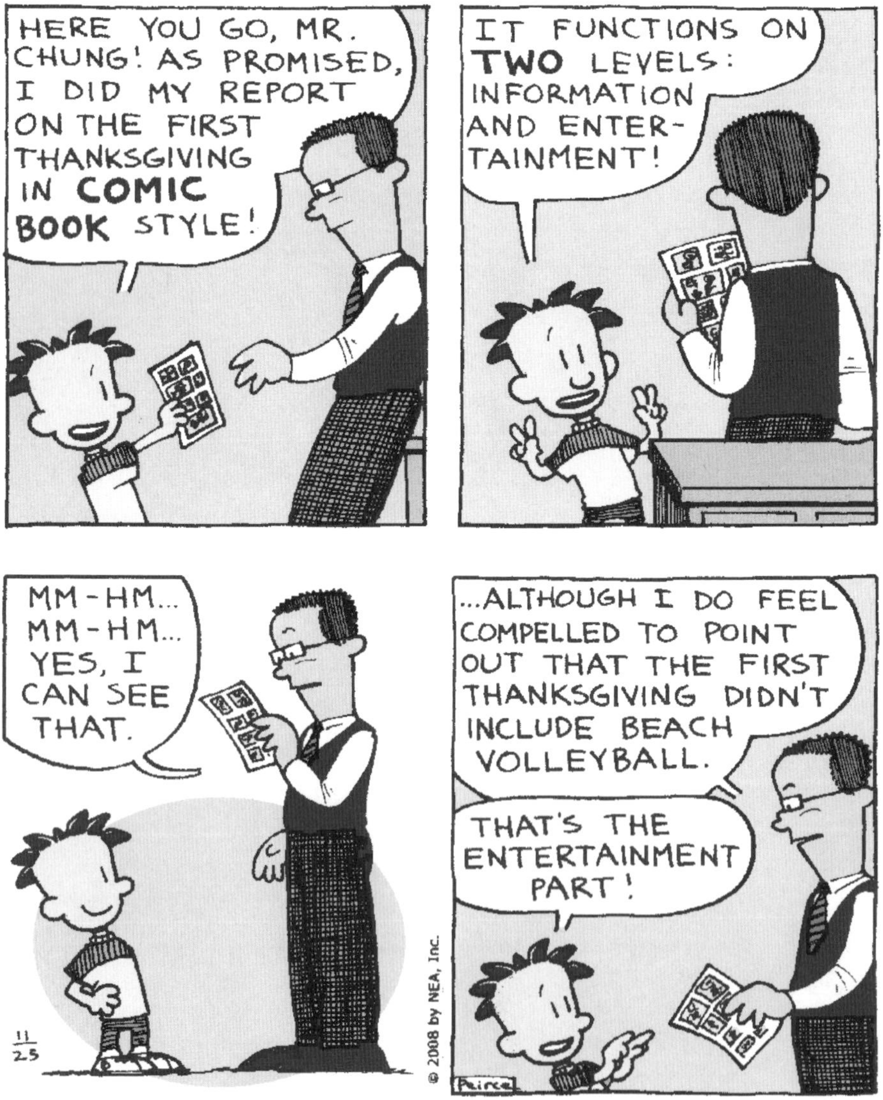
HERE YOU GO, MR. CHUNG! AS PROMISED, I DID MY REPORT ON THE FIRST THANKSGIVING IN **COMIC BOOK** STYLE!
IT FUNCTIONS ON **TWO** LEVELS: INFORMATION AND ENTERTAINMENT!
MM-HM... MM-HM... YES, I CAN SEE THAT.
...ALTHOUGH I DO FEEL COMPELLED TO POINT OUT THAT THE FIRST THANKSGIVING DIDN'T INCLUDE BEACH VOLLEYBALL.
THAT'S THE ENTERTAINMENT PART!
11/25
Peirce

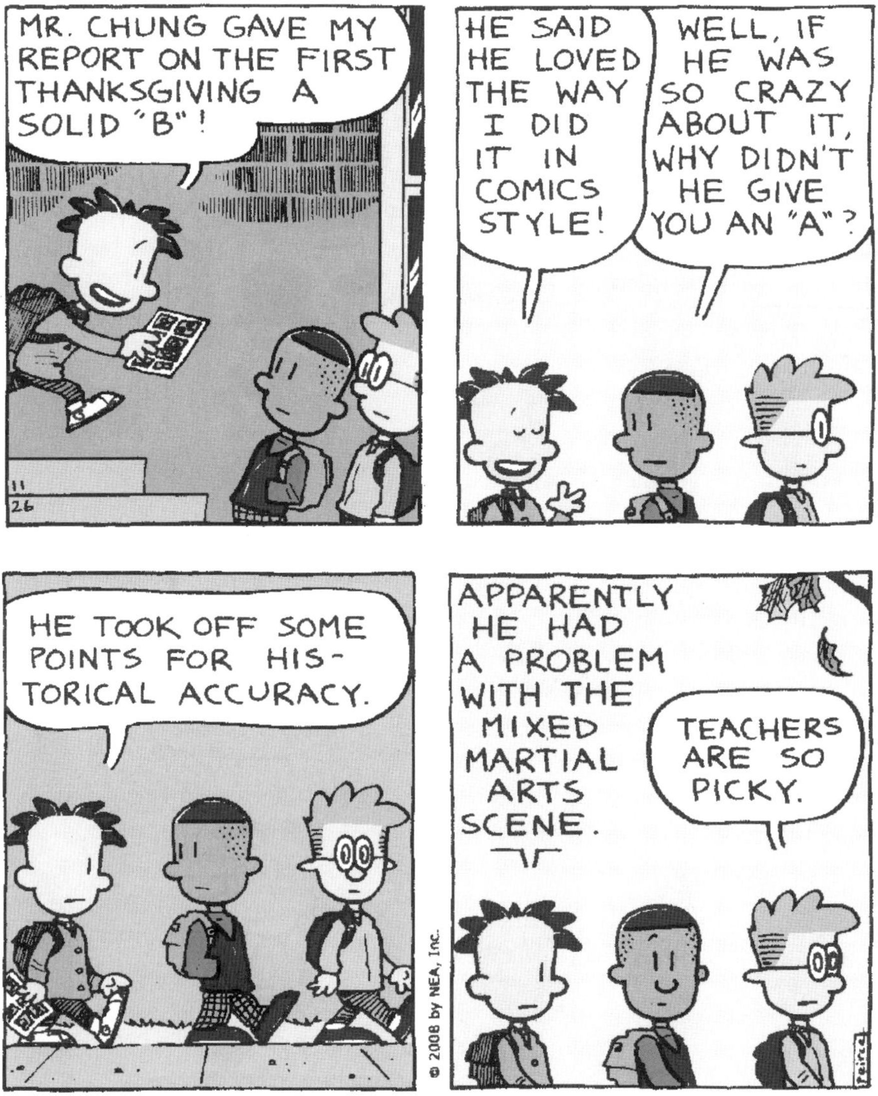
MR. CHUNG GAVE MY REPORT ON THE FIRST THANKSGIVING A SOLID "B"!
11
26
HE SAID HE LOVED THE WAY I DID IT IN COMICS STYLE!
WELL, IF HE WAS SO CRAZY ABOUT IT, WHY DIDN'T HE GIVE YOU AN "A"?
HE TOOK OFF SOME POINTS FOR HIS-TORICAL ACCURACY.
© 2008 by NEA, Inc.
APPARENTLY HE HAD A PROBLEM WITH THE MIXED MARTIAL ARTS SCENE.
TEACHERS ARE SO PICKY.
Peirce

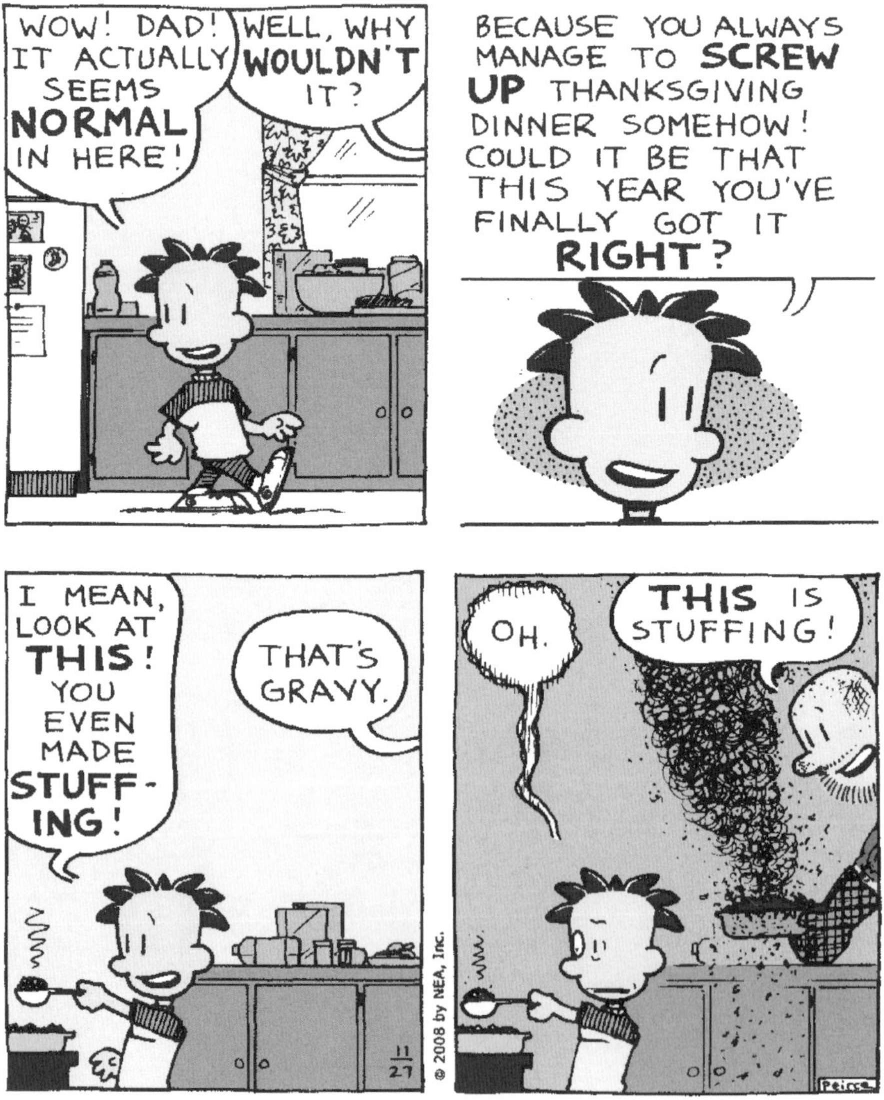
WOW! DAD! IT ACTUALLY SEEMS **NORMAL** IN HERE!
WELL, WHY **WOULDN'T** IT?
BECAUSE YOU ALWAYS MANAGE TO **SCREW UP** THANKSGIVING DINNER SOMEHOW! COULD IT BE THAT THIS YEAR YOU'VE FINALLY GOT IT **RIGHT**?
I MEAN, LOOK AT **THIS**! YOU EVEN MADE **STUFF-ING**!
THAT'S GRAVY.
11 27
© 2008 by NEA, Inc.
OH.
THIS IS STUFFING!
Peirce

OH, THE PAIN!

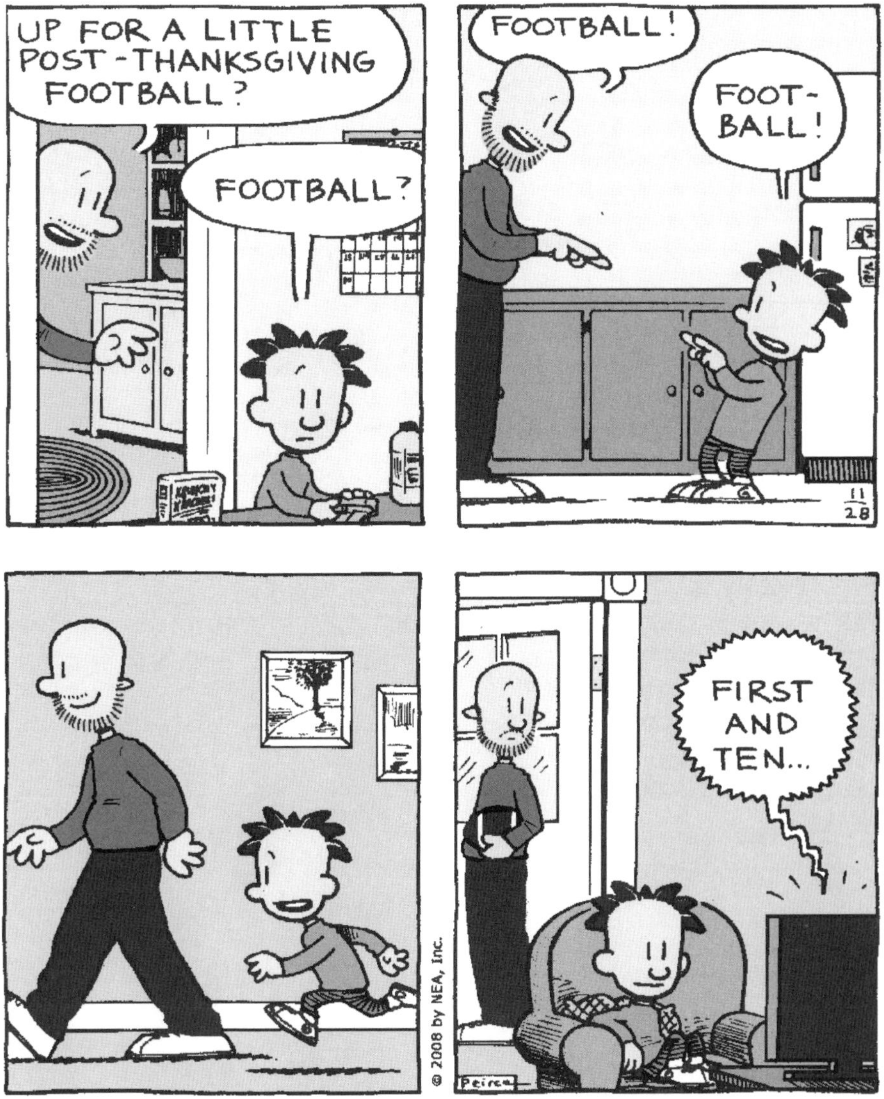
UP FOR A LITTLE POST-THANKSGIVING FOOTBALL?
FOOTBALL?
FOOTBALL!
FOOT-BALL!
11 28
FIRST AND TEN...
© 2008 by NEA, Inc.
Peirce

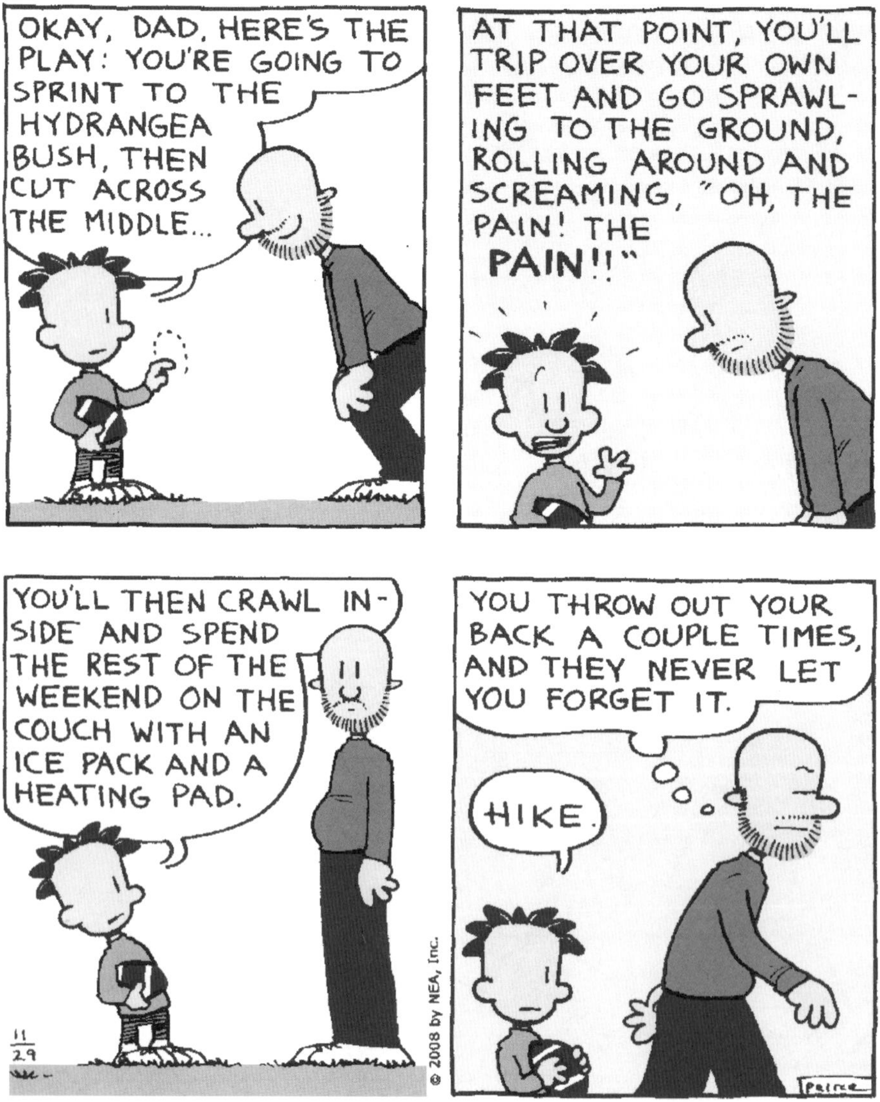
OKAY, DAD, HERE'S THE PLAY: YOU'RE GOING TO SPRINT TO THE HYDRANGEA BUSH, THEN CUT ACROSS THE MIDDLE...
AT THAT POINT, YOU'LL TRIP OVER YOUR OWN FEET AND GO SPRAWLING TO THE GROUND, ROLLING AROUND AND SCREAMING, "OH, THE PAIN! THE **PAIN!!**"
YOU'LL THEN CRAWL INSIDE AND SPEND THE REST OF THE WEEKEND ON THE COUCH WITH AN ICE PACK AND A HEATING PAD.
11/29
© 2008 by NEA, Inc.
YOU THROW OUT YOUR BACK A COUPLE TIMES, AND THEY NEVER LET YOU FORGET IT.
HIKE.
PEIRCE

THE MEANING OF WOOF

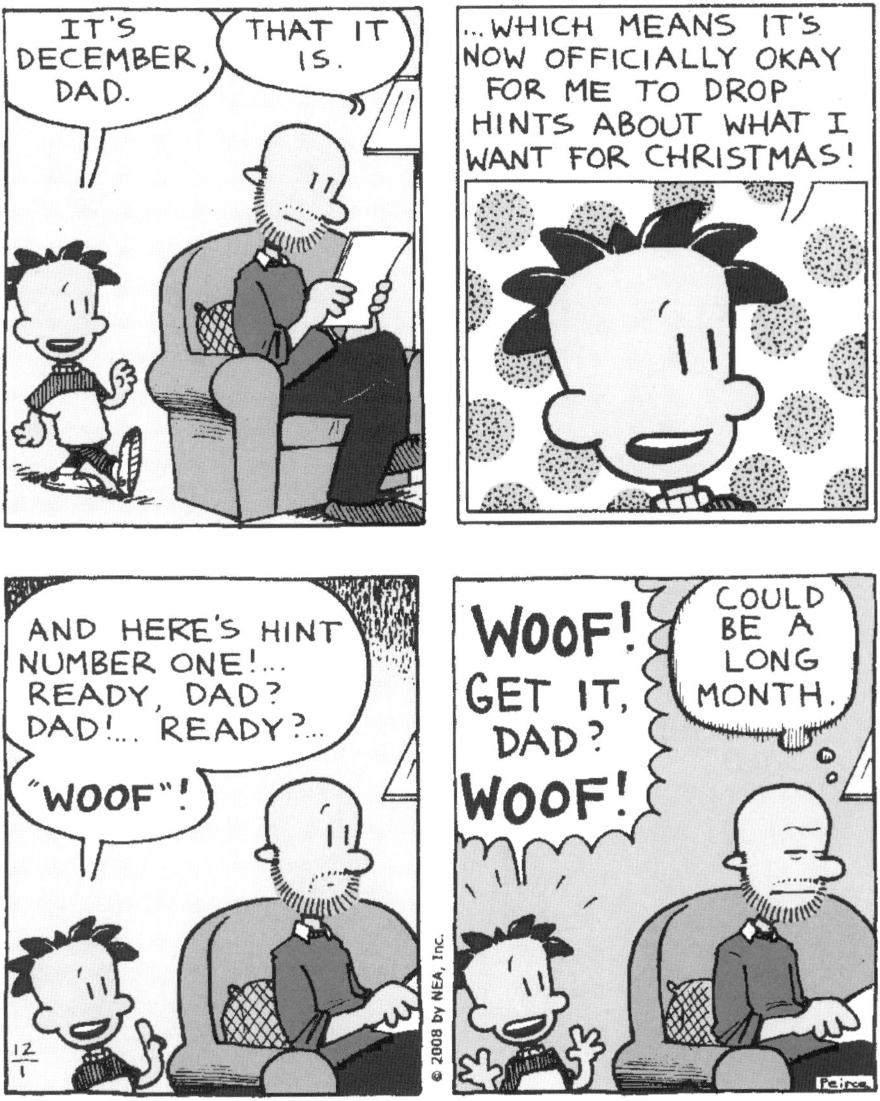
IT'S DECEMBER, DAD.
THAT IT IS.
...WHICH MEANS IT'S NOW OFFICIALLY OKAY FOR ME TO DROP HINTS ABOUT WHAT I WANT FOR CHRISTMAS!
AND HERE'S HINT NUMBER ONE!... READY, DAD? DAD!... READY?...
"WOOF"!
12/1
© 2008 by NEA, Inc.
WOOF! GET IT, DAD? WOOF!
COULD BE A LONG MONTH.
Peirce

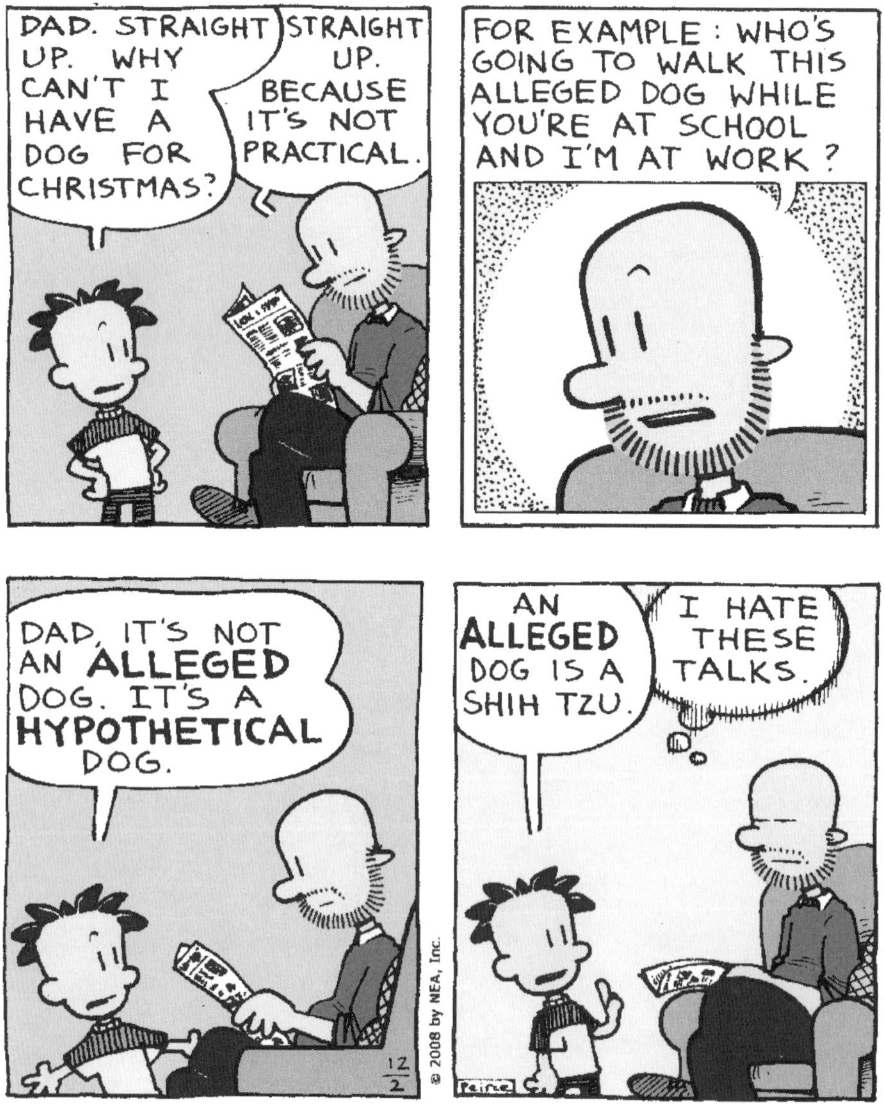
DAD. STRAIGHT UP. WHY CAN'T I HAVE A DOG FOR CHRISTMAS?
STRAIGHT UP. BECAUSE IT'S NOT PRACTICAL.
FOR EXAMPLE: WHO'S GOING TO WALK THIS ALLEGED DOG WHILE YOU'RE AT SCHOOL AND I'M AT WORK?
DAD, IT'S NOT AN ALLEGED DOG. IT'S A HYPOTHETICAL DOG.
AN ALLEGED DOG IS A SHIH TZU.
I HATE THESE TALKS.
12/2
© 2008 by NEA, Inc.
Peirce

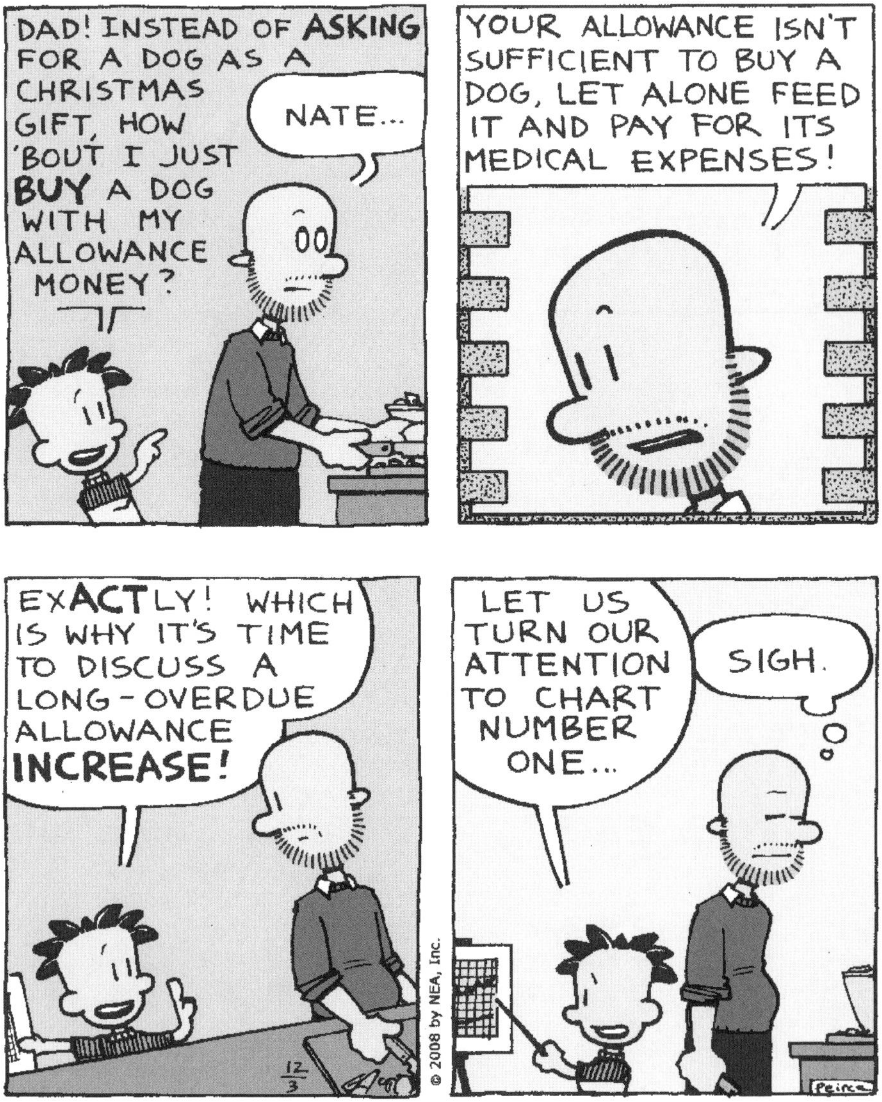
DAD! INSTEAD OF **ASKING** FOR A DOG AS A CHRISTMAS GIFT, HOW 'BOUT I JUST **BUY** A DOG WITH MY ALLOWANCE MONEY?
NATE...
YOUR ALLOWANCE ISN'T SUFFICIENT TO BUY A DOG, LET ALONE FEED IT AND PAY FOR ITS MEDICAL EXPENSES!
EX**ACT**LY! WHICH IS WHY IT'S TIME TO DISCUSS A LONG-OVERDUE ALLOWANCE **INCREASE!**
12/3
© 2008 by NEA, Inc.
LET US TURN OUR ATTENTION TO CHART NUMBER ONE...
SIGH.
Peirce

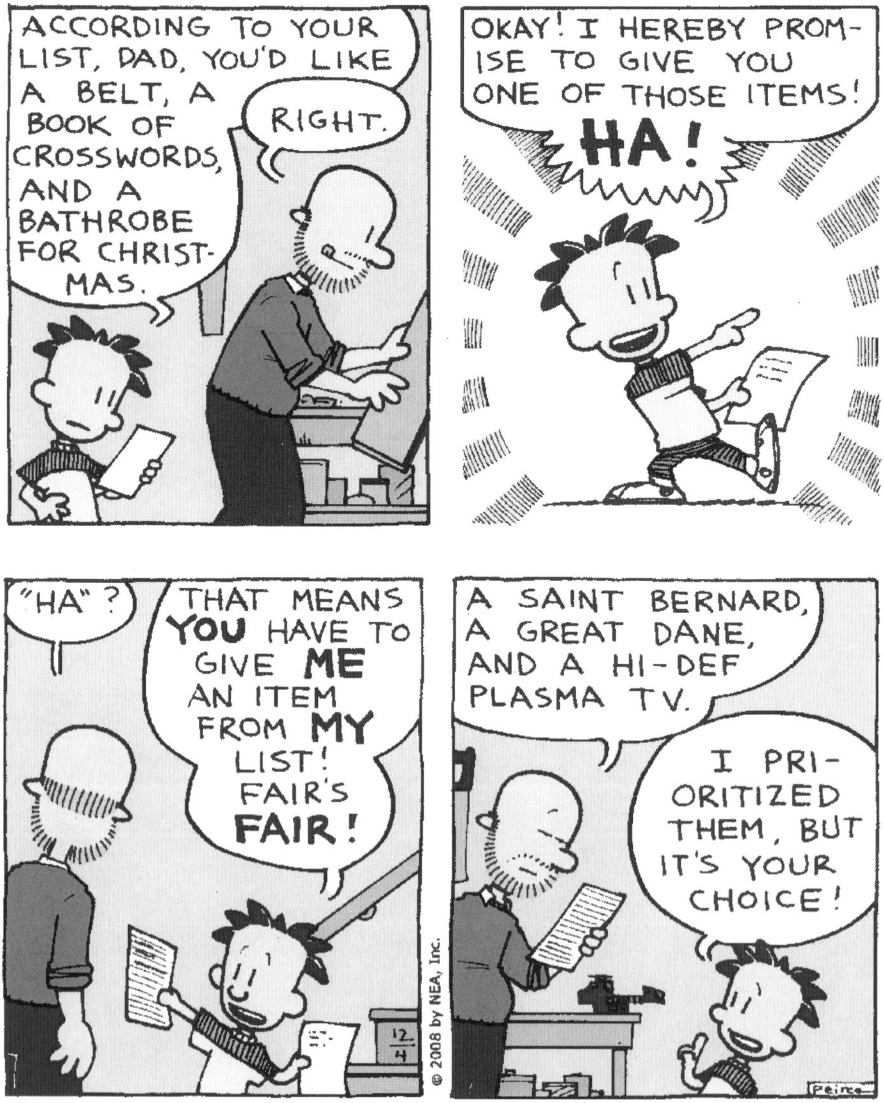
ACCORDING TO YOUR LIST, DAD, YOU'D LIKE A BELT, A BOOK OF CROSSWORDS, AND A BATHROBE FOR CHRIST-MAS.
RIGHT.
OKAY! I HEREBY PROM-ISE TO GIVE YOU ONE OF THOSE ITEMS!
HA!
"HA"?
THAT MEANS YOU HAVE TO GIVE ME AN ITEM FROM MY LIST! FAIR'S FAIR!
A SAINT BERNARD, A GREAT DANE, AND A HI-DEF PLASMA TV.
I PRI-ORITIZED THEM, BUT IT'S YOUR CHOICE!
12/4
Peirce

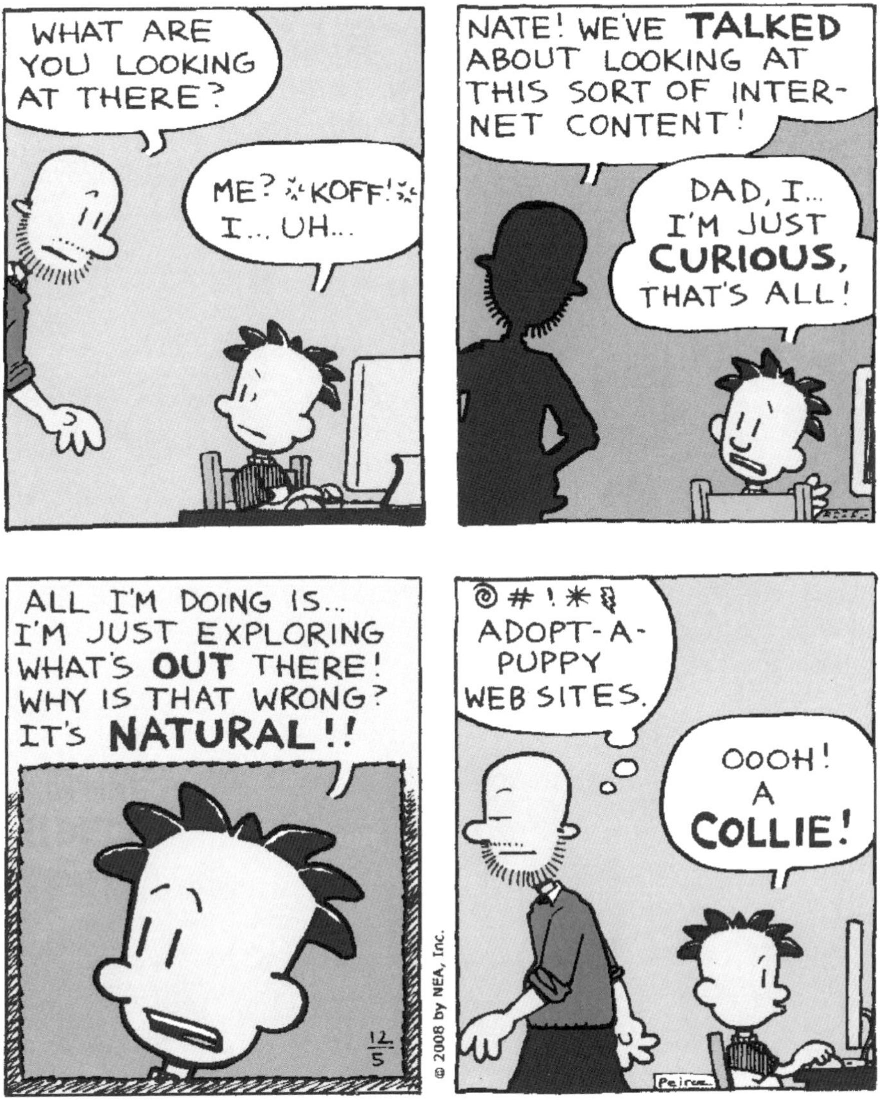
WHAT ARE YOU LOOKING AT THERE?
ME? KOFF! I... UH...
NATE! WE'VE TALKED ABOUT LOOKING AT THIS SORT OF INTER-NET CONTENT!
DAD, I... I'M JUST CURIOUS, THAT'S ALL!
ALL I'M DOING IS... I'M JUST EXPLORING WHAT'S OUT THERE! WHY IS THAT WRONG? IT'S NATURAL!!
12/5
© 2008 by NEA, Inc.
@#!*
ADOPT-A-PUPPY WEB SITES.
OOOH! A COLLIE!
Peirce

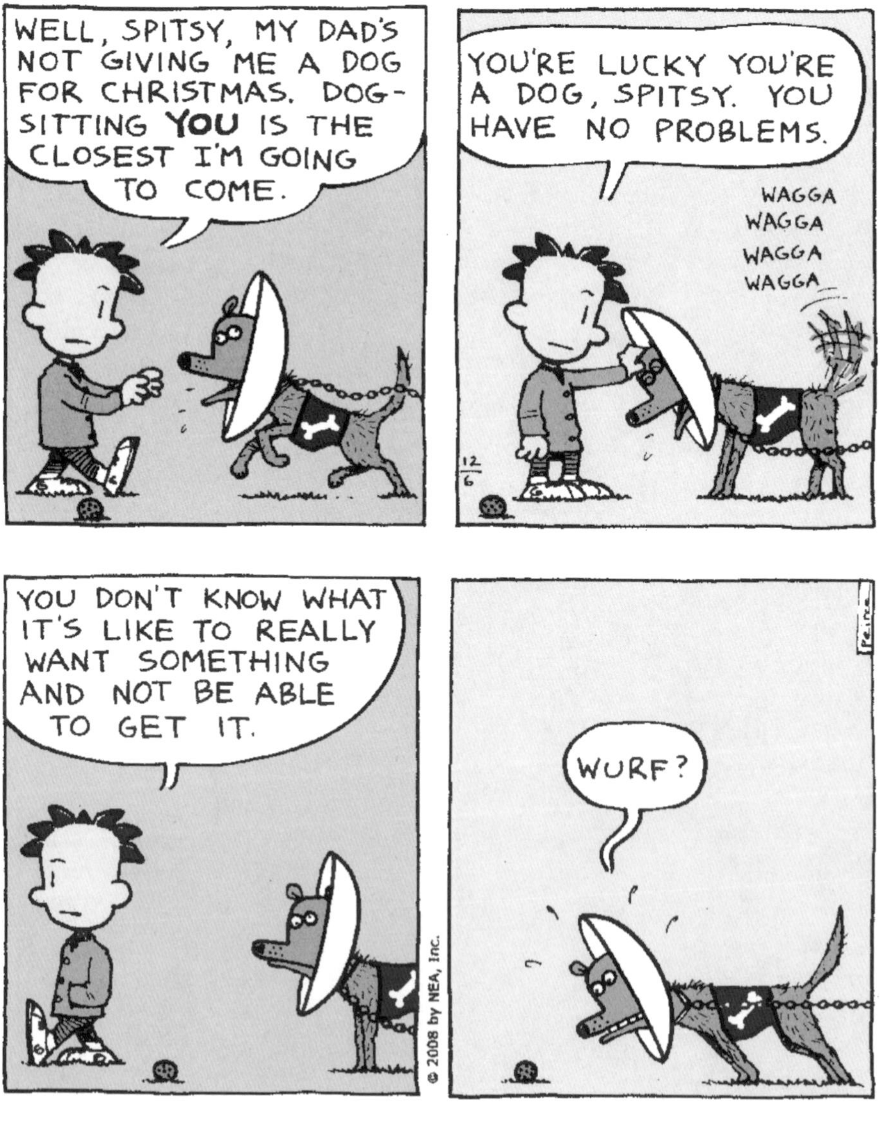
WELL, SPITSY, MY DAD'S NOT GIVING ME A DOG FOR CHRISTMAS. DOG-SITTING **YOU** IS THE CLOSEST I'M GOING TO COME.
YOU'RE LUCKY YOU'RE A DOG, SPITSY. YOU HAVE NO PROBLEMS.
WAGGA WAGGA WAGGA WAGGA
12/6
YOU DON'T KNOW WHAT IT'S LIKE TO REALLY WANT SOMETHING AND NOT BE ABLE TO GET IT.
© 2008 by NEA, Inc.
WURF?
Peirce

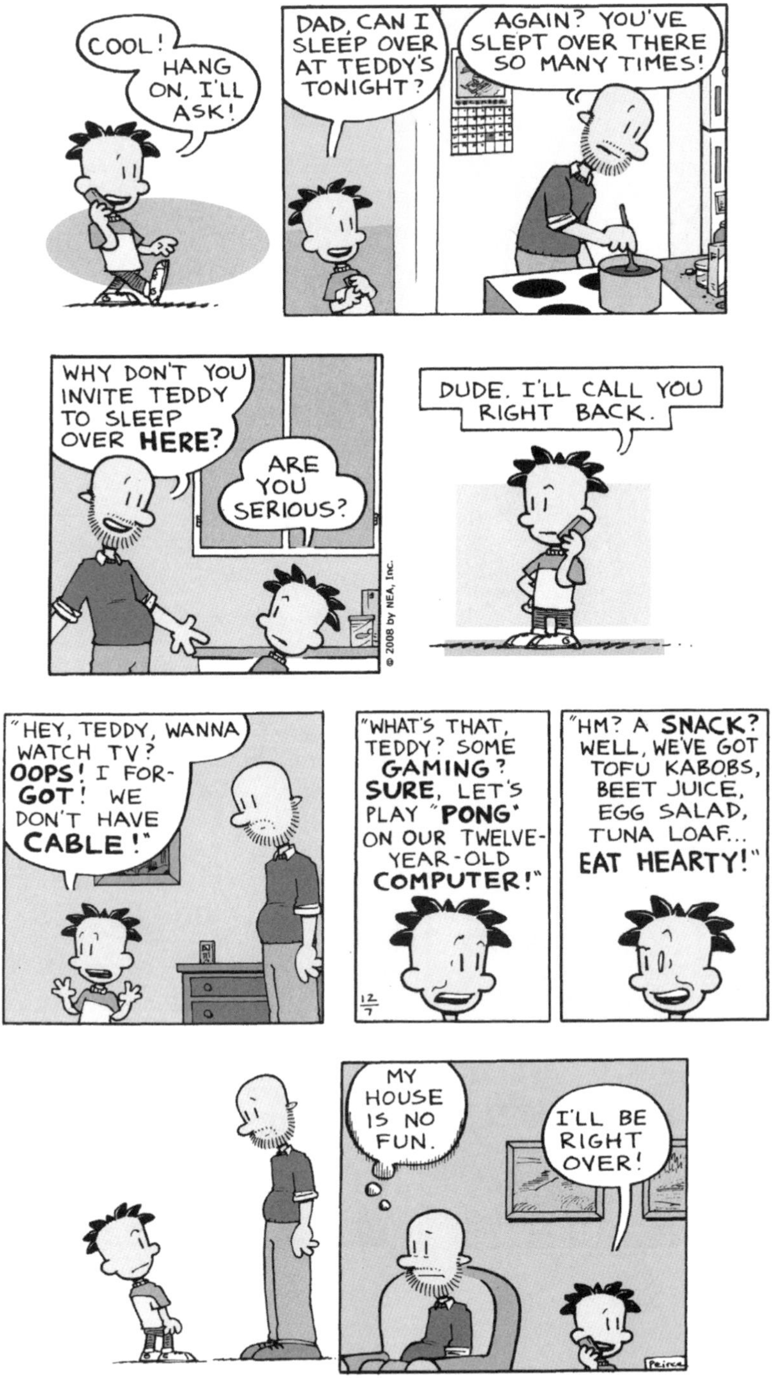
COOL! HANG ON, I'LL ASK!
DAD, CAN I SLEEP OVER AT TEDDY'S TONIGHT?
AGAIN? YOU'VE SLEPT OVER THERE SO MANY TIMES!
WHY DON'T YOU INVITE TEDDY TO SLEEP OVER **HERE**?
ARE YOU SERIOUS?
© 2008 by NEA, Inc.
DUDE. I'LL CALL YOU RIGHT BACK.
"HEY, TEDDY, WANNA WATCH TV? **OOPS**! I FOR-**GOT**! WE DON'T HAVE **CABLE**!"
"WHAT'S THAT, TEDDY? SOME **GAMING**? **SURE**, LET'S PLAY "**PONG**" ON OUR TWELVE-YEAR-OLD **COMPUTER**!"
12/7
"HM? A **SNACK**? WELL, WE'VE GOT TOFU KABOBS, BEET JUICE, EGG SALAD, TUNA LOAF... **EAT HEARTY**!"
MY HOUSE IS NO FUN.
I'LL BE RIGHT OVER!
Peirce

KISS THIS JOINT GOOD-BYE!

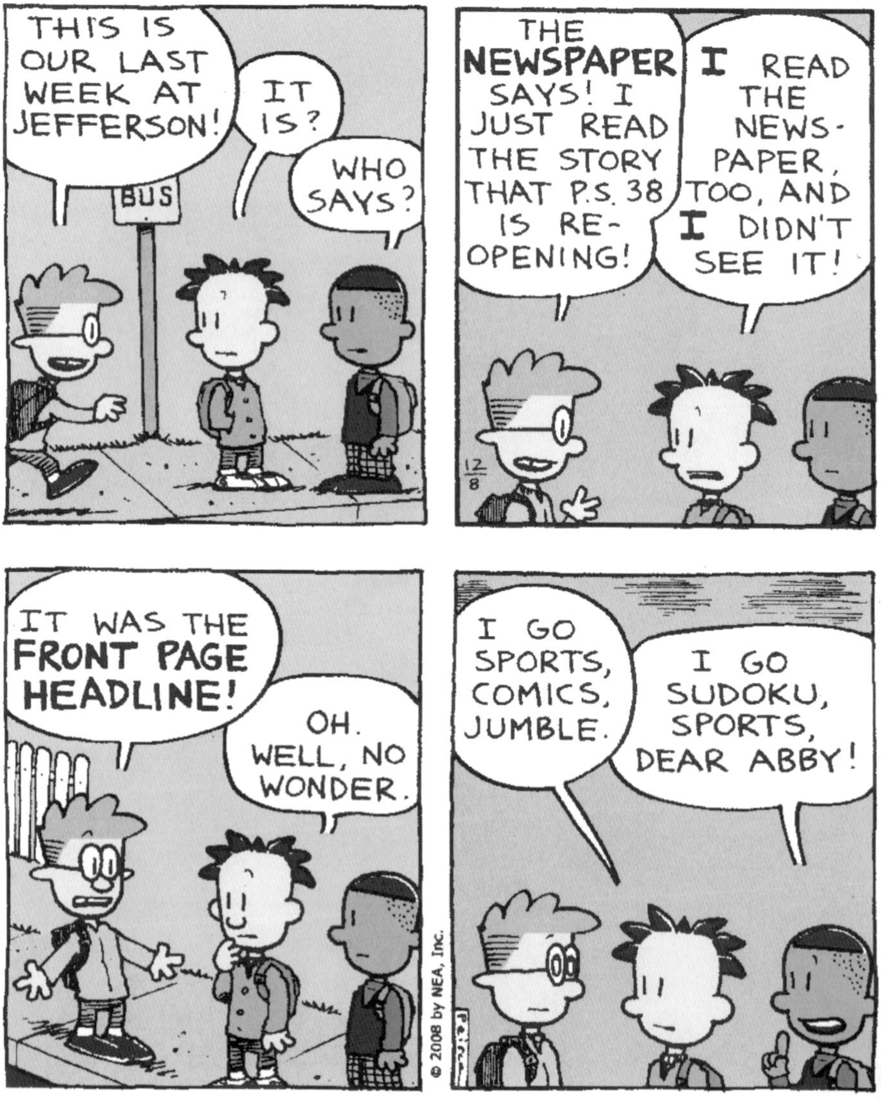
THIS IS OUR LAST WEEK AT JEFFERSON!
IT IS?
WHO SAYS?
BUS
THE **NEWSPAPER** SAYS! I JUST READ THE STORY THAT P.S. 38 IS RE-OPENING!
I READ THE NEWS-PAPER, TOO, AND **I** DIDN'T SEE IT!
12/8
IT WAS THE **FRONT PAGE HEADLINE!**
OH. WELL, NO WONDER.
I GO SPORTS, COMICS, JUMBLE.
I GO SUDOKU, SPORTS, DEAR ABBY!
© 2008 by NEA, Inc.

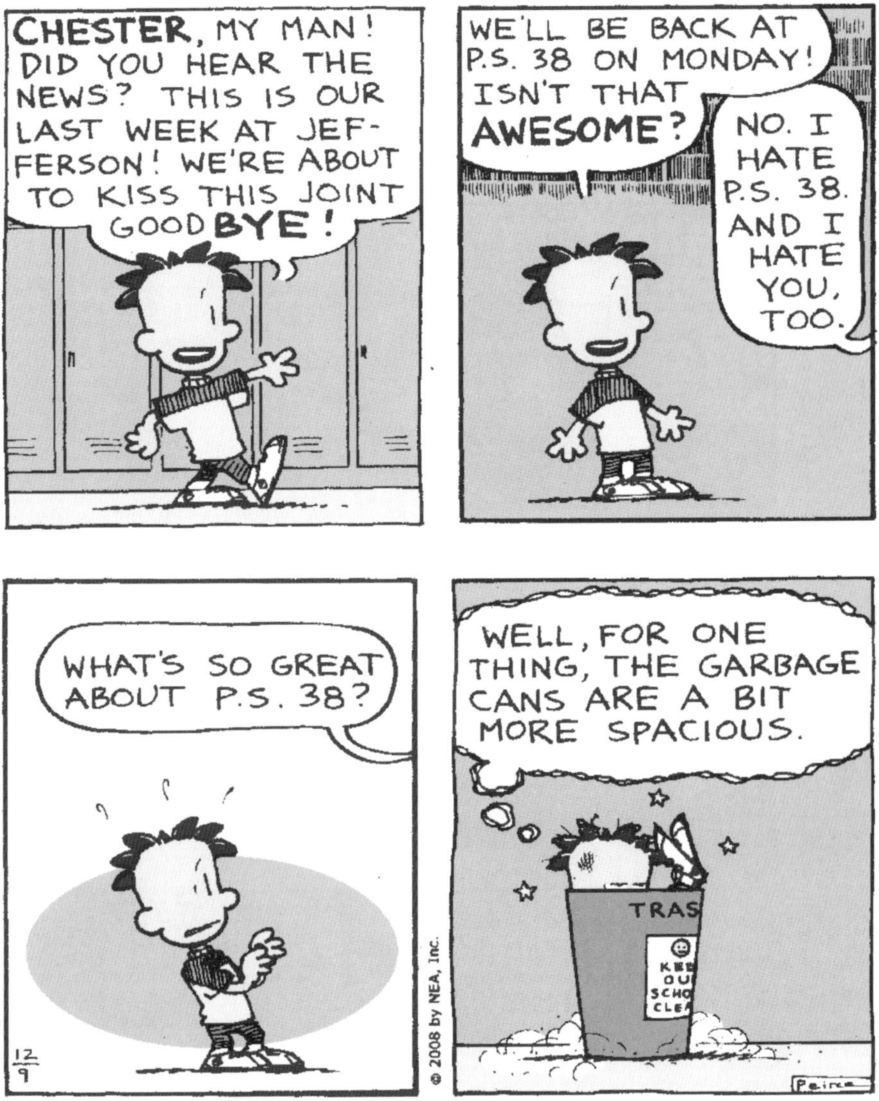
CHESTER, MY MAN! DID YOU HEAR THE NEWS? THIS IS OUR LAST WEEK AT JEFFERSON! WE'RE ABOUT TO KISS THIS JOINT GOOD BYE!
WE'LL BE BACK AT P.S. 38 ON MONDAY! ISN'T THAT AWESOME?
NO. I HATE P.S. 38. AND I HATE YOU, TOO.
WHAT'S SO GREAT ABOUT P.S. 38?
WELL, FOR ONE THING, THE GARBAGE CANS ARE A BIT MORE SPACIOUS.

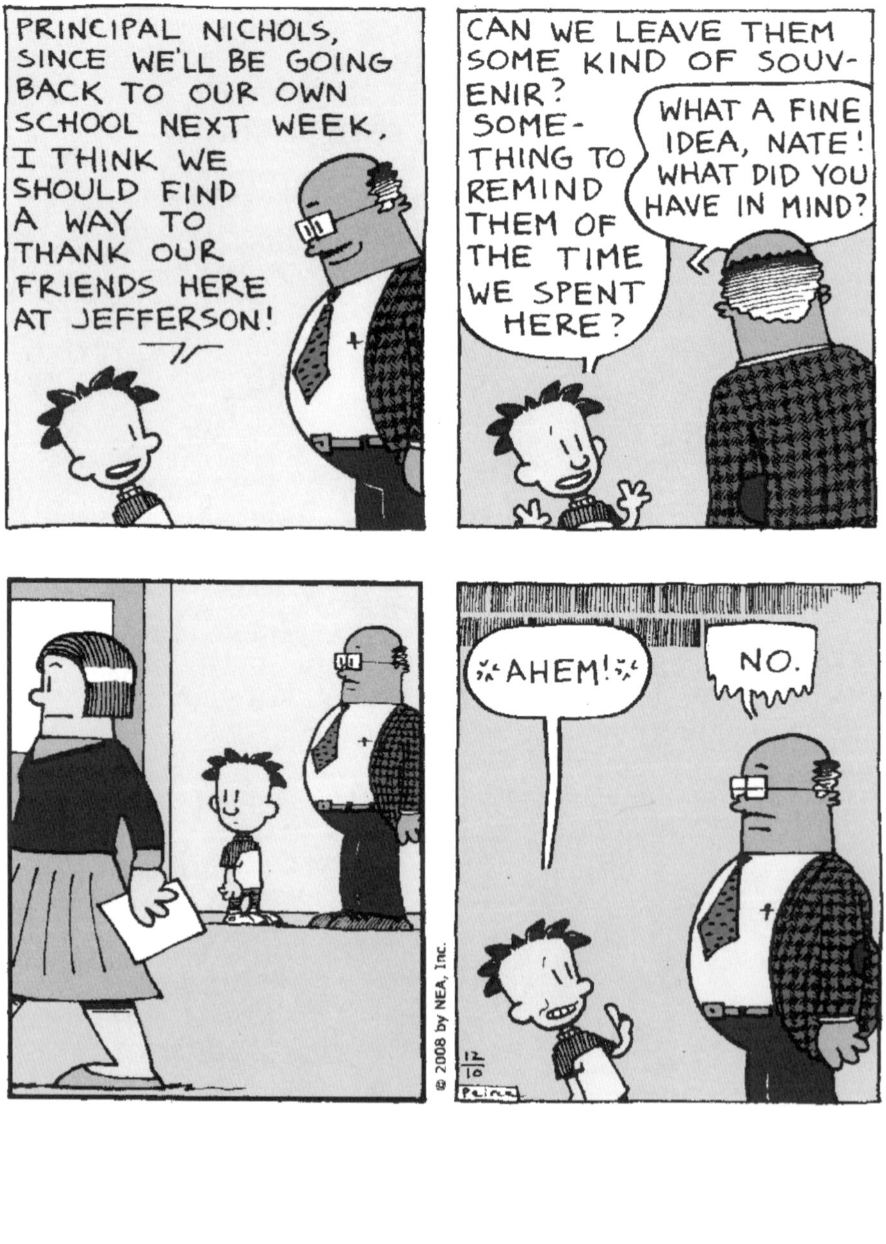
PRINCIPAL NICHOLS, SINCE WE'LL BE GOING BACK TO OUR OWN SCHOOL NEXT WEEK, I THINK WE SHOULD FIND A WAY TO THANK OUR FRIENDS HERE AT JEFFERSON!
CAN WE LEAVE THEM SOME KIND OF SOUVENIR? SOMETHING TO REMIND THEM OF THE TIME WE SPENT HERE?
WHAT A FINE IDEA, NATE! WHAT DID YOU HAVE IN MIND?
AHEM!
NO.
© 2008 by NEA, Inc.
12/10
Peirce

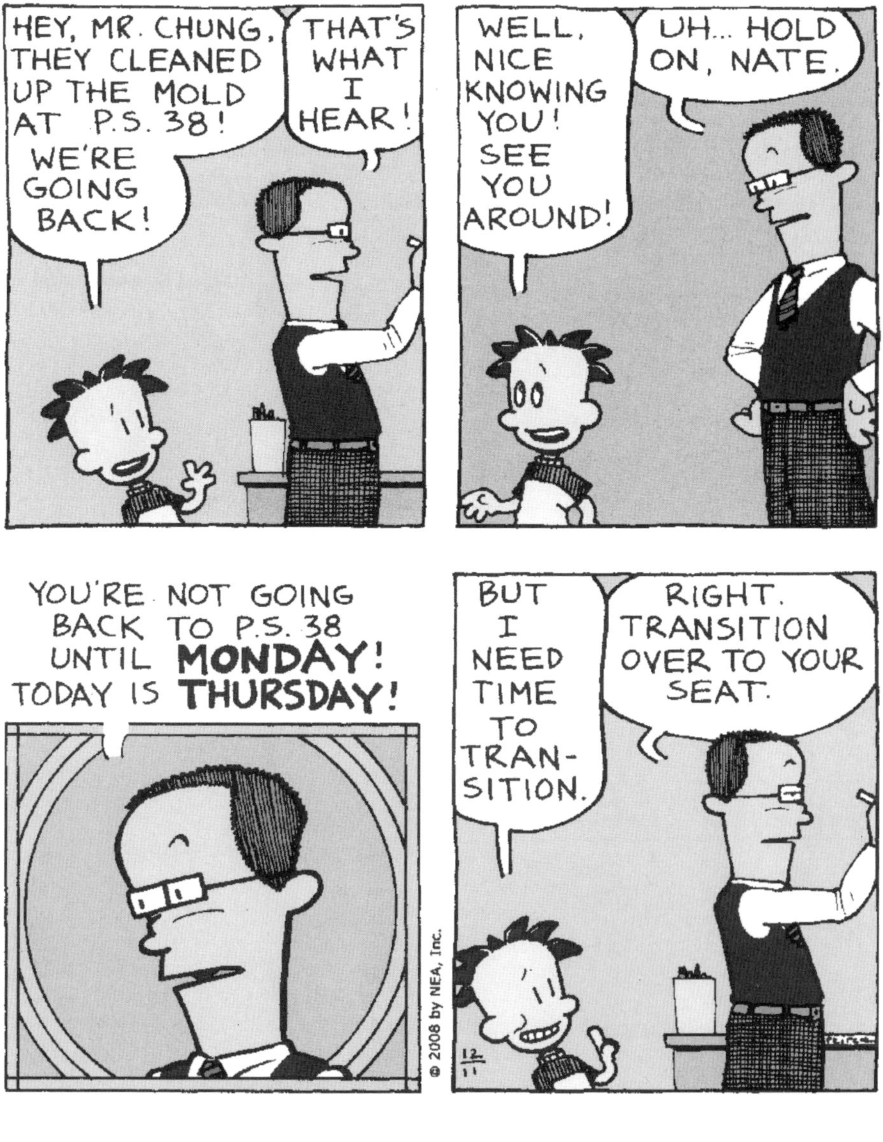
HEY, MR. CHUNG, THEY CLEANED UP THE MOLD AT P.S. 38! WE'RE GOING BACK!
THAT'S WHAT I HEAR!
WELL, NICE KNOWING YOU! SEE YOU AROUND!
UH... HOLD ON, NATE.
YOU'RE NOT GOING BACK TO P.S. 38 UNTIL **MONDAY**! TODAY IS **THURSDAY**!
BUT I NEED TIME TO TRAN-SITION.
RIGHT. TRANSITION OVER TO YOUR SEAT.
© 2008 by NEA, Inc.
12-11

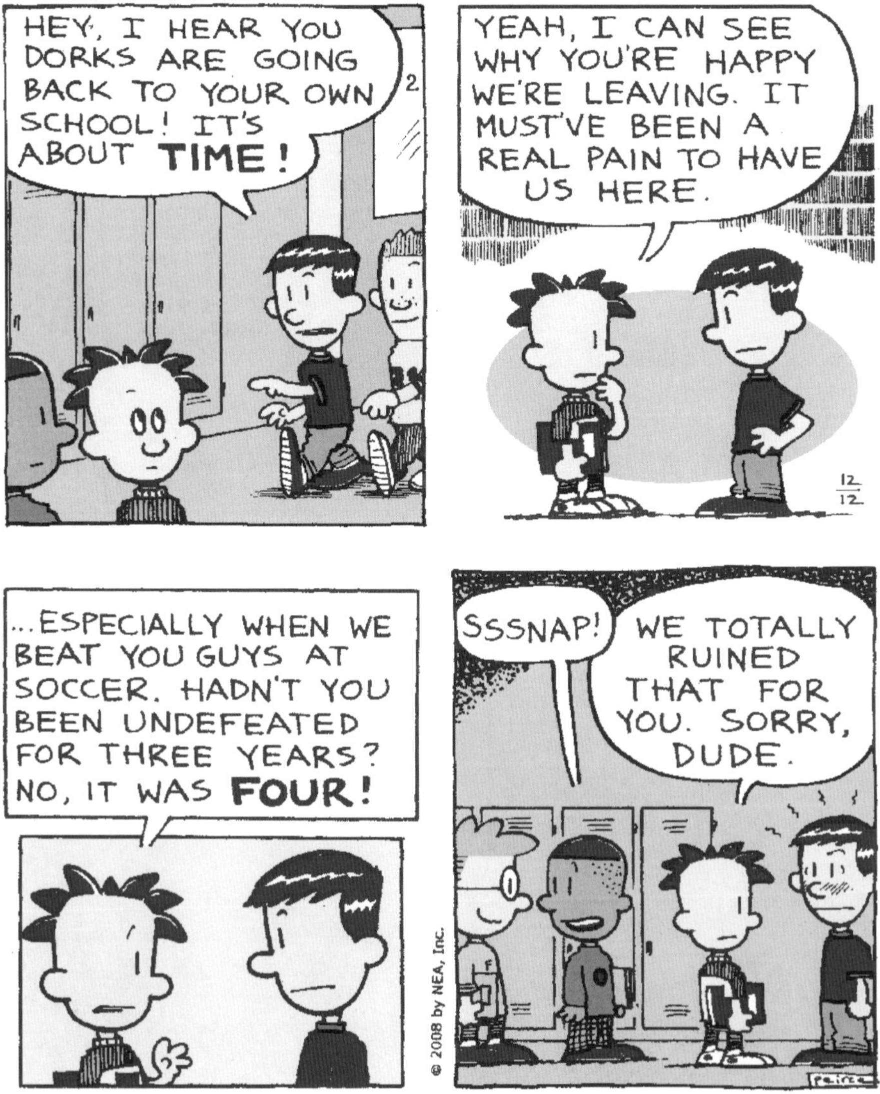
HEY, I HEAR YOU DORKS ARE GOING BACK TO YOUR OWN SCHOOL! IT'S ABOUT **TIME!**
YEAH, I CAN SEE WHY YOU'RE HAPPY WE'RE LEAVING. IT MUST'VE BEEN A REAL PAIN TO HAVE US HERE.
...ESPECIALLY WHEN WE BEAT YOU GUYS AT SOCCER. HADN'T YOU BEEN UNDEFEATED FOR THREE YEARS? NO, IT WAS **FOUR!**
SSSNAP!
WE TOTALLY RUINED THAT FOR YOU. SORRY, DUDE.
© 2008 by NEA, Inc.

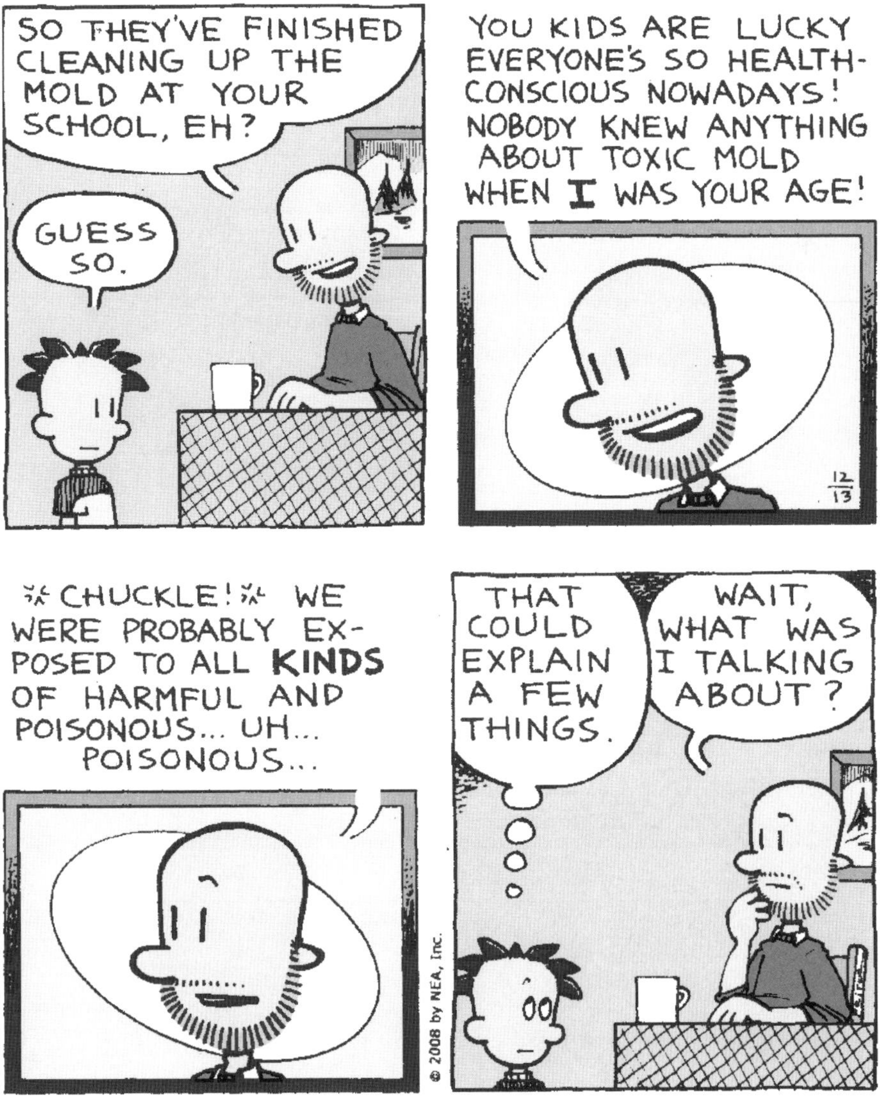
SO THEY'VE FINISHED CLEANING UP THE MOLD AT YOUR SCHOOL, EH?
GUESS SO.
YOU KIDS ARE LUCKY EVERYONE'S SO HEALTH-CONSCIOUS NOWADAYS! NOBODY KNEW ANYTHING ABOUT TOXIC MOLD WHEN I WAS YOUR AGE!
12/13
CHUCKLE! WE WERE PROBABLY EX-POSED TO ALL KINDS OF HARMFUL AND POISONOUS... UH... POISONOUS...
© 2008 by NEA, Inc.
THAT COULD EXPLAIN A FEW THINGS.
WAIT, WHAT WAS I TALKING ABOUT?

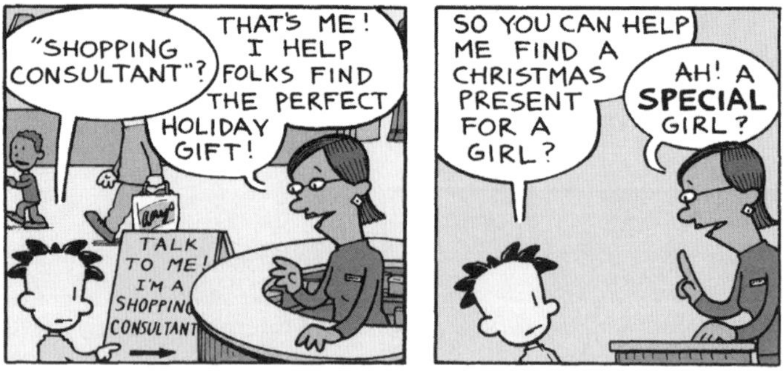
"SHOPPING CONSULTANT"?
THAT'S ME! I HELP FOLKS FIND THE PERFECT HOLIDAY GIFT!
TALK TO ME! I'M A SHOPPING CONSULTANT
SO YOU CAN HELP ME FIND A CHRISTMAS PRESENT FOR A GIRL?
AH! A **SPECIAL** GIRL?

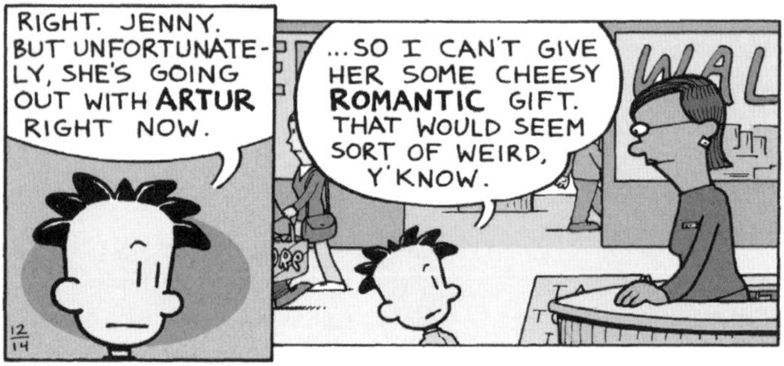
RIGHT. JENNY. BUT UNFORTUNATE-LY, SHE'S GOING OUT WITH **ARTUR** RIGHT NOW.
...SO I CAN'T GIVE HER SOME CHEESY **ROMANTIC** GIFT. THAT WOULD SEEM SORT OF WEIRD, Y'KNOW.
12/14

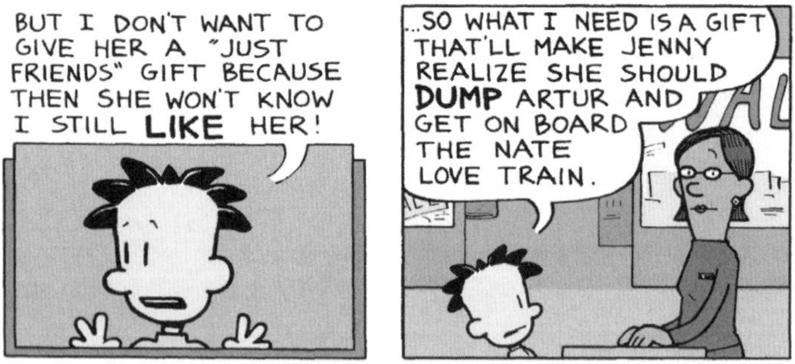
BUT I DON'T WANT TO GIVE HER A "JUST FRIENDS" GIFT BECAUSE THEN SHE WON'T KNOW I STILL **LIKE** HER!
...SO WHAT I NEED IS A GIFT THAT'LL MAKE JENNY REALIZE SHE SHOULD **DUMP** ARTUR AND GET ON BOARD THE NATE LOVE TRAIN.

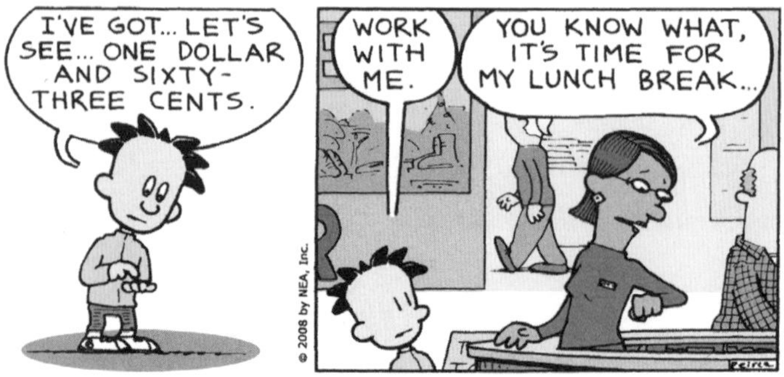
I'VE GOT... LET'S SEE... ONE DOLLAR AND SIXTY-THREE CENTS.
WORK WITH ME.
YOU KNOW WHAT, IT'S TIME FOR MY LUNCH BREAK...
© 2008 by NEA, Inc.

HOW BAD CAN IT BE?

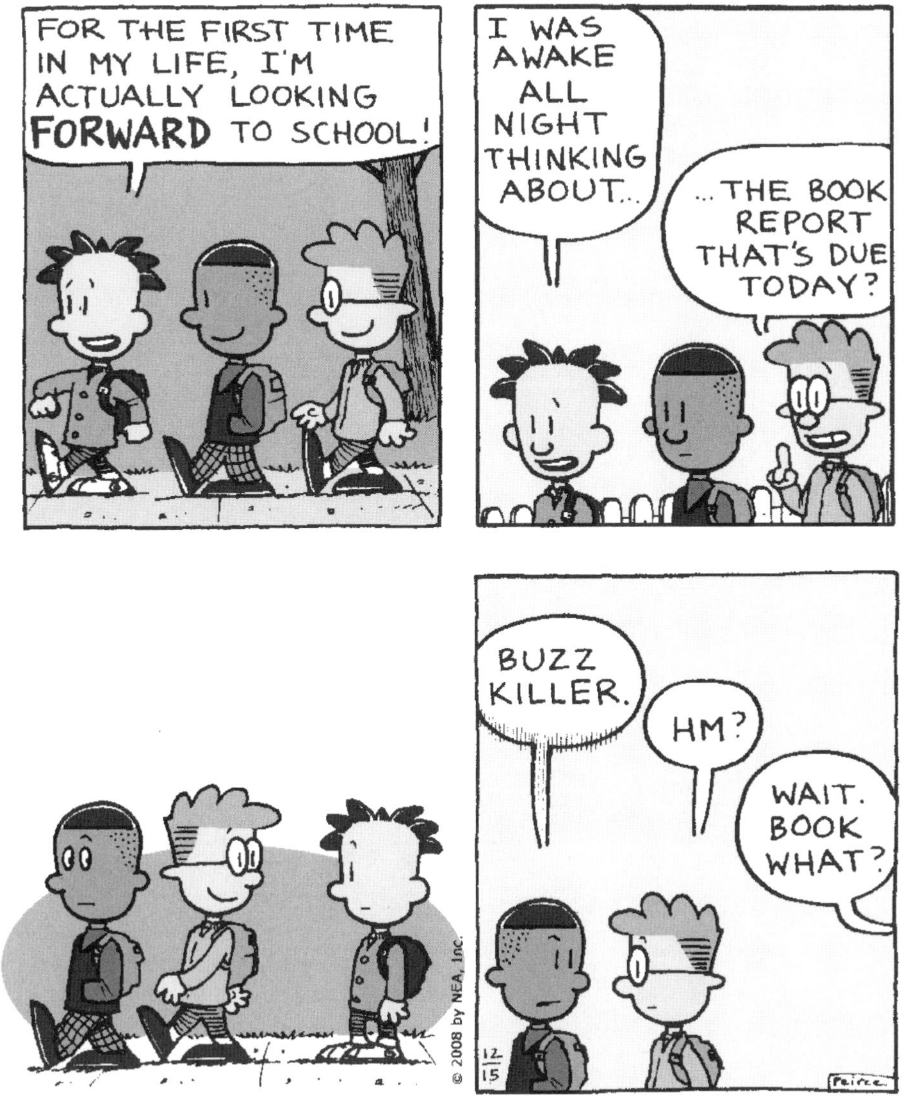
FOR THE FIRST TIME IN MY LIFE, I'M ACTUALLY LOOKING **FORWARD** TO SCHOOL!
I WAS AWAKE ALL NIGHT THINKING ABOUT...
...THE BOOK REPORT THAT'S DUE TODAY?
BUZZ KILLER.
HM?
WAIT. BOOK WHAT?
© 2008 by NEA, Inc.
12 15
Peirce

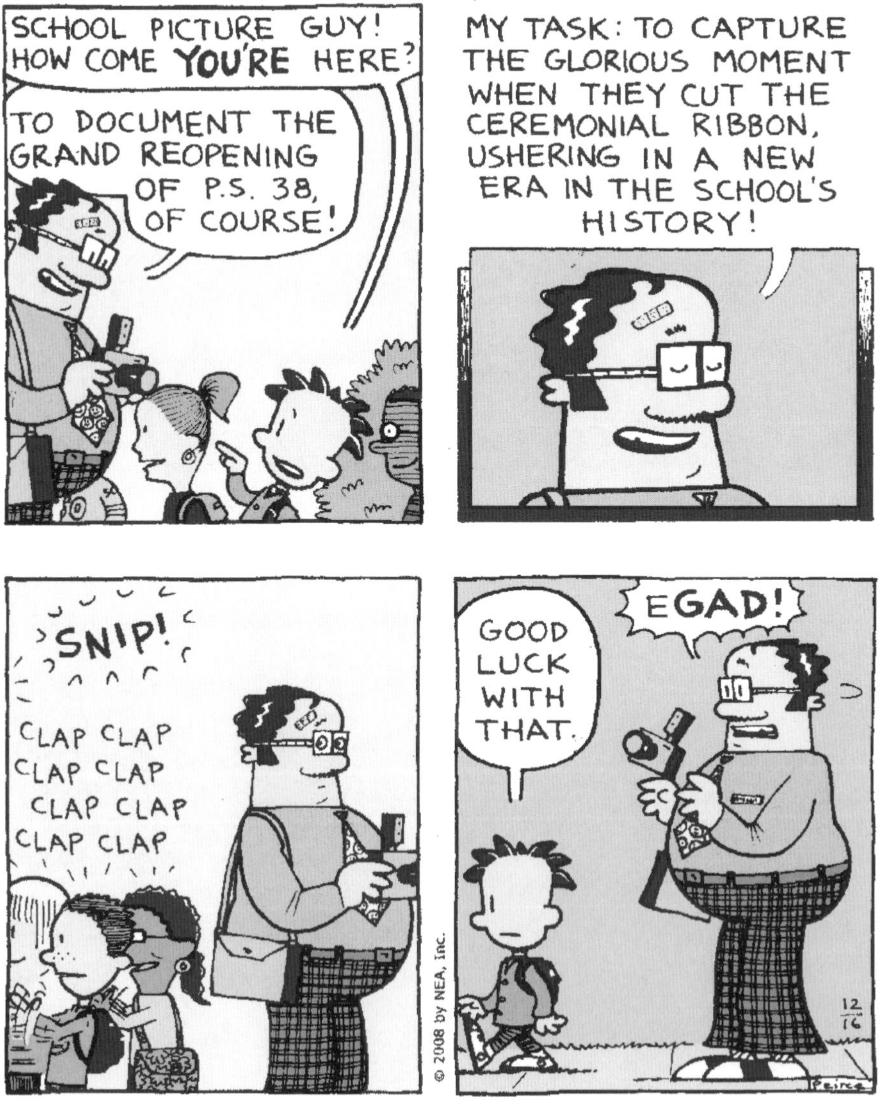
SCHOOL PICTURE GUY! HOW COME YOU'RE HERE?
TO DOCUMENT THE GRAND REOPENING OF P.S. 38, OF COURSE!
MY TASK: TO CAPTURE THE GLORIOUS MOMENT WHEN THEY CUT THE CEREMONIAL RIBBON, USHERING IN A NEW ERA IN THE SCHOOL'S HISTORY!
SNIP!
CLAP CLAP CLAP CLAP CLAP CLAP CLAP CLAP
© 2008 by NEA, Inc.
GOOD LUCK WITH THAT.
EGAD!
12/16

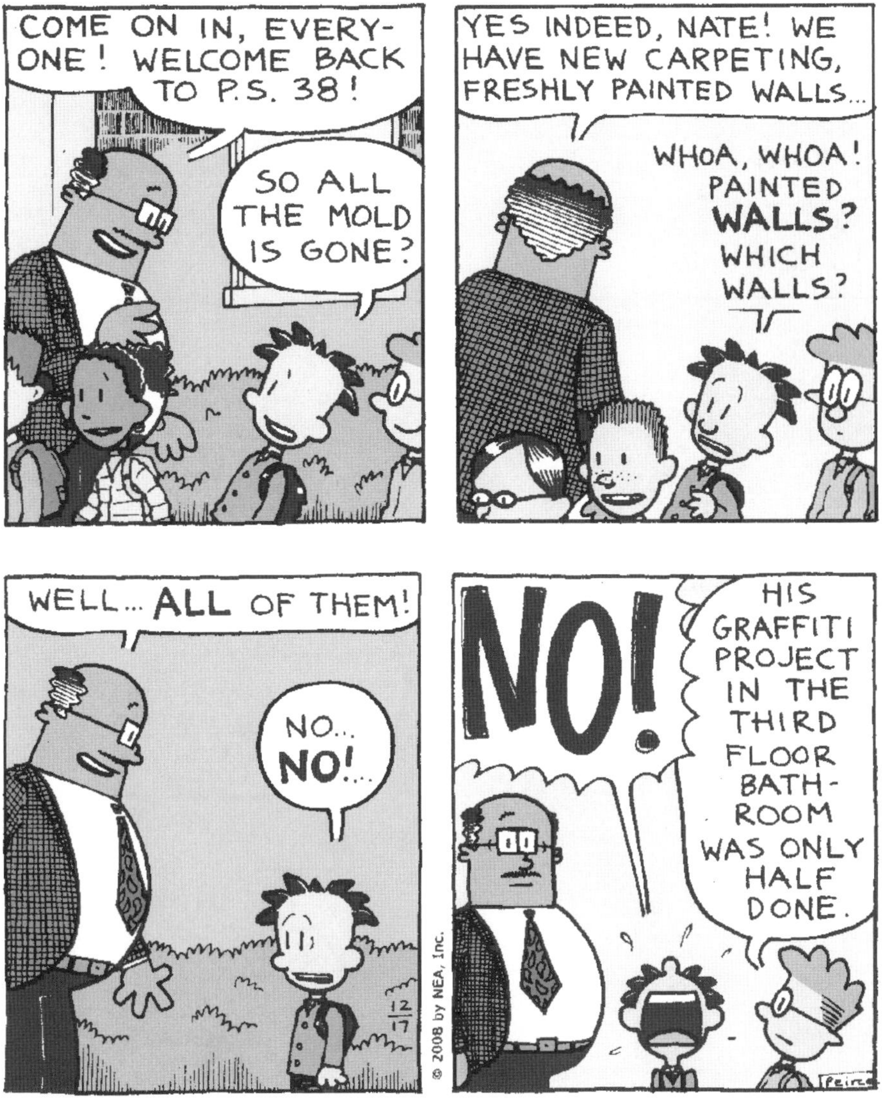
COME ON IN, EVERY-ONE! WELCOME BACK TO P.S. 38!
SO ALL THE MOLD IS GONE?
YES INDEED, NATE! WE HAVE NEW CARPETING, FRESHLY PAINTED WALLS...
WHOA, WHOA! PAINTED **WALLS**? WHICH WALLS?
WELL... **ALL** OF THEM!
NO... **NO!**...
12/17
© 2008 by NEA, Inc.
NO!
HIS GRAFFITI PROJECT IN THE THIRD FLOOR BATH-ROOM WAS ONLY HALF DONE.
Peirce

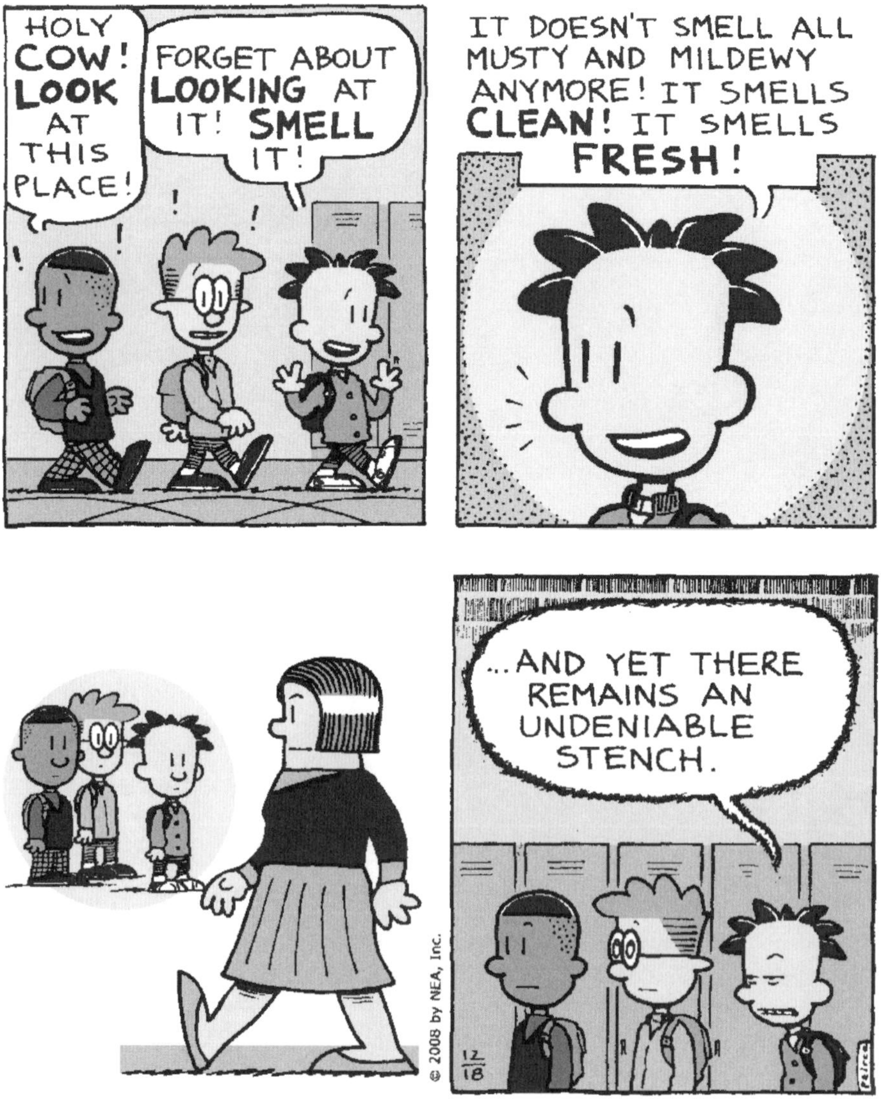
HOLY COW! LOOK AT THIS PLACE!
FORGET ABOUT LOOKING AT IT! SMELL IT!
IT DOESN'T SMELL ALL MUSTY AND MILDEWY ANYMORE! IT SMELLS CLEAN! IT SMELLS FRESH!
...AND YET THERE REMAINS AN UNDENIABLE STENCH.
12/18

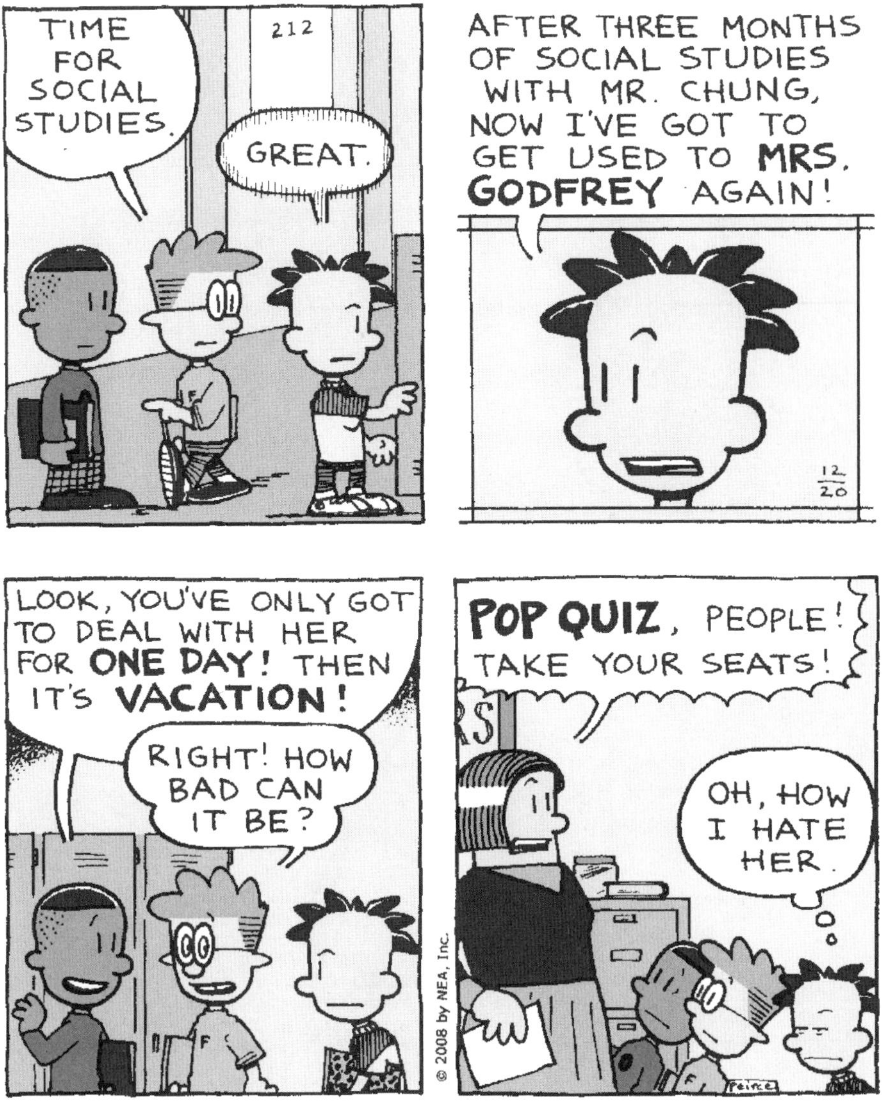
TIME FOR SOCIAL STUDIES.
212
GREAT.
AFTER THREE MONTHS OF SOCIAL STUDIES WITH MR. CHUNG, NOW I'VE GOT TO GET USED TO MRS. GODFREY AGAIN!
12/20
LOOK, YOU'VE ONLY GOT TO DEAL WITH HER FOR ONE DAY! THEN IT'S VACATION!
RIGHT! HOW BAD CAN IT BE?
© 2008 by NEA, Inc.
POP QUIZ, PEOPLE! TAKE YOUR SEATS!
OH, HOW I HATE HER.
PEIRCE

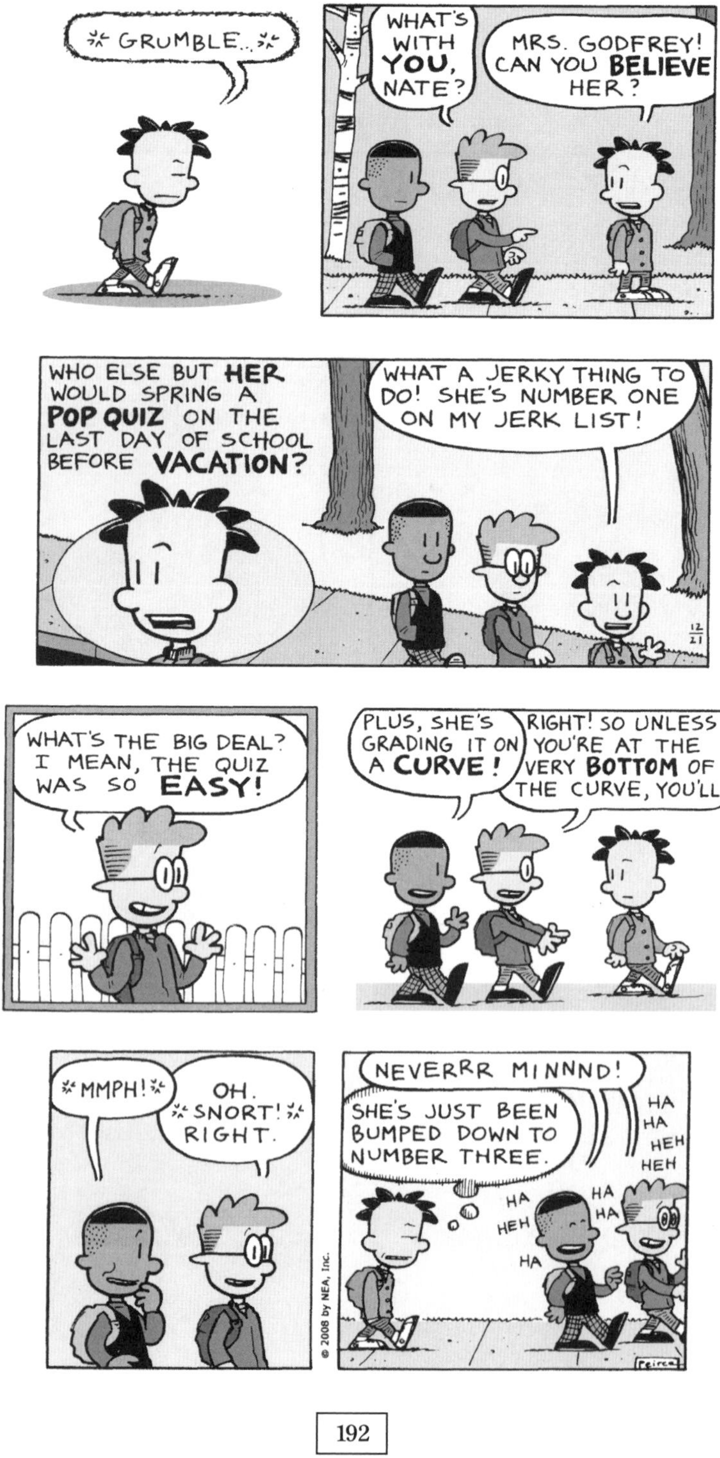

GRUMBLE...
WHAT'S WITH YOU, NATE?
MRS. GODFREY! CAN YOU BELIEVE HER?
WHO ELSE BUT HER WOULD SPRING A POP QUIZ ON THE LAST DAY OF SCHOOL BEFORE VACATION?
WHAT A JERKY THING TO DO! SHE'S NUMBER ONE ON MY JERK LIST!
12/21
WHAT'S THE BIG DEAL? I MEAN, THE QUIZ WAS SO EASY!
PLUS, SHE'S GRADING IT ON A CURVE!
RIGHT! SO UNLESS YOU'RE AT THE VERY BOTTOM OF THE CURVE, YOU'LL...
MMPH!
OH. SNORT! RIGHT.
© 2008 by NEA, Inc.
NEVERRR MINNND!
SHE'S JUST BEEN BUMPED DOWN TO NUMBER THREE.
HA HA HEH HEH
HA HEH HA
HA HA
PEIRCE

HOUSE GUEST PEST

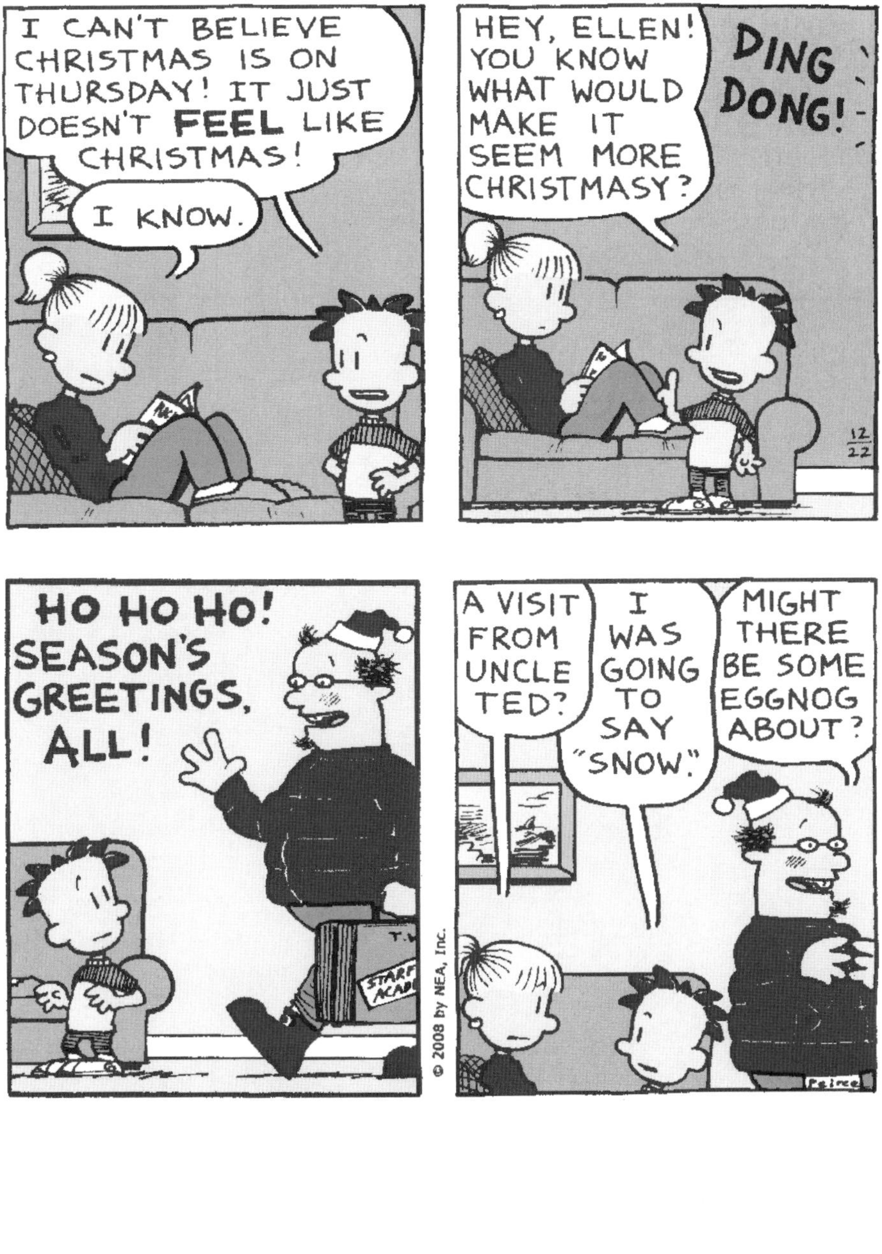
I CAN'T BELIEVE CHRISTMAS IS ON THURSDAY! IT JUST DOESN'T FEEL LIKE CHRISTMAS!
I KNOW.
HEY, ELLEN! YOU KNOW WHAT WOULD MAKE IT SEEM MORE CHRISTMASY?
DING DONG!
12/22
HO HO HO! SEASON'S GREETINGS, ALL!
© 2008 by NEA, Inc.
A VISIT FROM UNCLE TED?
I WAS GOING TO SAY "SNOW."
MIGHT THERE BE SOME EGGNOG ABOUT?
Peirce

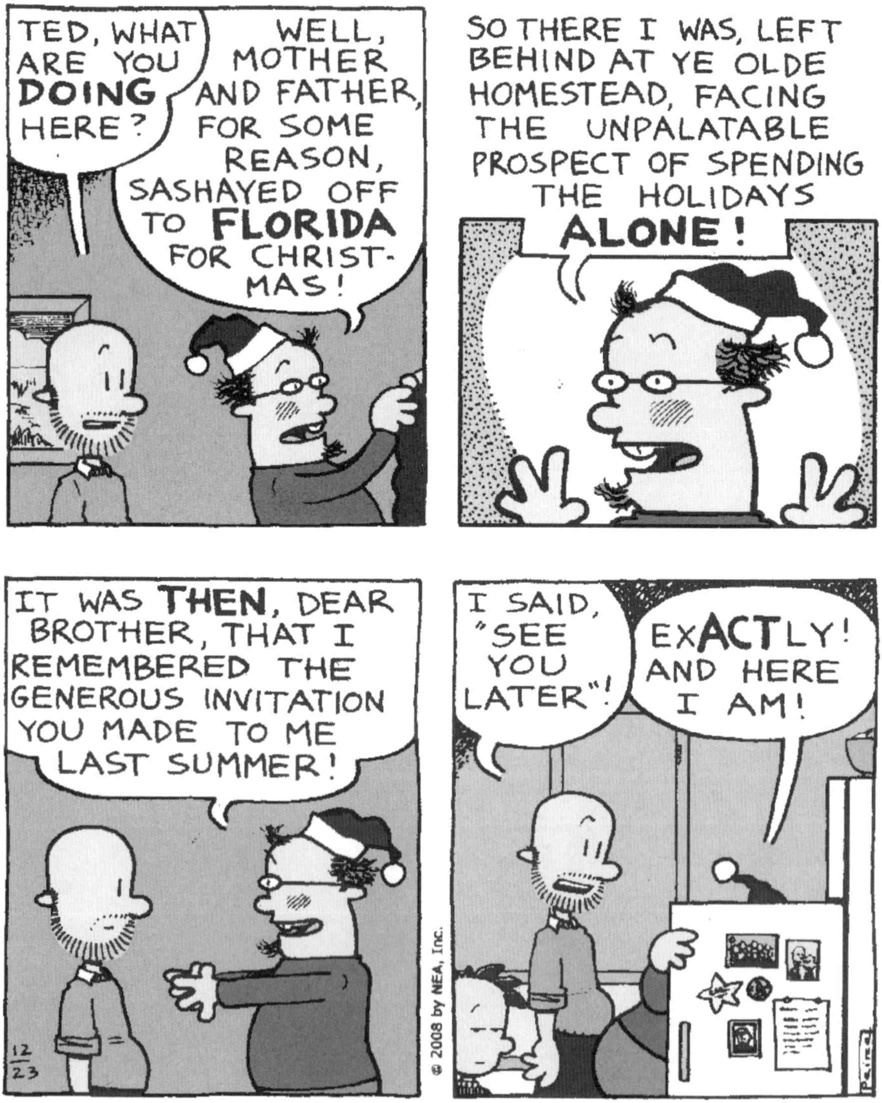
TED, WHAT ARE YOU DOING HERE?
WELL, MOTHER AND FATHER, FOR SOME REASON, SASHAYED OFF TO FLORIDA FOR CHRIST-MAS!
SO THERE I WAS, LEFT BEHIND AT YE OLDE HOMESTEAD, FACING THE UNPALATABLE PROSPECT OF SPENDING THE HOLIDAYS ALONE!
IT WAS THEN, DEAR BROTHER, THAT I REMEMBERED THE GENEROUS INVITATION YOU MADE TO ME LAST SUMMER!
12/23
© 2008 by NEA, Inc.
I SAID, "SEE YOU LATER"!
EXACTLY! AND HERE I AM!

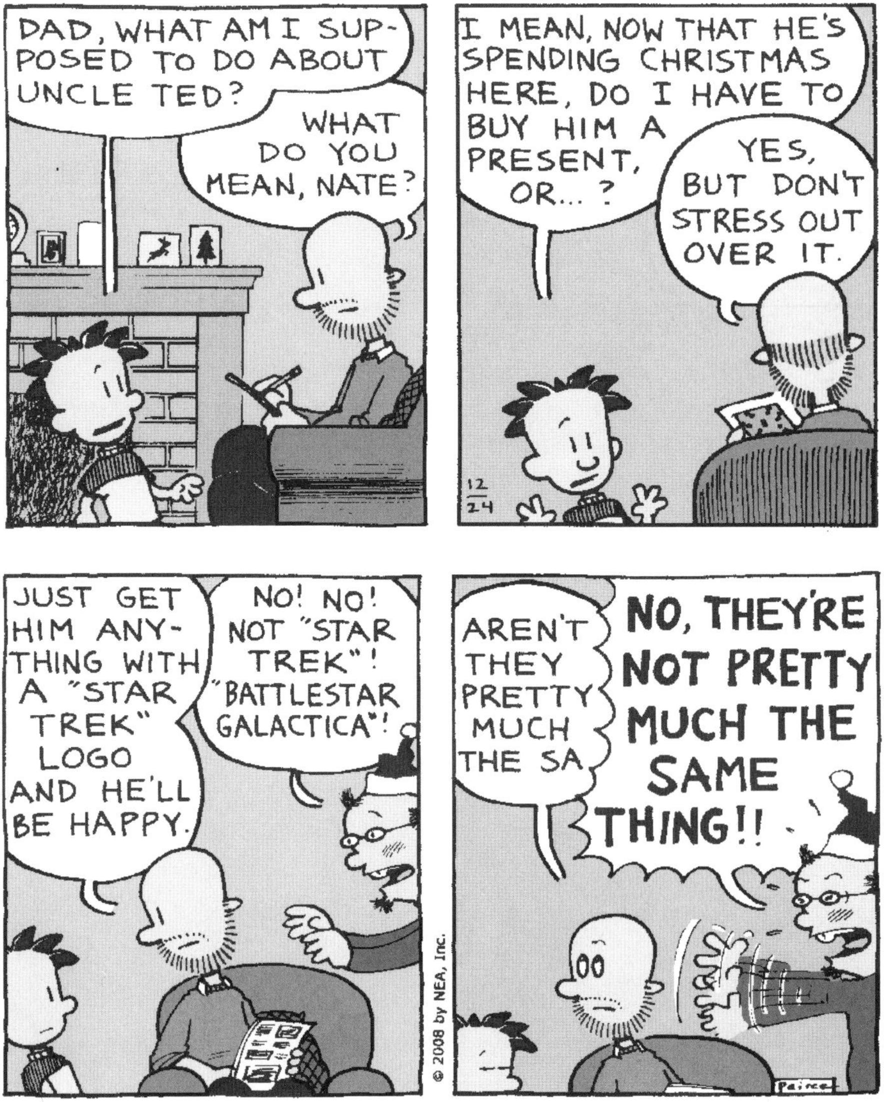
DAD, WHAT AM I SUP-POSED TO DO ABOUT UNCLE TED?
WHAT DO YOU MEAN, NATE?
I MEAN, NOW THAT HE'S SPENDING CHRISTMAS HERE, DO I HAVE TO BUY HIM A PRESENT, OR... ?
YES, BUT DON'T STRESS OUT OVER IT.
12/24
JUST GET HIM ANY-THING WITH A "STAR TREK" LOGO AND HE'LL BE HAPPY.
NO! NO! NOT "STAR TREK"! "BATTLESTAR GALACTICA"!
© 2008 by NEA, Inc.
AREN'T THEY PRETTY MUCH THE SA
NO, THEY'RE NOT PRETTY MUCH THE SAME THING!!
Peirce

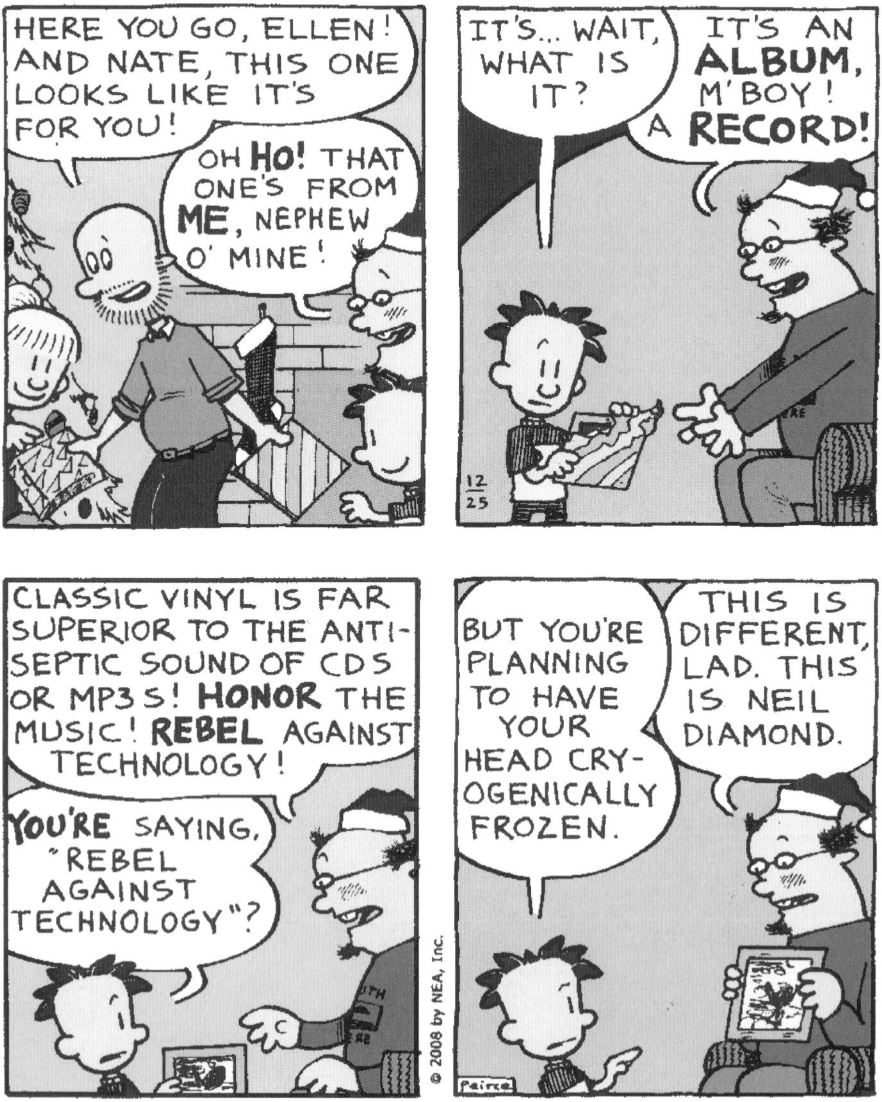
HERE YOU GO, ELLEN! AND NATE, THIS ONE LOOKS LIKE IT'S FOR YOU!
OH **HO!** THAT ONE'S FROM **ME**, NEPHEW O' MINE!
IT'S... WAIT, WHAT IS IT?
IT'S AN **ALBUM**, M'BOY! A **RECORD!**
12/25
CLASSIC VINYL IS FAR SUPERIOR TO THE ANTI-SEPTIC SOUND OF CDS OR MP3S! **HONOR** THE MUSIC! **REBEL** AGAINST TECHNOLOGY!
YOU'RE SAYING, "REBEL AGAINST TECHNOLOGY"?
© 2008 by NEA, Inc.
BUT YOU'RE PLANNING TO HAVE YOUR HEAD CRY-OGENICALLY FROZEN.
THIS IS DIFFERENT, LAD. THIS IS NEIL DIAMOND.
Peirce

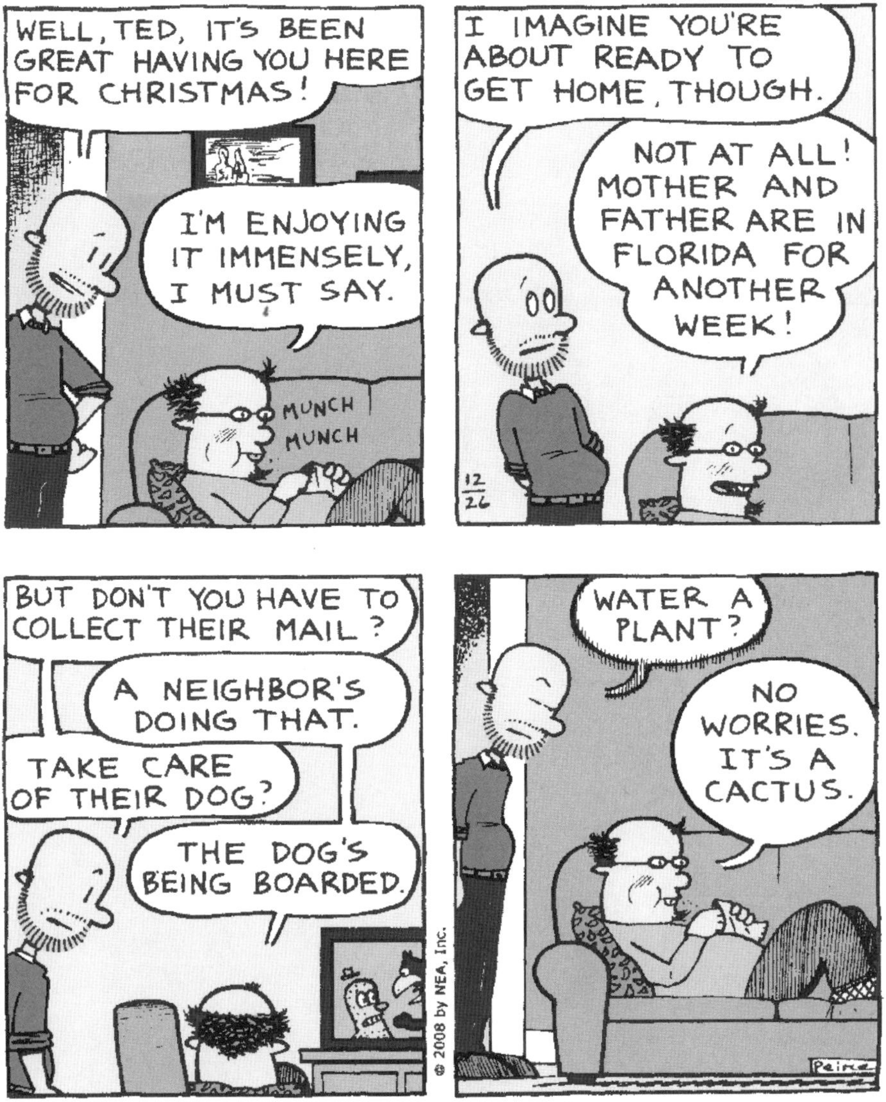
WELL, TED, IT'S BEEN GREAT HAVING YOU HERE FOR CHRISTMAS!
I'M ENJOYING IT IMMENSELY, I MUST SAY.
MUNCH MUNCH
I IMAGINE YOU'RE ABOUT READY TO GET HOME, THOUGH.
NOT AT ALL! MOTHER AND FATHER ARE IN FLORIDA FOR ANOTHER WEEK!
12/26
BUT DON'T YOU HAVE TO COLLECT THEIR MAIL?
A NEIGHBOR'S DOING THAT.
TAKE CARE OF THEIR DOG?
THE DOG'S BEING BOARDED.
© 2008 by NEA, Inc.
WATER A PLANT?
NO WORRIES. IT'S A CACTUS.
Peirce

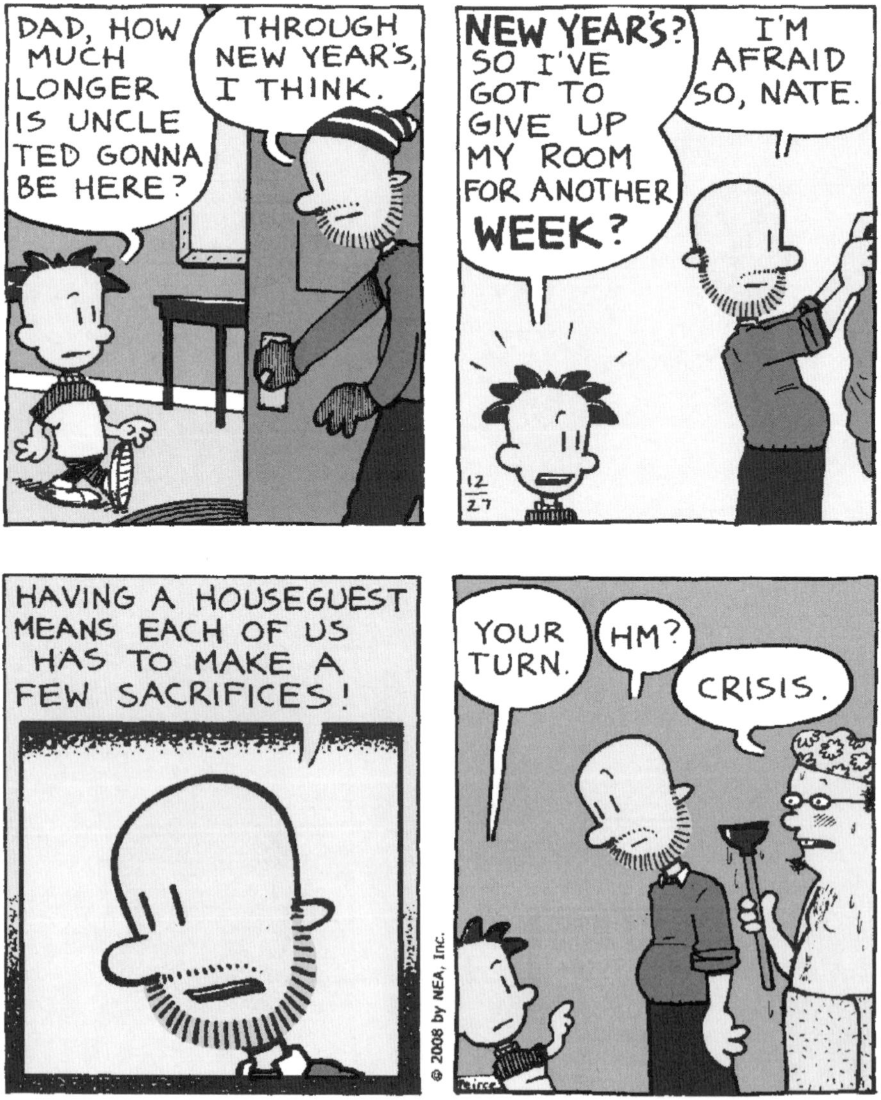
DAD, HOW MUCH LONGER IS UNCLE TED GONNA BE HERE?
THROUGH NEW YEAR'S, I THINK.
NEW YEAR'S? SO I'VE GOT TO GIVE UP MY ROOM FOR ANOTHER WEEK?
I'M AFRAID SO, NATE.
12/27
HAVING A HOUSEGUEST MEANS EACH OF US HAS TO MAKE A FEW SACRIFICES!
YOUR TURN.
HM?
CRISIS.
© 2008 by NEA, Inc.

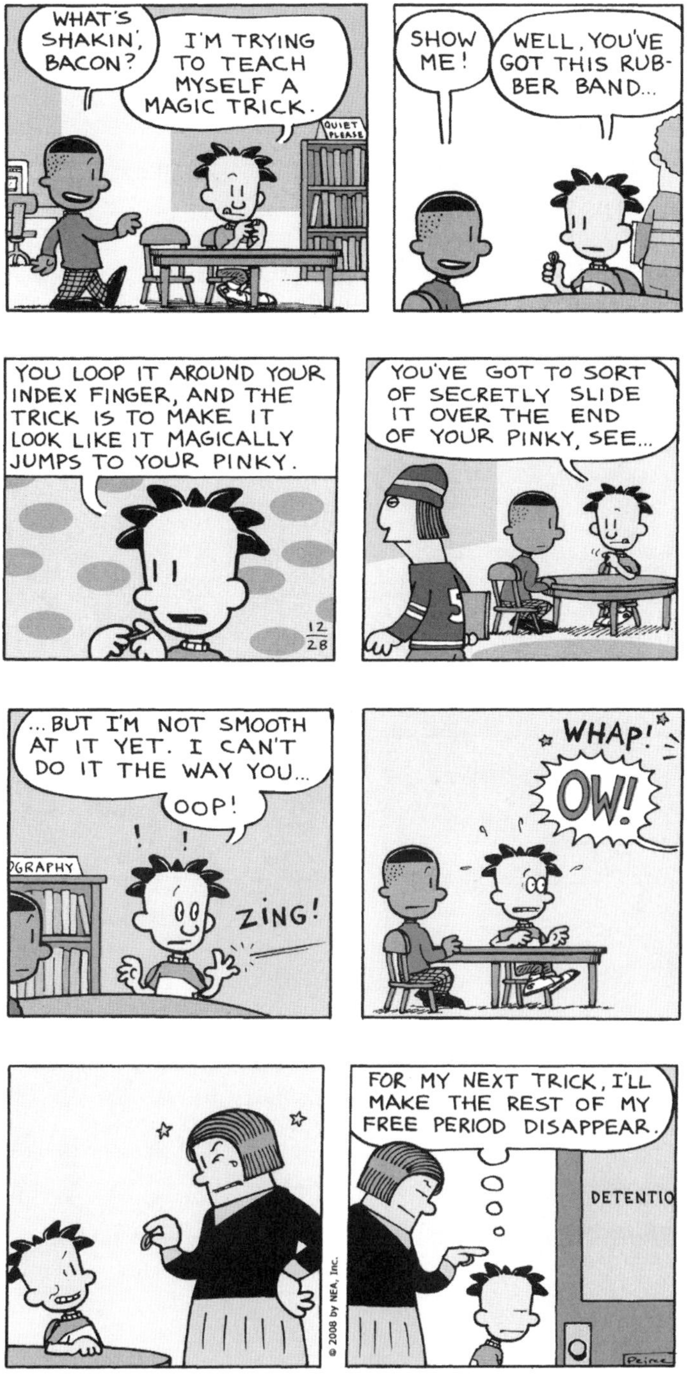

WHAT'S SHAKIN', BACON?
I'M TRYING TO TEACH MYSELF A MAGIC TRICK.
QUIET PLEASE
SHOW ME!
WELL, YOU'VE GOT THIS RUBBER BAND...
YOU LOOP IT AROUND YOUR INDEX FINGER, AND THE TRICK IS TO MAKE IT LOOK LIKE IT MAGICALLY JUMPS TO YOUR PINKY.
12/28
YOU'VE GOT TO SORT OF SECRETLY SLIDE IT OVER THE END OF YOUR PINKY, SEE...
...BUT I'M NOT SMOOTH AT IT YET. I CAN'T DO IT THE WAY YOU...
OOP!
!!
ZING!
WHAP!
OW!
© 2008 by NEA, Inc.
FOR MY NEXT TRICK, I'LL MAKE THE REST OF MY FREE PERIOD DISAPPEAR.
DETENTIO
Peirce

NO MORE MONOPOLY

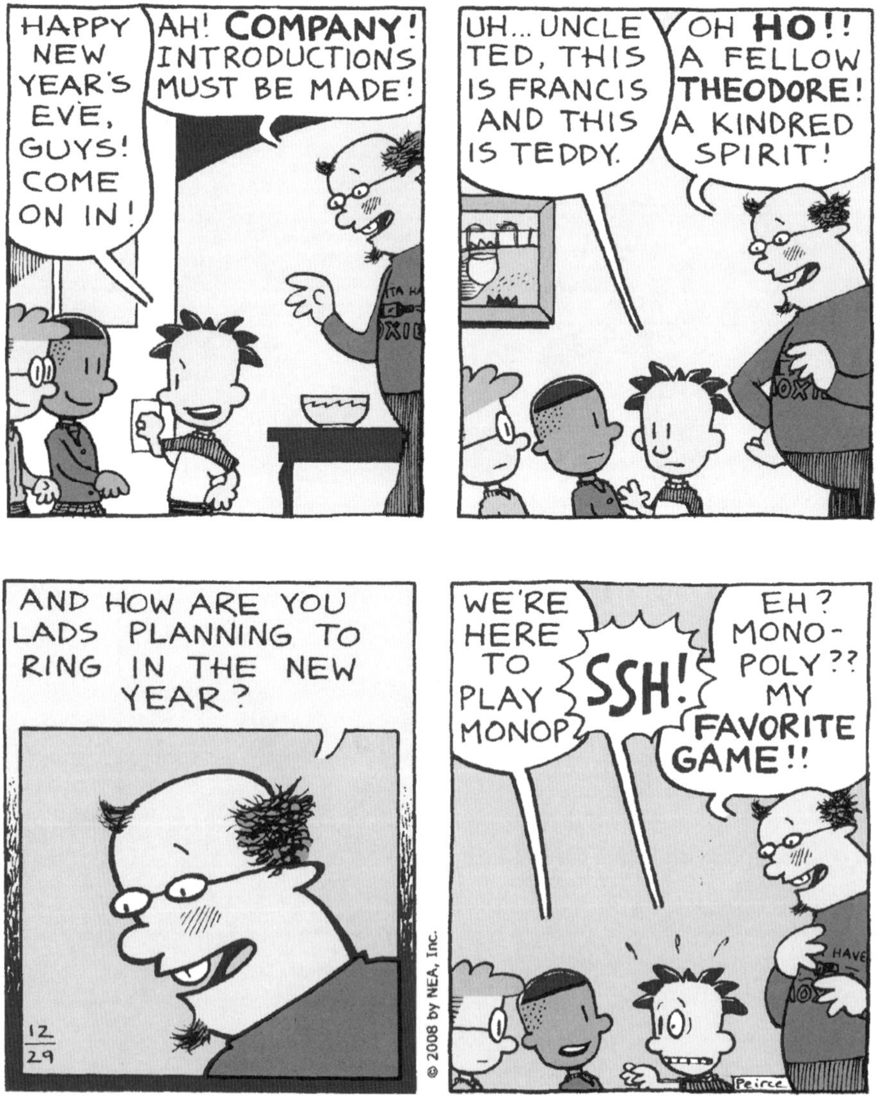
HAPPY NEW YEAR'S EVE, GUYS! COME ON IN!
AH! COMPANY! INTRODUCTIONS MUST BE MADE!
UH... UNCLE TED, THIS IS FRANCIS AND THIS IS TEDDY.
OH HO!! A FELLOW THEODORE! A KINDRED SPIRIT!
AND HOW ARE YOU LADS PLANNING TO RING IN THE NEW YEAR?
12/29
WE'RE HERE TO PLAY MONOP
SSH!
EH? MONO-POLY?? MY FAVORITE GAME!!
Peirce

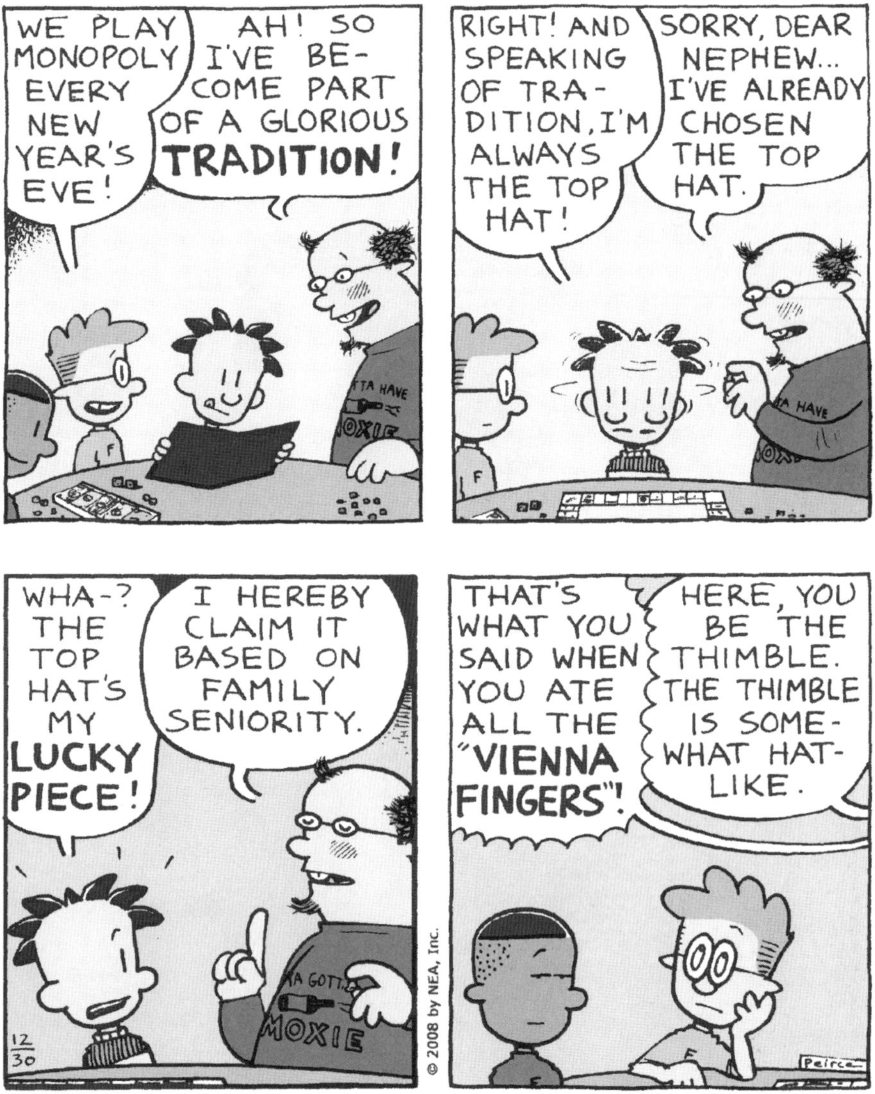
WE PLAY MONOPOLY EVERY NEW YEAR'S EVE!
AH! SO I'VE BE-COME PART OF A GLORIOUS **TRADITION**!
RIGHT! AND SPEAKING OF TRA-DITION, I'M ALWAYS THE TOP HAT!
SORRY, DEAR NEPHEW... I'VE ALREADY CHOSEN THE TOP HAT.
WHA-? THE TOP HAT'S MY **LUCKY PIECE**!
I HEREBY CLAIM IT BASED ON FAMILY SENIORITY.
THAT'S WHAT YOU SAID WHEN YOU ATE ALL THE "**VIENNA FINGERS**"!
HERE, YOU BE THE THIMBLE. THE THIMBLE IS SOME-WHAT HAT-LIKE.
12/30
Peirce

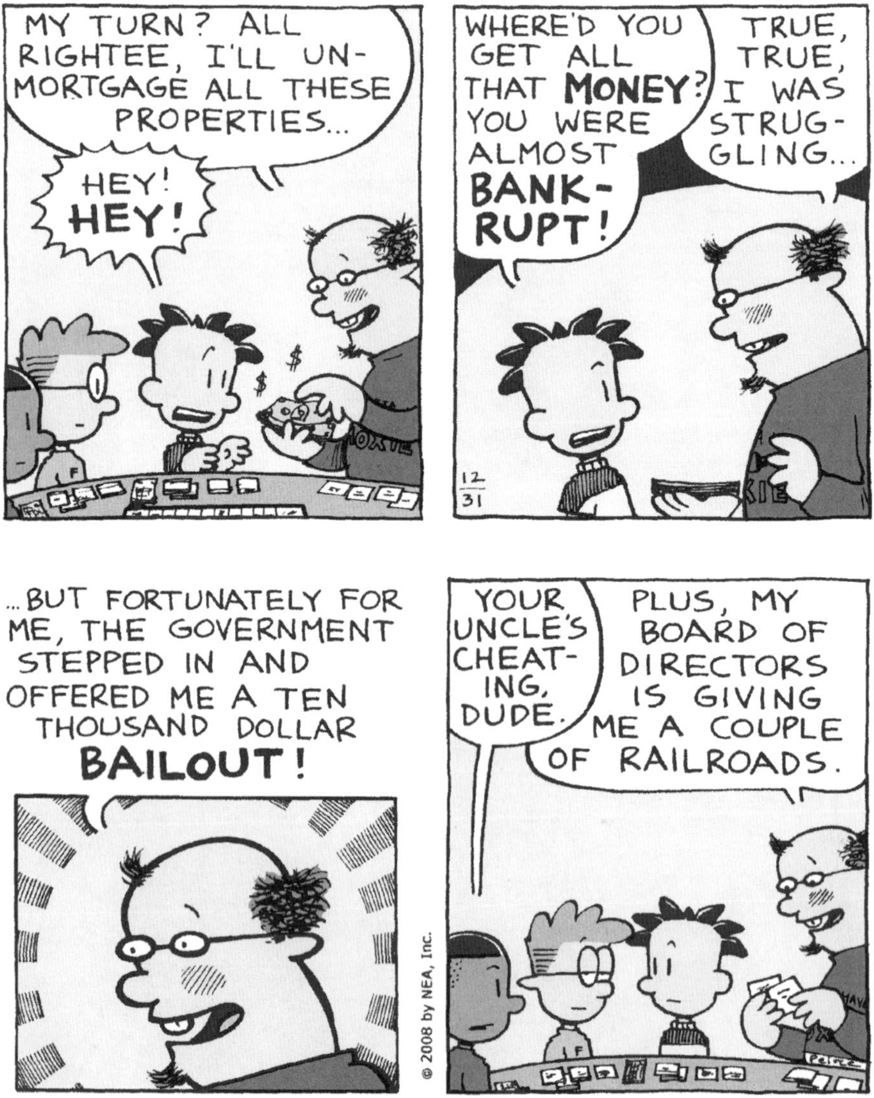
MY TURN? ALL RIGHTEE, I'LL UN-MORTGAGE ALL THESE PROPERTIES...
HEY! HEY!
WHERE'D YOU GET ALL THAT MONEY? YOU WERE ALMOST BANK-RUPT!
TRUE, TRUE, I WAS STRUG-GLING...
12
31
...BUT FORTUNATELY FOR ME, THE GOVERNMENT STEPPED IN AND OFFERED ME A TEN THOUSAND DOLLAR BAILOUT!
YOUR UNCLE'S CHEAT-ING, DUDE.
PLUS, MY BOARD OF DIRECTORS IS GIVING ME A COUPLE OF RAILROADS.

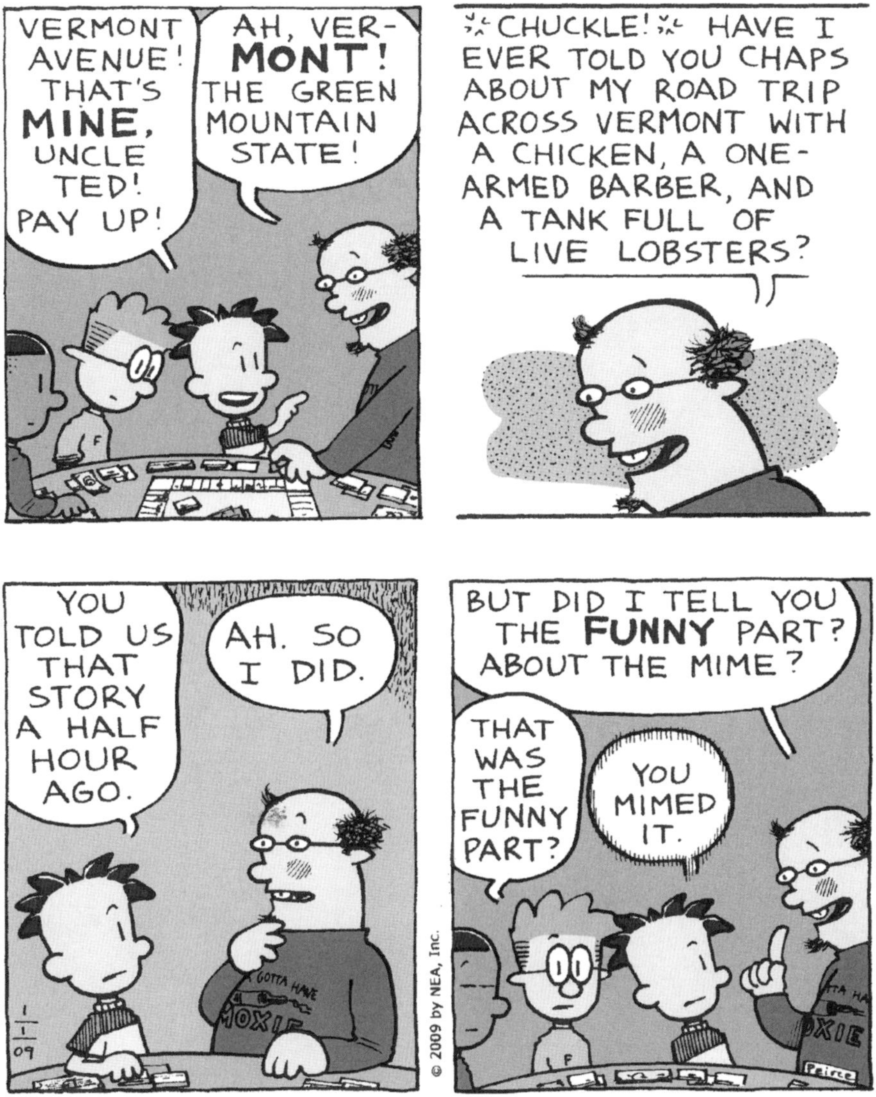
VERMONT AVENUE! THAT'S **MINE**, UNCLE TED! PAY UP!
AH, VER- **MONT**! THE GREEN MOUNTAIN STATE!
CHUCKLE! HAVE I EVER TOLD YOU CHAPS ABOUT MY ROAD TRIP ACROSS VERMONT WITH A CHICKEN, A ONE-ARMED BARBER, AND A TANK FULL OF LIVE LOBSTERS?
YOU TOLD US THAT STORY A HALF HOUR AGO.
AH. SO I DID.
1/1/09
BUT DID I TELL YOU THE **FUNNY** PART? ABOUT THE MIME?
THAT WAS THE FUNNY PART?
YOU MIMED IT.

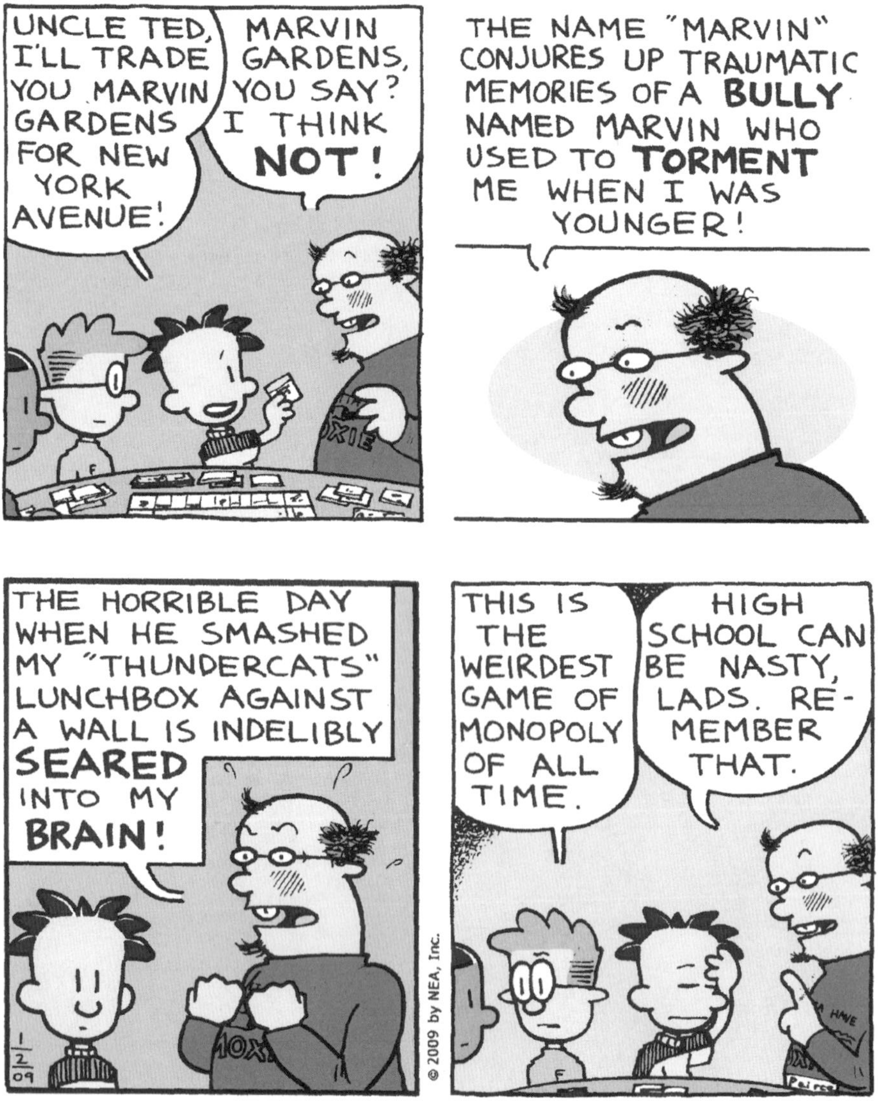
UNCLE TED, I'LL TRADE YOU MARVIN GARDENS FOR NEW YORK AVENUE!
MARVIN GARDENS, YOU SAY? I THINK **NOT**!
THE NAME "MARVIN" CONJURES UP TRAUMATIC MEMORIES OF A **BULLY** NAMED MARVIN WHO USED TO **TORMENT** ME WHEN I WAS YOUNGER!
THE HORRIBLE DAY WHEN HE SMASHED MY "THUNDERCATS" LUNCHBOX AGAINST A WALL IS INDELIBLY **SEARED** INTO MY **BRAIN**!
1/2/09
THIS IS THE WEIRDEST GAME OF MONOPOLY OF ALL TIME.
HIGH SCHOOL CAN BE NASTY, LADS. REMEMBER THAT.

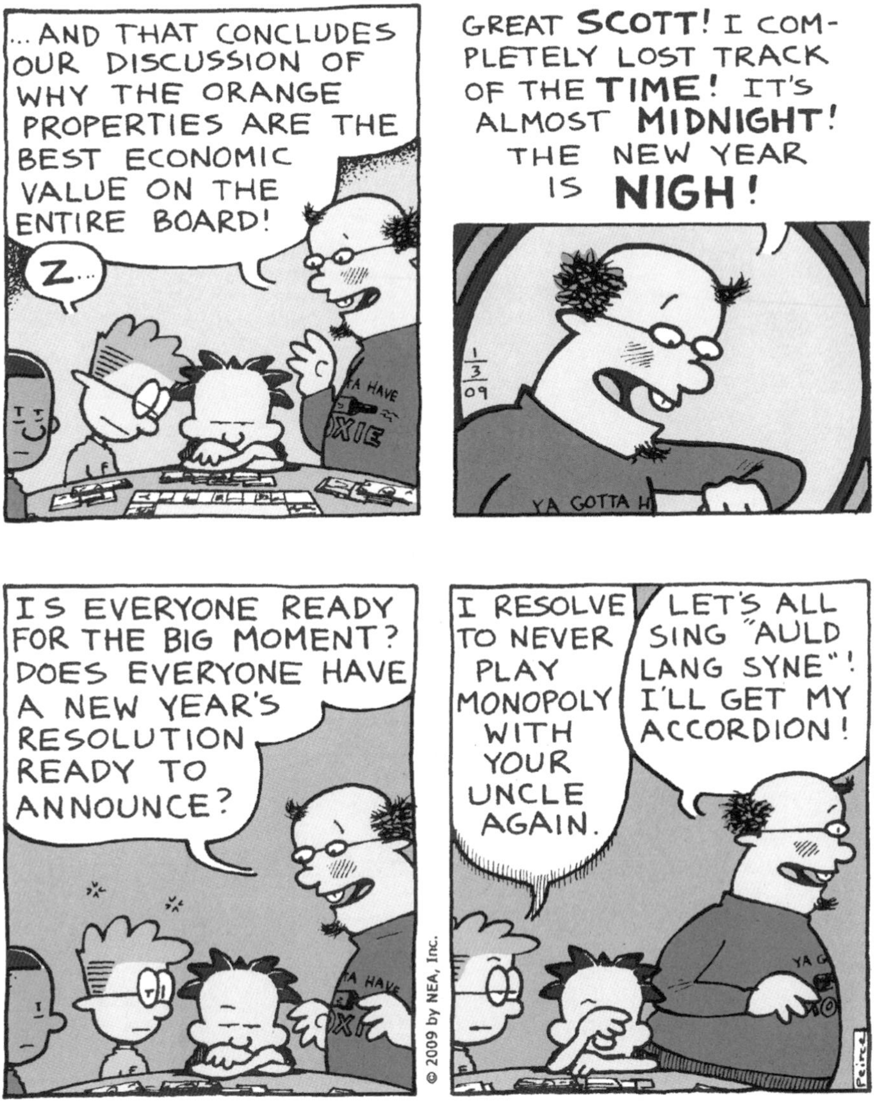
...AND THAT CONCLUDES OUR DISCUSSION OF WHY THE ORANGE PROPERTIES ARE THE BEST ECONOMIC VALUE ON THE ENTIRE BOARD!
Z...
GREAT SCOTT! I COMPLETELY LOST TRACK OF THE TIME! IT'S ALMOST MIDNIGHT! THE NEW YEAR IS NIGH!
1/3/09
YA GOTTA H
IS EVERYONE READY FOR THE BIG MOMENT? DOES EVERYONE HAVE A NEW YEAR'S RESOLUTION READY TO ANNOUNCE?
I RESOLVE TO NEVER PLAY MONOPOLY WITH YOUR UNCLE AGAIN.
LET'S ALL SING "AULD LANG SYNE"! I'LL GET MY ACCORDION!
Peirce

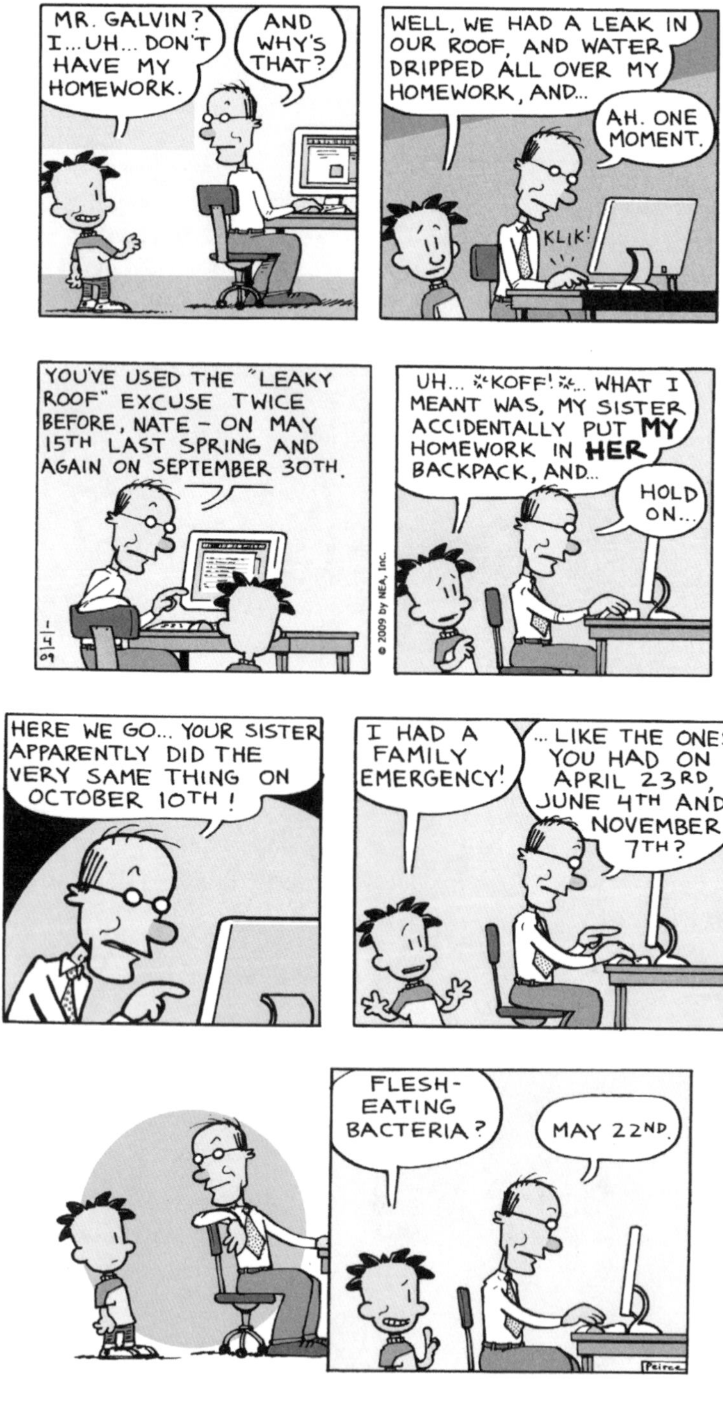
MR. GALVIN? I... UH... DON'T HAVE MY HOMEWORK.
AND WHY'S THAT?
WELL, WE HAD A LEAK IN OUR ROOF, AND WATER DRIPPED ALL OVER MY HOMEWORK, AND...
AH. ONE MOMENT.
KLIK!
YOU'VE USED THE "LEAKY ROOF" EXCUSE TWICE BEFORE, NATE - ON MAY 15TH LAST SPRING AND AGAIN ON SEPTEMBER 30TH.
1/4/09
© 2009 by NEA, Inc.
UH... *KOFF!*... WHAT I MEANT WAS, MY SISTER ACCIDENTALLY PUT **MY** HOMEWORK IN **HER** BACKPACK, AND...
HOLD ON...
HERE WE GO... YOUR SISTER APPARENTLY DID THE VERY SAME THING ON OCTOBER 10TH!
I HAD A FAMILY EMERGENCY!
...LIKE THE ONES YOU HAD ON APRIL 23RD, JUNE 4TH AND NOVEMBER 7TH?
FLESH-EATING BACTERIA?
MAY 22ND.
Peirce

MAKE IT OR BREAK IT

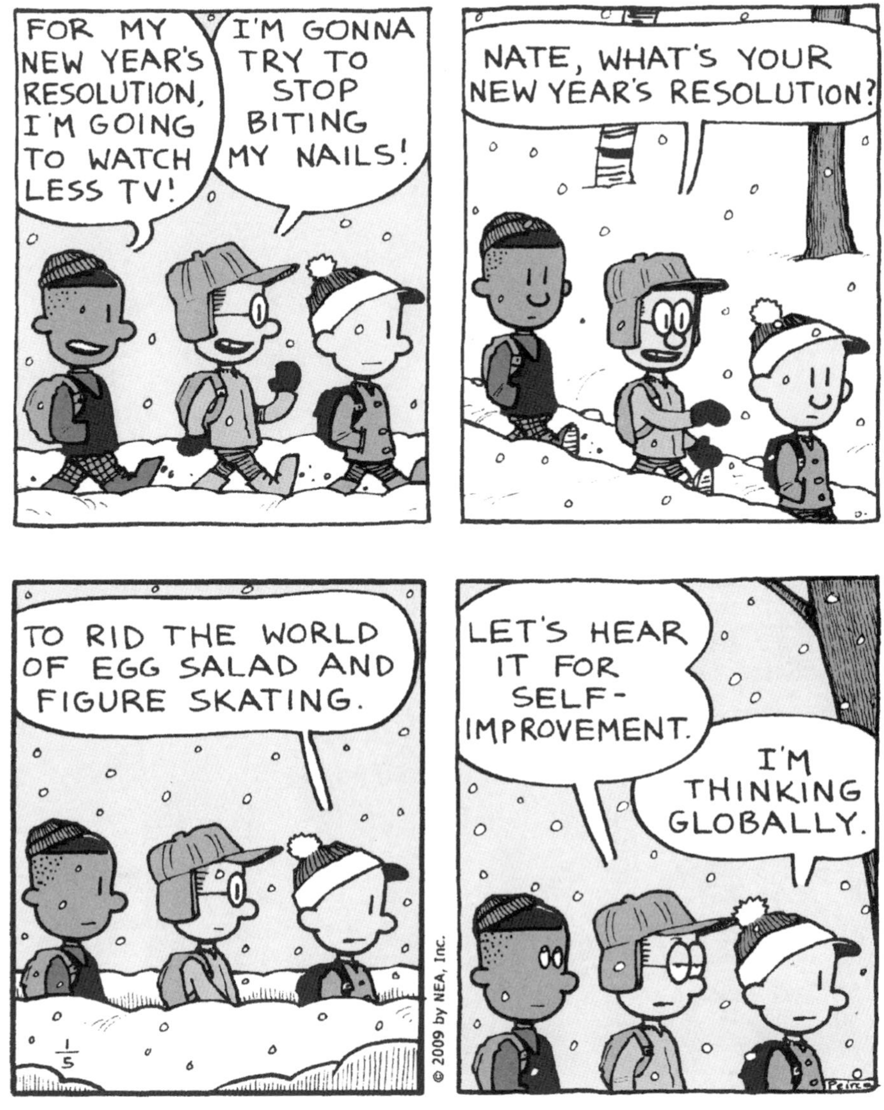
FOR MY NEW YEAR'S RESOLUTION, I'M GOING TO WATCH LESS TV!
I'M GONNA TRY TO STOP BITING MY NAILS!
NATE, WHAT'S YOUR NEW YEAR'S RESOLUTION?
TO RID THE WORLD OF EGG SALAD AND FIGURE SKATING.
LET'S HEAR IT FOR SELF-IMPROVEMENT.
I'M THINKING GLOBALLY.
1/5
Peirce

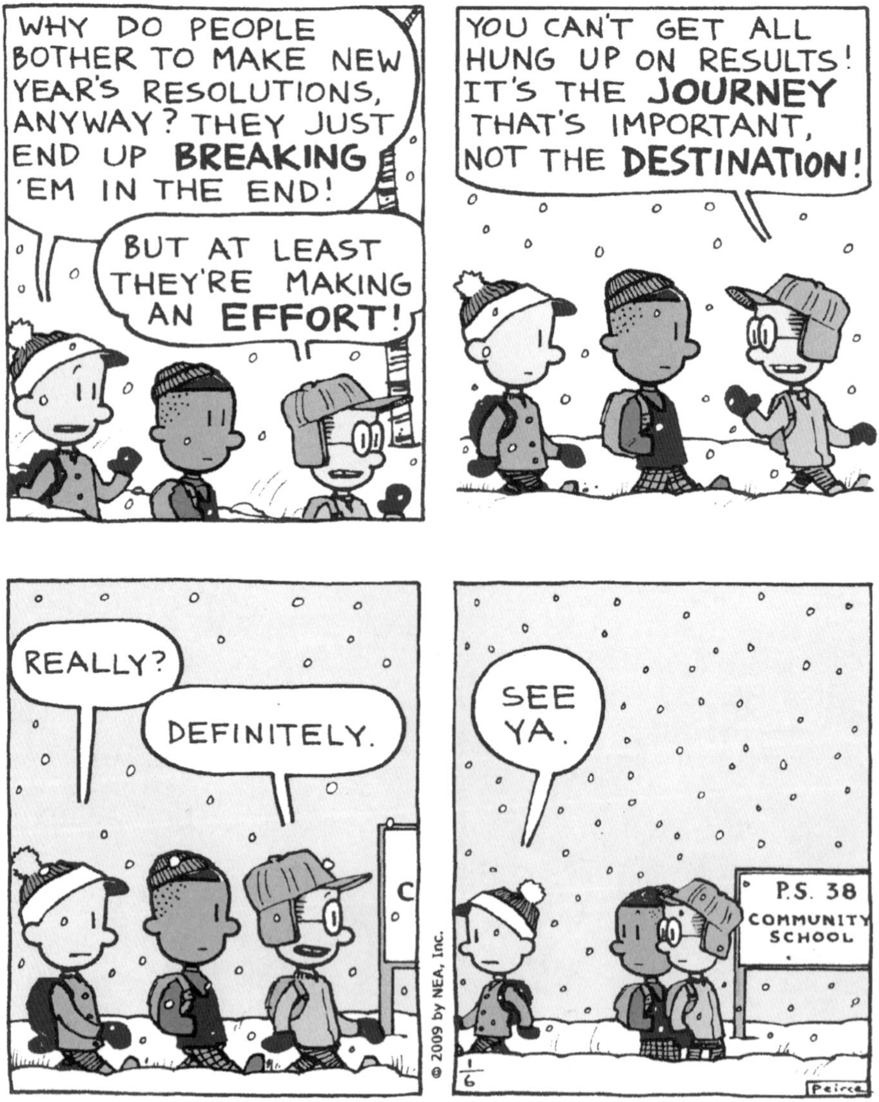
WHY DO PEOPLE BOTHER TO MAKE NEW YEAR'S RESOLUTIONS, ANYWAY? THEY JUST END UP **BREAKING** 'EM IN THE END!
BUT AT LEAST THEY'RE MAKING AN **EFFORT**!
YOU CAN'T GET ALL HUNG UP ON RESULTS! IT'S THE **JOURNEY** THAT'S IMPORTANT, NOT THE **DESTINATION**!
REALLY?
DEFINITELY.
SEE YA.
P.S. 38
COMMUNITY SCHOOL
© 2009 by NEA, Inc.
1/6
Peirce

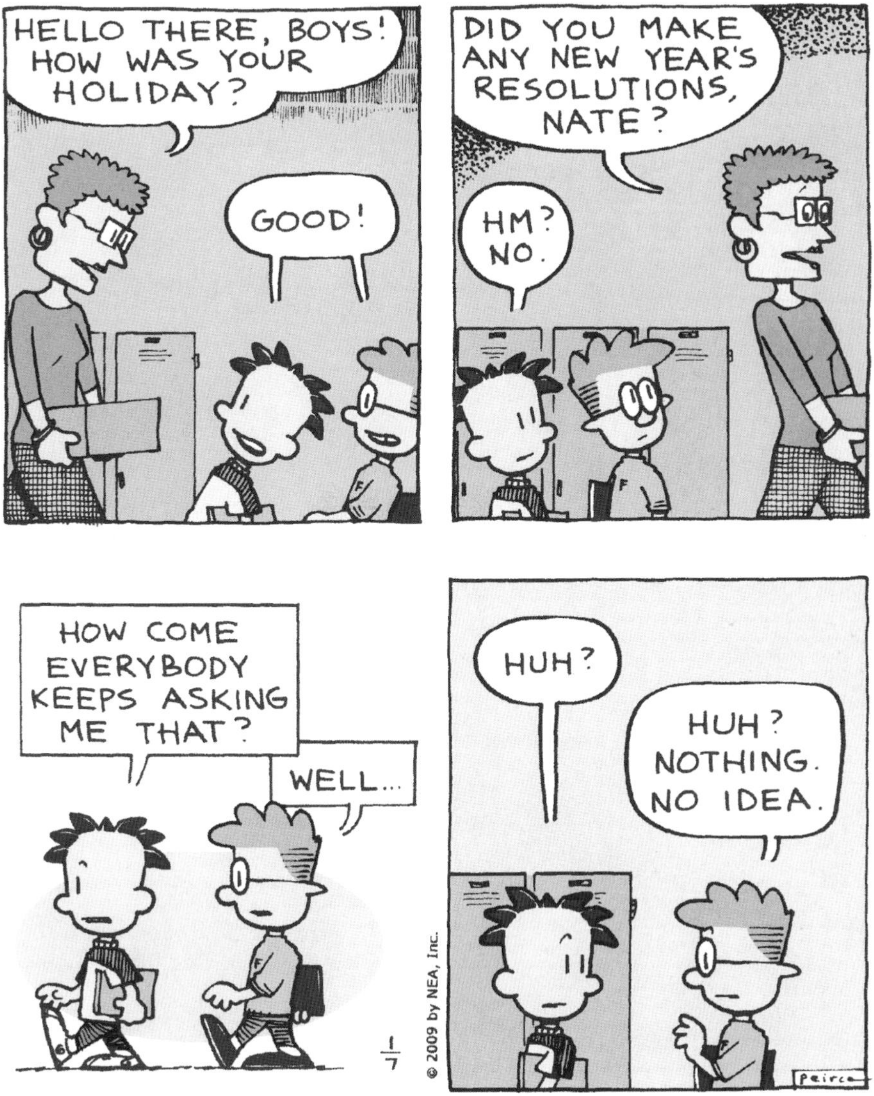
HELLO THERE, BOYS! HOW WAS YOUR HOLIDAY?
GOOD!
DID YOU MAKE ANY NEW YEAR'S RESOLUTIONS, NATE?
HM? NO.
HOW COME EVERYBODY KEEPS ASKING ME THAT?
WELL...
HUH?
HUH? NOTHING. NO IDEA.
1/7
© 2009 by NEA, Inc.
peirce

PET NAMES

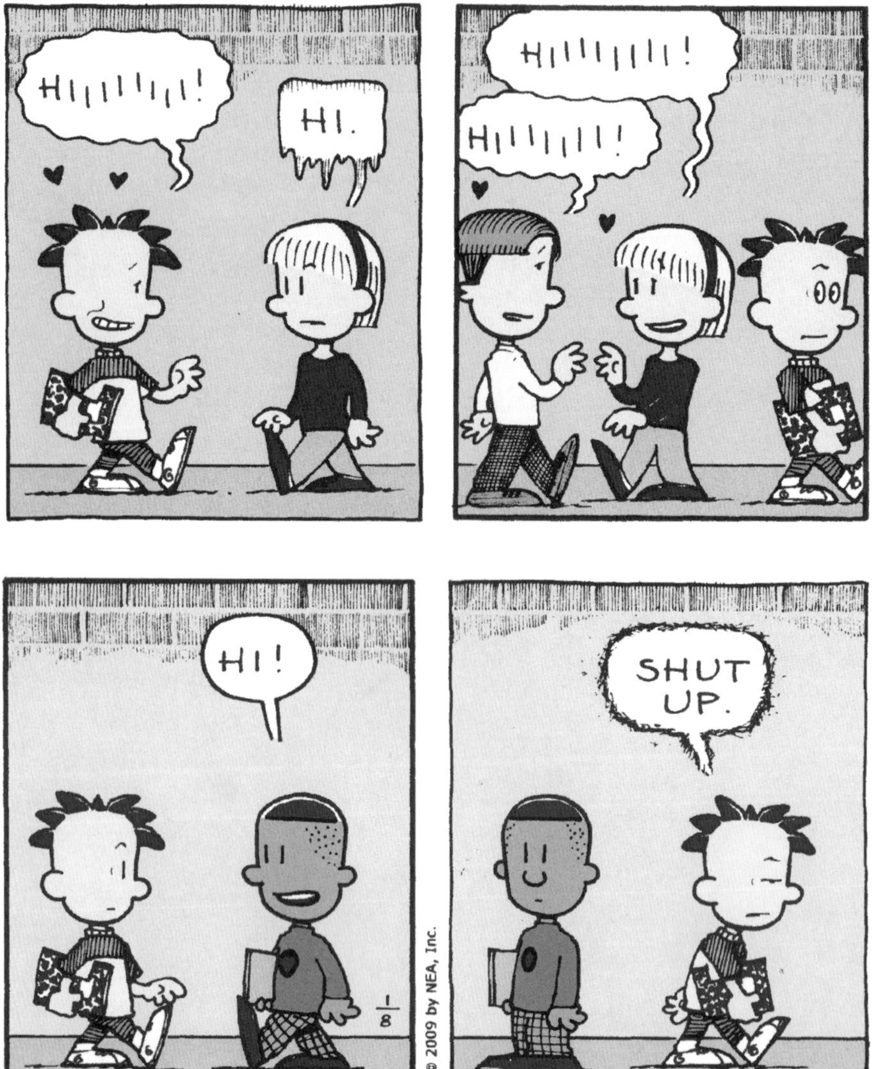
HIIIIIII!
HI.
HIIIIIIII!
HIIIIIII!
HI!
SHUT UP.
1/8
© 2009 by NEA, Inc.
Peirce

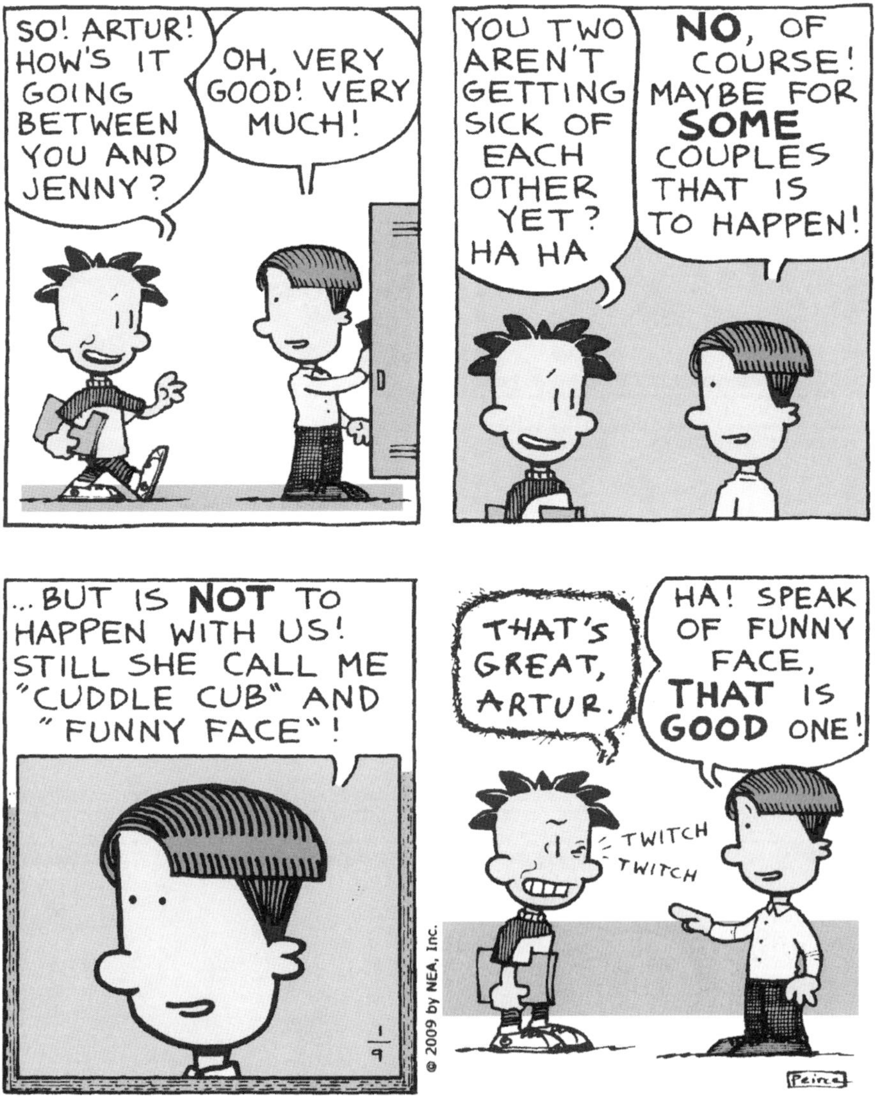
SO! ARTUR! HOW'S IT GOING BETWEEN YOU AND JENNY?
OH, VERY GOOD! VERY MUCH!
YOU TWO AREN'T GETTING SICK OF EACH OTHER YET? HA HA
NO, OF COURSE! MAYBE FOR SOME COUPLES THAT IS TO HAPPEN!
...BUT IS NOT TO HAPPEN WITH US! STILL SHE CALL ME "CUDDLE CUB" AND "FUNNY FACE"!
THAT'S GREAT, ARTUR.
HA! SPEAK OF FUNNY FACE, THAT IS GOOD ONE!
TWITCH
TWITCH
© 2009 by NEA, Inc.
Peirce

WHAT A PRETTY FACE!

Nate's dad has framed some of Nate's self-portraits. Draw yourself doing the same things as Nate!

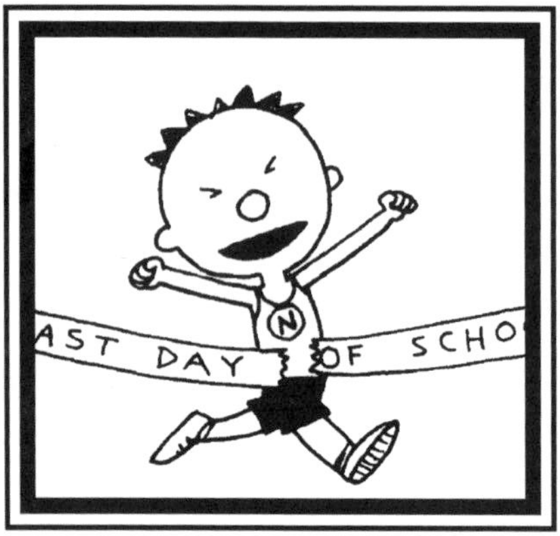
AST DAY OF SCHO
N

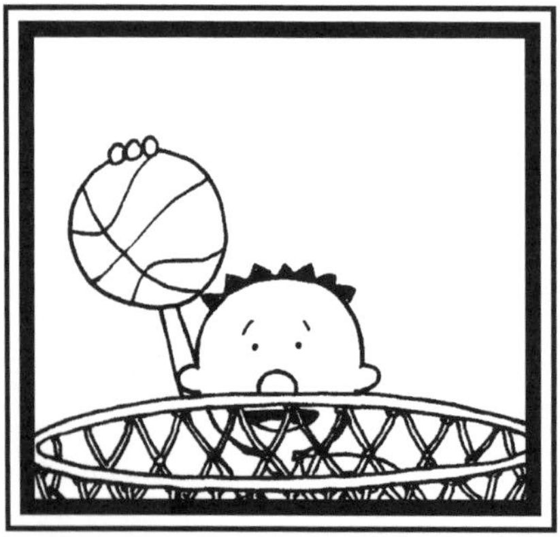

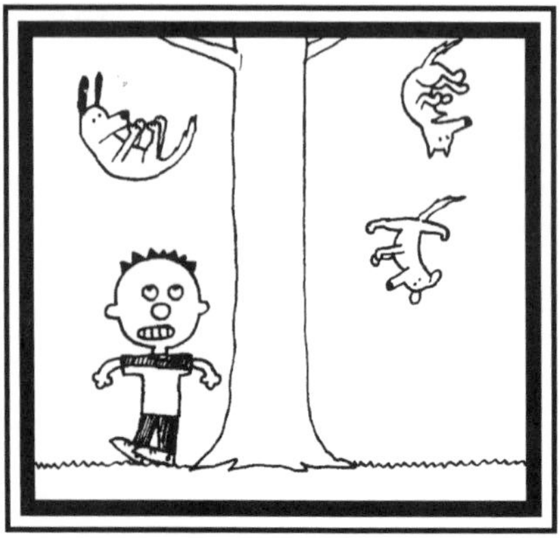

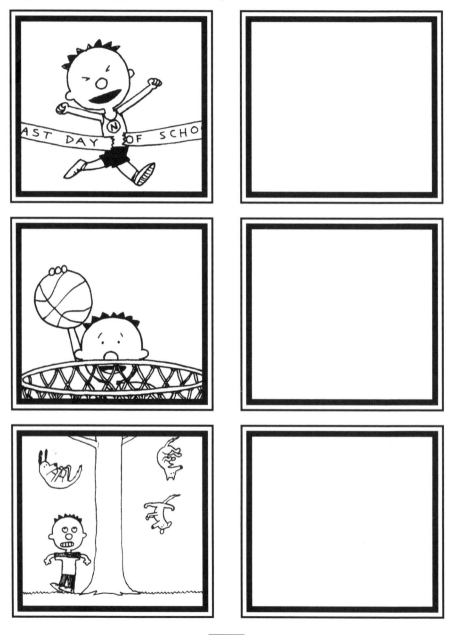

RHYTHM & RHYME

A picture is worth a thousand words. Fill in these limerick poems and create your own, all inspired by Nate's Sunday strip art!

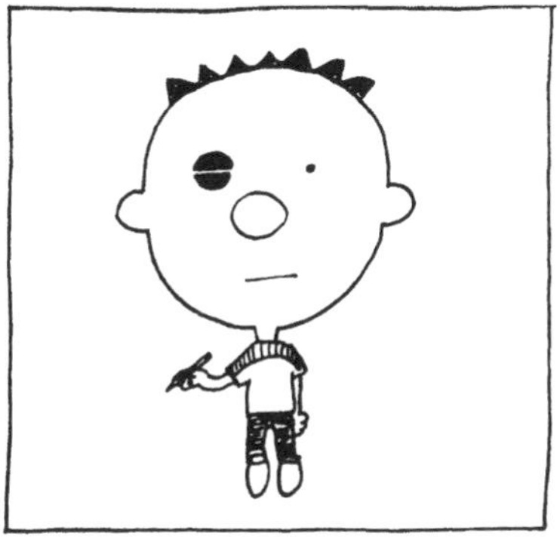

Nate is a pretty swell guy
But one day a ball flew into his _____.
It made him quite sad,
Though he couldn't get _______,
He did yell "Why, ball, _______?!"

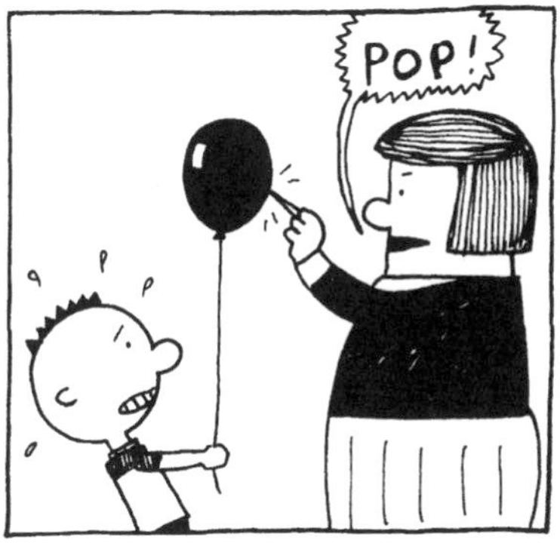

POP!

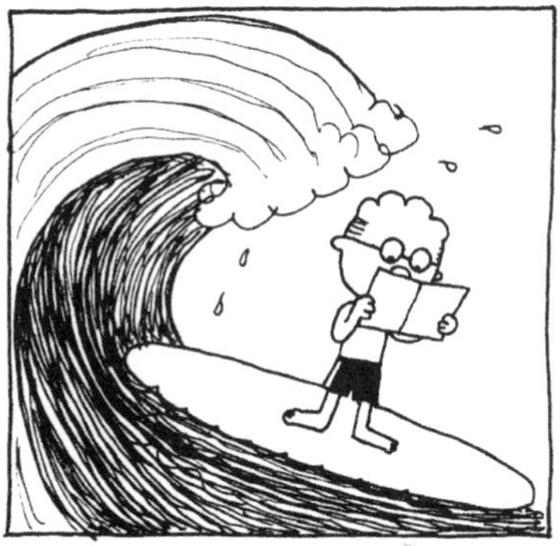

Francis loves to read most of all
Even on a wave standing _______.
I'd be willing to bet
(If the book didn't get _______)
He wouldn't notice a _______!

AWESOME ANNOUNCEMENTS

Have you suffered through those BOOORING announcements at school? What would you say if you had the microphone? Change it up and shout out something FUN!

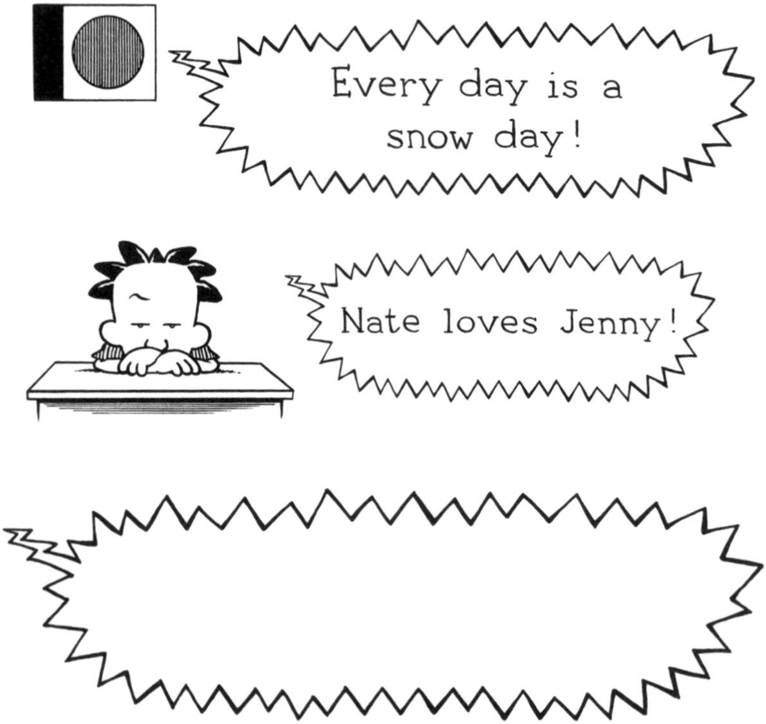
Every day is a snow day!
Nate loves Jenny!

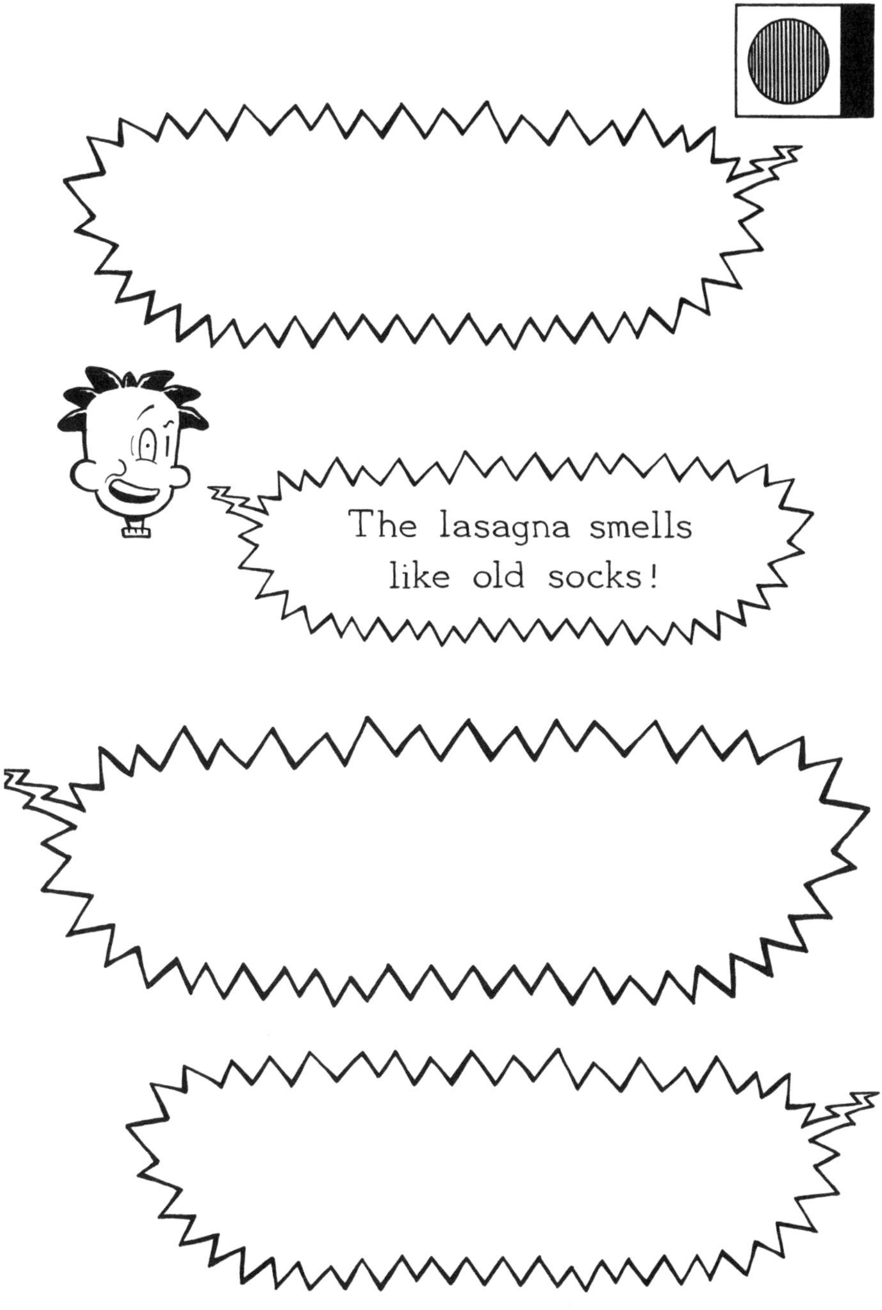
The lasagna smells like old socks!

NATE ≠ NEAT

Have you ever scrambled the letters in your name to see if they spell anything else? Well, **I** have. And guess what: **MY** letters spell **N·E·A·T!**

Pretty ironic, right? Hey, I realize I'm not exactly Joe Tidy. **EVERYBODY** knows it. But that doesn't stop Francis, who color-codes his underwear, from pointing it out about a jillion times a day.

Your desk is **DISGUSTING**. You have paint on your shirt. Oh, and you have Cheez Doodle stains all over your face. What a SLOB you are!

Francis has been telling me to clean up my act since I poured applesauce down his pants back in kindergarten. Of course, I've always ignored him. But then last week my sloppiness got Francis in trouble... and he **NEVER** gets in trouble!

I felt so bad about it, I decided to actually try to get neater. And thanks to

I'm **VERY** disappointed in you.

Oops.

Teddy and his uncle Pedro, the hypnotist, it's working... **TOO** well. All of the sudden, I'm starting to act **JUST LIKE FRANCIS!** Frankly, I think I'm losing my mind.

You're doing **GREAT!**

I'm FLIPPIN' OUT!

"*Big Nate* is funny, big time."
—Jeff Kinney, author of *Diary of a Wimpy Kid*

BiG NATE FLIPS OUT

#1 NEW YORK TIMES BESTSELLING AUTHOR
Lincoln Peirce

What a **MESS!**
Read all about it in
BIG NATE FLIPS OUT!!

Lincoln Peirce

(pronounced "purse") is a cartoonist/writer and *New York Times* bestselling author of the hilarious Big Nate book series (www.bignatebooks.com), now published in twenty-five countries worldwide and available as ebooks and audiobooks and as an app, Big Nate: Comix by U! He is also the creator of the comic strip *Big Nate*. It appears in over four hundred U.S. newspapers and online daily at www.gocomics.com/bignate. Lincoln's boyhood idol was Charles Schulz of *Peanuts* fame, but his main inspiration for Big Nate has always been his own experience as a sixth grader. Just like Nate, Lincoln loves comics, ice hockey, and Cheez Doodles (and dislikes cats, figure skating, and egg salad). His Big Nate books have been featured on *Today* and *Good Morning America* and in the *Boston Globe*, the *Los Angeles Times*, *USA Today*, and the *Washington Post*. He has also written for Cartoon Network and Nickelodeon. Lincoln lives with his wife and two children in Portland, Maine.

BiG NATE

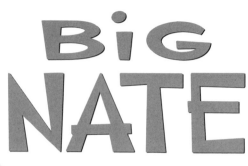

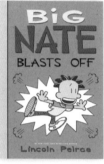

BiG
NATE
BLASTS OFF
Lincoln Peirce

Hardcover Book ISBN
978-1-5321-4521-6

COLLECT THEM ALL!

Set of 10
Hardcover Books ISBN:
978-1-5321-4520-9

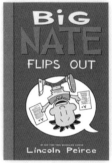

BiG
NATE
FLIPS OUT
Lincoln Peirce

Hardcover Book ISBN
978-1-5321-4522-3

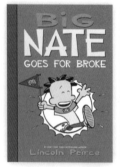

BiG
NATE
GOES FOR BROKE
Lincoln Peirce

Hardcover Book ISBN
978-1-5321-4523-0

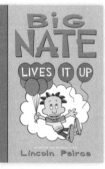

BiG
NATE
LIVES IT UP
Lincoln Peirce

Hardcover Book ISBN
978-1-5321-4524-7

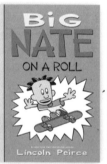

BiG
NATE
ON A ROLL
Lincoln Peirce

Hardcover Book ISBN
978-1-5321-4525-4

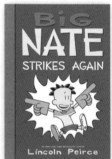

BiG
NATE
STRIKES AGAIN
Lincoln Peirce

Hardcover Book ISBN
978-1-5321-4526-1

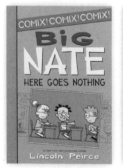

COMIX! COMIX! COMIX!
BiG
NATE
HERE GOES NOTHING
Lincoln Peirce

Hardcover Book ISBN
978-1-5321-4527-8

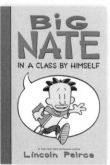

BiG
NATE
IN A CLASS BY HIMSELF
Lincoln Peirce

Hardcover Book ISBN
978-1-5321-4528-5

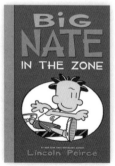

BiG
NATE
IN THE ZONE
Lincoln Peirce

Hardcover Book ISBN
978-1-5321-4529-2

COMIX! COMIX! COMIX!
BiG
NATE
WHAT COULD POSSIBLY GO WRONG?
Lincoln Peirce

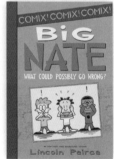

Hardcover Book ISBN
978-1-5321-4530-8